THE LAST THING he wanted to do tonight was to have sex with a beautiful virgin.

Tony stopped walking from the stage to the dressing room and scratched a lock from his head at that uncharacteristic thought. He slumped with a sigh against the dingy black hallway wall.

How had it come to this? He actually was dreading the idea of fondling the virgin he knew awaited him just a few steps and a door away.

When you put it on demonically notarized legal paper with a schedule, sex just didn't end up being as much fun as it used to be. The contract had sounded unbeatable at the time—fame and fortune for him and his band. And what he paid in return was a reward in itself.

The price?

Deflower one virgin after each performance.

By midnight...

PRAISE FOR
SACRIFICING VIRGINS

"...a collection that absolutely sucked me in, devoured my soul, and left me an undead husk, eager to be used and abused some more...Some of it is beautiful, and some of it is shocking, but it's all powerful."

– Beauty In Ruins

"*Sacrificing Virgins* is disturbing in the best sense of the word... The stories lingered, poking and provoking when I tried to move on to other things."

– The HorrorReview

"*Sacrificing Virgins* by John Everson is a wide-ranging collection of short stories that are long on imagination and originality. His style is the darkest of dark, erotic and delightfully sharp... Everson always delivers a brilliantly twisted tale. His delivery will make you squirm."

– The Horror Zine

"I am ashamed I have never read anything from John Everson before. Why didn't someone tell me about this guy? Wow. *Sacrificing Virgins* is Everson's fourth collection and contains twenty-five of the darkest, most sexually perverse stories I've ever read, and I mean that as a complement...Definitely recommended, if you think you can handle the hard stuff."

– Cemetery Dance

"I can honestly say there was something I liked and enjoyed in each and every story, something that very rarely happens when I'm reading a collection of shorts.. Well worth a read for horror fans."

– Scarlet's Web

"Everson has a terrifying and vivid imagination, and the tales he spins are gripping and enthralling. So, it's no surprise to discover he is a master of the short story as well. *Sacrificing Virgins* is a collection of twenty-five horrifying and visceral shorts that even the heartiest of horror fans will have a hard time putting down... If you're a fan of short stories and horror, this is a Must Have collection for your library."

– Shattered Ravings

"*Sacrificing Virgins* is an eerie collection of 25 short stories, sure to ensure you sleep with the lights on for many nights after devouring every deliciously demented word."

– Crowgrrl Entertainment Source

"*Sacrificing Virgins* is a collection of 25 stories from the Stoker Award-winning author and serves as a good example of the range of his talent. There are stories that will make the reader think and others that will make the reader scream in terror."

– Atom Bash

"...one of the better horror collections that you are going to find."

– Examiner.com

SACRIFICING
VIRGINS

To Kevin
Thanks for reading!
all my crazy Stories

JOHN EVERSON

SACRIFICING VIRGINS

B O O K S

NAPERVILLE, ILLINOIS

~2017~

SACRIFICING VIRGINS

Published by Dark Arts Books
www.darkartsbooks.com

ISBN-13: 978-1543252538
ISBN-10: 1543252532

INDIVIDUAL STORY COPYRIGHT INFORMATION

DARKARTS
B O O K S

For Geri

TABLE OF CONTENTS

FOREWORD

Legally Yours

LAST YEAR MARKED my 20th anniversary as a published horror and dark fantasy fiction author. I guess that means this year, my stories are officially legal and can finally hunker down on a barstool without a fake ID to talk about the good old days. You know, the days of dot matrix printers and story submissions that required postage stamps.

I spent the first half of my writing career printing out and snail-mailing short fiction to just about any magazine or anthology that published dark tales. I pored over the classified ads, looking for magazines to submit to in the back of *Writer's Digest*, and lived for the day each month when *Scavenger's Newsletter* arrived in the mail—*Scav* was a saddle-stitched 'zine that carried updated listings from all of the tiny magazines and small presses around the country that were looking for submissions. A batch of the more twisted things I created during that period were collected by Delirium Books in 2000 in my very first short fiction collection (and very first book!), *Cage of Bones & Other Deadly Obsessions*. A lighter (both in weight and tone) collection from Chicago's Twilight Tales followed, *Vigilantes of Love*, in 2003. And then in 2007, one of my favorite small presses, Necro Publications, issued my *Needles & Sins* collection. There was a time that I looked at that third book as my last word in the short form. I had begun publishing novels by then, and that collection held much of what I thought were my best short stories. For a while, I didn't think I had another short story in me. Nothing more to say. I was done here.

But...of course...I did, and I wasn't.

It's been eight years since that last collection, and there have been a half dozen new novels since then. But there have also been shorter tales. Twice as many as would fit into this book, in all honesty. I've always felt the short story can pack the best horror punch; it's the perfect conduit for capturing strong feelings and emotions. And so, now and then, instead of writing a novel chapter...I spend the day working on a short story idea that catches my imagination.

In reading through these pieces, I was instantly transported back to where I was when I wrote some of them. I remembered why. And often, they left me feeling the same way I did on the day that I finished writing them. These stories speak to me of different things. Hopefully they'll speak to you too...though the colors they leave in your head will be a little different than what they painted...or were painted from...in mine. And that's the beauty of fiction. They'll be different for you than they are for me. And that will make them yours.

There's a story here that I wrote after reconnecting with some old friends in a shot-and-a-beer bar in Denver ("Fish Bait") and a story I wrote after a brush with tinnitus after a really loud SXSW show (thanks for "Eardrum Buzz" Nashville Pussy!) There are creepy stories here that I wrote specifically to read for all-ages audiences on Halloween ("The Tapping" and "The Pumpkin Man"). And there are stories that I wrote because I wanted to go really over-the-top, like "Whatever You Want" and "The Eyes" and "Sacrificing Virgins". The latter two I read at Gross Out fiction contests many years ago at World Horror Conventions.

There are quiet ghost stories and erotic horror tales. A touch of humor and a touch of melancholy. There are also off-shoots here from three of my novels. "Ligeia's Revenge", using the title character from my novel Siren, was originally written for an Italian webzine and was only officially published prior to now in Italian translation. "The Pumpkin Man" originated the mythology that was used a couple years later to write my novel of the same name. And "Field of Flesh" offers a different entrée into the world of my novel NightWhere. They all stand on their own as stories, but fans of those novels will (hopefully) enjoy another glimpse into those worlds.

There is a short bit of flash fiction that I wrote for a benefit anthology ("Faux") and a vaguely Lovecraftian piece that I wrote partly on a pad of paper on Miami Beach at night, after building sand castles that afternoon with a boy who didn't speak English ("Star on the Beach"). I am very fond of all of these stories, for different reasons. They take me back to Miami Beach and The

Stars Our Destination Bookstore in Chicago, and Austin, Texas, and Resurrection Cemetery and World Horror Conventions in Seattle and Kansas City and San Francisco. One story takes me back to when I was just six or seven years old, and used to dig clay out of the earth behind the shed of my parents' first house to fashion homemade dinosaurs.

These stories all have moments that resonate with very specific, special feelings for me.

I hope that after you read them, they'll mean something special to you, too.

– John Everson
Naperville, IL
February 2015

SHE FOUND SPRING

IT TOOK A LONG time before Eric grasped the connection. The first time it happened, he was exhausted from cleaning the backyard. It was still March, but an unseasonable fifty-five degrees outside, so he'd spent the day raking leaves away from the fence and trimming shrubs and willow branches so that a month from now, when it all bloomed out, the yard would look neat.

He'd collapsed on the couch in the family room with a beer, and the next thing he knew, it was dark. The lights in the house were all out and the moon colored the brown back lawn in fairy light; ethereal.

Or maybe it wasn't the moon that did that.

Maybe it was the woman, who walked through his garden, glowing as if from her own inner light. Her blue-white feet were bare, and her face beamed with both light and pleasure. The garden was yards away from the back sliding glass door, but Eric could make out nearly all of her features from where he sat. She walked around the old willow tree, trailing her hands through the spray of its branches, and then hugging its center in an odd show of seeming affection.

Then she pulled away from the tree and walked towards the house. Towards the glass doors that Eric watched her through.

The closer she got to the house, the more nervous he felt. At first, it had simply been a joy to watch this phosphorescent creature dance under the moon. But now, she clearly had him pegged as a destination.

What did she want? Eric wasn't sure he wanted to know. He got up and walked to the sliding glass door and reached a hand out to check the lock. It was set. She was only a few feet away, so close that he could see the faint dark hairs that wisped away from the rest and brushed across her face in a fan. So close that he could see the glint of moisture against the dark when she licked her lips, and he could see the wrinkles of the white gauzy dress as it clung and shifted across her tummy and showed the flesh ripple there with every step. She seemed to almost walk naked in the night, but then the gauzy dress shifted again and she was hidden...just a woman moving closer and closer to his house in the night.

Eric reached for the switch that flicked on the outside lights. The twin spotlights on the opposite sides of the house suddenly filled the yard with hard yellow light, and the lantern light next to the sliding door on the outside did the same.

Instead of illuminating the woman though, they seemed to tear her apart. As the lights beamed on, the woman lifted her arms at Eric, as if begging for an embrace, or salvation. And then just as he registered her dismay, she was gone, and all he could see was the dead brown grass of winter outside his door, speckled faintly with the new green of spring.

He didn't sleep easily that night, but in the light of morning, he convinced himself that the woman had been the figment of the overactive imagination of an overworked lonely guy. He soon forgot the woman in white, and the spring disappeared into summer and then fall until winter killed the year again.

Winter seemed as if it were there to stay. This March was much different than last year—the grass had been buried beneath a foot of snow now for two weeks, and Eric cringed at the TV report on Saturday night that said more snow was due to fall throughout the day on Sunday. He had to travel on Monday morning, and worried about either getting snowed into his house, or having the airport close once he got there.

Neither was a good option.

He went out late Sunday afternoon, as dusk began to fall, to clear the driveway once more, hopefully making it easier for him to get out in the morning. The snow had not shown any sign of stopping, the driveway easily had three or four inches since he'd cleared it after lunch.

Sometimes it sucked to live in the Midwest.

Eric pushed the shovel and staggered back when it hit a crack in the asphalt beneath the snow. He tossed that load of white onto the tall bank already at the edge of the drive and then pushed the shovel again across the drive. Slowly he scooped the uncharacteristically late snowfall off of his driveway onto the also uncharacteristically high bank of snow that still sat on the edge of his drive. It had been a really cold, long winter.

He was nearly to the foot of the drive when he happened to look up from what he'd been doing. He could see the backyard from here, and his garden. He wondered if anything would manage to return from root or seed in a few weeks when spring finally came, given the harshness of this winter.

That was what he was thinking when he saw the sparkle of something more than snow in the air near the garden plot. Something that looked like *nothing* at first—a flutter of icy crystals on the breeze. Then, with every swirl, it became a something. A glimmering, real person...

Eric rested the shovel on the icy drive and stared at the woman walking towards him, clad in only a moonlight dress, all sparkles and vagaries...he could see the flow of her milky calves as they stepped through the snow atop his garden. He could see the press of her chest through the top of the dress, which seemed thin as tissue to his eye.

A woman dressed in tissue was walking barefoot across the snow to him.

Eric didn't know whether to run to the house or to run to her. He did neither. Instead, he stood and watched her approach. The darkness felt heavier all around them and as she stepped through the snow at the side of his house, Eric realized that this was the same woman he had insisted was just a figment of his exhausted imagination a year before.

She walked closer, and he could make out the dark brown pools of her wide-open eyes, and the wavy mane of brown hair that flowed over her shoulders as she came faster across the snow, blue-white flesh ready for embrace...

A car rounded the corner of 88th Street and its beams bore hard across the snow around his house and up the drifts of snow to kiss the feet of the garden woman. As they did, the woman in white seemed to dissolve, her face a surprised mask of anger and frustration.

For a few seconds, she'd been just feet from where Eric stood, and then, with a wavering double flash of light, she was gone.

The moment left him with a cold in his chest that wouldn't thaw...he kept thinking about that split second when she reached out for him...and then she'd come back with zero.

Cold. Gone.

She'd disappeared like the flakes of snow that shimmered and held there a moment, and then fell to the ground.

It hadn't been his imagination *this* time...or was it?

The questions kept him awake that night, and on the way to the airport the next morning, he found himself still thinking about the look of angered surprise on her face when the car lights had driven her away. But soon his attention was refocused on the business of his business trip. And then with the busy coming of spring, the strange vision again disappeared to the back of his memory.

He thought fleetingly about the ghostly woman a few weeks later as he turned over the still-hard soil of his garden. Both times he'd seen her, she'd appeared from this general area of the yard, it seemed. He'd picked the spot for the garden when he moved in because it was just out of the range of the tree roots of the old willow, and one of the only spots in the yard where the sun shone full enough through the trees to let the tomatoes grow. He had brought in bags of peat and manure the past three seasons to try to soften the ground, but it still remained difficult to turn over. He looked at the willow and wondered if the tree had something to do with the manifestation. Eric didn't remember his mythology, but it seemed like he remembered the willow as some kind of spirit-friendly tree?

He made a mental note to look it up on the Internet, but by the time he'd finished planting the bean and squash seeds and tomato and pepper plants, dusk was falling and his neighbor hung over the fence and invited him out for a beer. Eric cleaned up, went next door and didn't think again for a long while about the ghost and the willow tree. Life had a way of always moving quickly on...

❦

Dusk brought the faint reflection of stars to the frost on the ground of Eric's backyard. It was another cold snap in March, and his breath instantly fogged the cold glass as he stood staring out at the shadowy landscape of frozen grass and bare, twisted tree limbs. The winter had flown by as his day job sent him to bed exhausted and beat-up from the days, night after night. Nevertheless, he was more than ready for spring. In his heart, he felt worn out and constantly tired. He blamed it on the season, and prayed that with the return of spring, he might feel better. But he feared that in reality, he was just growing old. Used up.

The tea in his mug (brewed from dried peppermint sprigs that grew behind the willow) was lukewarm, and Eric began to turn away from the window to take it to the microwave. But a flash of something caught his eye. He turned his attention back to the yard, and for a third time, he saw her.

She moved quickly across the frost, and Eric backed away from the glass. He remembered that the glow of headlights and the flash of his backdoor spotlight had driven her away the past two times he'd seen her. Not wanting her to disappear instantly, he reached behind him and clicked off the table lamp near the couch. He was curious to know what she would do...what she wanted.

And then she stood outside of his sliding glass door, long brown hair rimmed in moonlight, white dress clinging to her like fairy gauze. Her eyes stared at him, as if questioning. She lifted one blue-white calf and then her bare foot was through Eric's window, and in a heartbeat, the rest of her followed.

Eric dropped the mug to the carpet.

"Who are you?" he whispered. She didn't answer, but instead flew towards him, moving across the room in seconds to stand silent within reach of his embrace.

His heart beat like a hammer and his arms were paralyzed as he stared into the faintly liquid eyes of the ghost. He could vaguely make out the outline of his sliding glass door through the pale glow of her skin. Part of him wanted to reach back and flick the light back on...but he couldn't move. From his throat, he managed a tortured whisper of "Why...?" But the room remained completely otherwise silent. The ticking of the kitchen clock was painfully audible as the woman slowly raised a hand and put a finger to Eric's lips. And then she placed the same hand flat on his chest.

He looked down and saw the shine of his belt through her thin luminescent arm. What did she want, why did she touch him? He could feel the strangest tingle beneath her hand, but no pressure of flesh. Was she sucking the blood from his heart?

She only paused there a second, and then removed her hand from him and began walking down the hallway. She paused once and looked back over her shoulder, as if waiting for him to follow. Eric found that his panic had relaxed, at least enough so that he could move again, and after a moment's hesitation, he began to follow. As soon as he did, she turned and continued walking deeper into his house, through the hall and around the corner and into his bedroom. As he rounded the doorway, he saw that she crouched next to his bed. One translucent arm pointed to the dark beneath.

What did she want? For him to crawl under the bed? Eric stood at the entrance to the room and watched her point repeatedly towards the space beneath his bed. Her eyes flashed with anxious need, as if it was a matter of life and death that he follow the clue of her ghostly fingers.

Eric shrugged and decided to play along and move the bed to see what she was pointing at. Absently he reached to the wall to flick the light on, so he could see what he was doing and…

…in a heartbeat, she was gone.

"You stupid shit," he cursed himself out loud. "How could you be such an idiot!" He turned the light off and waited in the empty room for a few minutes, hoping that she would reappear before walking back to the family room and looking outside towards the garden and the willow. He waited, but in his heart, he knew that she was gone for the night. She hadn't reappeared after the light had taken her the past two times, and so he supposed she wouldn't this time either.

Finally, he turned the lights in the house back on, and cleaned up the tea from where he'd spilled it on the carpet. Then he went back to his bedroom and moved the bed away from the wall. Dust bunnies rolled along the back wall, but it was the discolored wood a couple feet away from the wall that he stared at. Part of the reason he'd placed the bed where he had when he'd first moved in was because he'd noticed that spot in the floor. It looked as if someone had cut into the hardwood at some point, pulled out a square, and then replaced it with not-quite-the-same wood. He'd assumed that someone had needed to dig through the floor to fix a utility line at some point in the home's past, and had ruined the original flooring doing so.

Now he wasn't so sure.

Eric went and got a crowbar from the garage. He slipped the edge in the groove between the new square of flooring and the rest.

He pushed back on the other end of the tool, and the square shifted. Eric rocked the metal bar just a bit, and then pushed again, and the entire square of five strips of hardwood lifted as one. It clattered to the floor upside down, and he saw the flooring had been nailed together with two other thin boards. It was a doorway into the ground without handle or hinges. And beneath where it had lain, was a dark hole.

Eric peered inside. Six or eight inches below the flooring, a number of things rested on a small blue-and-green-checked blanket. He lifted them out, one by one, and then pulled the blanket from where it rested on the concrete of his foundation as well.

Then he sat back and looked more carefully at what he'd found.

A stack of faded black-and-white photographs, taken in a wide variety of locales. He recognized the Grand Canyon and Times Square amid many other less obvious locations. The common element of them all was a smiling woman with dark eyes and hair. She looked like the kind of girl who laughed easily and hugged hello. She looked a lot like the woman who had pointed to the space beneath his bed.

Her name was Emma Hodgson. At least that was what he surmised after reading the name on the prescription bottle that he had pulled up with the other things. And when he opened the small leather-bound book titled simply Diary, on the first inside page it read, *These are the private thoughts of Emma Hodgson.*

He noted quickly that the slim, loopy handwriting in the diary did not match the jagged script within a small notebook that had also been tucked into the "vault". The notebook held a man's writing.

Eric gathered the books and blanket, the bottle and a necklace and a jewelry box with a ruby ring inside, and took them out to the family room. After setting his bed to right, he began to read the story of Emma and Jerry Hodgson.

This house is everything I ever dreamed of, Emma had written early in the book. *We're so far from anyone, we could run naked as a jay through the backyard and nobody would ever know. It's a sanctuary. Jerry's going to plant some trees so that in a few years we might have some shade; there was nothing but scrub grass and the willow here when they built the place.*

The entry was dated April 22, 1954.

The early entries extolled the beauty of the prairie and eventually bemoaned the fact that a new house was going up a little ways down the road. They'd no longer be alone in their wilderness. Emma wrote about Jerry's new job at Goldstar, selling appliances, and about how much he loved her spaghetti, and about how they often they sat in the afternoon or at night in their family room looking out on the grassy plain behind their house, frequently watching falcons hunt rabbits.

But by 1957, Emma's entries grew shorter, and her mood less upbeat. She complained of headaches and sickness and more. *I don't want him to worry,* was her frequent explanation for why she told these things to her diary, but kept them from Jerry. Eventually, Jerry apparently noticed that her slim form had grown bony and her smiles turned from cheer to grimace. In December of 1957, he forcibly took her to a doctor, despite her protestations that they couldn't afford it.

They came home with two bottles of pain pills and the memory of the doctor's expression of hopelessness.

In February of 1958 she wrote, *It hurts to breathe, it hurts to eat, it hurts to live. It's killing Jerry to watch me die. He's been so good to me, trying to keep me warm, making sure I take my medicine so that the pain goes away, a little bit. I don't think this can drag on much longer in any event. Every night when I say good night to him, in my heart I say goodbye, just in case. But I so hope to see the spring come one more time. If I could just see my hyacinths bloom one last time and the goldfinches return...*

Jerry's notebook told an equally painful story. The short version was, he'd lost his job before Thanksgiving and had no family to turn to as his wife grew more ashen and frail by the day. He couldn't afford the morphine, and so he sold off his possessions, one by one, to buy them rice and milk and medicine. After he sold their car, he spent two and a half hours walking down the country roads back from town in a snowstorm. That was on February 16, 1958.

On March 21st, 1958, he wrote:

Emma screamed all night. I couldn't do anything but watch her and rub her head with cold rags. Her fingernails drew blood on my arms. But this morning, she got her wish. The green she's been watching all week finally burst into color—the purple hyacinths she planted the spring we moved here have bloomed. I carried her outside so that she could smell them, in the grove she dug near the willow. When I brought her back in the house, she fell asleep on the couch, and there was a smile on her face for the first time in weeks. I hate to admit it, but I cried then. I sat in front of my wife and cried, and she didn't hear me; she's too far gone. That's when I went to the kitchen and poured all of the morphine pills into her broth. It's not right that she suffer anymore. I can't do anything else for her. Today, she got what she's been praying for—she found spring. Tonight, I'll send her home to heaven.

On March 22nd, Jerry wrote simply, *I laid her in the earth by her hyacinths. I have no money for a coffin or a stone or to bury her in the cemetery...but her flowers will mark her place.*

The next entry was dated two months later, and was equally brief.

I can't stay here any longer. The bank threatens foreclosure, and the electric company turned the power off last week. This is no longer my home, it's her resting place. I will place these memories of her someplace safe, and say goodbye. Emma found her spring, now I have to find mine.

There were no other entries, though the ink was blurred on that final page, as if it had gotten wet. Perhaps from tears.

Eric felt chilled as he closed the notebook. He looked at the date on his phone and nodded. It was March 21st. Fifty-three years to the night that Emma had died. On a hunch, he looked up his calendar on the computer to see when his business trip had been the year before, when he'd seen her walk towards him as he shoveled snow from the drive. He'd left on the Monday, and been shoveling snow Sunday at dusk…March 21st.

He couldn't narrow down the previous sighting to a date, but he knew it had been an unseasonably warm day in March…

Eric marked March 21st on his calendar so he would re-member, and set it to repeat on the same day every year. The entry simply read *Emma Hodgson*.

～∞～

Over the next few weeks, Eric researched the history of his house, and found that it had been built in the early '50s. Its first owners had been a young couple named Jerry and Emma Hodgson. Four years after purchasing, both had disappeared, and when the mortgage was six months in arrears, the bank had reclaimed the property and sold it to another couple who owned it for the next thirty-one years, while a subdivision grew up all around them. Two more owners had held the property before Eric bought it. In all his searches, he never could come up with an answer to where Jerry had gone.

Eric finally researched the mythology behind willow trees too, and found them closely identified with the feminine aspect and intuition and deep emotions, as well as with dreaming, en-chantment, rebirth and spring.

Fitting, he thought.

～∞～

That summer, Eric didn't plant his vegetable garden. In-stead, he cleared the topsoil off the area he'd been planting. Not far from the willow tree, at the edge of his garden plot, he found a large round boulder buried a couple feet below the soil. He dug carefully around it, focusing on the area pointing away from the boulder…he guessed that stone would likely be a poor man's headstone.

The clay didn't get any easier to turn over the deeper he went, and Eric's shoulders were aching when he scraped away another thin layer of orange clay to reveal a ragged edge of some kind of material. He chipped away at the ground until more of the fragment was revealed. It appeared to some kind of white silk.

He worked more carefully then, and little by little, he freed the material from the soil...and then his shovel scraped ever so slightly against something that wasn't dirt. It could have been white rock, but Eric knew better. He climbed out of the hole and got a small garden hand shovel, and carefully carved the earth until the vertebrae and jaw were revealed. A half hour later, he sat back in the hole, and stared into the black pits that remained of Emma's eyes.

Her skull stared back at him, sightless in the cool earth. Beneath the sweat streaming from every pore, Eric shivered. "I'm sorry, Emma," he whispered at the skull beneath his garden. "But I had to know for sure. I won't bother you again."

Gently he pressed the dirt back over her face, and then climbed out of the hole. He cut a branch of lilac from the bush nearby, and tossed the fragrant purple flowers into the hole in offering. Then he filled the grave back in, and lifted the boulder out of its pit so that it visibly marked her resting place clearly once more.

Eric replaced his garden plot with a stand of lilies...

∽

Eric read Emma's diary cover to cover that summer, walking the yard to try to find places and views she described. Everything was different now, with houses now all around. But the willow remained, and just as she described doing more than fifty years before, he frequently rested there, content in the summer shade beneath its rain of branches. Somehow, in his focus to plant a proper memorial on her grave, his own personal ennui and exhaustion disappeared. How could he feel empty inside when others had experienced so much worse? He still had his life, and his warm house and the comforts of a million things that Emma and Jerry had never even imagined.

∽

In the fall, he filled the entire area with hyacinth bulbs.

∽

On March 21st, Eric was ready. He was as nervous as a boy on a first date—so afraid that he might be stood up. But when the dusk came down after a warm day and the stars came out, once again Emma rose from her grave beside the willow, and walked towards the place where her life had loved.

Eric waited for her there on the couch facing the sliding glass door. He sipped a bottle of winter ale, and smiled as the glowing woman in white stepped through the glass and across the carpet to join him.

For a time, the two of them simply sat there, staring out the glass at the shadows of a hundred hyacinths blooming atop her grave.

And then Eric began to speak, quietly in the dark room. The ghost of Emma Hodgson turned her face to meet his own as he began to tell her the story of her house—of all of the things that had happened here in the years that she had been away. He told her of the cycle of rebirth and death, again and again. She slipped a glowing hand into his own, as Eric told stories of love, and loss...and spring.

In Memoryum

They say the memory is the first to go. That was his first thought as he turned his head from one side of the pillow to the other, and recognized…nothing.

Jayce got up from the sagging mattress and wondered where his memory had slipped away to. His lower back spasmed as he walked across the tiny room, nearly spilling him into the yellow-rimmed window shade he'd crossed to open. He caught himself with a shaking palm on the wall, gasping at the pain and the sudden dizzying speed of his heart. Two inches to the left and he might have fallen forward, full force, and put his hand through the glass, and after his hand, maybe his whole body, unless his neck hung up on a jagged shard and left his body dangling there on the inside of the room while his lifeblood spilled down his severed neck and the fractured glass to pool on the pavement below.

Or was there pavement? Jayce shook his head, trying to clear the cobwebs. He didn't remember. He didn't know where the room was or what was beyond it, or how he'd gotten there in the first place.

The shade pulled down and released like a slingshot, clattering around and around at the top of the battered wooden window frame. Jayce squinted at the sudden influx of sun. Blinking away tears, he leaned forward to look outside.

An empty parking lot. Tufts of grass split the graying surface. To the left, Jayce could make out the rusted base stanchions of some kind of large signpost, and to the right, a single car overran the yellow guidelines of a designated parking space. The lot seemed to end at the back of an abandoned field, which stretched on to disappear into a stand of trees far away on the horizon.

Jayce turned back from the window and took a closer look at the room itself. There wasn't much to look at. A single bed, with a thin mattress that had obviously seen the press of many a heavy backside. A green floral comforter dragged off to the floor where he'd thrown it, and the only other piece of furniture was a dark brown nightstand topped by a thrift shop lamp and a $5 traveler's alarm clock. The red LED read 11:21. From the growl of his gut, he also assumed that it had been some time since he'd last eaten. Though he couldn't remember when or what that last meal might have been.

There were no other personal effects in the room, but Jayce found a set of keys in his pants pocket. The world felt skewed, everything tilted forty-five degrees. He stared at the keys and wondered what doors they opened. He wondered who he was. He knew his name, and when he touched his arms, they felt familiar. Right. But everything else felt gray.

Jayce stepped through a doorframe into a tiny bath, and plunged his hands into the water from the sink faucet, splashing his face again and again. When he looked up into the mirror, he saw a face dripping with exhaustion...deep-set eyes ringed by shadowed purplish circles, and a patchy growth of beard spread like a rash across wide cheeks. Lips cut through black stubble like a pale river. It was a face that Jayce didn't recognize. But then, he had no mental picture of himself at all to compare it to.

He looked closer, trying to remember. Despite its fatigue, the mug that stared dully back at him didn't look that old, just a worn-down thirtysomething, not the ancient creaking geriatric his back and limbs and mind seemed to indicate he might have physically become. Jayce wiped the water and his frown on a dingy white hand towel, and decided to see what lay beyond the room.

∽

The keys in his pocket started the car in the parking lot. But Jayce didn't know where to go. He edged it out onto an empty side road, *Clandestine Road*, the sign read. He laughed at the irony of that. Behind him the vacant shell of the building he'd awoken inside loomed like a cutout prop against a gray sky. These moments hardly seemed real, yet, no matter how many times he tried pinching his skin, or biting his tongue, he did not wake up. Nor did he remember. At least, he didn't remember what he had done yesterday, or what people called him, but he did remember learned motor skills, like walking and opening doors and driving a car.

In a haze of time, he even vaguely remembered once getting his driver's license, which allowed him to drive the car...speaking of which...

Jayce pulled to the side of the road and put the car in park. Then he pulled out his wallet. If he had a license, he at least would know where to go home to, since it included his address. So long as he hadn't moved recently.

In moments he had discovered his address, and cross referenced it with a map from the glove box. The morning fog lifted as he navigated his way home, stopping once at a gas station to find out exactly where he was starting from, since Clandestine wasn't on the map. He laughed at that.

The gray morning fog had lifted by the time he stepped onto the wooden porch of the small bungalow he apparently called home. He froze for a second as he slid a key into the lock. What if he was married and there was a woman inside whom he didn't know? Or worse yet...what if he was divorced and he no longer actually lived here?

The lock clicked, and before he could think of any further debilitating scenarios, the door had creaked open. He stepped inside, shutting it quietly but firmly behind him. He knew in an instant that nobody was home. The air hung stagnant, stale, yet spiced with the hint of cumin.

He quickly saw why when he stepped past the empty dining room table and into the narrow run of the kitchen.

One long counter, meant for a cook's workspace, was littered with empty Thai takeout boxes. As he stepped into the room something small and brown darted away from one of the boxes to slip in between the creamy counter backsplash and the kitchen wall. From the corner of his eye, Jayce thought he saw the dash for safety repeated elsewhere around him. He shivered and left the room to the bugs.

Upstairs in the bedroom, he found a rumpled mess of pale sheets wound inside an ocean-blue comforter. Elegant gold thread slipped and curled in subtle filigree patterns across the thick bedcover; they glimmered like firefly capillaries in the dull light as he threw the sheets up to cover the crushed mound of pillows. Apparently he hadn't cooked *or* made the bed in a while. He ran a finger across the dark wood of a woman's dresser and stared at the gray silt that had collected there. Or dusted or cleaned.

He reached around a ceramic statue of the Virgin Mary to pick up a picture frame from the dresser. The frame enclosed an action shot, rather than a portrait. He recognized a younger version of the face he had seen in the mirror this morning. Broad cheeks with a shadow of time turning to whiskers. Thick black eyebrows pulled back against an unmanageable tousle of hair. He was laughing in the photo, as was the woman whose shoulder he draped an arm around. One long lock of cinnamon hair obscured her right eye, but her left held the secret mirth of a cat's eye. Emerald and squinting at whatever moment they shared. Captured in that second when all the two of them could do was gasp for air from laughter, while holding back the tears of life. He searched his memory for some clue, but his brain remained mute. His heart did not turn over. Jayce felt no connection at all to the picture or the woman.

Next to the frame was another, this one a posed portrait of a small child. A boy judging by the outfit. The toddler knelt in front of an obviously fake fall photo backdrop, chubby hands locked together atop a small stepladder with a collage of red and orange and browned leaves behind him. From the light of the photo, it appeared that the child's eyes were green. *Like his mother's,* Jayce guessed.

I knew these two well, if I kept their pictures on my dresser, he supposed. Girlfriend and her kid? His own wife and son? He realized suddenly that there was a ring on the fourth finger of his left hand.

God! Jayce slammed his fist down on the dresser and a bottle of woman's perfume shivered on the edge of a small shelf next to the mirror. It fell and shattered on the wood below and the room filled with the dizzying scent of gardenias and vanilla.

Jayce breathed in the scent and gasped.

...black lace slipped high and stark on the cream of her thigh, and he moved his lips farther, up into the warmth of her, tongue teasing at her sweetness as he inhaled that warm elixir of her sex. Her

*fingers twined in his hair, pulling him closer as he tasted her heaven
and breathed in her perfume, lust mixed with the lush of gardenias,
woody vanilla spiced with love. His eyes flickered at the intensity of the
moment, as she pressed harder against him and filled the perfumed air
with the soft cry of her pleasure...*

In a flash the moment was gone again, and Jayce staggered
backwards, resting against the bed. He pressed a palm to his
cheek, and closed his eyes again, trying to delve deeper into the
memory, farther into the moment unlocked, and then stolen
away again. But now he only smelled the overpowering thickness of spilled perfume, and presently he went to the bathroom
to find a washrag to sponge up the spill before it ruined the
wood. It was his dresser, he supposed, so he might as well take
care of it.

He opened the bedroom and kitchen windows and cracked
the front door to let in a breeze. The air chilled him to the bone
and the furnace kicked on and ran and ran. It couldn't keep up
with the first breath of winter. But the cold braced him, woke
him. He'd been in a fog since he'd woken this morning in the
strange bed, and now he needed a plan. Something had happened to him, and he needed to find out what. Was he in danger? Where was his wife, and, he supposed, his son? Who could
he call to find out?

He glanced across the room and saw the black-and-silver
answering machine station sitting on an end table, one receiver
poking its thin plastic antennae at the ceiling. A red light flashed
incessantly, a heartbeat demanding notice.

Jayce reached out to touch the button to hear the message
and then hesitated. His neck grew instantly cold. What if he
didn't want to know?

He *needed* to know.

*"Hey, Jayce. It's Bill from work. You remember work, don't you?
We remember you...but we haven't seen you this week. Or heard from
you. And well... Listen, I'm sorry about this, I really am, but...you
brought this on yourself man. I mean—we were really understanding
after Becky and...well, you know. But...it's been months now, Jayce.
And you're not any better. We never know when you're going to turn
up...or if you're going to turn up at all. I talked to you about this last
week and you promised that was the last time. Well...I'm afraid this*

is the last time. We've gotta pull the plug and get someone in here who's here, Jayce. I'm really sorry about this because you're a nice guy and I know it's been a lot to handle but...um...well listen, I'll see you around, I'm sure..."

So...he'd apparently gotten himself fired from...wherever it was he worked. He would have called back and found that much out at least, but the phone said *unlisted number* on the call log.

Jayce closed the door and the kitchen windows. He was now cold inside and out. Stacking the partially empty takeout cartons one inside of the other, he cleared the kitchen counters of debris, wiping up the food and stains with a wet paper towel.

That was when he found the notepad by the kitchen phone. The edges of the top sheet were covered in scrawled notes, and doodles. *Thai Bonsai—555-1223* read one note, which matched the name on the boxes he'd just thrown away. *Saturday at 8* read another note, without further description. Who knew what he'd been planning for Saturday. Or even which Saturday.

Jean says quote is no read another. And *Nothing lasts* still another. As he searched for a memory to explain them, to find context, Jayce wondered if all the notes people scrawled by their phones were so oblique. At least to a stranger. And he was a stranger, at the moment. A stranger to his own life.

At the bottom of the sheet, hedged off in the corner by a triple crosshatched box, was another phone number, this one surrounded by a single explanatory note: *She can help.*

Jayce picked up the phone, and dialed the number. He didn't know what "she" could help with. But at the moment, he'd take any help he could get.

A cool female voice answered on the fourth ring. "How can I help you," she asked.

"I'm not really sure," he said. "I can't really remember how this all started..."

He was surprised at her answer. "That's a great start..."

The road seemed vaguely familiar as Jayce wound through the city following the directions the woman had given.

After a while, he realized it was more than familiar. He pulled through the narrow steel gates and drove into the parking lot of a building that teased the sky in a defiant thrust.

Jayce wondered if he'd taken the same parking space as he'd

left earlier this morning. Shrugging and curious, he exited the car and walked towards the building where he'd awoken just hours before.

The parking lot was still empty, but for his car.

⤸⤹

The door opened just a crack and Jayce could see the shadowed glint of a large brown eye through the narrow opening. "It *is* you," she said, and a chain clattered metallic against the door as it opened farther. "Come in," she said.

Jayce stepped inside, but didn't immediately follow her after closing the door. The room was exactly as he remembered it from this morning, only now, there was a woman inside...and that made everything about the space different. She wore only two thin strips of black lace lingerie above and below a tightly cinched corset. Jayce followed the bob of the dangling corset laces as she crossed the room and sank to the bed. She patted the mattress beside her and beckoned him over.

"Come here," she said in the lowest melody of near-silence. He obeyed her, taking her all in as he came to stand beside her and then joined her on the bed. Her eyes watched him, wide and brown as a doe's, lashes unblinking. A haze of lushly black hair cascaded over her shoulder, broken in its midnight by a thick strand that glowed as red as neon. As red as her glossed lips. As red as the balm that traced and overwrote the thin seam of her eyebrows.

She was a black cherry, lush and waiting for him. But why? And waiting for what? She had not been terribly surprised when he'd called, and seemed to recognize him when he stepped into the doorway. Jayce instinctively knew as she slid a hand easily up his back and shoulder that he'd been with her the night before. Here. In this bed. He couldn't remember a minute of it. Which was a shame. As he looked closer at her vanilla-scented skin, he knew that she must have been very good. Perhaps a once-in-a-lifetime partner.

"I don't know who you are," he said suddenly.

A tiny flicker across her lips.

"I don't know why I was here last night with you."

She blinked, but did not deny his supposition.

"I don't really know anything anymore."

She nodded, and this time grinned, exposing a smile that could have lit the room. "That's good," she said. Her voice was honey mixed with cloves—sweet but edged in dark peat. She pulled him against her and ran cool fingers up his temples.

"Let's keep it that way."

Jayce could feel his body relax, the frustration of the day fading out of him with every stroke of her fingers. She pressed him back to the mattress and he laid his head against the pillow. She coiled around him like a velvet robe, her thighs slinky and warm against his, the tight cinch of her waist hard against the place where he grew hard, and the swell of her chest a cushion that both called him forward and pressed him down. He breathed her in, and the scent of vanilla suddenly filled the room. Vanilla and gardenias, like this afternoon, when he had... When what?

He wondered, the press of her lips now whispering something to his ear, and then the light flick of her heat warmed his lips as her tongue teased him.

"What about this afternoon?" he asked aloud, and she shushed him, pressing against him with all her body. Her hands ran up and down his ribs and arms, and as she did he felt strange, disoriented. The room seemed to swim in the heady scent of...of...

"No!" Jayce pushed her back and off him, and the woman nearly fell to the floor at his violence.

He shook his head, struggling to clear the cobwebs that had grown across his vision like cotton. "What are you doing to me?" he said, and slapped his own face. In a heartbeat she was there, kissing his reddened cheek, but this time he did not succumb. He backed away and put out a hand to keep her at bay. She crouched on legs creamy as vanilla, her chest flushed cherry red, and heaving now. Her lips were wet, and she licked them nervously. "I need to kiss you," she begged, and crawled forward again, pushing her way around his hand. He tried to fend her off but she was faster, darting through his fumbling hands to sink a wet, pink tongue quickly between his lips.

Jayce felt the world rush away, and everything tasted...hot. His thighs itched and his eyes refused to stay open. He tasted something warm and smoky, something sweet, something vanilla…

Jayce shoved her away again, disengaging violently from her kiss. She surged back instantly, and he yelled again, "No!"

She took his shoulders between her hands, trying to pin him between the wall and her chest, and he slipped one arm free.

He slapped her, hard, across the face. This time, she did fall back, and off the bed.

Jayce leapt after her, and before she could get up, he cuffed her wrists with his palms and held her to the floor. She twisted and thrashed against him, but he used his weight to hold her down.

"What did you do to me?" His voice grated as he struggled to remain on top. "Why was I here last night? Why can't I remember anything?"

"Let me go," she hissed back. "I did what you paid me to do."

"Tell me," he insisted.

"I'll do better than that," she said. "Let me go and I'll show you."

He released her, and pushed back to sit on the floor as she sat up herself, rubbing her wrists. Her face was still dark where he'd slapped her. She was so fair-skinned it would probably bruise. The thought disgusted him. He was no woman beater. Or was he? He couldn't remember enough to know.

"What is this place? Who are you?" he said, calmer now.

"Call me Lethe," she said, not easing the tension of her body as she faced him. Her voice betrayed a sadness that stretched deeper than any physical pain. "You came to me for help. Let me help you again." She reached out a hand to him but he batted it away.

"Let me," she said. "This time, I will help you remember, since that is what you wish."

This time, he let her touch him, and as she ran fingers up his face, and around his neck to draw him close, he felt his pulse quicken. The fuzziness in his mind began to fade back, and his mind seemed to…tighten. Lethe's eyes gazed into his own, and he could see his own reflected back at him, gray eyes wide with fear and a growing pain.

Her tongue slipped into his mouth again, and her fingers began to undress him as his own fumbled with the string of her corset. With every breath he shared with her, with every touch of his skin to hers, his world grew sharper.

He remembered his parents, Lois and Bill, and the cottage that they still kept in Michigan. For no reason, he found himself thinking of skinny-dipping with a blonde girl down at the quarry on one dark amazing night when he had come home for the weekend from college. He'd gone to the quarry alone for a late-night swim, and found himself an hour later exploring the cool skin of a beautiful girl who had come to the lake for the same reason. Escape from the problems of the day. Freedom from everything that had gone before. Instead they had become entangled in each other. A new problem, if a sweet one.

As he thought those words, Lethe suddenly became clearer to him. He had come to her for the same reason. He remembered unzipping the back of her thin black dress and watching in amazement as it fell to the floor.

"The only way out is in," she had said, and wrapped her arms around his shoulders, pressing her bare chest to his shirt. "I hope you don't mind coming in."

He'd let her undress him and lead him to the bed, tears forming in his eyes as he thought about why he'd come and felt a rush of guilt for what he was doing. Becky was gone now, but still...he was paying a woman to...

To what...?

Lethe had led him again to the bed, and he kicked off his pants, as she shrugged out of her corset. She slid to the sheets next to him, wearing only black stockings, barely breaking their kiss the whole time they'd undressed each other.

The scent of her hair tickled his nose and he realized it smelled like the perfume of his wife. She wore vanilla. Had worn vanilla, the last time he'd kissed her. But that time Becky had smelled not only of vanilla, but of iron. And her lips tasted strange and cold as he pulled away. His hands had been smeared in her blood, but he couldn't stop from pressing them to his face, to wipe the horrible tears from his cheeks. Across the room, Danny lay dead too. Like his mother, they had carved things in his flesh, something that only Jayce would understand.

The memory stabbed into the deepest pit of his heart like a coil of barbed wire, and he broke from Lethe's kiss to cry out.

"This is why you came to me," she whispered, pulling him back. "You don't have to remember all of it now. I can take it away again."

Jayce put a fist to his eyes and shook his head. "I have to know now." Then he pressed Lethe to the bed, and forced his tongue back into her mouth.

"It wasn't your fault," Lethe gasped, pushing him back. "You didn't kill them."

He kissed her again, gripping the fullness of her breasts in desperation, not desire. But she let him use her, and in seconds, as his thrusts built to a point of unbearable need, the worst of it came upon him with the wave of his orgasm.

The laughter froze on his lips. He'd been chuckling at the radio DJ's banter since he'd turned the key off in his ignition, and that laughter stayed with him right up until he saw the bloody handprint slapped against the buttercream wall of the living room. He called out for his wife, and before the echo faded from his voice, he had dropped his empty coffee thermos and a sheaf of papers from work to the carpet as he ran through the kitchen, following a trail of crimson smeared on the carpet, across the tile, and occasionally, with a long, scrabbling fingerprint, down a wall.

Jayce was crying before he found the bodies.

The blood led him on. It stopped sometimes, and then pooled heavily where she'd fallen to rest before forcing herself up and onward, up the formerly white carpeted stairs and down the hall. He knew as soon as he hit the landing where that blood would lead. Her palm and fingerprints scratched and smeared in long digs against the hallway carpet. The tears were already to Jayce's chin when he stepped into the nursery.

Becky lay nude and still at the foot of Danny's crib. The carpet around her had darkened. Her hands clutched at the rails of the baby's bed, but it looked as if she had been unable to make it that final three feet. Her face was wet with tears, but it was the blood that Jayce couldn't stop seeing. Because the blood didn't come from just a stab, or gunshot wound.

It came from two letters and three numbers carved deep into Becky's back. Jayce could see the white of bone shining through the oozing gore around her spine.

AS032.

That was all that her back said. But the numbers were fatal.

Jayce moved closer, forcing his eyes away from his wife to look into the bed where she almost, but couldn't quite, reach.

"Jesus," he cried aloud, when he saw the still form of his little boy. The crib bars were coated with blood, and the sheep and cows on the bedsheets appeared slaughtered in the sea of red. How could one baby have held so much life?

"Oh God, Danny," Jayce had cried, barely seeing, but not stopping until he held the still form of his sticky, lifeless boy against his chest. After a moment, he crumbled to the floor with the tiny corpse to sob beside the body of his wife.

His fingers traced the wound that was already almost dry on his son's back. From the amount of blood smeared on the baby's hands and across the bars of the crib, he knew that Danny had been carved alive, just as Becky had been. The fuckers had left him their living note, and coldly walked away. Jayce had not killed his wife or son, Lethe was right in the literal sense. But they were condemned by his actions.

AS032.

Danny's back bled the code just as Becky's did.

AS032 was the last sequence in the passcode to the account that Jayce had been siphoning from for the past six months. And someone had, apparently, gotten wise. Someone who could never go to the police to complain.

"You lived in fear for months," Lethe whispered to him, kissing his earlobe gently. "You were paralyzed with it. Nothing worked. There was only one way."

Jayce nodded. The memories all came back. The agony of his unconfessed guilt. The fear that at any moment, from any corner, they would finally step out of the darkness to end his life. The insomnia. The jumping at every creak and crack. The horrible, racking tears that came without warning at work, in the car, as he made breakfast...

In a flash he saw the flyer again that he'd found at the back of the free weekly paper. *In Memoryum*, read the headline. *Let* *us remove those troublesome memories inside your brain with a kiss. What we give you here, you'll want to remember...but we'll make you forget. Ask for Mistress Lethe to receive a $20 discount.*

The address was in the city's red light district, but Jayce had called anyway, and quizzed the woman who answered about whether they could really make a person forget. In the end, he set up the appointment.

"You're a hooker," he whispered.

Lethe raised one eyebrow, shrugged. "And you're a thief. You hired me to take away your memories. I did."

"But you..." He pointed at her stockings, her discarded corset.

"The only way out is back in." She smiled. "My gift is forgetfulness. But you must be close to receive it."

Jayce slumped on the bed, pulling his arms around his knees in a fetal hug. The images of his wife and baby, carved with the code of his trespass, was now overlaid on everything he looked at. He closed his eyes, and the blood still was there. He remembered now, why he'd lost his friends, and his job after the murders. The picture wouldn't leave. AS032. Carved in his family's flesh. In his mind's eye forever.

"Why did you take the money?" Lethe asked.

"For them," he said. "For Becky, Danny. I didn't think a little bit here and there over time, would be missed. I wanted to give Becky a new house, a place where Danny could run..." His voice trailed off.

"And now?" she asked.

The tears came again, hot and fast, raining down his cheeks to drip across his thighs. Jayce rocked on the bed, crying without restraint, his voice gasping in tortured hitches as he begged the air for forgiveness. "I'm sorry," he moaned. "So, so sorry."

"You didn't mean it," Lethe said.

"I miss them so bad," he cried. "I don't want to forget them. But all I can see is their blood."

"Sometimes, you have to be reborn to go on," Lethe said. She stretched her arms out to him, and lay back on the bed, slowly spreading her legs for him to move between.

"The only way out is in," she said once more.

Jayce rubbed the tears from his cheeks, and looked through

the bloody memory of AS032 to see the beautiful woman who offered herself before him.

"I have to forget," he said, gritting his teeth against the sobs. "I need to forget."

He took Lethe in his arms, and pressed himself desperately against her, inhaling her scent and drowning his guilt in the warmth of her touch. She kissed his tears, and then his lips. Through the window, the dull red glow of the neon sign that blazed *In Memoryum* to anyone on Clandestine Road, lit his way to her.

Everything blurred, and Jayce pulled away, just for a moment, to stare down into the dark pools of Lethe's eyes. She did not blink.

"Goodbye, Becky," he said. A tear fell to wet Lethe's cheek. "Goodbye, Danny."

The earthy scent of vanilla teased him forward, and he kissed Lethe once more, as the room slipped away.

BAD DAY

I CAN REMEMBER the very first time I heard the news report on them. A commentator made a joke of it. "Paul Hughes," he said, "had a bad day today."

That was something of an understatement, to say the least. Paul Hughes had just been fired from pushing paper literally the day after his wife filed for divorce. He made the news because in the aftermath of this personal implosion, he was walking, no doubt somewhat disconsolately, in the forest near Brave River. As he moped along a walking trail some kind of insect attacked him. The commentator speculated that the buzzing sound of the creature at the back of Hughes's earlobe led him to jump, slap at the back of his head and consequently lose his balance to fall to the concrete walking path below. He ended up in the hospital after a cardiac arrest left him thrashing on the riverbank with said insect crushed in a chitinous orange paste to the back of his head.

It wasn't really funny, but I laughed. The poor guy lost his wife, lost his job, and now, might lose his life because a hornet or something "took advantage" of him at the wrong moment.

That was the last time I laughed.

In the beginning, everyone thought they were some strange, exotic breed of roaches. They measured about two inches long, and like the roaches or palmetto bugs of the Deep South, were bronze-tinged, dark as well-cured tobacco. They were quickly dubbed Luna Roaches, because they flew in clouds on the wind at twilight and descended on the city in a swarm that blotted out the light of the moon. What bugs flew at night? Nobody really asked that.

The warnings went out quickly. Don't stay out after dark. Don't let your children stay out playing after school. Don't leave your windows open.

Don't, don't, *don't.*

The media told us to hunker down and hide, cuz the killer roaches had come to town.

Of course, they didn't say it that way. But while some of us laughed at the story of Paul Hughes flailing about and ending up in a coma because a bug dive-bombed him, we lost our sense of humor really quick when swarms of them began to attack people on the streets at night.

We didn't know what they could do, at first. Didn't know what they wanted. Initially, the concern was that they could carry some kind of virus or disease.

Who would have guessed that what they brought us was so much more? And so much worse?

"Kara, come inside," my wife shouted. Our little girl was only five, but already she was a handful. Sometimes I was glad that I had to go to work every day and sit in an office. While I lived for the hours that we played together, and she giggled and kicked and fought against my tickle bombs, I knew I could never spend the day with my baby and keep up with the girl. She was a handful of laughter and energy, while I felt like a slow-moving anchor of molasses shellacked in tar. I was tired after lofting her in the air a few times like a rocket and rolling about on the floor with her before pronouncing bedtime. I played with her an hour or two a day, while Jenna had her for the other twelve.

The city was under alert now; for the past few nights swarms of the Luna Roaches had descended on the streets in a bizarre attack of buzz and wings and biting venom. Those who fell prey to the things were taken to hospital, but couldn't be revived. Neither did they die. The doctors quickly learned not to try to pry the roaches from the flesh of the bodies they brought in. While the victims were comatose when they came in to the hospitals with the bugs on their necks or skulls, when the insects were removed, the low level of neural activity dropped to virtually none. If you removed the bugs, you turned the patient into a human vegetable. But if you left them attached to the host, the victim lay in the hospital in a coma. The difference seemed negligible, but as we soon learned, the difference was great.

Jenna slammed the sliding door like a shotgun behind Kara and my little girl ran right into my arms.

"How's my baby?" I asked, lofting Kara in the air like a juggler's bag. She giggled and screeched, kinked bronze hair flying in the air like her mother's had once, when I'd had the energy to lift and twirl Jenna around like so much paper. Now, I'd be lucky to dance around her mother, let alone lift her. A combination of her own gain in "stature" and my own declining energy. We'd had Kara late in life, and frankly, the kid wasn't making me feel younger, as people had promised. I felt every strain in my back these days as I twirled her in the air and when I looked in the mirror in the morning I saw every age line darkened by another night of worry when she was sick.

I'm getting too old for this, I told myself more and more often. I didn't dare broach those thoughts to Jenna, whose pallid complexion and dark bags beneath her eyes spoke for themselves. She lived in the trenches of child-rearing. I only dabbled.

Kara giggled as I twirled her in the air and asked again, "How's my baby?"

"Good, Daddy," she said, throwing her arms around me, and then pushing off my shoulders to raise moon eyes at me. Knowing she had my attention, she said seriously, "Daddy, there were bugs by the swing set!"

In another time, such a statement from a child would have raised an eyebrow with a smile. But now, today, in an age of Luna Roaches that rendered their victims either comatose or vegetable, I spun my daughter in the air and ran my fingers up under her hair, praying with every pounding beat of my heart that I would find nothing beneath those copper locks.

My hand met only the cool skin of a child and I set her to the floor before slumping myself into a chair, exhausted from the onset of panic. My wife hadn't moved an inch during our conversation. She held her breath. And when I nodded that everything was okay, she closed her eyes and put a palm to her chest.

"What kind of bugs?" I said, as Kara's moon eyes stared up, smiling at mine.

"Ladybugs!" she proclaimed and ran into the living room laughing and singing, "Ladybug, ladybug fly away home…"

∞

If only the Luna Roaches had been ladybugs. If only they had flown away home. But they hadn't.

Paul Hughes was one of the lucky ones. Apparently, as he'd slapped and fallen, he'd killed the bug before it set its hooks in him. He was shaken. He was physically injured. He was depressed by the disaster of his life.

But he recovered from the bug's bite. Thinking about his situation, I bet he was later sorry for that. Then again, he never really had the chance. The news reported that he died of a heart attack just a couple days after regaining consciousness from his ordeal. His bad-luck streak could have been legendary.

The hospitals were quickly growing overcrowded with those who had not recovered. Instead, bed after bed filled with bodies that were neither dead, nor, in a rational sense, alive. Oh, they lay there breathing. Their hearts beat out a predictable circadian rhythm, but behind their eyes…nothing stirred.

Within a week of the first Luna Roach swarm sighting, the hospitals were out of beds, and emergency wards began forming in the gymnasiums of high schools and colleges.

Nobody liked roaches…but few people were so afraid of the things that they wouldn't go out after dark.

They should have been.

∞

The Luna Roaches were legion. The true meaning of that struck me on a Tuesday night as I walked the five blocks from our house to the library. Kara had forgotten to return *The Book of Five Cows* that day after school, and was distraught that if I didn't get it back to the library she'd have a fine. Welcoming the opportunity to stroll through the neighborhood on a warm summer night, I took the heavily illustrated volume and started down the sidewalk. I was passing the park just a couple blocks down from my house when I saw them.

A silver-white cloud rose like a mist from thousands of blades of darkened grass, and a sibilant hiss filled the air. In a moment, the sky was a mass of pinwheeling, shimmering dust motes. They ascended like a flock of startled pigeons, and then after gaining their bearings in the sky, momentarily blocking the light of the moon from which they took their name, they turned their shivering antennae on me.

I saw the shift; one moment, the swarm drifted aloft startled and unsettled. The next, they had a direction. And that direction was my head. As they began to shimmer towards me, a million Luna Roaches on the trail of a new victim, I looked around for a safe place. I'd seen plenty of the creatures over the past few days, but never so many in one place. They turned the sky a slithering arm of silver, and its fingers were reaching for my head. When I saw the shadowed house not too far away, on the corner lot near the park, I nodded to myself. And ran. Where else could I find shelter?

My ears cringed at the chittering sound that grew louder behind me as I shot up the flagstone walkway to the weathered old colonial like a bloodhound, determined to nab my quarry before the things behind me nabbed my back. And my quarry, in this instance, was safety. When I got to the doorway of the house, I found its entryway unlocked. I didn't hesitate in throwing open the screen door and diving in, as a flurry of shimmering wings beat the air in a hungry hiss behind me. Many of them crashed into the screen as it slammed shut, unable to turn, and I breathed a sigh of relief on the floor as the soft crashes echoed in the air behind me.

"Wow," I whispered, tossing the thin hardcover book on the floor in front of me. "That was close."

I lay on the floor for a couple minutes, breathing heavily and occasionally glancing back at the cloud of angry bugs still slamming against the door behind me. Finally, I pulled up my legs and pulled myself into a crouch to see where I'd ended up.

That was when I saw her.

The owner of the house, or at least that was what I assumed she was, sat as still as a statue on the couch facing the foyer where I'd landed.

"Did you see that?" I asked. "The damn things came at me like a swarm of killer bees!"

She didn't say anything.

"I'm sorry I let myself into your house like that, but I didn't know where else to go," I apologized.

Behind me, the soft flutterings and keening insectoid cries and smacks against the screen of the door were abating. In front of me, the woman stood, still saying nothing.

She stepped forward.

"Just let me wait here a second, until I'm sure they're gone," I said, picking the library book up. "Then I'll get out of your house."

She stepped forward again. Her eyes didn't blink.

"Um, ma'am?" I said. Fear began to grip at my bowels. What had I walked into?

She put another foot forward, and now I began to panic. She moved with the halting stiltedness of a robot still discovering its joints. And she hadn't blinked since the moment I'd looked up and noticed her staring blindly ahead from her seat on the couch. How long had she sat there, waiting for me to fall into her house? What would she do when she reached me? She was only feet away.

I jumped towards the door and she changed direction to follow. There were still a few Luna Roaches circling in the halo of light like moths outside the screen, but I didn't hesitate. I launched my way into the twilight and ran back up the street towards my home.

Kara's library book could be late. I'd be happy to pay the fine.

∽

That was the night the hospitals emptied. And the churches. And the school gymnasiums. All of the places where the volunteers from the Red Cross and a wide range of other medical saviors had stacked the comatose victims on cots and blankets in hopes that someday they would awake again.

That was the night that they did.

When I got home, breathless and confused at what had just happened, Jenna didn't give me time to speak. When I dove into the family room, she instantly pointed at the TV and whispered, "Look." The news anchors were raving.

"Around 7 p.m. tonight, the victims of the Luna Roaches began to walk. But it's as if they are walking in their sleep. They don't speak, and they won't stop, no matter what gets in front of them. We've had reports from every part of the city; it's happening everywhere, all at once. The scene is like something out of a movie. An hour ago, there were thousands of victims, all in a mass coma, and now...now..."

The co-anchor lost it. "Now the dead walk!" she exclaimed.

"What do you think it means?" Jenna said. She put an arm protectively around our daughter.

"I think that this is a really bad day."

I was only partly right; it was actually a bad night. And a strange one. By morning, after frantic eyewitness news reports flooded the television stations and people barricaded themselves in their homes in panic, it had gotten even stranger.

You wouldn't think that thousands of people could get up one night, walk out into the streets all at once and then disappear, while the eyes of millions were upon them. But that was what happened that night. The coma victims got up from wherever they lay, walked out into the street, and as the rest of us ran inside and panicked at their single-minded, staggering gaits and blank, black gazes, they kept on walking. By the next morning, nobody could quite answer exactly where they'd gone.

On my way to work that next day, I drove by the house I'd hidden in the night before near the park. The front door was wide open. I bet to myself, that nobody was at home. But I didn't stop to find out.

The chatter went on for days. The networks played an endless cycle of footage of blank-eyed men and women and creepily vacant children staggering out of hospitals and churches and walking down the center of the street, feet padding along strangely straight as they strode the dotted yellow lines out of town.

There was one image that haunted me, especially. They played it again and again, and every time, inexplicably, I began to well up. There was nothing inherently wrong with the picture. It was just a little girl, maybe eight or nine years old. She wore a red T-shirt that had a giant thumbprint stenciled on it. And she walked down the street, on the way out of town. Her hair was long and ratty brown, and tousled in so many knots, the father in me knew they'd be hours to comb out, and many yelps of hurt. I don't know exactly what it was about her. Maybe the way her big brown eyes drooped and looked hopelessly tired. Maybe it was the way she walked, listless and slow, but with a horrible, unrelenting purpose ahead. Or maybe it was the way she dragged her ragged brown teddy on the asphalt as she walked. The stuffed animal had probably been her favorite toy days before, something she tried to feed and cuddle and hug. And now its head bumped on the ground, silently thumping, thumping, thumping with each small step she took. Her hand didn't let go of its leg, but neither did she care that she was dragging the toy to death.

Tears filled my eyes at the image and I looked away. At that moment, a thrumming sound filled the house, as if it had begun to hail. Something was pounding on the shingles and the windows all around the house.

"Daddy," Kara said, running into the room. "There's a bug on my bed."

I scooped her up in my arms and took her back to the room, the noise still echoing overhead and all around. Somewhere I heard glass shatter.

"There" she pointed, and on the middle of the pink Hello Kitty bedspread sat an abomination. At least two inches long, the Luna Roach sat still, smack in the center of my baby's bed. Its wings shimmered in the yellow light like a gold haze, and it crept forward as I entered the room, heading for the shelter of her pillow. I set Kara on the floor, pulled a tissue from my pants pocket and brought my hand down on the bug. With a scoop, I enclosed it in the tissue and squeezed. The crunch of the thing's body was audible, and the warm wetness of its insides bled through the tissue to squish against my hand. I threw the mess into the toilet in the hall bathroom and flushed, rinsing my hand as if I'd touched poison in the sink.

From the other side of the house, my wife screamed. Wiping my hand on my jeans, again I scooped up Kara and ran. When we got there, Jenna lay on the floor, arms clenched around her-self in a desperate hug. When she saw me, she pointed to the living room window. "They're getting in," she whispered.

Sure enough, on the floor near the windows and streaming around the coffee table were dozens of Luna Roaches.

"Stay here, don't move," I told Kara and set her on the couch.

Then I started stomping.

When the room was a glistening mess of bug guts and bro-ken wings, I finally reached the window and pulled the drapes aside. The glass on one of the side windows had broken, and insects were still crawling up and over the jagged glass to drop into the room. The room hummed with their high-pitched, ulu-lating trills. I reached back and grabbed a throw pillow from the couch, stuffing it roughly into the hole that had been my win-dow. Its threads caught on the edges of the glass, and when I was certain the room was airtight again, I continued my stamping campaign until I felt sure that every keening bug was dead. The carpet was a mess of orange goo, and Jenna still hadn't moved from the floor.

"Mommy's asleep" Kara pronounced, and I realized my wife had fainted.

"Let's put her to bed," I said, and with Kara holding on to my leg, I grunted, groaned and eventually staggered aloft again with her mother in my arms. I tucked Jenna under the covers as carefully as she normally tucked Kara, and checked to make sure she was still alive. Her slow, steady breath whispered gently in my ear, telling me that shock had sent her into more peaceful dreams than I was wont to have. When I looked up, my daugh-ter stood at the edge of the bed, brown eyes brimming with salty concern. Her cheeks glistened, and I could see her tiny chest shivering with fright.

"Will Mommy be okay?" she whispered.

"She'll be fine," I promised. "She's just scared and tired. Let's climb in with her and get some sleep, too, okay?"

Kara nodded. I scooped her up and slid her into the center of the bed and climbed in beside her. Once beneath the sheets, it didn't take long before I heard the long slow rhythm of my baby's deep sleep breathing kick in as she clung to her mother's back. I thought about waking Jenna to make sure she was okay, but then decided she was better off just to sleep, while she could. Lord knows I couldn't. I wished that I could join the two of them, but instead I lay awake, listening to the light rain of bugs battering against the roof and windows of my house for what seemed like hours. My ears magnified every creak of the house into the echo of an imaginary phalanx of roaches advancing on my bed. I kept itching at phantom touches on my head and legs and hands, driving myself crazy with the idea that a new attack of insects would descend to smother us there in the bed at any moment. At some point, long past midnight, the sound finally quieted and the house grew quiet. I put a hand on my baby's shoulder, and eventually fell asleep myself.

It was the last good sleep I can remember having.

⌒∞⌒

"Daddy," Kara said, pushing tiny hands against my shoulder. "Daddy, I'm hungry and Mommy won't get up."

I blinked heavy lids open and squinted against the glare. The sun was fully up in the sky and the room glowed with the searchlight of morning. Kara sat in the middle of the bed in her Candy Kids nightgown, dark hair tousled, but eyes bright as the sun.

"Daddy?" she said again.

I rolled over and hugged her, and then prodded Jenna. Nothing happened.

I pushed against her back again, and then pressed my head to her side. She was breathing.

"She won't wake up, Daddy. I'm scared."

"Let her sleep," I said, slipping out of the bed and grabbing Kara in my arms. "Let's go have some cereal and let her sleep."

I tried to sound boisterous as I said it, but inside, my heart was dissolving like ice on the beach. I knew why Jenna wouldn't get up. A chill went through me as I thought about it. God, we'd slept right next to her. But I knew if I moved her hair aside, I'd find the shell of a Luna Roach attached to her neck.

I choked back a tear as I reached for a box of breakfast cereal in the cabinet and Kara settled herself on a chair at the kitchen table.

Jenna was not going to be waking up. Kara would probably never have her mom make her breakfast again.

The TV was playing snow. Snow on almost every channel. There was one local access channel still broadcasting, with a wide-eyed, disheveled man screaming into the microphone. "They've come back," he kept saying. "They've come back and there's only one way to stop them: aim for the head. It's the roaches, you've got to smash the roaches…"

As I watched him babble, the door behind him opened, and a stream of people entered the studio. They surrounded the man, who leapt up on a chair and grabbed a microphone stand, holding it out like a cattle prod. Then he began swinging it wildly, like a bat, again and again until he finally connected with someone. The stand hit a woman right in the back of the head, right where the Luna Roaches loved to fasten. The woman went down. But then so did the man. There were hands all over him suddenly, and a buzzing sound slowly filled the room. I heard him scream just before a hand covered the lens of the camera, and then that station turned to snow too.

There were still cable stations playing old sitcoms, but none of the local networks were broadcasting. The same with radio. At last I understood what they meant now by corporate "canned" radio. Only the FM channel programmed by someone a thousand miles away on the left coast still played the latest singles from U2 and Green Day. And I knew it was because they had programmed the schedule days before. Nobody was working the boards right now.

For the first time since I'd seen the news story about Paul Hughes, I truly panicked. I felt the ice in my belly, and struggled not to fall to my knees and tremble like a baby *in front of* my baby, who was holding my hand and counting on me to be strong, to make things all right.

Except that I couldn't.

Not even close.

In the other room, Kara's mom was turning into some kind of a zombie in her sleep, and outside, the world was awash with buzzing, swarming death.

There was no way out.

"Daddy, can I have more milk?"

Blinking back tears, I opened the refrigerator, and pulled out a carton. I wouldn't look at the missing person picture on its side. Soon, we might all be missing.

∞

"We're just going to take a little ride," I said, as I buckled Kara into the seat belt.

"But what about Mommy?" She quailed.

"Mommy needs her sleep. We'll bring her back some dinner later."

It killed me to lie, but I had to get her out of here. I had to get Kara out of the city.

As we pulled out of the garage, I saw the door from the house open, and Jenna stepped out onto the concrete behind us. Thank God Kara was buckled in and couldn't look in the rearview mirror. Her mother looked ghastly.

Her eyes were vacant.

I hit the gas and squealed out onto the street. I don't know where I thought we were going to go. Somehow it seemed like this was a local problem; if we could just get out of the city and into the country, everything would be normal again.

We never left the neighborhood.

I pulled out on Highland and turned on to Norfolk to get out of the subdivision...but a block before I reached the main road, the way was blocked.

They moved slowly, but they were moving. And they were moving inward, a barricade of bodies ten and twenty deep. They strode towards us, honing in. When one turned, all of the others followed, as if driven by a single mind. When I looked in the rearview mirror, I saw they were behind us as well. Surrounded.

I stopped the car to think. The bodies didn't stop. They

came forward, slowly, inexorably. Their eyes were dark, and unblinking. I could see the tan shadow of Luna Roaches trembling on the necks of some of them as they stepped forward, one shambling shoe at a time.

"Daddy," Kara said. "They're getting closer."

Her hand gripped my shirt-sleeve and my heart crawled into my throat. I had to do something…but what? I had no idea. I could try to plow the car through a phalanx of still seemingly human bodies but I had no faith that I would get that far. If we left the car, we were doomed for sure. The mob stretched as far as I could see, in every direction. Were we the only regular humans left in the neighborhood?

"Daddy," Kara repeated. "They want to come in."

The first one had finally reached the car. He was an older man, I'd guess sixty-five or seventy. His hair was white as salt on his head and his lips thin as parchment. He leaned his pale, too-slack face into Kara's window and leered, teeth exposed and rotten.

The pounding began then. And from all around us a hum began to wail.

First the old man began to smack his head against her window. And then from the back window an answering echo, as one of the other Luna Roach automatons began to slap slack fists against the glass. An answering thud joined from my side of the car. One old woman threw her body onto the hood of the car and tried to claw her way up to the windshield. When a gnarled finger grasped at the windshield wiper I turned the control to full and watched the steel and rubber arm bat her tentative grasp away again and again.

But nothing was going to keep them away for long. Kara held on to my arm tighter and tighter as the car began to shake.

"Daddy, what are we going to do?"

The metal of the passenger door suddenly creaked and squealed. The golf pin of a door lock snapped, the plastic vanished to the floor.

"I don't know what to do," I finally admitted, as the door wrenched open and six arms reached through the breach towards my baby girl.

"Daddddddy!" she screamed.

I pulled her closer, but the hands gripped the fabric of her shirt and pants and then, next to my ear, the glass exploded. Another hand reached through the broken glass to bat at my head.

"Kara, hold on," I begged, grasping for her.

But she was gone.

From outside the car I heard her screams. I dove after her to follow, but before I had my feet on the ground a dozen fists pounded into my neck and back and shoved me to the asphalt. Through a field of swaying bodies and limbs I saw Kara raised above the mob, and then Jenna appeared, arms held out to take her.

"Mommy!" Kara cried, arms outstretched.

My wife scooped my baby up, and Kara hugged her tight. Jenna stared at me over our little girl's shoulders, and a look of victory flickered in her eyes. For the first time in my life, I was sickened by seeing my wife smile. But then, strangely, that smile grew confused, uncertain. It turned to a frown. Her eyes squinted like they did when she got migraines. I could see the muscles on the backs of her arms begin to tense and shiver as she gripped Kara tighter. Then she opened her mouth, not to kiss our baby, but to scream. I heard it clearly over the cacophony of the mob.

That was when the Luna Roach slid out from the wet cavity between her eyeball and her eyelid. Kara saw the bug and recoiled from her mother, but Jenna only held our baby tighter, as the roach walked to the edge of Jenna's nose and poised there to stretch its wings. Then my wife's whole face convulsed and began to change. Her skin crawled and swelled; her whole body began to visibly tremble. Jenna's face exploded at that moment, as the hive of Luna Roaches nesting and gestating in her brain finally clawed their way free of her flesh and bone and took to the air. A cloud of blood sprayed the sky as her eyes and flesh caved in like undermined sand to the angry mandibles of a thousand trapped and buzzing bugs. As the first spurts of blood misted, a black-and-tan cloud of buzzing wings instantly hid the sudden ruin of her features, as Luna Roaches lit from her exposed flesh to swarm around the bloody mess of her eyes and the sticky, shredded cartilage of her nose, which hung by a thread down her face.

I launched myself forward to save Kara, but the arms and feet of the mob held me down as my baby beat tiny hands against Jenna's gore-streaked shoulders, trying to escape. Against all sanity, her blinded, broken mother did not fall or let go. A buzz of wings multiplied in the air, and a cloud of Luna Roaches hovered like a bee swarm around my baby's screaming, horrified face. I screamed for her, holding out a helpless hand that was quickly stomped to the ground. Something in my arm snapped as it met the asphalt, but louder than my own cry was Kara's shriek. I swear that she called for me, but the street was alive in screaming and calls for help. Whether she called my name, or something else, in seconds, it was all over. Kara lay quiet and still, limp and blood spattered in what had been her mother's arms. But I knew, even if my baby never really did, that those were not Jenna's arms any longer. Luna Roaches darted across my baby's face, sampling her innocence with their nervous, hairy feelers.

The crowd drew back from me, setting me free from where they'd pinned me to the pavement and I stood up outside the car, cradling my arm and staring at the crowd of blank eyes that glittered like obsidian in the descending night. Silence fell like midnight fog around us, as the mob grew still, and the moment pregnant.

"What *are* you?" I whispered. "What do you *want*?"

One of the men stepped forward, and tentatively opened its mouth. A growling sound came out, and then a word. "Jeessst." It said in a voice like shifting gravel. Its unblinking eyes fluttered at the sound and it seemed to smile. Understanding dawning.

"Jeessst yur legs," the man said, the words coming out slowly before it stepped forward. Its face looked pleased. "Jeesst your arms."

"And what do I get in return?" I asked.

"Us," someone else growled.

From above I heard the fluttering drone of thousands of translucent wings.

"Where did you come from?" I asked.

"The places you have never gone," came my only answer, a whisper from the crowd. And then the cool teeth of a Luna Roach settled onto my spine. For a moment I struggled, hoping to throw it off. But then the ice slid through my brain, and I felt the world go quiet.

As I slid back to the ground, I wondered what would become of my body. And of all the bodies that surrounded me. Normally in a symbiosis, the predator used the host to serve as a nest for its offspring.

Oh God, I cried, as my body went numb. What would gestate and grow inside of Kara. What would hatch from my poor, sweet baby?

What would climb out of my own swollen belly after I had been used and used up? Or would they use me like Jenna?

I prayed that the chittering sounds I heard in my brain would take any knowledge of that away. Already, I could almost understand what the keening, droning noises I'd been hearing now during the nights meant.

Eat. Eat.

Kill. Eat.

Spawn.

Paul Hughes was lucky. His bad day had ended a long time ago now, before things really did get bad.

Mine was only just beginning.

NAILED

SOME PEOPLE FOUND their sex toys in adult catalogues and others in seedy bookstores. But Natalie found hers…in her garden.

No, she didn't harvest a cucumber for her nightly pleasure. Or a warty squash (*studded—for her pleasure!*) But she did find something deep beneath the roots of her tomato and pepper plants that extended deeper into the heart of her house than her kitchen.

Something that got its roots in her…

The sun felt good on her back as she pulled weeds in the "back forty", as Crisofer liked to call it. She always left the T out of his name because she thought it sounded more "come hither-ly". Right now, she wasn't feeling very "come hither-ly" though. She wore a loose old T-shirt and ratty jeans so that she could kneel in the mud, and as she did so, pulling weeds and digging holes with a hand shovel beneath the exceptionally hot August sun, she felt the sweat beading and dripping from the nape of her neck and down her spine to slip and drip into the crack of her ass.

Sweat on a body could be sexy in some situations, but this definitely wasn't.

Natalie tried to pry the roots of a thistle out with her gloved hands. But it wasn't budging. The sweat kept streaming down her back as she dug and pulled and dug some more. Her hands followed the thick white root farther and deeper into the gray-caked concrete that was the earth of her garden. She needed to have a truck of loam or manure dumped back here this fall for next year. This earth was too hard from topsoil to clay.

When the ground suddenly gave way and the shovel sank down until the spade head completely disappeared, Natalie straightened up, and yanked her hand and shovel from where they had suddenly been swallowed.

The thistle "tree" of a weed fell over to the ground.

Natalie looked down into the pit she'd dug. And saw a small tunnel at the bottom of the hole. It opened farther into the earth beneath.

"What the hell..." she murmured. It was a phrase that Crisofer always said.

She reached a gloved hand into the hole, and felt the hair on her arm tremor when it sank deeper into the dirt. She stretched until her shoulder touched the top of the ground.

"Whoa," she whispered, as the cold of the air beneath the ground made the hair on her arm stand up. When the shiver reached up her arm and into her spine, she pulled her hand out of the hole and shook her head. "What the hell," she said again.

Then she stood up and really got busy with the spade.

In a few minutes, the place where the stubborn thistle had been was no longer visible. Instead, an opening the size of a manhole cover had quickly revealed itself. And a few minutes later, when the pile of dirt thrown to the side of her healthy-looking Big Boy tomatoes had grown to knee deep, Natalie stopped her work, wiped the streaming sweat from blinding her eyes and looked down.

She whistled.

But there was nobody around to hear.

After all, she and Chris had moved here to get *away* from the monotonous drone of civilization. They were really only about forty-five minutes out of the "loop", but that drive down the expressway for a bit and then off onto country roads made all the difference. Many people had a longer commute from the city into the congested suburbs, but they'd opted for a route that led instantly to nowhere... And they liked it that way. It didn't take as long as you'd think to work your way down the backroads to get into "the country". At least not when you headed steadily straight northwest of the city. Of course, when Chris was gone for days on business trips, their little love nest in nowheresville seemed very remote indeed to the person left turning on the porch lights at night. And that person would be Natalie.

But right now, Natalie was staring into a hole in her garden. A hole that seemed to open on a good-sized cavern. She carefully prodded with the spade and expanded the hole, wondering how far it extended. The garden butted up against a slope of silt that formed the hill leading up to their house; at the bottom, a long creek wound through the edge of their property, its water protected from view by a heavy growth of scrub bushes and trees. The hole she'd found seemed to extend up under the silt hill. Maybe the creek bed had buried it long ago, whatever it was...

Natalie worked at the edges of the hole and little by little it gave way until she had a three-foot-wide entrance to a darkened cave in the earth uncovered. She poked her head into the dark tunnel a couple of times, but couldn't see anything past the periphery... That was when she dropped the spade and ran back up the hill to the house to find a flashlight.

She wasn't going to get lost in the dark...but she *was* going to explore the hole that spied on the roots of her garden.

The narrow tunnel turned out to extend beneath the hill that led to her house. The floods and debris of decades had apparently built up a covering of mud that had obliterated the entrance, but Natalie had revealed the edges...and found her way inside.

And inside...was old.

She moved a flashlight back and forth like a pendulum as she made her way, first in a crawl and then a crouch down the path that led away from the hole in her garden. She hadn't gone too many steps into the earth when she saw the colored stones. They were placed on the ground, as if meant as a sort of gated periphery. Turquoise and ruby and slate-colored, they were fist sized and placed in a semi-circle of three rows. Beyond that, though, was what interested Natalie.

Bones.

Laid out on the dusty gray ground was a skeleton of old bones. Old human bones, she had to assume, from the look of the arms and legs and skull. Around the whitened bones were other things.

Strangely carved bits of wood and colored stones and twisted ropes of twined twigs and other unidentifiable things that looked both organic and very old—desiccated.

Natalie stepped into the weird buried cavern and bent down to touch the forehead of the skull that lay in the midst of the open space. It didn't move. But she whispered anyway…

"I'm not here to disturb you," she said in the narrow space.

That was when she saw the rusted spikes between the bones of the skeleton's hands. And the decayed bits of rope that still circled the wrists and ankles of the long-dead figure.

Why had someone staked and roped this person to the ground? Natalie wondered. She said "this person" in her head because she couldn't even tell if it was a he or a she.

The hair stood up on the back of her neck, and she stepped back from the skull. "Who were you?" she whispered. Natalie crouched on her haunches and looked at the skeleton lying on the earth, deep beneath her house. On a whim, she reached out and pulled the frayed twine away from the bones of the skeleton's wrists, and then did the same to the rope that remained around its ankles. That was when she saw the stone.

It lay between the thigh bones of the skeleton. Unlike some of the other stones and bits of debris, this was a carefully formed, sculpted piece of rock—rock so smooth and polished it looked like marble. It was mostly cylindrical, almost a foot long, Natalie thought, as she stared at its shape there in the dirt. The white stone stood out sharply from the dirt of the floor it rested on, and the shape stood out more. On one end, two round circular shapes had been carved. If they'd been rectangular, she would have compared them to a gun handle. Only…they were round. Like balls in a skein, stretched away from the thing that held them fast.

On the opposite end of the cylinder, the shaft was capped in a faintly mushroom-like shape, a softly carved rounded triangle of stone.

Natalie reached down and pried it from the soil. As her fingers curled around the long center of its shaft, she felt her heart trip. She held her breath and turned the thing first one way and then the other in her hands. Her fingers clung hard to the smooth surface of its center and she could feel her face blushing in the dark as her blood pounded faster. There was no question about what this thing was that she'd found.

It was a dildo. A carefully carved, ancient sex aid.

She looked at the bony remains of the long-dead body on the ground beside her and whistled. "Did they crucify you for using this, or *making* this?" she whispered in the shadowed chamber. She turned it over in her hand and ran the tip of her index finger over the "head" of the stone implement. "Well, you got nailed, that's one thing for sure…"

Again the hair on the back of her neck stood up, as if a snake had slithered across her skin. Natalie gripped the ancient sex relic hard and trained the flashlight in her other hand back and forth across the ground. Slowly, she began to back out of the room and into the narrow tunnel that she'd entered the buried room through.

When she wiggled her way back out into the sunlight and the garden, she stood on the edge of the plot and looked around at the weeding she'd been doing. She knew that she should get back on her knees and pull more of the weeds that were choking out her fledgling squash vines. But that pragmatic idea didn't hold water for a second. Instead, Natalie trembled as the words "get back on her knees" ran through her head. She absently ran a finger up and down the stone shaft in her hand and thought about going back to the house and getting out of her sweaty clothes. She thought about what the thing in her hand might have been used for once. And as she did so…she felt the sweat gather faster, trickling down her back and siphoning down into the channel of her ass.

Natalie blinked twice, fast. It was almost as if something snapped inside her. And then without another thought, she was walking up the hill and back to the house. Once she got inside, after she stripped off her clothes in the bedroom, turned on the water and stepped into the shower in the master bath, she reached for the shampoo…and realized she still had the stone in her hand.

Thinking fleetingly of hygiene, but even more of how amazing the sensation might be, she squeezed her shampoo over the smooth white stone and with her fingers spread it all around the cool carved surface. When it was fully slicked in soap, she held the ancient dildo by its carved balls and began to stroke her hand up and down the shaft, urging the soap along it to kill a millennium of bacteria. At least, that was the conscious thought she told herself. She was cleaning the relic, she thought, as the stem where its balls were, moved ever closer to her body until the stone cock pressed against her groin and seemed to emanate *from* her. In moments, she stood beneath the spray of the shower with the stone cock protruding from her body as if she were an excited male. Her hand worked the thing as if she could coax cum from a stone.

She felt overcome with lust in those moments, her eyes closed, her body...somewhere else. And then hesitantly, shakily, she turned off the water, halfheartedly toweled herself off, and then went and lay down on the bed without dressing. Instead, she reached into the nightstand for a bottle. She repeated the actions she'd done with the soap, and the room filled with the scent of baby oil as she lathered the polished stone head of the thing in her hand before she slipped it between her thighs. Slowly.

Slowly.

But then faster. For a moment, she felt almost as if the room had slipped away, and she was being taken hard and rough by a thin man in a room with colored stones...

∞

Natalie didn't weed the garden anymore that day.

∞

"What's for dinner?" Crisofer called a couple hours later, and Natalie woke with a start on the bed.

She felt fuzzy and groggy, but when consciousness really kicked in and she heard her husband's voice and suddenly realized that there was a hard piece of cool stone in her hand, her eyes went wide as the events of the afternoon came back to her. Quickly she rolled out of the bed and dropped the stone phallus into the nightstand. She fled to the bathroom, and pulled a robe from the door. She met Crisofer in the kitchen a minute later, apologizing profusely about falling asleep on the bed after being out in the heat.

"Can we maybe just go out for pizza?" she asked.

He smiled that lopsided grin he had, and said, "Sure. Since I'm headed to Cincinnati tomorrow, that will give you some easy leftovers for tomorrow."

When Natalie woke the next morning, she felt guilty. As if she'd cheated on her husband, who stood just a few feet across the room, straightening his tie in the mirror. He'd tried to put the moves on her after they got home from dinner, but she'd begged off, claiming a stomachache. In reality, she had a crotch-ache, after pounding a foot-long piece of rock inside her for a good chunk of the afternoon. Even now she could feel the sting-ing ache of "overuse" and didn't look forward to her next trip to the toilet.

All that said...

Something inside her ached for Crisofer to leave the house so that she could open the nightstand drawer again.

Natalie closed her eyes and wished the thought away. She was a whore!

No. She hadn't slept with anyone. But...

"Goodbye, sweetheart," Crisofer said, bending down to kiss her. He looked so good in his sharp white shirt and black-and-silver tie. "I'll be back on Wednesday."

"Good luck," she smiled, and then snuggled into the pillow. "I'll be here when you get back!" she promised.

"Better be," he said, and in a flash he and his suitcase had fled from the room.

Natalie waited until she heard the back door close before she reached into the nightstand. Just barely waited.

Her hand trembled as it darted from beneath the sheets to grab the handle of the drawer. She wrenched it out and seconds later, the cool head of the stone artifact was slipping along the silken skin of her inner thigh.

Moments later, eyes closed and hands busy, Natalie felt her skin suddenly chill. It was a weird feeling, with the blood surging through her groin and her hips arching up to meet the bank of her hands. Her body was more than warm; she was on fire as she shoved the ancient sex toy inside her and yet…her skin suddenly goose bumped as the air shifted around her. The breeze felt wonderful against her fevered skin, and yet…strange. Her bedroom was a closed space. The window wasn't open, the door to the rest of the house…mostly shut. There could be no breeze here…

Natalie opened her eyes to the dim morning light and saw the strangest thing. A man, moving in the air just above her body, writhing with the same motions as her own. His face was sallow and thin, his mustache dark against the gray shadows of dawn. But his eyes glimmered with their own light in the depths of his face. When he opened his mouth to silently moan, Natalie felt her own climax near, and she moaned with him, giving voice to his orgasm. She knew how strange this was, and yet, she couldn't stop, not now.

And when she did stop, at last, sated and hot and damp…she collapsed to the pillow and looked up at her strangely indistinct lover and saw…

That he was not there.

Oddly enough, the moment that he was gone was the moment when the fear first iced her veins.

In a span of just a few seconds, she had felt her climax coming and opened her eyes to see a man above her, and she had briefly reveled in the intensity and the forbidden. And now… he was gone, and Natalie began to shiver uncontrollably. For a second, she wondered if he had ever been there at all.

She threw the phallus in the drawer and hurried to the shower, anxious to wash away the strange moment with hot water and soap. Lots of soap.

∽∾

It took a pot of coffee before Natalie felt up to admitting to herself that she was scared. Like…arms shivering as you walk when it was not even remotely cold out kind of scared. Luckily the sun was bright and the day warm…and after a bit, she donned a pair of loose shorts and a light T-shirt and went out to the yard to putter around a bit. She pulled weeds along the edge of the house and considered trimming the evergreens in front before wandering back to the long patch of garden area down the hill. Of course, if she was honest, this was really where she'd been headed from the moment she'd stepped outside.

She had to know more about the place that hid beneath her garden. Beneath her house. *What* had she brought to her bed?

The hole in the garden remained, and Natalie slid her body through that space in the dirt without a thought for ruining her clothes. She'd come with the intention of going belowground. She was hidden from the sun, below the roots of her tomato plants, in seconds.

She came again to the room with the dead bones, and the rocks and…the wishes.

She knew the room was filled with wishes as soon as she entered. They whispered in her ear like poison.

I wish your mother would choke on her tea and die.

I wish your lover would stick his cock in a mousetrap that he thought was a whore.

I wish you would eat the first piece of meat you meet, even if he was human and weak…

She ignored the odd voices and instead looked for something beyond the empty bones that bled from the floor. But the underground crypt was empty. The only things there were the bones of the dead person in its center. And the glimmer of the rocks set in a circle just beyond. Natalie didn't know what to think of those. They almost seemed to be a barrier to the outer world.

She knelt next to the long-dead form half absorbed in the soil and felt a stirring in her loins as the jeans slipped over her panties. It began as a faint itch, but soon she felt stiflingly hot, and the sensation spread up between her thighs and along the valley of her ass and past that sensitive dirty place and then up her backbone. It was a torrent of feeling, a prickly warm irritation that demanded to be scratched…

Natalie stripped off her shirt and used it to wipe the trail of sweat down her back. But as soon as the cotton touched her skin, she burned inside like scalding water. She dropped the shirt and unbuttoned her jeans as the fire cooled above the waist and spread to the places where her clothes kissed.

She cried out at the sensations that coursed across her skin; molten lava chased with frozen cactus needles. The intensity of the sensation only stilled when she ran her hands across her skin. She discovered this solution to the heat, as she stripped off her panties and bra. Soon she crouched on her knees in the cave and kneaded her breasts and belly to relieve the heat, and then her ass and thighs. Her fingers were a flurry of motion, but when they slipped between her legs, well, that was when the heat turned to ecstasy. She saw the face of the sallow man on the ground, his lips ghostly flesh atop the bones. Natalie whimpered and lay down next to him, yearning to get closer, yet still afraid to feel his ghostly touch.

He smiled at her and nodded, urging her to come closer, closer. The wish voices whispered louder all around, exhortations to grovel and groan. They whispered sexy things…and horrible things.

Fuck the dead and taste the bread
Death is life and life is dead
Lick his ass and find your place
Stick your tongue into his face
Suck the juice of broken skin
And suck the teeth of open sin
Spill your pleasure in the mud
And be the slut you yearn to love

The smile of the sallow man grew as Natalie pressed first her fingers inside her, and then rubbed her wet crotch against his pelvis bone. Her eyes fluttered closed as the voices sang sing-song rhymes of nakedness and depravity, and her body burned with pleasure at every movement she made. Natalie groveled and pressed her lips to the open skull mouth of the dead man, and shivered at the touch of her lips to the empty teeth bone of the fossils there. She could taste his dust like spice, and something *like* a tongue sprouted inside her mouth, pressing its way deeper inside her. She sucked his ghostly tongue like a cock until her throat filled with something that was strangely both acid sour and honey sweet.

She gagged on the taste and instinctively rolled away, but the bones of the ancient thing came with her, almost as if he were pinned inside her as she'd tried to move away. And then as her eyes opened, she realized he *was* inside her...his mustache was ghostly soft against her lips, and his eyes empty black like doors into nowhere. The bone of his femur had somehow separated from the rest of his skeleton in their tussle, and her hand had been working it against her clit as if it were the stone dildo she'd left in the house.

"Mine mine all mine..." she heard a chorus of voices wail, as the cave grew dark, and the man leaned down to kiss her one more time.

When Natalie woke, she was cold, and felt disgusting. Her thighs and belly were covered with smears of dirt, and an old bone lay cold against her belly. She shoved it to the side and rolled to a crouch, looking all around the shadowy space. But it was silent. Something cool and viscous had gelled across her cheek, and she wiped it away with the back of her hand.

Natalie pulled her jeans from the ground and stabbed her leg in the leg hole, nearly falling over before she got the pants pulled up to her thighs. She pulled the shirt over her head in a flash, grabbed her underthings and fled the cave.

The afternoon was already waning when Natalie half-ran, half-stumbled her way back to the house. She stripped right back out of her clothes and turned on the shower as hot as it would go before stepping in to soap and scrub the mud from her flesh.

When she stepped out, her skin glowing red, she felt a little better. But as she dressed and walked around the empty house, fixing leftover chicken and rice for dinner, her mind kept seeing what had happened during the afternoon over and over again.

"Jesus," she said seemingly a million times. "How *could* you?"

Feelings washed over her like a kaleidoscope. Self-loathing and disgust and depression and then the creep of carnal excitement as the memories of the sensations returned...and then loathing again...

She barely ate her dinner, but popped one of Crisofer's Coors Lights and downed it almost in two swallows.

The house had grown dark as she'd eaten and fretted, and Natalie sat down on the couch in the living room with the empty bottle in her hand. The windows were black as her mood. But then in the distance, she saw something shimmer orange and red...a distant car light...or maybe a fire.

She stared at the faint light outside and sensed that it was growing closer. And then the hair on her arms stood up, and she knew that it was *definitely* closer. Natalie stood up and walked slowly backwards, away from the approaching flame. Then she turned and ran down the hall to her bedroom, and slammed the door behind her.

Heart pounding and feeling flushed, she sat down on the bed and put her head between her hands. "Oh my God," she murmured. "What have I done?"

The temperature in the room suddenly rose, as if the furnace had kicked on and run for ten minutes in a closed space.

Natalie's eyes widened as she felt sweat drip from her forehead to her arm. It rolled down the faint hair and dropped to the bed, but soon another drip followed. She could feel the heat breathing down her back like flames.

"Leave me alone," she cried out, and rolled across the bed to wrench the nightstand drawer open.

The stone phallus lay there, white and ready.

She picked it up and cradled it in her palms, and instantly felt the heat dissipate.

"It's mine," she whispered to the air. From somewhere far away she heard more voices crying. "Mine," they argued.

Natalie smiled and set the stone on the bed, as she stripped her shirt and pants off. Part of her was screaming inside, in complete disbelief that she would do this again. Twice in one day lowering herself to…whatever this was.

But when she lay down on the bed and pressed the cool, slippery smooth head of the phallus between her legs, those thoughts disappeared as she felt her reward. All she could whisper as waves of beautiful heat and pleasure surged through her nerves, making her legs shiver and her belly heave, was, "Mine… mmmm mine."

When Crisofer got home a couple days later, he found Natalie lying naked and curled in a ball on their bed. He stepped over a line of colored stones near their doorway and picked up the sheets from where they lay crumpled on the floor, and draped them over her. He saw that her feet were smudged with dirt, and frowned. Natalie was far too neat to ever climb in bed with muddy feet. WTF.

"Wild night," he said softly, running his fingers through her hair. One of Natalie's eyelids fluttered open, and she grinned feebly. "Had a hard time sleeping while you were gone," she said. And seconds later, her face went slack, and she dozed off again.

"Wow," Cris said, backing away to quietly unpack his suitcase. He turned off the lights before stripping down and walking to the bed where his wife lay, seemingly comatose. He slipped in beside Natalie and draped an arm around the smooth skin of her waist, then moved his hand up her arm. His fingers brushed against something cold and hard in her hand, but then whatever it was slipped out of her grasp and thumped on the floor. Cris thought about getting up to see what she'd been holding, but the warmth of the bed won against his desire for neatness. He'd get it in the morning. Or she would.

Comforted by the warmth and smell of her, he instantly began to drift off to sleep himself. But after a few minutes, the warmth of her became *too* warm, and he rolled away. He pressed his face into the pillow, searching for a comfortable position.

But even moving over to the cool sheets didn't take away the heat. Cris tossed and rolled, and finally threw the sheets completely off of him. Sweat beaded on his forehead.

"What the hell," he whispered, and got out of bed to get a glass of water from the bathroom.

When he climbed back in the bed, Natalie didn't budge. But Cris grew increasingly hot. Soon he was lying on his back, face to the ceiling, sweat dripping down his cheeks and pooling on his chest. His breathing increased and his skin flushed.

He almost thought that the air at the corners of the room was growing a faint, wicked red.

"What the hell," he gasped, as the skin across his entire body suddenly felt like a fingertip pressed to a hot frying pan.

It may have been the smell that woke her. Natalie's eyes peeled open, and as she struggled to wake, her nose wrinkled in dismay. She rolled onto her back.

The source of the smell was in her bed. Inches away.

The blackened husk beside her didn't look much like her husband. But still, somehow, she knew him. The hair had shriveled into ringlets and ash around his skull, and his blue eyes had yellowed and dried in pits beneath a face warped by dozens of blisters and singed as if held to a blazing flame.

His body seemed made of ash, and Natalie opened her mouth to scream. But then held it in. She knew what had burned her Crisofer to char. She knew almost instantly. She had felt that heat herself.

"Why," she whispered to the air.

"Mine," an invisible sound answered.

Natalie shook her head and got out of bed. Naked, she walked to the line of stones she'd taken from the tomb the day before and replaced at the doorway of her bedroom. She had guessed the meaning of those stones, and figured she had only set the thing free by taking the stone back to her bed. With his phallus in the drawer and the warding rocks restricting the doorway, he was trapped inside her room, for when she needed or wanted him. Or so she had surmised.

"No," Natalie said, tears running down her face as she picked up the stone cock from the floor where it had dropped during the night. She placed it gently in the nightstand drawer.

"Mine," she said. And then she stepped out of the room, closing the door behind her, leaving both of her lovers behind.

THE EYES

THEY'RE PROBABLY GONNA die, so they might as well have a little fun with it, right? I always offer them this game: "If you can drive the needle into the white of your eye—not the colored part in the center—and then pull it out of your head without puncturing that precious gooey fluid sac in the middle...I'll let you live."

Only one person has ever actually risen to that challenge and survived...and my current candidate seemed unlikely to join her. Jake thrashed and tried to scream in the converted gynecologist's chair he was strapped into, but the ball gag sealed his anger in. I held out the foot-long needle to him and said again, "Touch the needle to the side of your eyeball and push. It'll feel a little slippery at first, until the tip really sinks in and penetrates the eyeball. Then give it a good tap with your hand—not too hard, or you'll puncture your brain. That won't feel good at all..."

I paused so he could think about that a moment, and then explained.

"What you wanna do is, knock it in about an inch, so you get the tip of that needle all the way through the back of your eyeball. Remember, if you hit the cornea, you're disqualified. I want you to skewer the eye on its end, and then pop it out of its socket. I'll cut the optic nerve for you, if it doesn't separate on its own."

In my hand, I showed him the exacto knife. In that instant, it almost looked like his eye might fall out of its socket all by itself, he was glaring at me so hard.

"Last chance," I said. "C'mon, it's a game. It'll be fun." This was the tough part for most—would *you* really consider jamming a needle in your eye and then pulling the thing out to live? Or would you rather just die?

Believe it or not, more women took the needle from me than men. Higher pain threshold, I guess. It was ironic but men are usually pussies about pain. I kinda hoped Jake would fail, because I had an experiment I wanted to try involving his testicles, his eyeballs and about a foot of his still-living intestine. So, I have to admit, I really didn't want him to win.

Jake took the needle. He touched the point to the side of his eye, which was crying...that would only make the going more slippery. He gave the back of the needle a quavering thump with his free hand, and this time he screamed loud enough to get past the red rubber ball in his mouth. His whole body convulsed and shook in the chair like an electrocution. The needle stuck out of his eye like a dart. Blood streamed down his face like red Kool-Aid.

"Pull it out," I reminded him, and with two shaking hands, he grabbed the needle and tried to rock it to the right and left, so as to pop the eyeball out of his head. His screams had turned into rhythmic panting shrieks and finally I yelled at him, "Do it!"

With one good yank, he separated the eyeball from the socket so hard that the optic nerve snapped instantly and hung like saucy spaghetti down his cheek. The jelly of his once-blue cornea slid like thick snot across the bridge of his nose. I took the skewer from his hand and *tsked*.

"Sorry, Jake, you ruined the center. I told you not to do that. You lost, my friend."

"Brenda? Let me have the spoon."

I snapped the restrainers back onto his arms and accepted the grapefruit spoon from Brenda. In a second, I was pushing the serrated edge down beneath the lower eyelid on his good eye. The spoon slipped in easy, and with just a little wiggling, I got it all the way under his eyeball. Then I gave the handle a good pull and popped Jake's second eyeball into my hand. His face was really bloody now, and two raw meat sockets stared at me and my soon-to-be snack.

But I told you there was a game afoot. Here was the fun part. I wanted to play a little taste test with Brenda. Taking the exacto, I cut a slit across Jake's ballsack and removed the slippery white testicles. *Nothing like the salty taste of man-oysters in the back of your throat to get the mood going*, I thought.

As Jake's screaming and thrashing quieted, fading to uncon- scious tremors, I cut open a six-inch slash right across his bellybutton, reached my hand inside, and pulled out a length of gory, slippery-slick intestine. I'd made him fast for the past three days, but I looked inside the steaming pink flesh just to make sure there was no shit surprise there, once I cut out myself a good length. I didn't want to have to wash out impurity if I didn't have to—cleaning the guts took away the flavor and I wanted them fresh.

Finally, as Jake lay dying in the chair, I snipped his bloody intestines into four short lengths and stuffed the ragged holes in each with either an eyeball, or a testicle.

I skewered each one to make a plate of cannibalistic hors d'oeuvres, and called for my lovely bride.

"Tasting time," I said. "Get 'em fresh and hot before they die!"

I gave her the man-oyster stuffed gut first, and she licked her lips before touching the bloody flesh to her lips. Then she slid the still-pulsing meat into her mouth. She chewed, and made a confused, though not unhappy face.

"What's this?" she asked.

"A little something special," I said. "Jake Oyster Surprise."

She raised an eyebrow and chewed some more. She shrugged, as if to say, "I've had better." Then I gave her an eyeball-stuffed gut.

When she bit down this time, you could hear the wet *pop* as the cornea gave way and all that gooey good stuff turned to a delicious bloody iris jelly in her mouth.

"Mmmmmmm mmmm good," she moaned, nodding.

Her happy eyelids fluttered over empty eye sockets and she grinned, strings of pink gut still sticking like Coney Island taffy through her teeth. She looked as happy as the day I had fed her her own baby blues.

"Oh, without a doubt," she sighed. "The eyes have it."

SACRIFICING VIRGINS

THE LAST THING he wanted to do tonight was to have sex with a beautiful virgin.

Tony stopped walking from the stage to the dressing room and scratched a lock from his head at that uncharacteristic thought. He slumped with a sigh against the dingy black hallway wall.

How had it come to this? He actually was dreading the idea of fondling the virgin he knew awaited him just a few steps and a door away.

When you put it on demonically notarized legal paper with a schedule, sex just didn't end up being as much fun as it used to be. The contract had sounded unbeatable at the time—fame and fortune for him and his band. And what he paid in return was a reward in itself.

The price?

Deflower one virgin after each performance.

By midnight.

Not a problem!

The contract stipulated that to meet the terms, the virgins thus deflowered must be those that would be delivered by "The Messenger" to his dressing room. It also guaranteed that they would be "pleasing to behold".

Tony had always liked 'em young, so this worked out well. Since they had to be good-looking virgins, the girls The Messenger brought almost always were young—you didn't stay a virgin for long if you were hot! And the whole virgin thing saved Tony from worrying too much about STDs with the girls. He hated condoms.

What could be a sweeter deal? There were always hot, tight babes willing to do whatever he wanted after every show when he was pumped full of hype and adrenaline. It was just what he needed. And he did his best to ignore the suspicion that the girls provided were somehow drugged. They seemed alert, but *no* girls were that pliable. Hell, there'd been one he'd tied to the chair, gagged, poured a pitcher of beer over her and then invited in a couple members of the crew for a gang bang (after he'd given her a Miller douche and deflowered her himself, of course). When he took off her gag and handed her over to The Messenger at midnight, she had smiled dumbly at him and said, "Thanks."

He'd had every female model there was at this point it seemed—except for the dumpy sack of potatoes kind. The band was selling millions of CDs and spent half the year touring all parts of the world, so he'd fucked virgins from France, Melbourne, Rio, Moscow, New York and everywhere in between. Redheads, blondes, platinums, goth chicks with cropped raven hair and farm girls with sunny smiles and big tits. And every one a tight, ready-to-be-popped virgin.

Each night after a show it was the same. He returned to the dressing room to find a naked bit of tail just waiting for him to nail. He'd have an hour or so usually before the 12 o'clock chimes struck and his business had to be over. Then the nasty-looking dwarf Messenger appeared at the door to lead his latest sacrifice away.

It sounded like an awesome life. But Tony was tired.

Or bored.

Maybe both. He considered asking the band to cancel the next few months of its tour to take some time off, but he knew it was a foolish dream. If they quit now, it was only cuz they were breaking up. They were booked on an arena tour for the next six months straight. It was worth millions in the hand and untold millions in future sales.

A splash of light fell across the hall and a gnome-like head poked out of his dressing room.

"Better unstrap that instrument and get to performing," said the growling little Rumpelstiltskin. Tony had never asked its name, but that was how he referred to the little man in his own mind.

"Boss sent you something special tonight—says you're acting bored and ungrateful. Says you been performing like a geriatric sprinter against the Olympic team—no staying power."

Rumpelstiltskin cackled and Tony pushed off from the wall and resignedly moved towards his dressing room.

"I'm coming, I'm coming," he murmured.

"Boss's hoping you'll be doing just that," the imp laughed again.

Tony pushed past the little man and closed the door behind him, locking the creature out. Not that locks had any real impact on the little devil, but it made him feel better. He performed *music* for an audience, not sex.

Tony looked at the bed and grinned in spite of his reservations. The "boss" *had* sent something special. She was lying stark naked, head propped on a blue paisley throw pillow, left knee crooked, legs apart to display the object of Tony's mission in all its raw, pink glory. She was built like a track star—lots of leg and a taut tummy, with small, but ample breasts (*more than a mouthful's wasted*, he thought). Her nipples were wide, just as he liked, and matched the auburn crop that crowned her head and arrowed down from her belly. Her features were elfin fine, but her lips were full, and Tony felt a thickening in his tight black leather pants.

Maybe this wouldn't be so bad after all, he thought and then stepped closer.

"Hey," he said, not knowing what to call her. She didn't reply.

"Stoned?" he asked in a louder voice.

Still nothing. He reached out to shake her by the shoulder and drew back his hand in a flash. She was cold to the touch.

Clammy. And stiff.

She was quite dead.

Tony yanked the dressing room door back open and looked for The Messenger.

The little man was talking up a groupie near the stage door. Tony knew she was a groupie with one glance, since her boobs were falling out of one of his band's concert T's, which had been ripped specially to show off her cleavage. But most telling was the fact that she didn't seem to mind the dwarf's face anchored in her crotch. Some chicks'd do anything to get backstage—including servicing perverted dwarfs.

"Hey," Tony yelled again. Rumpelstiltskin looked around, a scowl on his face.

"You've got yours," he snapped and turned away. But the groupie wasn't so easily distracted.

"Tony DeBruno!" she screamed. "Oh... My... Gawd." She started to push past the dwarf, who gave a disgusted look, anchored his hand between her legs and shoved. The groupie and her three-inch black spike heels disappeared with a scream down the back stairs.

"What do you need?" he asked, suddenly standing right in front of Tony. He pointed to a nonexistent wristwatch. "It's after eleven thirty, you know."

"She's dead," Tony complained.

"Well, when you've had all the rest, you've just got to do the best," the creature laughed. "Enjoy."

"But how can I..." Tony began, but then shut up, since The Messenger had disappeared.

Tony returned to the dressing room and looked the girl over again. He was definitely not into necrophilia, but she was attractive, no question about that. Milky-white skin, full lips. He imagined in life that she had been quite the sucker with those pouty kissers.

The clock on the wall read 11:39, and Tony paced the room, considering. The contract stipulated that he had to deflower the virgins sent to him by midnight, or he lost it all. The wording was vague on this point, but he could guess that "all" included life, as well as fame. You didn't fuck with the devil and not pay dearly at some point.

So he had no choice here. He had to slide it in between the legs of a dead chick. Tony shook his long bleached hair and let out a low moan. Why had he gone in for this? He'd enjoyed playing in the band even before they were famous. And even if the money sucked and the fame was missing, he'd never had a problem getting some bar slut to go home with. Why had he ...?

A hand slapped his face.

His own.

"No time for what ifs and whys," he told himself out loud, and began to unbuckle his pants.

"You won't mind if I don't waste time on foreplay, will you, hon?" he asked, stroking himself erect—which turned out not to be difficult if you just looked at her and omitted the minor unappetizing detail that she was dead. Then he crawled onto the bed with her.

As he climbed closer, he realized that she smelled. It was faint, but the cloying scent of something like rotting hamburger clung to the air about her. Tony began to breathe through his mouth and with one hand levered himself into the groove between her thighs.

He pushed himself at her, and felt a much tighter resistance than even most virgins. Death didn't exactly make you ready and willing, he supposed.

He lay heavier on top of her and thrust, and as he pressed down on her with his chest, her mouth loosed a sudden cloud of rotten air. Tony choked in spite of trying to keep his nose closed, and thrust again, but he was making no headway (so to speak).

"Ahh shit," he declared and rolled off of her, his erection gone and his stomach suddenly nauseous.

He turned his head away from her and took a deep breath to clear his lungs, and then took a closer look between her legs. Maybe rigor mortis had closed her off to him? He fingered her to see how tight she truly was, and it wasn't too hard then to find the problem.

She'd been sewn shut.

Stitched up by a devil with a sense of humor, the thread matched the auburn crop of her pubic hair.

"What the…" he moaned aloud, voice breaking. "I've gotta cut her open? Shit…why would a dead girl need a chastity belt?"

Tony got off the bed and picked up his pants. He kept a pocketknife on his keychain, and while he was sure its makers never envisioned unthreading dead virgins as one of the 1001 uses they advertised that it had, he flipped the blade open.

"Use one thousand and two," he murmured, bringing its blade to bear on the thread between the dead girl's labial lips. "Readying dead virgins for necrophilia."

He sliced downwards, careful not to take her delicate tissues with the thread, though why he should care at this stage, he didn't know.

It was difficult at first; the stitch had been very tight and close. But one by one he sawed through the barrier threads, and grinned with satisfaction as he saw the glint of something shiny begin to leak out of the hole he'd broken. Finally, halfway down the girl's cleft, he gave a fast flick and opened the last stitches with one slice.

And froze.

That glint of shininess was oozing from her vagina now that he'd set it free, and it wasn't feminine mucous.

It was a stream of maggots.

A score of them exploded from her to land squirming and stinking on the bed. And instead of slowing, the stream increased. Dozens of the white slimy worms slipped out of her in seconds, some of them choosing to crawl up through her ruddy hair or to hug the inside of her thighs.

Tony coughed and covered his mouth with a hand, choking down vomit. In horror, he backed off and away from the bed, still holding the knife, which had one-half of a tiny squirming maggot stuck to its tip. He dropped it and his keys to the floor.

"Oh God, oh God," he cried. The clock read 11:54. "What am I gonna do?"

The stench of her now filled the room and it was everything he could do to keep from puking. But he watched the second hand spinning slowly around the clock face and shook his head.

"No you don't," he said, and again went to his pants. Contract didn't say he couldn't wear protection when he came. Just said he had to come. And he knew there was an old condom in his wallet. You never knew when you might run into a chick who wasn't a devil-provided virgin.

Closing his eyes for a minute, he pushed the images of the maggots away and brought to mind the image of the last blonde he and the crew had gang banged. With a frightened urgency, Tony worked himself hard enough to slip the rubber on. Then he moved to the bed and got in push-up position over the girl, trying not to let any part of his body except his cock make contact with her. He guided himself towards her and thrust forward, feeling something squish as he tried to enter her virgin walls. In his head he knew what his cock was mashing, and it wasn't a hymen.

He shook the thought away, and stared at her breasts, which still looked suckable and warm, despite her condition. He pushed himself again to slip inside her, and coughed when the result was an expulsion of fetid air. It would help if he could at least kiss the girl, he thought, and looked up from her tits to see a creamy yellow maggot worming its way out of the corner of her mouth.

"Ahh shit, shit, shit!" he cried and rolled away from her again, cock flaccid and breath coming in dangerous gasps. "I can't do this. I can't!"

The clock now read 11:58. He didn't know if he'd gotten deep enough inside her to make her no longer qualify as a virgin, but he hadn't consummated the deed and that was definitely part of the deal. He looked down and grimaced at the yellowish scum that discolored the head of the condom. With his hand, he tried to stroke his cock erect again, but if anything, it pulled deeper inside him, like a hiding tortoise head.

11:59.

Still yanking his maggot-slimed penis, Tony stood at the side of the bed and looked at the virgin. The freed worms were now happily canvassing her entire body with their spasmodic up and down inchworm motions. A steady stream issued now from her lips and pooled in the cavern of her throat. Her thighs and the bed between them were alive with fly spawn and even the rosy tips of her nipples boasted one curious worm. Another twitched from between the toes of her right foot, and then fell with a plop to the sheets.

Tears ran from Tony's eyes, which were torn between staring in horror at the rotting girl and at the second hand of the clock, which inched from the 30 to the 40 to the 50, 55 and finally...

The door burst open and Rumpelstiltskin sauntered in, his face covered by the most profound grin Tony had ever seen. The Messenger was looking forward to becoming The Executioner.

"What's a matter, can't get it up?" the dwarf taunted. He hitched at his belt. "Need me to do the deed for ya? It won't fulfill yer end of the bargain, but hey, what's a little worm meat between friends, eh?"

"She's dead," Tony said. There didn't seem to be anything else he could say.

"What's your point?" the dwarf laughed. He was giving her a gynecological examination. He looked up, still grinning and announced, "She's still a virgin."

"She's full of maggots!" Tony cried.

"You think *that's* bad? Wait 'til you see what the boss has got waiting for you below."

"That's not fair," Tony pleaded. "The contract didn't say anything about them being dead."

"Yeah, well, it didn't specify nothin' about them being alive neither," Rumpelstiltskin cackled. "And anyway, they all die pretty quick once you're done with 'em anyway."

"Die?"

"Sure." The dwarf grinned, wrinkles nearly swallowing his beaming emerald eyes into the folds of his leathery face. "Lots of 'em slit their wrists, especially after they pump out some kind of six-armed monstrosity. Others just kind of corrode away. Boss figures they're either fertile fer his kids or ought to be fertilizer for someone else's."

"His kids?" Tony frowned. "What are you talking about?"

"Talking about the Boss's seed," Rumpelstiltskin said. "You carry it inside you. Been carrying it to women all over the world for years. And the Boss's seed don't plant any happiness, let me tell you! You think he's been having you sacrificing virgins just for your own fun? But you can see for yourself; Boss'll have what's left of those girls waiting for you down below."

The dwarf looked at the clock, which now read 12:03.

"How would you like to shuffle off? Something memorable, I imagine. 'S a shame when rock stars just slip away in their sleep. No headlines there. Wanna slit your wrists and write a goodbye message in your blood? Maybe OD on some choice heroin? How about drink yourself out—choke on your own vomit?"

The dwarf tapped a long gnarled finger to his lips.

"Naw, I'm getting too habitual about this, we've done all those. How about…"

Tony bolted from the room, without even slowing to pick up his pants. The dwarf followed at a more leisurely pace, pointing his finger "up" when Tony reached the stairs the groupie had fallen down. Instead of following her path, the singer's feet suddenly turned and took the stairs towards the roof.

The Messenger hopped happily up the granite steps and a smile cracked his hide from ear to ear as in the theater attic,

Tony tried to dig his feet in but found himself unable to stop from running headlong toward the giant air circulation fan.

"Yes," the dwarf said to himself. "Decapitation is a nice choice. Haven't done one of those in…literally…ages."

As Tony's head punched through the barrier screen to meet the slicing blades, the Messenger winked out to meet him on the other side. He had lots of new girls for Tony to meet.

And none of them were pretty—or virgins—anymore.

WHATEVER YOU WANT

IT WAS THE shiny metal of her belt that first drew my eye. They say it's women who are entranced by things that glitter, but don't fool yourself. Guys have eyes too. And the silver jiggle of her hips as she walked back and forth in front of me all night served as a homing beacon. I couldn't *not* look. I couldn't *not* see the delicate tendrils of the tattoo that rose in a sensual tease from beneath the back of her skirt. I couldn't *not* see the black shadow around her eyes that pronounced her a "dark soul" and I couldn't *not* see the way her black T-shirt crept up above her hips as she walked, sometimes showing just the faintest hint of winter-white skin and other times fully revealing the dark pit of a bellybutton. I stayed at the bar a long time; I took a lot in. And no matter what I asked for; she only smiled, her eyes creasing almost closed as she answered, "Whatever you want."

I knew she was curious about me before midnight; she came to my table more than those of any of her other customers, and her eyes glinted white as she laughed at my painful jokes and made a point to stare at me deeply, attentively, slavishly. Sometime around my fourth or fifth beer I asked her to sit down with me.

"Whatever you want," she said, and slid into the booth with me. I put my arm around her thin shoulders and asked, "You won't get into trouble with your boss, will you?"

I could feel her shrug. "I was just taking care of a customer," she said innocently.

"Makes me wish there was more on the menu," I said.

"*You* can order off-menu," she answered. She turned her head towards mine, clearly inclining for a kiss. I bent to give her one, and she licked her tongue across my lips like a cat and pulled back before I could meet her.

"May I take your order, sir?"

"I'll take the public hand job with a French kiss," I laughed. She didn't.

A cool palm slipped against my belly and down below my belt. Warm lips brushed across my ear, moving to my mouth, as her voice promised everything. "Whatever you want," she said.

∞

I took her home when she got off work. I don't even think we said a word to each other after I shut the door to my apartment before she had completely shed her clothes on my living room floor.

"I'm not sure I tipped well enough for this," I murmured as her lips slid from my nipples to my groin. Her hands worked my belt loose and then freed the rest. The warmth of her lust engulfed me and I moaned.

"What would you like, baby?" she asked. Her voice sounded too young for her actions.

"I'd like to bend you over the daybed," I gasped, "and take you from behind."

"Whatever you want," she promised again, and stood up. In moments, I was treated to an easy study of the ornate bat-like tendrils of that tattoo above her ass, and my fingers roamed freely across the cool naked skin of her backside. I could feel every hair on her body, every pore. And more surprisingly, every scar. Her back was a mess of them. Faint, most were, but as I pressed myself tight against her, cleaving to her, I could see a lattice of her past.

A violent past, from the look of it. I had a vision of her tied against basement walls, a leather-clad man with a whip poised behind her. With every lash he created new scars.

They made me inexplicably excited and my intensity increased. It wasn't long before we had both collapsed atop each other on the daybed. I slid my fingers through the tangled black hair over her ear and whispered, "Stay here with me tonight?"

In the morning, she still looked good. But now the romantic shadows that had hid the intensity of her scars was gone. She slept next to me, still nude, the curve of her ass slipped out of the sheets as I shifted, and I studied the crisscross of jagged white lines that led from above her shoulder blades down past her waist to twist like barbed wire around the globes of her warm and very willing ass. I slipped a hand across her chest to feel the warmth of a breast, and she answered with a faint groan, rolling back towards me, delivering herself into my touch. The road-map of scars continued across her middle, and now I saw that some of them were deeper below the lines of her nipples. Her belly remained mostly unmarked, but her ribs might have had fishhooks pulled across them at one time.

"What happened?" I asked, trailing a finger across the faint indentation of one deep scar.

"He loved me," she said simply.

I didn't know what to say to that. So I didn't say anything.

Her name was Kerstin. I didn't know that until I went to drive her home. But I got to know the sound of it a lot better over the next few weeks. She spent a lot of time at my place, and after her Friday night shift, she even spent the rest of the weekend.

It was probably our third full weekend together when my neighbor decided to make good on his threat to build a bookcase for his living room wall. The hammering woke me up, but it was the high-pitched whir of the circular saw that made Kerstin's eyes go wide.

I thought she was frightened of the sound at first, and then her lips were covering mine. The saw next door oscillated through the wall, growling high and hungry as it slipped through whatever wood Mike was repetitively slicing. Probably making the shelves for his case, I thought. The sound vibrated in my bedroom, which was on the other side of his main room wall. Kerstin's tongue pressed hard in my mouth, and then she rolled and I felt the warmth of her engulf my cock. She was already dripping with excitement, and she'd only just woken up.

Afterwards she grinned sheepishly. "The sound of a saw just gets me going," she said. "Don't ask me why. But if you ever want to get me hot...just rev up a blade for a minute. I know, it's weird."

She rolled her eyes and I could tell she was embarrassed and afraid of what I'd say. Then she turned the tables and asked me, "Is there anything weird that gets you off? Anything you've always wanted to do but were afraid to try?"

I thought of the whir of a saw and the splash of blood as it bit into flesh instead of wood and shivered.

I shrugged. "I don't know," I said. "I guess I've always thought it would be hot to do it in public, in an elevator, or in the back booth of a bar or something."

She raised an eyebrow. "A little exhibitionist, eh?" Then she put her hands on my chest and pushed me back to the bed. Rising above me, snowy-white breasts inches from my face, she bent down until her nipples brushed against the hair of my chest. "You can do better than that," she whispered.

"A threesome would be hot," I began, and her lips twisted.

"Vanilla," she said. Her mouth leaned close enough to mine for me to feel her breath. "What really turns you on when you're all alone?" she said. "What gets you hard that you'd never admit to your best friend?"

I thought of my old girlfriend's accident, and blinked it away.

"Well, why would I admit that to you?" I grinned.

"Because I'm not your friend," she whispered. "I'm your sex toy."

I felt my cock stir at the same time as my stomach twisted. She *was* my friend. I really had begun to care about her. I had...

"Whatever you want," she interrupted my thoughts. "You'll never have this chance with anybody else. Just tell me. Do you want to beat the woman you fuck? Do you want to piss on her face before you make her suck you off? Or maybe you need the other side of the play... Do you want to lie down in the middle of a circle jerk and feel the rain? Would that make your cock shake? Do you want me to fuck all of them before I let you inside me? Do you want to find yourself a sixteen-year-old Lolita and plow her evil young pussy while I hold her down for you? Do you want to wear panties? Do you want to be tied up? Do you want to shave a woman clean? Do you want to cut her before you cum? Do you want to get it on with a dead girl?"

I don't know what made me say it. Maybe I just wanted to stop the stream of embarrassing perversions that dripped from her lip like cum. Tantalizing and wicked. Maybe it was the dead girl thing and I just jumped on what I thought would be an innocuous weirdness.

"I would love to fuck a goth girl in a coffin," I breathed.

"Now you're getting the idea," she said.

∽

The next night, Kerstin picked me up and drove me across town in the dark. She didn't say anything, and refused to answer when I asked where we were going. She wore a short black skirt and a black satin blouse opened three buttons down to show the creamy swell of her breasts against a black silk bra. I knew why when we pulled into the parking lot of a Funeral Home and around the back.

"You can't be serious," I said as she pulled up to the back door.

"It's after-hours and I know someone who works here," she said, holding up a key. "I can make your dreams come true."

"No way," I resisted. "I was only joking…"

"Come with me," she said, and got out of the car. I followed her, still protesting, but she ignored me.

Kerstin led me through the back entry of the funeral home into the heavy silence of thick carpet and sob-absorbing wall hangings. This was a place that could absorb any noise, from a scream to a furtive cry. It certainly had plenty of opportunities to mask pain.

She led me away from the viewing rooms down a flight of stairs. Then we entered a doorway at the end of the hall, and she turned on a wall switch to illuminate the room. Several coffins were displayed in-line, from high-grade metal bronze boxes to ornate varnished wooden ones, with red velvet lining the insides.

Kerstin walked between the staged boxes, leading me to the end of the line, a wooden coffin with its lid propped up.

"My friend left this for you."

In the coffin lay a naked girl. A naked dead girl. She was dark-haired and young and pale. Her eyes were rouged black. Her breasts looked strangely cold and yet…enticing. I wasn't sure if it was due to the attentions of her embalmer, or her own hygiene, but her pubes were shaved clean. She looked plastic and fuckable at the same time.

"Her funeral is tomorrow," Kerstin offered.

"No," I said, backing away from the dead girl. "I didn't say I wanted necrophilia." I turned to look at Kirstin, panicked. "I said I thought it would be kinky to fuck in a coffin, but not to fuck a dead girl, no way, I'm not into that, I mean, that's just fuckin' twisted and now someone you know thinks that I want…"

"Shhhhhh." She pressed a finger to my lips. "Come here."

She pulled me away from the dead body and led me to an empty coffin. Its lid was also lifted, and the silky white cushions inside looked decadently rich. Kirstin pulled my shirt over my head and unbuckled my pants before I could think twice. And then as she stripped herself, she told me to climb inside. There was a stepping stool already in place, and I did what she commanded, my heart beating in a mix of fear and excitement.

The silk felt cool against my skin, and when Kirstin rose above me, and slid in atop me, it suddenly felt warm in an electric ice against fire way.

Then she reached up and pulled the lid closed and sealed us in the black of a portable crypt. My skin chilled, even with her flesh breathing against my pores.

"Whoa, girl," I whispered. "I don't know…"

"It's just you and me," Kirstin said, spreading her legs to encompass mine. She whispered in my ear, trying to set a mood, "You are deep in the grave in a cemetery at night…buried alive…there is only me to fuck. For eternity. The dead are all around us. Can you get it up?"

She laughed wickedly, and it wasn't her scenario, but rather something in her pitch got me excited. In minutes we were both breathless and sweating… The heat of our tomb only beaded more water on our skin and we slid against each other in a twisted scene that was as wrong as it was hot.

When it was over, Kirstin nuzzled against my ear and whispered, "You fucked me in a coffin…but I know you wanted more."

There were images in my mind, and a pang of fear, and then she just held me, and we didn't speak for a while. When she raised the lid, and helped me out of the humid coffin, she didn't give up.

Kirstin took my hand and led me to the coffin of the goth girl corpse. "I know this is what you wanted, even if you thought you were joking, even if you thought this wasn't at all what you meant…this is what you wanted. And I'm here to give it to you."

"No," I said, my heart pounding. The girl's lips were blue, and my lover was here with me, warm…pink…insistent…

"Get in the coffin with her," Kirstin said. "That's all I ask. Do that much for me. If you don't want to do anything else, you don't have to. But let me see you lying with a dead girl. How many times do you have a chance like that?"

I can't tell you why I did it. Actually I can, but I won't admit it. I climbed, naked, into a coffin with a dead, pretty, cold, young girl.

"Hug her," Kirstin urged.

And I did.

"Kiss her," Kirstin whispered. I could see my girlfriend's nipples were erect. She was getting off on this.

"Press yourself between her thighs," Kirstin urged, and I halfheartedly said, "No." But I did it anyway. Her skin felt cool and almost rubbery as I pushed an insanely hard hard-on up towards that shaven delta. After what I'd just done with Kirstin, I didn't see how I could even get it up again. From behind me, I heard Kirstin whimper in excitement. "This might help," she said in my ear, and then her hand, dripping with some kind of lubricant, slid between my groin and the belly of the dead girl. She stroked me until I was slick, and then stepped back to watch.

It was a while before we left the funeral parlor.

∽∽∽

It was only after that when Kirstin finally invited me to her place. I was still feeling a little nauseous about the night before when she picked me up and asked me if I liked girls with scars.

"I like you, don't I?" I answered. I'd never forced the issue to find out more about her scars. But now I acknowledged them.

"You love me." She smiled. "That's how I know you're going to enjoy this."

"Huh?" I questioned.

"You'll see," Kirstin said. "She's really sweet."

"She?"

"My roommate. She's like, the Queen of Scars."

My stomach trembled. And my cock did too. But I had no idea what waited for me at my girlfriend's.

The apartment was a penthouse suite. At one point, it had probably been the recreation hall for the building, and then someone had thrown up a couple walls to carve in a couple bedrooms and a bath, and suddenly you had a spacious, still mostly open living space. The hardwood on the floor looked a hundred years old, but I had to admit, it was an awesome-looking place. To the right, as you stepped inside, was a small but modern kitchen, with shiny oak cabinets and a stainless steel sink. A half-wall divided that from a bedroom. To the left was a living room, with couches and TV. Someone had installed modern can lights in the white ceilings, which shed a subdued orange glow across the whole of the main room, which had been painted a deep, dusky brick red. Candles flickered against the walls on top of a combination TV / stereo wall unit. Lying on the couch angled across the center of the space in front of the TV, was a woman. I could see a long trail of black hair fanned across the arm cushion. Her leg V-ed up against the back of the couch as she lolled, watching TV.

"Alexis, we're home," Kerstin called. The girl on the couch popped up, or at least part of her did. She pushed herself up with a hand that looked…wrong, but before it dawned on me why, I saw the V of her right leg slip down as the stump of her left leg push out into the space above the floor. She had nothing below the knee. That's when it occurred to me what was wrong with her hand: no fingers.

"Hey," she called, in a soft, but liquid voice. "Missed you. Is this my competition?"

Kerstin took my hand and led me to the couch. "Not competition, Lex. Spice of life."

"You just want someone with two good arms," Alexis complained.

"That would be a benefit for some things," Kerstin agreed, pushing me down on the couch at the end of Alexis's good and bad legs. "Can I get either of you something to drink?" She looked at me and warned, "Don't have any beer, but plenty of liquor."

"Absinthe?" Alexis asked.

"Starting early tonight?"

The dark-haired girl shrugged.

"Got any bourbon?" I asked.

She offered Knob's Creek and I took her up on it, sans ice. As Kerstin busied herself in the kitchen, Alexis turned her attention to me. She pulled her stump back onto the couch so that its smooth end nearly touched my thigh. I could see the jagged pink lines where the flesh had been stitched together.

She pressed the bare foot of her other leg against my thigh. It was missing all but her big toe. What kind of accident had she been in? I wondered.

"Kerstin tells me you like girls with scars," Alexis said. She raised her head to watch my reaction. Her eyes were that piercing color of blue that looks almost likely to be unreal. Her face showed the pocks and gouges of glass spray, or knife play...who knew?

"Well, I..." I stammered.

Her lips spread in a slow, easy, knowing smile. "It's okay," she said. "I know what you did last night. You may be a little shy, but I think you're one of us. And I want you to look at my scars. Go ahead. Touch them."

She pushed her stump closer, and massaged my leg with her mangled foot. I put my palm on the flesh where her left knee should have been, and traced the lines in the skin there. A shiver ran up my back as a memory passed my mind and my hand clenched gently around her flesh. I could feel my cock getting hard instantly.

"Why do they turn you on," she asked softly. "Do you like to give them?"

"No," I said, jerking my hand back. I wondered what she would think if I told her, but then I admitted, "Nothing like that. My first girlfriend was in a car accident, and I guess after I got used to her scars...I started to see them as a turn-on."

"Hmmm," she said.

Kerstin came back with the drinks, and the conversation only got weirder. It didn't take but a couple rounds before Alexis asked Kerstin, "Can we go back to your room now?"

Kerstin helped her friend up, and acted as her crutch as they walked together across the floor. "Aren't you coming?" Kerstin called over her shoulder at me.

I didn't need a second invitation, but I excused myself to stop in the bathroom first. The granny-tiled room smelled mildewy, and a pile of presumably damp towels lay on the floor. One looked to have the dark stains of blood on it. Where there were women, there were always towels with blood, I thought. Then I noticed the alcohol on the sink. Nosy, I opened the cabinet beneath, and looked inside. There were more bottles of alcohol there, and boxes of surgical gauze, fastening tape, and a variety of other medicinal-looking boxes. The cabinet looked like the supply chest for a hospital. Shaking my head, I took care of my business and returned to the girls.

Alexis sat on the edge of the bed, and reached out for me, pulling me near as Kerstin watched.

"Undress me?" she asked. "I think you'll like what you see."

I looked at my girlfriend, who smiled. "We share everything," she said simply. Minutes later her mouth joined mine in tracing the fractured skin of Alexis, who moaned on the bed beneath us. Her body was a spider web of history. A thousand cuts, a hundred pock-holed stabs. There was more pink than flesh tone to her torso. I was so entranced in the ruin of her that I didn't even notice when Kerstin took my pants off and began to use her lips on me.

We were awake for a very long time.

∽

I liked Alexis. She was funny in a very under-spoken cynical way. I spent the next few days at their apartment, becoming more and more enamored of them both. They were completely warped women, both of them, and for the first time in my life I truly felt like I could share all my own kinks and dark fantasies with someone. I knew they would both understand. Alexis started telling me the origins of her scars. She'd point to one gnarled indent in her belly and smile dreamily as she explained, "This was Jim's. Our first weekend away together. He used a pocketknife." And then another time as my tongue traced a longer, more angry line. "That was Jim's last one," she said. "He used a box cutter." I could instantly imagine the blood pouring across her belly from the cut, and winced. "We had such a good time that night," she said, drawing my face up with her lips with her good hand. "He had so much blood on him by the time we were finished…" her voice trailed off and she smiled at the memory.

She *was* the Queen of Scars.

I slept with both of them nearly every night for the next two or three weeks before Alexis said to Kerstin, "Let's go to my room tonight." I didn't think anything of the change immediately, until I stepped into the other bedroom just off the living room. I'd never been in it before; the door was always closed. When Kerstin turned the light on, I gasped. The single ceiling fixture was covered in a red-tinted glass, giving the whole room a bloody glare. The walls were covered with some kind of foam board (soundproofing, I learned later), and the floors were sheeted in plastic. The bed was sheeted in black, and as we laid Alexis out nude upon it, the contrast of her skin looked shocking. The red light played off her scars weirdly…her whole body might have been perspiring blood from the way the light and shadows played.

"You two get started," Kerstin said, and pushed off the bed as I slid my hands over Alexis's chest, cupping one beautiful breast, and then one ruined mound, its nipple cut off and clumsily stitched back together. I'd learned why her scars all looked so pronounced. She never went to the hospital after her sado-masochistic exercises, but stitched them at home, these days with Kerstin's help. Hence the hospital-supply chest in the bath.

Alexis's finger-shy hand was kneading my butt when the electric whine of a circular saw broke the silence of the room. I jerked away from a kiss, but Alexis only grinned, and pulled me back. "It's just Kerstin," she said, pressing my head to the scars of her ruined breast. "She gets off on the sound."

I relaxed then, remembering the time in my apartment. The sound got closer, and when I looked up from Alexis's embrace,

I saw Kerstin sitting next to the bed naked on the floor. The smooth steel handle of the circular saw was kneading her crotch, as her fingers revved and relaxed on the trigger. Not your usual vibrator, I thought, and went back to using my own brand of vibrator on Alexis. She was wet and more than ready, but after I entered her, she turned her mouth from mine to say to Kerstin, "My turn?"

"I *knew* you wanted it." Kerstin grinned, and stood to approach us with the saw.

"What are you doing?" I said, freezing my rhythm.

"Don't worry," Kerstin said. "Just be still. All she needs is a little lubrication. Just a taste."

With that, her fingers tightened on the saw and she moved the blur of the blade closer and closer to us, a centimeter at a time. I could feel Alexis's breath on my neck; it was coming in shorter, faster gasps, and I started to pull away, but she hissed at me, "Please don't move."

She pressed her mouth to my shoulder and I felt her teeth clench hard on my flesh as the edge of the saw finally kissed the skin of her thigh, just an inch from my own skin. Her body tensed and trembled. She gave out a slight moan as the blade bit, and blood welled instantly to stream down her skin. And then Kerstin dropped the blade and began masturbating herself on the floor as Alexis rolled me onto my back and mounted me savagely, grunting in both pain and pleasure with every movement. I could feel the wetness of her blood lubricating our act, and she reached down with a hand and smeared the red across her chest and my own before falling down hard on me, climaxing, her motions spastic and desperate.

I felt that same sick feeling as I had after the coffin incident on the following morning when I woke up in the red room between them and I saw the ragged wound on Alexis's leg. The perverse pleasures of the night before came back in a rush. I should have run. But in some sick way, I loved them both even more.

I didn't even think of leaving.

∽∞∽

The next night, Kerstin handed me a black leather flogger, its multiple leather strips tipped with small shards of metal. Then she pressed her hands onto two rings suspended near the far wall of Alexis's bedroom. "Lex can't do this very easily anymore," she whispered. "Don't be gentle. Tonight you'll make your mark on both of us."

I took the flogger from her and turned it over in my hand, shaking my head. I didn't want to hurt her. But I knew she needed to feel it...she needed the pain it gave. I flicked it against her naked back a few times, and Kerstin laughed.

"Hit me like you mean it," she said.

The next stroke was harder, and she flinched. The crack of the leather on her skin sent a thrill down my lower back. I hit her again, and I could see the skin reddening already from the last slap.

"That's it," Alexis encouraged, from behind. "Punish her."

On the next crack, I felt the ends of the barbed leather catch slightly on her skin before pulling away, and beads of blood rose on the skin between my girlfriend's shoulder blades. Kerstin moaned, and twisted in obvious pain against her cuffs. "Don't stop," she begged.

Sweat was beading on my forehead. My armpits were damp. I felt something raw coursing through my groin. Power. Evil. Sadism. Alexis moaned on the bed behind me as Kerstin's cries mounted in front.

I didn't stop.

When I was done with Kerstin, her back a bloody mess of red weals and broken skin, she staggered over to a toolbox across the room and returned with a large set of wire cutters. On the bed, Alexis was writhing in excitement, her ruined hand missing between her legs. "Take it," she gasped, over and over. "Please."

When Kerstin put her cutters against the end of Alexis' foot, I pulled her back. "You can't," I cried.

"It's what she wants," she answered. "And I won't, you will. She wants this to be your mark. We talked about it earlier today."

"No," I said. "No fuckin' way."

"I'll help you," Kerstin promised, and pulled my hand to the softness of her breast, before clasping it to the handles of the cutters.

"Please," Alexis begged me from the bed. "I need it."

"We need you to do these things for us," Kerstin said, looking into my eyes. I saw a desire there harder than stone and darker than war.

Together, we cut off Alexis's last toe. I won't detail the things we did with her after that, before Kerstin dressed the wound.

∽

After that night, I didn't feel nauseous about anything we did together anymore. It was all consensual, right? I pressed my fingers into their wounds and kissed them both, reveling in the shiver of their pain as much as they did themselves. The thoughts I once had kept buried about my old girlfriend's scars were tethered no longer.

We had begun our descent into the circles of hell. They were far ahead of me, but quickly I shed all of my inhibitions and caught up. Maybe I surpassed.

A few weeks later, we pooled our money and bought a tiny house out in the middle of nowhere, but still just thirty or forty miles from Kerstin's bar and my day job.

We built our own private dungeon in the little frame ranch's basement, and that's when things really got weird.

The night she cut off Alexis's other leg, Kerstin was ready with morphine and stitches. I couldn't do it, as depraved as I'd become. I literally cried when I saw the blood spray as the saw bit down and Alexis screamed so hard my ears still rang in the morning. We buried the leg in the yard, and for the next three weeks we fucked like a twisted trio of wounded rabbits, while Alexis screamed between us alternately in pain and pleasure. Eventually she healed. It was the celebration of our first anniversary together.

My fixation with her stumps only increased now that both of her legs were shorn, and I began to whip Kerstin not only on her back, but across her thighs and breasts as well, taking care not to hit her on flesh she couldn't cover at work. But I quickly overprinted her lattice of scars. She abandoned her body to my growing sadism. She took to wearing layers of clothing when she left the house, as she was always bleeding and oozing from somewhere.

"Front or back," I'd ask, as she handed me the cat o' nine tails.

"Whatever you want," she'd always say. Later, I would lick pink scars on the stumps of Alexis's legs before cleaning Kerstin's wetter wounds with my tongue. There were times that I thought I was in the heaven of hell. My daydreams were filled with scars and blood and writhing women who lived for both.

I killed Alexis on Christmas.

I didn't mean to. We were taking her arm off with the saw, and I think we waited too long to bandage her up, after. But Alexis kept screaming in pain at the same time as insisting that I fuck her. The three of us were covered in her blood when Kerstin finished her orgasm with the butt of the saw as I came inside a bloody, screaming Alexis.

The next morning, stitched, bandaged and morphined… Alexis was blue. She did not wake. She had wanted to give me a special Christmas present and I'd elected this year to take it. It was the last gift she would give.

Kerstin and I wept and held her dead body for an hour before we finally left her in the slaughter room.

"We'll bury her in back," she pronounced later that day.

"Are you serious?" I said.

"We can't very well call an ambulance and report it as an accidental death, can we?"

Good point.

"I can get us a coffin, even," Kerstin said, her voice paper thin. "I have connections, you know. And he'll think it's just another kink."

That night, she pulled into the driveway in a rented SUV with its seats removed. A plain brown coffin in the back. I helped her bring it in the house, and together we laid Alexis out in it. A private wake.

"Take her one last time," Kerstin begged me. "She would want you to."

It didn't take too much urging for me to lie with our Queen of Scars one last time. And another.

We kept her in the living room for three days before I could let her go.

∽

Things changed after Alexis was gone. She was our center, the perversion we'd revolved around. Kerstin and I started pushing the envelope on each other then. She would threaten to cut me with the saw, its teeth just inches from my neck, before collapsing into a masturbatory fugue on the floor beside the bed.

I started bringing a razor to bed, and I dragged it across her skin deeper and deeper by the night. The flesh of her back and chest was black with scabs and swollen with infection. She oozed foul fluids when I pressed my body against hers. Her eyes took on a strangely haunted look as she continued to taunt me to hurt her more.

The morning I woke up tied to the headboard was the final nail. As my eyes fluttered open, and I realized what was going on, looking from one hand to the other and flexing my fingers, I heard the saw start up.

"I need a piece of you," Kirstin said in a low, sex voice. She brought the blade up to my chest, and then down the length of my arm.

"No, Kerstin," I begged. "Please don't do this. I can't live without my arm."

"Whatever you want," she whispered sweetly, and then the pain lanced through my little toe.

When I was done crying and she'd bandaged the wound, Kerstin kissed me. Deeply. With more passion than she'd had in weeks.

"So many things to cut." She grinned, running a finger down my armpit and out to my palm. "But we'll save the best for last," she said, toying with the root of my cock with her other hand.

"I should be able to get weeks and weeks of use out of it before it's time."

That time was never going to come. Kerstin was used to dealing with masochists; people who wanted to be cut. She never tied ropes to hold people who didn't want to be held. And I didn't.

It only took a couple days before she tied one of my wrists just a little too loosely before she went to work. I was ready for her when she got home from work. I stayed in bed and feigned bondage. So well, in fact, that she stripped and straddled me before she knew anything was amiss. She bent to kiss me, and the shriveled remains of my severed toe trailed across my chest. She'd threaded it onto a thin chain to create a gruesome pendant.

"I love you," she breathed. The warmth of her breasts slipped softly across my chest hair. On the surface, it probably looked or sounded romantic. But you could see in her eyes, that Kerstin was lost. Broken. Searching for something to fill in the hole Lex had left in her. In both of us.

I knew there was only one answer for her. She'd been getting closer and closer to it for years. And I was the one who would give it to her. It was something I had been getting closer and closer to for years too.

I flipped the ropes off my wrists and grabbed her around the waist, quickly changing our positions to pin her to the bed.

She was surprised at first, but she didn't really struggle very hard when I twisted the ropes around her wrists.

I looked down at the ugly gashes across her breasts and the bruises on her ribs. At the yellowing stains left by the lashes on her upper arms. At the long ragged pink tracks of pain that crisscrossed her thighs.

"How…" she began to ask, as she tested the ropes. They held.

"You don't tie a very good knot," I explained. "But I do. Remember that night you asked me what I secretly fantasized about doing? My darkest dirty secret?"

She nodded. And I could see in her eyes a new spark of fear and…I think…the first flash of excitement in a long time.

"I don't know if I could have admitted it to myself back then, not really," I said. "But you've freed me."

I walked over to the dresser and picked up the saw.

"I told you I once had a girlfriend who was covered in scars. But I didn't tell you why we broke up."

"Why?" Kerstin asked. Her voice was very small. She moved so easily from subjugator to slave.

"Because she died," I answered, stepping closer to the bed with the saw. I revved it once, and I saw the muscles in her thighs clench. Her fingers touched the sheets and trembled.

"Her father worked at a lumberyard, and one day he'd gone to work and left his lunch on the counter. Becky—that was her name—drove it out to him, because her mom didn't want him going hungry that day. She went into the plant and saw her dad working on the big saw down in the pit so she walked over. She couldn't just call to him, because the place was too loud with machinery. Thing was…Becky didn't walk very steady because of the car accident that gave her all those scars. And the day she went to give her dad his lunch…one of her legs decided to just… give out. It happened sometimes. She'd be walking along and she'd just…fall.

"It picked a rotten time to give out this time though; she was on the stairwell just above where her dad was working. He had no idea she was even there—you couldn't hear anything in that place but the sound of the cutting. He had no idea until she fell right there on the big log he was guiding through the saw, and that blade bit right down into the middle of her without slowing speed a hair. I used to wonder if he even knew who it was that he'd helped chop up before her head rolled down the sawdust trough to stare up at him from his feet."

Kerstin's eyes were bugging out now, fascinated and afraid at the same time. "Oh my God," she murmured.

"Yeah," I said. "Can you imagine sawing your own daughter in half? I was pretty broken up at first. But then I started having these dreams about it. Only, it wasn't her dad at the saw when she fell. In my dreams, it was me. I masturbated a lot thinking about how she must have looked there on the floor, sawed in half…"

"Oh God," Kerstin said, spreading her legs wider. She glistened with excitement, and I put my finger on the saw's trigger again. She visibly responded to the sound, but this time, I didn't relax my finger.

"I never wanted a dead girl the way you thought," I said, moving the saw closer, finally admitting my darkest fantasy to myself. I don't even know if she would have tried to close her legs if I hadn't tied her ankles. In any event, I had, and she couldn't. But I knew that she was twisted just for this. I was twisted just for her.

"Whatever you want," I heard her whisper as the whining teeth of the saw moved steadily closer to her most vulnerable parts.

I think she orgasmed as the blade ate into that pink flesh. I know she was moaning the closer I brought it, and the first scream she let go sounded like the big O. After that…the screams sounded a lot less happy. Either way, they didn't last very long.

Some of her ribs were hard to cut, but steel blades and electricity prevailed. In the end, I lay down there on the wet bed with her. In her. Between her. I kissed her blood-spattered lips and felt my own insanity rise fully, freed at last. Her eyes were vacant, but I knew she was happy wherever she was. Violated completely at last. Her lips were still warm. This time, she wouldn't heal.

When I fell asleep that night, I didn't dream at all.

Because all my dreams were real.

GRANDMA WANDA'S
BELLY JELLY

EVEN THE SLOGAN was inane:
It won't stick to your heart or make your thighs swelly
But it's sweet as the twinkle in the eyes of lil' Nelly
It's Grandma Wanda's great Belly Jelly!

God was I sick of hearing that name. You'd think old Grandma Wanda had a fifty-percent market share or something.

Not likely. The prune-complexioned granny produced this stuff in the basement of her little suburban house and only released a few hundred jars a year.

Oh, but those jars…

People paid a hundred bucks a pop for them. *Before* the resale scalpers came into the picture. Naturally it wasn't long before the real jelly manufacturers wanted a piece of the action. We could have made her a millionaire overnight. Her face (well, actually, we would have gotten a sweeter-looking granny for the labels) would have smiled from the aisles of supermarkets from Greenwich Village to Key West.

But Grandma Wanda had turned up her mottled, discolored close pin of a nose and grunted. "Uhh-uhhh."

There were plenty of closed-door meetings about Grandma Wanda. Bet on it. We were not the only bread spreaders who wanted the rights to the recipe. Marketing boys sketched kindly looking aproned matrons and syrupy slogans to present to the old bat in hopes of converting her.

Money didn't talk. "Uhhh-uhh."

Ad slicks met with crumpling. "Uhhh-uhhh."

The old warhorse patriotic good-of-your-country speech raised an eyebrow but no salute. "Uhhh-uh."

"We have to buy her out before Fucker's," our CEO shouted in his affectionate vernacular for our arch rivals in morning manna.

The offers were made.

The offers were countered.

The counters were topped.

Grandma Wanda spread a slick of translucent crimson jam across the contracts, folded them neatly and shoved them back in the breast pockets of our sales force.

"Uhh-uh," was the extent of our negotiation effects.

Which put me in my current position: Street corner of Eigel and 5th, powdered sugar stains on my gray trousers, a stale reek of sweat and frustration bouncing from me to the Caprice's upholstery and back again, like some vile game of scented racquetball. I'd been in this car a long time.

Grandma Wanda, however, had been in her house even longer.

I knew she had to come out sooner or later, and I only wished she'd chosen a more interesting neighborhood to set up shop in. At least then I would have had something interesting to look at while I waited for her knob to turn, the car to rev and her 1954 Ford to cough its way onto the street and away from her house. She and the car made a well-matched team: rusted, beat-up, old and indomitable. If she'd driven a tank, I wouldn't have batted an eye. But the Ford was close enough.

I'd been watching the stationary hunk of road armor since last night, and the arches of my eyelids were threatening to give way. Their architect couldn't argue very much against the idea. The suburban street stretched ahead of me like a gray ruler: straight and evenly dotted with houses of similar size and shape and color. Geometrically positioned parkway trees and driveways divided the suburban yardstick. I had waited in vain for that tedious sameness to be interrupted by the salacious stride of a young teenage girl, or even by the aged but titillating sunbathing of a not-too-far-to-pot housewife.

But the neighborhood was as sterile as its construction.

When the choking cloud of blue smoke drifted past my lookout post, I almost missed it. But the backfire startled me into spilling coffee on my crotch, and I looked up just in time to see Grandma Wanda's prune-veined cheeks go chugging past me. Ten seconds later, I was out of the car and heading nonchalantly up her driveway (as nonchalantly as someone can be when wearing a dark stain of coffee and a sticky smear of sugar on one's crotch).

I ducked past the creaking wooden gate and tiptoed up the rotting deck behind Wanda's house. At that moment, one of the obstinately invisible sunbathers of the past twenty-four hours decided to step out into the yard next door.

She waved, brown-freckled breasts bouncing like untethered water balloons back and forth. She was maybe forty-five, false blonde, and a dermatologist's dream: Every inch of her body was tanned a dark leathery brown, and I mean every inch. There were only about three palm's worth of skin on her that she didn't have exposed and she was obviously proud of this fact. She jiggled herself from doorstep to fence in seconds.

"Hiya," she called, resting forearms on the fence and sticking out her derriere so that I couldn't help but notice her physique. It wasn't bad, but I'd guess from the amount of dark freckles on her face and chest that skin cancer was a bet no bookie would take odds against. I nodded in her direction and smiled, but she didn't take the hint.

"You a friend of Wanda's?" she asked, cocking her head like a bird. Vulture, perhaps.

I nodded.

"Nephew, actually. She told me to stop by and wait for her," I lied, pulling out my skeleton key and praying the door wouldn't be stubborn. "I'm picking up some jam," I added.

She grinned and rubbed her stomach invitingly.

"Mmmm, I do love that Belly Jelly! But ya know, any boy of Wanda's is welcome to wait at my place," she offered, slowly pushing browned breasts over the rail of the fence. "I like a little company now and then."

"Thanks for the offer, ma'am," I said, wondering if I should try to slip in a quickie next door after I left Wanda's. "Maybe I'll stop by later, if it's okay."

She frowned, wide lips drooping like a pornographic clown's.

"Suit yourself," she said, and slipped the already thin strap of her bikini bottoms into her ass as she walked away from me.

Slowly, for emphasis.

Wow.

I had never believed the tales of bored suburban housewives, but maybe the false symmetry of the streets bred bizarre behavior. Certainly Wanda was no normal granny, from what I'd seen.

My key slid into the lock and sifted through the tumblers with ease. I took a last glance at the bare backside of Wanda's neighbor, now reclined on a plastic cushion, and stepped inside.

I started in the kitchen.

Where else would you look for a jam recipe?

It was a kitchen like any other grandma's: Its white Formica countertops were lined with spices, potholders and jars of flour, sugar and who knew what else. A warm yeasty odor, like fresh-baked bread hung in the air. But there were no dishes in the sink, and no recipe books lying about. The fridge was dotted with those ridiculous magnets shaped like ears of corn and pieces of fruit. I'd never understood why people paid money for a kitschy kitchen. Then again, I'd always had an urge to open fire with a shotgun on those yard ornaments spotlighting people's bent-over backsides.

I didn't spend too long in the kitchen before marking it off as dry. Wanda had to have a larger place for canning her jam anyway, and I'd always sort of figured she used a basement. I know my grandma used to keep preserves in the cool damp confines below her kitchen. Maybe Wanda cooked and canned there.

The stairs weren't too hard to find. A door opened right off the kitchen onto a narrow descent of dark wooden steps. I felt around for a light and found a string, loosely tied to a hook in the wall. I pulled it, softly at first, and then with a harder tug. A bare bulb screwed into a rough-wood ceiling flickered on at the bottom of the steps.

My first step creaked so loud my heart turned over like a rusted-out '68 Chevy. I looked behind me and listened hard, paranoid now that as soon as I made it to the basement, the ol' bat would walk in the door behind me.

"You get caught, and we don't know ya'," my boss had told me right out. Just the sort of corporate loyalty I expected. And yet I was here anyway. If I didn't get caught, there was a huge bonus waiting for me in an unmarked envelope in the safe behind the CEO's red leather recliner. I had counted the zeros myself. This was a trip worth the risk. And hell, what could an old lady do against me anyway, aside from calling the police and reporting my license number, if she'd noticed the car? I almost whistled as I descended the rest of the stairs.

Wanda's basement reminded me of a cave I'd once gone through on a tour. As I reached the bottom of the stairs, I shivered with the clammy cold that seeped immediately through my still-damp pants and shirt. I guessed it was good for the jelly to stay in a natural refrigerator, but I couldn't imagine that the old lady spent much time down here. I know I wouldn't. Not by choice, anyway.

The floor of the basement seemed to be natural rock. Lord knows, digging a deep enough hole to put in a basement was difficult around here, with bedrock being about one foot down. But usually when they did dredge one out, they concreted it too. The floor sloped off to the right from the end of the stairs, and I decided that right couldn't be wrong. With a quick look back up the stairs to the cheery light above, I ambled deeper into the darkness. I quickly realized that the other strange thing about this basement was that there were no windows. It was as if the house had been built atop a cave. And as I looked up at the ceiling, I wondered if that was really so far-fetched. The ceiling was not planed out as the floor had been, and instead, outcroppings of smoothed red and tan stone crept along in tides of tension.

So I was in a cave. What would the boys say to this one? Not only does the Granny refuse a cool million for her stupid jelly, but she hides in a dank cave with the recipe. Probably even stirs up the mix in a big black kettle.

I was startled out of my internal amusement by a noise upstairs. A door slamming.

SHIT.

"Hellooooo?"

I dove back for the stairs, crawling up them on all fours to try to spread out my weight and minimize their creaking.

"Wanda's nephew? Are you still here, hon?"

It was the damned nosy neighbor! I considered just hiding down in the basement and hoping she'd go away on her own... but if she came down the stairs, I'd be cornered.

No, I had to get rid of her quickly, and on the ground floor.

Quietly I rose to my feet and slipped through the door back into the kitchen.

"Helloooo?"

She'd moved to the stairs that I assumed led to bedrooms on the second level. I pushed the door slowly shut and stepped into the dining room behind her.

"Looking for me, ma'am?"

"Oh!" She jumped around, hands on her chest, still only marginally covered with a pink-and-yellow day-glo bikini. "You gave me a start. I had just about given up on ya."

She covered the distance between us before I could think of a response. And then she put her hands boldly on my crotch. My eyes must've bugged.

"Listen, I noticed outside that you'd spilled something on your pants here." She rubbed the appropriate (or inappropriate) spot. "I thought I could just take these and clean 'em up for you while you're waiting for Wanda. I think she headed into town for some sugar."

With that she began unbuttoning my pants with one hand, while massaging my coffee stain with the other. I couldn't help but respond, which brought a grin from her.

"I might be able to help you with something else, as well," she said. Her voice had grown huskier, and rising interest aside, I had to help this sex-starved sweetheart to the door.

"I'd like it if you would, ma'am, but not just now."

I removed her hands from the waistband of my underwear, which she had dropped to her knees to pull down. She leaned in to breathe heavily on my Jockeys, looking up at me with a mouth ready to swallow Olympus. And I don't mean the camera.

I shook my head once more and readjusted my pants. She pouted and rubbed her chest provocatively as I rebuttoned myself, stubborn tent notwithstanding.

"I've got some business I need to take care of before Grandma Wanda gets home," I said. It was a lame excuse, but I kept picturing the zeros on the end of that bonus check. Transposed with the second hand of a clock, it made for an inspirational mental lever. Button it up and push her out, my greedy side intoned. I won't repeat what my other side said, but it had to do with finding out natural hair color and connecting light to dark freckles. The zeros won.

"I need to get some phone work done," I told her, leaning

forward to cup her chin. God she had big lips! "But maybe tonight?"

She shook her head. "My husband will be home in a couple hours."

"How 'bout tomorrow. Lunchtime?"

She brightened somewhat. Shook her head halfheartedly.

"If I'm home, maybe."

"Good. Let me help you up."

I took her arm and pulled her to her feet. She made sure to push her chest against me, and I ran a hand appreciatively down her backside. But kept steering her towards the door.

As I opened it for her, I bent to kiss her on the cheek.

"Tomorrow then?"

She turned her cheek away and sucked my lips inside her own. It was a hard, wet kiss. It left me breathless, and wondering if I really needed zeros for anything.

"Sure?" she whispered.

"Yeah."

The cellar felt even colder this time down, and it didn't help that I had images of Wanda's neighbor spread-eagled underneath me interrupting my concentration. I headed right once more and found that the stairs had apparently ended in a corridor, not a downstairs room. It narrowed as I walked, until it seemed that the ceiling and walls were but inches away from by head and shoulders. The bulb that hung at the bottom of the stairs barely illuminated this area, but I could see that there was a door just ahead. I reached out to open it, and the knob stopped dead.

Locked.

Damnit.

This was taking far more time than I'd planned. How long had the bimbo upstairs kept me? Ten minutes? And I'd been in the house five to ten minutes before that. If Wanda was just picking up sugar, she could be to the store and back in twenty-to-thirty minutes. I didn't have much time.

I pulled out my skeleton key and tinkered with the lock. This one wasn't budging as easily as the outside door. I could almost hear my "mission clock" counting down in my head.

And then the tumblers tumbled, and the door eased open.

I felt around on the wall inside, and found a light switch. Clicked it.

And swore out loud.

Granny didn't work in a dainty little old-fashioned kitchen. No sir.

The light switch activated a long fluorescent light fixture that hung over an island workstation in the center of the room. I know a thing or two about browning a good piece of beef, and I have to say, that long wooden counter, with its rack of expensive-looking carving knives off to one side got my hands itching to slice and dice something. A half empty box of mason jars sat on the floor nearby, and a gleaming stainless steel sink divided a huge countertop against the back wall. There was a row of dark wooden cabinets lining the wall above the sink. I stepped over and yanked a couple open to confirm by guess.

Yep.

The old bat's toothy face looked back at me from dozens of home-canned jars of Grandma Wanda's Belly Jelly.

The contents of these cabinets would bring me thousands on the open market. But they wouldn't tell me how to make more. I shut the doors and peered deeper into the room. The light yellowed and dimmed before reaching the far wall, but I could see there were racks of something over there in the shadows.

An old white refrigerator hummed against one rocky wall, the kind that you actually had to pull a handle down to release the door. Probably had been here since the house was built. Another door was tucked into an alcove in the wall near it, but that wasn't what held my attention. Instead, I noticed the strange array of thin clear plastic tubes running along the floor towards the shadowed rack. I followed them across the room and up a metal shelving unit. Each tube ended in what looked like a glistening, bloated sack. They smelled rank and heavily sweet at the same time.

I reached out to touch one with a fingertip and recoiled instantly. It was cool and slick with a slimy ooze of what I'd guess was decay. And it seemed to quiver when I touched it.

A lightbulb burst in the back of my head and I connected the name of Grandma's jelly with these lumps of bloated flesh on stainless steel bar racks.

Bellies.

She actually was fermenting the jelly in stomachs!

My own middle began to churn dangerously as the sour part of the smell hit home. I stepped back a pace.

What the hell was she mixing in there? I followed the tubing past the fridge and under the lip of the closed door. This one wasn't locked.

I wish it had been.

When I opened it, my nose was immediately assailed by an earthier, fetid odor. The stench of decay. Of death.

And laid out on a half dozen cots in the center of the room were the reasons.

Six men.

With their abdomens sliced open. Autopsies in progress, only the procedure seemed to have been put on hold for a bit too long. The flesh hanging from the open bellies to drip brown stains on the floors near each bed had long ago ceased to weep. But the chilly temperatures and lack of flies had worked together to keep the flesh of these men bearable. Barely.

The man nearest me was grossly overweight, and one blackened arm hung to the floor, its hand smeared in his own dried guts. His eyes were open, and though they'd filmed over a yellowish white, I still thought I could see the terror crying in them.

She had stolen their bellies to make jelly!

This was bad.

This was not a recipe the home office could adapt.

But who was going to believe me when I described this scene? Disemboweled men rotting on cots like discarded carcasses in a meat locker. Their bellies hosting some weird jelly concoction and connected to, what I now saw in the far corner of the room, was a hospital drip bag hanging from a hook embedded in the blue-gray rock walls?

"Care for some jelly, mister?"

I almost jumped onto the cot with the fat man.

Almost.

Grandma Wanda stood in the doorway. And unlike the toothy likeness on her jelly jar labels, this Wanda was not smiling.

"Maybe another time," I answered, edging farther back into the room.

"Well if you didn't come for my jelly, my guess is, you came to learn how to make it, eh?"

I didn't answer. But her voice was not in a tone that demanded, or even sought, reply.

"My guess is, you've realized by now why I really couldn't sell this little grocery list for mass production."

She laughed then, a not-particularly pleasant cousin of a cackle.

I continued to step backwards, a few inches at a time. I was near the third cot, and the air was growing thicker by the moment. I stifled the urge to gag, and Grandma Wanda finally stepped fully into the room. I intended to barrel past her just as soon as she moved a couple steps from the door. She was only about four foot eleven. How hard would it be to knock her out and clear the stairs. Even if she had a knife or a gun, which I couldn't see handy at the moment.

And then I noticed the face of the man in the third cot. Long nose, thick mustache, mouse-brown hair. I knew that man. As only a rival salesman can know another man.

I hated him.

And in a way, I loved him. We'd warred for years through jelly market penetration, favored distribution contracts, clever television slogans. Ted Mernier. From Fucker's. Apparently I wasn't the only jelly gigolo to come creeping around Granny's basement on the sly. Or maybe she'd lured him here with the promise of a deal.

No matter what the circumstances, Ted wasn't going to be sharing any panels with me this year in Cleveland at the Bread Spread Convention. His stomach just wouldn't be in it.

So to speak.

She saw me staring at Ted and grinned. The veins in her cheeks only seemed to deepen, spreading like an interstate system across the wrinkled states of her cheeks. "Seems your competition got the 'can't beat 'em, join 'em' philosophy. Care to devote your life to a greater purpose?"

Now.

I threw myself at the doorway and Wanda didn't even try to stop me. She stepped aside, that horrible grin still etched on her face like a Halloween mask.

I made it through the kitchen and down the outer corridor before I found out why.

"Hiya!" The brown-freckled bimbo from next door was sitting comfortably on the third stair from the top. And she was aiming a small pistol right between my eyes.

I stopped.

"Looks like I'm going to be having lunch on my own tomorrow," she sighed.

"You don't have to. Just let me up those stairs and I'll show you the best lunch you've ever had."

"Now you know I can't do that, sweets. You've been in Wanda's back room. Nobody who goes in that room comes back up these stairs outside of a jar 'cept Wanda and me."

She ran a tongue over her upper lip. "Pity though. You looked like you'd have tasted good."

"Oh, he still will, he still will," came a rasp from behind me.

I had an idea. If I could grab the old bat around the neck and gain a hostage...

I turned to see where she was and something cold struck me in neck. Like an icy bee sting.

Wanda was just two feet away. I could do it!

"Got him, Wanda," the bimbo keened as I reached for the old lady. She dodged me easily, strangely fast for an old woman.

I felt funny, thick-lipped, loose-limbed. The cold sting...

I reached my hand up to feel the area around the cool pain and found a small needle still poking from my neck. Tranquilized.

Giving up on Granny, I flipped back to the stairs. The room spun crazily, but I didn't wait for it to right itself. I launched myself up the wooden steps, cracking my shins on the lower ones in my haste and rapidly declining motor skills. Annie didn't move, just kept the gun leveled at my brain as I crawled the stairs towards her like a ladder, one hand at a time. When I reached out to grab her ankle and pull her down and out of my way, she mumbled something about "cute" and then brought the barrel of the gun down on my head. I probably would have dropped out of the conscious zone before reaching the kitchen table anyway, but she did speed it along by a few seconds.

My headache was the first thing I noticed when I came to. And then this weird burning in my belly.

I tried to lift my head to see where I was, and found that not only was my neck restrained, but my arms and legs appeared to be beyond my control.

"Are ya in much pain?" a disturbingly familiar voice asked. I tried to shake my head, which only made the rocky ceiling turn into a red kaleidoscope of pain.

"I used to be a nurse, so I know how to take out the lower nerves without much fuss. But I'm never sure about the upper half."

Grandma Wanda's wicked face loomed above my own. "Ya shouldn't go a poking around in folks' homes 'at haven't invited ya, son. Now look what it's come to. But don't worry. You'll come to some good use. I've got your tummy busy a-pickling up a new batch of jam right now."

"Oh my God…" I cried out, but she shushed me.

"I don't take for no swearing now. I'm trying to do you an honor here. I've sewed up all the ends of the intestines and what-not that I had to cut to take your tummy, so that you might last a couple days. I figure the least I can for a man who's given his all to my jelly is to let him taste some of what he's helped make. So far, I haven't been able to keep one of my donors alive quite long enough to get a taste, but I'm getting better. The chubby man over there lasted four days. Just a few more hours and he would have been able to sample his own jelly. Maybe you'll be the lucky one. Here, I'll prop you up a little, so you can see something."

The hazy pain collided like a car crash between my eyes and then the walls swam into focus. As did the open pit where my stomach used to lie. She saw me stare at my middle and nodded.

"I know it looks bad, but I'm no tailor. There's little point in trying to stitch you back together without a belly, so I just cauterize the main bleeders and let things lie. Now, is there anything I can get for you, while you wait for your jelly to be done?"

I couldn't think of a thing.

I Love Her

I LOVE HER. How can I explain it better than that? Every night, I come home from the Many Mammals Meatpacking plant, covered in the blood of a hundred sheep, slathered in the slippery juices that stick and drip from the loopy large intestines of a hundred pigs, peppered with the explosions of one hundred gas-bloated cow bellies.

But she doesn't care. Her love is thick, like the steaks carved from an Iowa corn-fed cow. Her love is ever flowing, like the blood that ripples in the slaughterhouse trough. Her love is the rich red drawn by a rose—one that has pricked and scratched away the flesh of your finger 'til the blood runs fast and bright over velvet white petals. Her love doesn't care that I smell like I've bathed in a fountain of feces, or that my hair is thinning…

Well, perhaps more than thinning.

Okay, bald.

Her love sees past the brown moles on my forehead, and the deep pockmarks on my cheeks. She doesn't care that I'm missing my left eye from that unfortunate meat hook incident. I know she would kiss the crooked scar there if she could.

She is the saint of one thousand acnes, the Madonna of my moles.

I love her.

Every night, when I come home bathed in the sewage of the slaughtered, she says to me, without judgment,

"You have no messages."

I admire her honesty. Another girl might have lied to me, said, "Someone called, but I forgot who. I'm so sorry." Or, perhaps, tried to change the subject entirely with false compliments: "I love that cologne you're wearing, is that Slaughterhouse 5?"

But no. She always tells the truth.

"You have no messages," she says.

I thank her, and ask how her day went. After a moment, I realize that she doesn't want to talk about it. Her concern is solely for me. She wants to hear about *my* day.

Once, after I discovered how to push her buttons the right way, she used to regurgitate the monotonous pitches of the day's telesales calls, one after the other after the other. I know she must have been so frustrated when they would demean her authority, her self-worth, her depth perception and instead of inquiring as to the solid state of her circuitry ask, "Is Mr. Mantain at home?"

I installed a telemarketer screening device this year to spare her from such mundane attacks on her ego.

And her time. I want her to enjoy her hours at home.

After all, I love her.

I love the way she blinks at me with her glowing red eye, when she wants to tell me about someone who called.

I love the way she puts my mother on hold or just cuts the old windbag off "accidentally".

I love the way she doesn't berate me for being out too late, or condemn me for my own brutally physical condemnation of so many animals. She knows that I wield the slaying hammer with ruthless efficiency, sparing them as much pain as I can. When I look into their wide brown eyes, I see the empty stare of my mother, and I know I must be quick.

Ahh...she asks for so little, but gives so much.

So you can imagine that when she does ask for something, I do everything I can to give it to her. Not that she ever asks for anything outright. She is not like some girls, who *want, want, want* and never fail to let you know it. You know the kind, the ones who reach around while you're giving them a hug to run their hands across your ass to see how much of a bulge there is in your back pocket. Oh, they pat the front pocket too, occasionally, but they always try the right ass cheek first. If that's sitting slim, so's your chance of unleashing for them the snake of eternal delight.

The eye that sees best in darkness.

The gopher of the Lilith hole.

The Tommy gun that is always cocked and loaded.

She's just not like that. You might say that's because she has no hands to reach for your wallet, but I know better. She's not like the other girls. And she never nags.

When the telemarketers got to be a pain for her, she never complained. Instead, she would say, with a calm matter-of-factness,

"You have fifteen messages."

I noticed, as the number seemed to grow each day, as my phone number was propagated exponentially to more and more telemarketing lists, that she began to pause before reciting the so-obviously-read-from-a-sheet-of-paper pitches on replacing my windows (*does the draft lift the hair off your head even after you shut your shutters?*) or fertilizing my lawn (*does your grass look more like the sandpit than the putting green?*). She would hesitate before burdening me with such intrusions. I know she only wants to protect my privacy, but is still obliged to report their messages. It's just her nature. But she pauses before doing so.

"You have fifteen messages. Message one."

...and she would wait. After a bit, really an electronic sigh, she would let the caller's voice come through.

"Hello, this is Johnson's Dig a Ditch service. Do you need a ditch dug? We bet we can dig a ditch down deeper than dozens of ditches you dared to dig yourself. We're the diligent dirt devils that don't..."

At this point, often, she just cuts them off.

Sometimes, she doesn't cut them off as quickly as I wish she would. And sometimes, she gets just a little too anxious to hold messages at bay.

Take Melissa. She runs the front office at work, and for three months now I've tried to have a drink with her. I've been to her house—a dozen times, I bet, fixing her faucets, cutting her trees, trimming her bushes. When I agreed to check out her bush, I'd hoped she'd really meant more than just her evergreens. But no luck so far.

"Message two."

"Hi, Ray, it's Melissa. I know I promised if you cut my lawn yes-terday that I'd go out with you tonight, but something's come up. I have a..."

Sam cut her off. She hates it when Melissa uses me.

Oh, I guess I hadn't mentioned her name. Sam.

Short for Samsung. She's oriental. You can tell by the slant of her receiver. Now don't take that the wrong way. Not that receiver. I would never talk about her private places in public like that. That's between her and the phone company. I never go there. Our relationship isn't like that.

Still, I love her.

I love the way her slim, sculptured body exposes itself to me every time I walk into the room. I love the way she winks at me, a sly coquette, when I'm watching Bot Wars on cable. I know she lusts after the hard silver carapace of Bart Bot, but I don't say anything. After all, I'm trying to date Melissa. And sometimes I watch Cinemax After Dark right in front of her. How could I complain about her harboring an appreciation of the fine phy-sique of another machine when I do that right in front of her?

Anyway.

As I was saying. I love her. She does so much for me, and she rarely asks me to do anything for her. She listens as I tell her about the cows that refuse to drop dead, even when my hammer has crushed their skulls three times. She feels for me when I tell her about the rendering room, and was especially sympathetic the day I cried in front of her when I explained how Charlie had fallen from his ladder right into the vat of boiling pig fat that was headed for the Crisco plant. Most guys search their whole life for a confidante like Sam, but I found her on the shelf of my neighborhood Best Buy.

Life's funny that way, sometimes, you know?

She doesn't say much, when I tell her the sinew-steeped sto-ries of my death-dealing days. But when she does, I listen. A few months ago, she played a message from mom for me, and was a lifesaver.

"You Have One Message. Message One."

"Honey, it's Mom, just checking in. Frank and I are looking forward to seeing you this weekend. Do you know, last night he gave me the sweetest gift—"

Sam cut her off right on that word. She doesn't say much, but when she does, it just hangs out there.

Gift.

I was stopping at Mom's for Mother's Day tomorrow and I had yet to purchase a potted plant or a pair of oven mitts or a subscription to the Meat of the Month club for her.

"Thank you so much," I told Sam, and slipped my blood-spattered shoes back on and headed out to the mall. She takes care of me, she really does.

Now and then, she even answers an occasional sales call, just to make a point. Usually, she'll let me know she's serious by the tone of her voice.

"You Have On-on-one Message. Messs-sssa-aage One."

I always listen especially close when she stresses a point like that.

"Hi, Mr. Mantain, this is Olsen Rugs calling. Does your carpet have the wear and tear of thousands of footprinmnnntttssss…"

She cut him off then, and I stopped walking away from her across the family room. Looking at the carpet, I saw the tracks left by boots that had bled a thousand carcasses that week, and it wasn't a pretty sight. I'd forgotten to take them off when I dropped my duffel bag on the milk crate and scattered the roaches that covered the cracked tile in my foyer.

That's how I know she's psychic. She saves the messages that will be needed, and discards the rest. She knew I'd track on the carpet.

"You have no messages."

I know that everything is good when she tells me this. We're in love, after all, and in love, no news is good news. News means she's leaving you for a man with a full head of hair and a red Mitsubishi two-seat convertible.

"You have o-on-one mess-ss-age. Message o-o-ne."

It's Melissa again.

"Hi, Bart," she says. *"Just looking out at the baby dwarf rose bush that you gave me. She's so full of pink buds, I love her. I think the Rose of Sharon next to her needs a trim though. Sharon's just branching out like crazy, and hanging over Rosie. I don't want Sharon to kill her."*

Sam cut her off again. I get the feeling she doesn't really like Melissa.

I didn't really think much about this one. Just called Melissa back and found out that the next time I cut her lawn, she wanted me to trim all of her bushes. I could do that. She'd have dinner with me next week, she promised. But the next night, I got another message. A clearer one. Sam spoke really meticulously, as if wanting to make sure I understood every word, and stopped the caller in the middle once more.

"You have o-on-one mess-ss-age. Mess-ess-ess-age one."
"Hi, Bart, it's me. Did you mention to Alice that you were doing yardwork for me? She came to me today and said that she was concerned that I might be taking advantage of you. I could just kill her—"

"I know she can be a pain sometimes," I told Sam, "but you've got to understand. I think she's the one. You'd love her too, if I could ever get her to come over. I know you would."

I didn't hear from Melissa for a couple days. Her lawn was trimmed, after all. Her bushes pruned. And then, one night, as I picked the gluey pink strand of a pig ligament from my shoulder, and washed the creamy beef fat fragments from my forehead, I heard another message stop suddenly.

"Mess-ess-ess-ess-ess-ess-age two."

"Hi, Bart. Me again. Listen, I know you sprayed the dandelions with that stuff to make sure they wouldn't come back, but I'm worried about Muffie. I think she's licked some of it and she's acting kinda funny. Do you think that stuff would...kill her?..."

Sam stopped the message again. Just hanging it out there.

...kill her

I stopped washing the gobbets of animal flesh from my face and neck and stared hard at the single eye in the mirror. It drooped and wouldn't look back at me. All of a sudden, I got it. She'd asked me three times now. I nodded. I knew what I had to do.

I put my work clothes back on, and laced up my boots. They'd been light tan when I first bought them, but now they were the color of heavy rust.

In the garage, I kept a sledge much like the one I used every day on the cows at work. I lifted it from its hook and weighed its heft in my hand, practicing my down stroke on the wooden workbench. I left dents a half inch deep in the hard wood.

It would do.

...kill her

I had to use all my skill. Right between the eyes, and with full, unflinching force. It would be hard, I knew—those eyes were wide and blue and blinked long lashes at me all the time. Usually just before she asked me for a favor.

But I had to do this. I'd make sure it was quick. When it comes down to it, I guess Sam is the only woman for me.

I love her.

She doesn't ask for much. And she never asks me to cut the grass or trim the bushes.

...kill her

Hammer in hand, I take one last look back into the family room. Her eye shines cool and red in the darkness. It occurs to me for the first time that we both have only one eye, Sam and I. We are so alike; a match made in heaven! Why had I been blind to it before? She is all I ever need.

"I'll be back soon," I promise, and shut the door.

EARDRUM BUZZ

"JOIN THE MISERY MACHINE Street Team!" the ad in the back of the music magazine read. "Inseminate the masses with Eardrum Buzz!"

Wes ripped the page out and filled in the coupon in seconds. The first Eardrum Buzz disc, *Misery Machine*, had permanently bonded to his car CD player a few weeks earlier. He didn't leave the driveway without the machine-gun attack of its bass drum rattling the dashboard. Eardrum Buzz remained anything but a household name, but Wes couldn't get enough of the power-saw drone of their guitars, or the manic fever squeals of their singer, Arachnid.

Yeah, they were a gimmicky band—all the members named themselves after bugs. But the fierce mind-drill power of their music was as insidious as a horde of marauding carpenter ants. And let's face it, nobody had designed a cooler-looking homage to insectoid life than Eardrum Buzz's *Misery Machine* CD cover's locust orgy—at least not since Journey had celebrated the scarab on multiple LP covers in garish reds, blues, and golds. Wes was hooked.

Join their street team and help bring the music of Eardrum Buzz to others? There was nobody more suited to that than Wes. At least, that was how he felt about it. So he sent in the coupon and waited to hear. Rushed home from work to check the mailbox every day for a week. The ad had said that only "a few would be chosen" in each city, and that the band would be in touch soon with those who were to be "The Swarm".

Every day he tossed catalogs and junk mail over his head as he rifled through the pile of mail, looking for something that would anoint him a "chosen" one.

And then the call came—but not through the US Postal Service—it was on his e-mail. He almost deleted it as spam. It said Eardrum Buzz was playing a show in a week at the Paranoid Lounge. He was invited to a meet-and-greet party beforehand. He was in! And he was going to meet the band.

Wes ran out to his car, cranked up the volume, and peeled his tires with a smokin' scream as he headed up the street to Rudie's Tap to share his luck with his friends.

He was "chosen".

⌒⌒⌒

"It's not that I don't like you," the goth girl said as she pushed him back two steps. "It's just that I don't want to know you."

With that, a swipe of black hair licked at Wes's nose and the mini-skirted tramp faded back toward the bar.

It was a swank bar. It was a private bar. The room was barely twenty feet wide...Wes had known friends with bedrooms this big. (Not many admittedly. But a couple.) Tucked in the back of the Paranoid Lounge, it put the front, for-business bar to shame. This was clearly the private-party portion of the Paranoid, and Wes was at a very private party. There were about a dozen other people in the room, and all of them had shown up within a few minutes of his arrival at the unmarked door behind the club. All of them holding slips of paper that announced, *Bring this with you for admittance.*

Wes had brought his, and now he stood, watching the black-haired skank walk away in the low light of the golden-wood bar. He waited to meet the band.

While the ad had said that drinks and hors d'oeuvres would be served, Wes had avoided the snacks. True to the band's crawly affectation, the silver trays on the side of the room were brimming with french-fried roaches, candied locust and honey-coated raisins—the raisins each gripped by an amber-coated giant black ant.

Wes ordered a Jack and Coke and waited.

The band was fashionably late. But they were also fashionably dressed. Arachnid wore a skintight black bodysuit, and a web of chains jangled from his arms to his chest. When he held his hands up above his head, it looked as if a web of silver joined him to himself. The other members of the band had their own style: Cicada, the drummer, was literally shellacked in black— Wes struggled to ascertain where his painted skin ended and his shiny black clothing began; he suspected there was very little clothing attached. And the lead guitarist, Scorpion, wore an atomic-orange bodysuit, and silver dangled from his ears like wind chimes. When he smiled, Wes could have sworn he saw fangs.

A creepy little man in a Metallica T-shirt slid up next to him and grinned…with the left side of his face. His right seemed as immobile as granite.

"You gonna spread the word?" he asked. Wes saw a trickle of sweat slip between the kinked and wild hairs of his mutton chop sideburns.

"Word?"

"You gonna sell the Buzz?"

"Yeah," Wes said, and moved away as quickly as the skank had ditched him just minutes before. "Yeah, I love 'em."

"We all do, yeah," the man said, nodding and flashing a row of yellowed teeth. "Love 'em to death we do, hmm."

Wes slipped back to the bar and ordered another Jack and Coke.

Arachnid finally appeared, as if from nowhere. He put two hands on the edge of the bar and pulled. In a flash he was standing on the bar; he raised a bloody-red glass to the room and toasted.

"To the Swarm," he called, and a dozen glasses raised in answer. "I love each and every one of you."

Someone yelled back, "We love you!" and Wes found himself raising his glass and downing a cool draught of liquor and fizz. He swallowed and felt the warmth in his gut.

"Buzz," called Arachnid, holding his glass high.

"Buzz," answered the small crowd, and downed another gulp.

The creepy little Metallica man—who was also bald as a cue ball—sidled up to Wes and held out a bowl of fried bugs. Wes wasn't sure what they were exactly, but he noted a lot of crusted golden-fired legs protruding from each of the inch-long, worm-thick forms.

"Brood," the man said, and Wes raised his hands in passing.

"Naw," he said. "I'm full."

"Brood!" the man said louder as Arachnid raised jangling chains again on the bar.

"Take our communion, if you will, and we will be your sponsors to the Church of Insectoid. With our music, and these children in your belly…our word will spread for miles and miles and miles."

"I don't think so," Wes said, waving him away. But the man didn't relent. He pushed the bowl insistently, and then the goth-skank came back as well.

"Chow down, baby," she whispered. Her eyes seemed to glow ice blue in the dim light of the room. She put two long fingernails into the container and then held a crusted insect to Wes's lips.

Maybe this was some kind of a hazing. A test, he thought. As the woman crushed a warm fleshy chest to his side, pressing closer to breathe on his neck as she held the french-fried bug to his lips, Wes felt his jaw drop. She took advantage and slipped in the crunchy insectoid morsel, at the same time leaning in to whisper, "It only hurts a little," she said. "And then…you *are* the music."

Wes could have sworn she spit in his ear, because he felt a cool slippery feeling in his ear canal as she bit at his lobe and hugged him. But then, as he turned to face her, she giggled and planted a kiss on his lips, forcing him to swallow the salty bug before she backed away to fade into the small crowd. Wes noticed that the girl made a few stops in the crowd, sidling up to people and then slipping away with a whisper. He didn't think much of it at the time, only shook his head to clear away the whiskey blur. Shit, he was fuck-faced, and the concert hadn't even started yet. Hell, he hadn't walked up and introduced himself to the band.

He moved toward the bar and Arachnid, and held out his hand. "Hi," he said, trying to make an impression on the singer. "I was a fan before you guys even thought of flying."

The singer opened his mouth to laugh, revealing a row of jagged, jewel-crusted teeth. "And I sucked blood before I was a vampire," he laughed, leaning forward to stare eye to eye with Wes. "Bring me more Brood," he whispered.

"I'll spread the word," Wes assented, nodding vigorously. "I have been already."

In just minutes the private party was over, and a door was opened to the main floor of the club. Wes pushed for a spot at the front of the stage and held it, turning to put his back to the stage monitor as he watched the club fill. The alcohol settled in his eyes, and the room swirled for a moment like a bad ride on a merry-go-round as he and the crowd waited for the band to take the stage.

By the time they did, Wes was slumped against the black fuzz of the monitor. The liquor had hit him harder than he'd expected, and the vibration of the lead guitar jolted him upright in surprise. He hadn't even registered the cheer of the crowd as the band strode onstage. But with the jolt of electricity in his spine as Scorpion chimed out the intro to "Fly for Your Life", Wes threw himself into the frenzy and jumped up and down like a pogo stick. The band accommodated, dealing out one manic anthem after another.

Wes sang—or screamed—every word for the next hour and a half.

At the end of the night, Wes went outside of the club to hail a cab. He hadn't driven—he knew that it was likely to be a buzz-buzz night—and he lived close enough that a cab ride was far more desirable than the chance of a DUI.

When he climbed into the yellow car, the cabbie asked, "Good show?" and Wes could only mumble, "Yeah…it's all a blur…and a buzz."

"A buzz?" the cabbie asked.

"Yeah…my ears feel like they're in the middle of a hive," Wes said, grinning. "Everything's buzzing."

The cabbie shook his head. "You better get some sleep."

In moments they'd pulled up to the curb of his place. With an unsteady gait, he approached his front door and remembered the cabbie's advice. "I intend to," he mumbled. "I intend to."

What he hadn't intended was to be awoken by the buzz in his brain. He'd barely gotten his clothes off before falling onto the sheets, but within minutes the alcohol blur shifted, and

Wes found himself staring at the ceiling as in his head a drone whined like wind through a tin whistle. The noise shimmered and buzzed like a living thing, sinuous and insistent. It didn't let up. And it wouldn't let him fall asleep.

At one point he rolled over and stared at the blue LED of his clock radio. 3:34. "Fuck," he moaned, rolling over and punching a pillow over the offending ear canal. "I've gotta be up in three hours."

⤫

"How was the show?" his workmate Trent asked as Wes slouched down the hallway to his office.

"Loud," he complained, holding a palm over his ear. "I can still hear it."

"Kiddin'!" Trent said, laughing. "Oughtta wear earplugs to those shows."

Wes nodded. "I know." He stopped a moment at Trent's doorway and shook his head, trying to clear the still-annoying hum from his eardrums. "I've woken up with my ears buzzing from a show before, but never this loud still. I should have stuffed some cotton."

Trent shrugged. "Hindsight and all that."

"Yeah. Ears are old. Can't take rock and roll the way they used to."

"You call that rock 'n' roll?" Trent shook his head. "I call that shit…shit."

"Bite me," Wes said and stepped past the doorway and into his own cube. He punched the computer *On* switch and almost sighed with relief when the machine whirred to life; its hard drive spun at just the right rpm to whine a sympathetic tone to the one frying Wes's brain right now. The effect was that he didn't notice the buzz in his head as much, since the same sound was sawing away outside of his head as well.

He did his best to ignore the steady drone in his ears that first day, but when it kept him awake again that night and was no better the next morning, Wes began to seriously worry. He knew the story of Pete Townshend and how he had to live with tinnitus, a constant ringing in his head, from loud shows. His stomach turned cold and hard at the thought of permanent hearing damage, and he did searches of tinnitus on the Internet, praying after skimming a few pages that he just had gotten what one website called "temporary threshold shift (TTS)" from the overexposure to the Eardrum Buzz's amplified guitars. His life had become a fuzz of constant humming distortion.

Often TTS dissipates within hours or days as the ear re-acclimates itself, one page read. *But in full-blown tinnitus, the patient can suffer the constant ringing and buzzing sound in the brain for the rest of his or her life. This can often lead to depression and, sometimes, suicidal impulses.*

Wes thought about the latter idea as he tugged hard on the skin of his earlobe, trying to open his ear canal wider and perhaps pop it so that the sound would go away. Nothing happened, except for the feeling of a bruised pinch on his already sore-from-pulling lobe.

"I can't live with this," he whispered, staring at the words on his computer screen and not comprehending them. "I can't concentrate."

He put both palms against his ears and pushed toilet-plunger style. Maybe he could push air into the ear to stop the buzz. The result was a pressure pain in the bowels of his brain, and he reluctantly gave up. Placing both palms on the desk, Wes took a deep breath and forced himself to stop focusing on the problem. He needed to forget the locust hum and read the words on the screen.

Fly with the swarm, he read, and shook his head to clear his vision. That couldn't be right. He stared harder at the lease paperwork. *Fryer with warming console,* it read. Wes put his head on the desk and closed his eyes. He needed sleep.

And silence.

∞

On the fourth day after the concert, Wes yawned ceaselessly. His eyes were shot through with red, and his head lolled periodically as his body tried to shut down, regardless of its position.

"You need sleep, man," Trent observed. "Tried taking any sleeping pills?"

"No, but that's a good idea."

"Remember, if the dose looks like it reads twenty-two, that's just because you're seeing double."

"Thanks. I think twenty-two might be the only thing that could put me out."

After work, he stopped at the supermarket to pick up a frozen dinner and some sleeping pills. The buzz had subsided some, but it was still there, coiled and hissing in his brain. It had snaked into his consciousness like a viper, and it would not leave its lair.

"I can't live with this," he mumbled in the analgesics aisle, and his eyes welled up as he stared at a bottle of sleeping pills. He was at his end. "I don't *want* to live with this," he whispered, and read the back of the bottle to see if it warned against a lethal dose.

When he looked up, the piercing, icy eyes of the skank who'd blown him off at the Eardrum Buzz party were staring back at his over the low aisle shelf. She looked startled when he caught her glance over the top of the Bufferin boxes and turned away.

"Wait," he said. "You can do that to me once but not twice. I'm Wes."

"Jen," she said. Her voice was brittle, with a melting point that Wes wasn't likely to reach.

"Sorry I spooked ya, Jen," he said. "But I saw you recognized me."

"We're both part of the swarm," she said, nodding. He noticed that her eyes looked as bloodshot around the edges as his own. And her perfect gloss hair from a few nights ago had a frizzy, static-cling look to it now. She was windblown, or buzz blown, around the edges.

"How are your ears?" he asked, not knowing quite what to say.

She jerked. "What do you mean?"

"Mine are still buzzing from that show last weekend," he complained.

"I'm fine," she breathed, and pulled something from the shelf to throw in her cart. "Spread the word."

And she walked away.

∽

The next day Wes saw the grizzled mutton-chop Metallica guy from the Eardrum Buzz party standing around the news-stand he stopped at each morning. As Wes paid for his paper, he saw the guy staring at him from over the top of a newspaper he was pretending to read.

Two in two days, he thought. Some coincidence.

Normally Wes did all he could to avoid trouble. But over the course of this week, his patience had grown thin. He didn't care about consequence anymore.

"Why are you spying on me?" he asked, walking up to the older man. From where he stood, the man sidled backward, as if trying to be unseen.

"I know you from the concert," Wes said, unconsciously pulling on the edge of his earlobe. The sound seemed to be growing as he remembered the night he'd first seen this loser. And now the guy was spying on him.

"You know nothing," the man hissed. As he approached, the man threw down his newspaper on the pile and darted away, melding into the crowd of briefcase toters and disappearing into the glass door of an office building.

In his head, Wes heard the buzz grow like the keening call of a locust swarm on a hot August night. He grabbed the light pole at the curb and held on as if he were on a ship in hurricane season. When he pulled his face away from the cold gray steel, its surface was wet, and the locusts laughed and buzzed behind his eyes.

Wes did not want to live like this.

He pulled out the bottle of pills and read its contents again. He could swallow the whole thing with a couple glasses of water, and then the buzzing would go away. Everything would go away. He closed his eyes and thought about going to the top of an office building instead, and jumping. He would fly for just a moment, like the bugs he swore he heard, before the sound would be gone for good.

He shook both thoughts away and walked on.

∽

On Friday, Wes couldn't stop the tears from streaming down his face. He cried as he bought his newspaper and cried again as he tripped and fell over a crack in the pavement, scattering his pages to the wind and the trample of commuter feet.

"I can't stand it," he moaned, writhing on the ground as if he were being bitten by a thousand fire ants. He shivered and jittered and put both hands to his ears. "No more."

Hands grabbed at his arms and pulled, tugging under his armpits until he had staggered to his feet. His eyes were swollen and blurry, but he could still make out the faces of his rescuers.

Goth-skank Jen. And the scraggly guy.

"Can you hear them?" he whispered.

Jen nodded. "You're the vessel of the swarm to come," she said. "And this is their time."

She reached a hand then to her own ear and tugged hard on her lobe. When she poked a long, black-painted fingernail into her ear to itch and clear the channel, Wes swore he saw a winged thing fly out, as if a beetle or fly had been feasting on the wax inside.

"Where are we going?" he asked feebly as they escorted him to a beat-up Volkswagen and shoved him into the backseat.

"For help," the man answered.

The car followed a winding road out of the city and past the docks and the warehouse district. Then it shivered off onto a gravel road that led to a small shack within spitting distance of the bay. As the woman helped him from the car, Wes complained, "I haven't slept, it's so loud."

She nodded and pointed up at the trees around them. "They never sleep."

It was then that Wes realized the trees all around them were alive with the sound in his head.

"I tried to take sleeping pills," he began, but she only laughed and pulled him toward the gray-boarded shack.

"They never sleep," she repeated.

"Will I ever have my hearing back right?" he asked. "I just want to go back to normal again."

Metallica Man laughed at that. "You're chosen," he said. "You'll never know normal again. Just the swarm."

With that, the man grabbed him around the throat and whispered, "Lie down" into his right ear.

"Why?" was all he could say.

"Eardrum Buzz."

They pushed him onto a cot, and as he lay there, face buried in a dusty pillow, Wes could hear the sound in his head chime and chitter, rise and fall like the whir of an engine. It called to the noise in the trees, and as it received an answer, its buzz grew more excited. The nagging pain in the back of Wes's head grew from dull to ice sharp and spread to pound like a nail gun into his forehead, hammering just behind his eyes.

I'm going to die, he thought. And the thought was good.

∽

Wes woke from a droning doze to the sound of boots. They clomped hard on the wooden floor and paced back and forth nearby.

"It's almost time," he heard a voice growl.

Wes opened his eyes and rolled to see the thin, saturnine features of Arachnid pacing near the cot. The singer wore his usual black leather pants and boots, and a tight, ripped T-shirt. On its black cloth surface, the white fangs of a spider opened hopefully.

"You did this to me," Wes accused, struggling to sit up.

Arachnid shook his head. "Not me," he said, grinning and pointing to Jen. "She did it. I just told her what to do."

"Why did you bring me here?"

"You want the buzz to stop, yes?"

Wes looked into Arachnid's too-black eyes and nodded.

"Then we must release the swarm." He lifted a pair of gardening shears from a small table and ran a finger down the sharp side of the blade. A bead of blood collected almost instantly on the tip.

It occurred to Wes that "releasing the swarm" was not a procedure he was likely to live through.

"Why are you doing this?" he asked, stalling.

"You were drawn to our music, right?" the singer said. His voice was almost gentle.

"Yeah."

"They *are* our music," Arachnid said. "They live within each of us; it is their sound that makes Eardrum Buzz."

"How do you live with it?" Wes whispered.

Arachnid leaned down, until Wes could smell the faintly licorice and hay scent of his breath. As Wes stared at the singer's discolored-brown and gold-flecked eyes, a small black form crawled from the man's ear. Its antennae shifted back and forth quickly, like the nervous jitter of a roach. Then, with a spread of brown-and-clear chitinous wings, the bug launched itself from the lobe of Arachnid's ear and flew up in a lazy circle to land somewhere in the shadow of the pitched roof.

"They're our children." Arachnid grinned. "We love them."

Wes's stomach churned as he realized that thanks to Jen's false kisses at the party, those same bugs were inside him right now. Growing inside his ears. Rubbing tiny hairlike legs together to sing in the center of his brain.

"Bugs don't live inside humans," he whispered. Hoping perhaps that by saying it the statement would be true. But he'd seen the evidence proving his theorem false just seconds ago.

"These do," Arachnid smiled. "They feed off of us just a little at a time. They can't live without us. That's why we're helping them find new hosts. Soon the swarm will be strong enough to fend for itself and find its own hosts. But right now...only one in a million survives."

"What do they eat?" Wes whispered.

"Brains." The singer laughed and pointed the shears at Wes's forehead. "Right now they're in there nibbling. Before long, if you incubated a few nests of them, you'd have a hole in your head as big as a baseball. Like our drummer, Cicada. He found them a couple years ago when he went on a rain-forest trip. But he's hosted so many that he's not much there anymore, ya know? That's why he never does interviews."

Arachnid drew a cold steel line from Wes's forehead to his ear.

"But you won't have to go through that. I know you haven't enjoyed our children. Jen and Orin have told me their song is driving you a little nuts. So we'll just set your brood free."

"Set them free?"

"Outpatient surgery," Arachnid said, laughing and brandishing the pruning shears. "Won't take but a moment. And when we're done...your babies will be free, and the swarm will have a fresh dinner."

"Dinner?"

"Your brains." Arachnid shoved downward with the shears like a spear thrust. But Wes had seen the tensing of his arms and rolled just in time. He jumped to his feet as Jen and Orin grabbed him from behind.

Kicking backwards, he heard a grunt of anguish from Orin, and as one set of hands released, he spun hard to his left, catching Jen in the breast with his elbow. Like a dancer he spun in a slow circle away from the three. He lost his balance in the momentum and staggered into the rough-hewn wall in the corner of the shack. Something rattled as he hit the wall, and Wes grinned when he darted a glance to see what. There was a rack of old rusted gardening tools screwed to the wall.

"Just what I needed," he whispered, and reached past a rake to nab a long, pointed spade from its hook.

Arachnid was on him before he had it fully in hand.

"Drop it," the singer hissed. Wes felt the bite of cold metal at his throat, and he twisted backward a step before letting his body crumple. The shovel thumped to the floor as he released it. Before Arachnid could follow through with a stab, Wes rolled into the singer's shins, knocking him off-balance. Wes grabbed the shovel again, and from a crouch on the floor he brought it around hard to finish the job his body had started. The edge of the steel connected with Arachnid's shins, and the singer went down hard as Wes leapt up.

Orin and Jen were waiting.

They circled him, hands outstretched to grab for his shovel, to disarm him. Arachnid moaned on the floor and clutched his leg in a fetal curl.

Orin came for him. Without thinking, Wes brought the spade up and around, catching the grizzled man in the side of his shiny head with the back of the rusted blade. The man went down with a low *whoof*.

Something scratched at his neck, and Wes gasped. Jen brought her fingernails around to claw at his eyes. Wes couldn't go forward without driving her nails into his brain, so he shoved hard in reverse, throwing his weight against her. She didn't expect the motion and fell back as he pile-drove her into the wall. Her body slammed hard enough to rattle the window.

Jen screamed. Not a little "there's a mouse" squeal of fear. Jen screamed a horrible, long, wrenching cry of anguish.

Wes turned to see why, and the reason fell to the floor as Jen staggered to the center of the room grabbing at her back. The rake rattled to rest, and Jen fell forward, five blooms of blood already seeping through the puncture marks in the back of her shirt. She was gasping for air, her screams cut short by a gurgle of fluid filling her lungs.

Wes backed away to the other side of the room. Orin lay where he'd fallen. A gory gash split the skin along his forehead leading to his ear. And around that ear clustered a handful of small, black, antennaed bugs. They buzzed quietly as more emerged from the black, bloody hole of Orin's ear. They shook the crimson free as they met the air and gathered on the man's cheek.

"Fuck," Wes gasped, and held a hand up to his own ear. The noise in his brain escalated when he covered the canal.

Jen was shuddering on the floor, trying to crawl toward Orin. But Arachnid was no longer on the ground with them.

Arachnid was back on his feet and moving slowly toward Wes with the shears. He was not smiling.

"It would have been painless," the singer growled.

"For you, maybe."

Arachnid launched forward and cut at Wes, who recoiled and tried to bring the shovel around. Too late. The blade slashed against his chest, cutting through the shirt and drawing a line of blood. He screamed and ducked as Arachnid brought the shears down again, this time aiming for his neck.

Wes threw himself sideways and rolled over the dead weight of Orin, disturbing the small swarm that had gathered on the man's face. Wes came to his feet in front of the door and with one hand felt behind him for the knob. It turned as Arachnid rushed at him. Wes pushed the door as the lock released, and fell back, stumbling down the step to the ground outside.

"You're not going anywhere," the singer yelled, limping after him.

Wes leapt to his feet and ran around the shack, waiting for Arachnid. He didn't wait long. The singer turned the corner, brandishing the shears.

But Wes's reach was longer. He held the shovel like a baseball bat, and as Arachnid lunged, he brought the heavy side around, and all those years of Little League paid off—in a spade. The metal tip of the garden implement connected dead on with a clang against Arachnid's skull. But this time the singer didn't just go down.

This time the shovel cleaved his skull just above the ear. Maybe it was because the generations of Brood he'd fed had weakened his skull, or maybe it was because Wes swung that shovel damned hard. But the top of Arachnid's head came off as clean as a Tupperware lid. With a slight pop.

As it did, a cloud of black wings filled the air, and the world was alive with the drone of an angry, surprised hive.

The Brood.

As the droning black bugs swirled into the air, a cloud of larger insects poured like smoke from the trees all around, and Wes was pummeled by legs and wings and chittering, buzzing smacks of bug.

The Swarm.

Wes dropped the shovel and ran.

He'd only gone a few yards when he realized...the swarm wasn't after him. They hadn't followed. The yard sounded like the inside of a beehive, but when he looked back he saw the center of activity. Arachnid's head.

More precisely, Arachnid's brain. The swarm...was feeding.

There was a pain then in his own head, and Wes felt dozens of tiny teeth biting. Something pushed through his ear canal, and legs pricked across the lobe of as it crawled out.

He swatted the side of his head.

His hand came away bloody and black.

"Oh God," he cried, and slipped down to his knees. His stomach threatened to puke. These things were really alive *in his head!* Then he felt the creepy plucking feeling again, and this time he didn't swat. There was a piercing cicada buzz, and a small black bug flew past his face. And then another. And another. They were leaving!

His brood was going to join the swarm. For dinner.

He stifled the gorge in his throat, and his whole body shook with horror as he forced himself to remain still, kneeling, and let them go.

When he got home that night, Wes took his Eardrum Buzz CD and threw it in the garbage. Then he reached for something older. Safer. He popped in a The The disc and sat down on the couch.

"Infected with your love," Matt Johnson began to sing.

"Uh-uh," Wes said, and hit the *Power* button on the remote. The stereo went dead.

"No more infected with your anything," he said.

As he lay back on the pillow, he realized that the drone in his head was finally gone. Mostly.

It was actually so quiet he could hear the silence.

It buzzed.

FIELD OF FLESH

EVERYONE KNOWS THE SAYING: Only the good die young. But the corollary is, only the bad live forever. And to crib from another really well known pop song, forever is a really long time.

I'm a neutral party. Or at least, that's what I always said. Call me a voyeur if you want. I call me a private dick. And I don't mean in the sense you're probably thinking. My dick *is* private, but I meant that in the parlance of 1950's noir movies.

I watch people.

I find out their dirty secrets, and bring them out of the closet and home to roost. And no, I'm not normally the purveyor of a cavalcade of clichés, but those timeworn phrases are perfect to illustrate my profession. I make money by watching people… usually people involved in nefarious activities.

The people who will live forever.

So I didn't blink when the woman in front of my desk said she wanted to pay me a retainer to go a sex club, find her husband and bring him home. It was not *exactly* something I'd done before, but I'd been asked to do stranger things. And been paid well for it.

In this instance, the setup was intriguing. I was to be a "white knight" in the dark cellars of kink. Apparently the client—who introduced herself as Patricia Delacruiz—had been attending a super exclusive bondage club called NightWhere for the past few months. Every month, she and her husband Lucas would receive an invite delivered to their home a couple hours before a session was to occur, with instructions on how to find the secret club. Because NightWhere, apparently, was never held in the same location twice.

Smart setup, I thought. Keep the lookie-loos out and the local constabulary off your back. Before any of the locals knew any wiser the club would have come and gone. So to speak.

"Here's the thing," Mrs. D informed me, with fingers entwined nervously on her lap. She was wearing a short black dress, and I could see the top of a garter belt holding up the black pantyhose she wore. I suspected I was meant to see that, so I ignored it. "They have a room where they torture people, and never let them leave. They have my husband, Lucas locked up there, and now I don't receive any invitations to come back to NightWhere, so I don't know where they are. I can't get back to the club to find him and get him out of there."

"Well, if you can't get back there, how am I supposed to?" I asked. Yeah, I know I'm a private eye, but...that doesn't mean I always want to do things the hard way. I wanted her to help me out a little. One thing I've noticed—people are usually more resourceful than they give themselves credit for being. I never pass up a little help.

"That part's easy," she said. My ears perked up at the word easy. It's a word I like. Eggs over easy, The Big Easy, women who are...you get the picture.

"I know a couple who go to NightWhere every month," Mrs. D said. "If you stake out their place at the right time, you could get their invitation, and use it to get in."

"Well," I said, thinking this one through. "That seems like a sound plan. But why couldn't you just ask them to take you? Or stake out their place yourself and snag their invite if they won't? It would be cheaper than hiring me."

"Because the doorman at NightWhere would recognize me. He'd know not to let me in. With you? You'd be a newbie, and they always have a few new recruits every month. He won't recognize you, but you'll have an invitation, so he'll think you're one of the newbies. So you could get in, find your way to the Field of Flesh, and set Lucas free. They'd never suspect what you were there for, until it was too late."

"Field of Flesh?" I asked. I wasn't sure I liked the sound of that. I tapped my Bic pen impatiently on the notepad. So far I hadn't written anything beyond a sketchy list:

sexy dame

easy

bondage club

find NightWhere

Call Tommy to see if bowling is still on for Friday night.

I needed to fill in the blanks on this assignment and then hustle it over to the bank to make sure her check cleared.

"Yes," Mrs. D said. "The Field is the place where they take people to torture inside NightWhere. You'll have to look for it, but carefully." She chewed her lip before continuing.

"The Field of Flesh is kind of the last resting place in Night-Where for voyeurs."

"So Lucas was a voyeur?"

Mrs. D uncrossed her legs, and then crossed them again, with her opposite foot now on top. She made sure to give me a long look at the shadow above her garters before settling back in the chair. She smiled, two cherry-red lips moist and full of promise.

Whatever she was promising, I didn't want. Except as it applied to money. Payment in cooch didn't pay my rent. As enticing as it may have been. From the sounds of it, she wasn't just second hand goods at this point; more like sixty-second-hand.

"He liked to watch," she admitted, dipping her head a little. I could almost imagine that she blushed. "He really liked to watch me."

"Hmmm," I said. "And now they've locked him up in the voyeur's prison?" I said. "What's he watching now?"

"He can see everything that goes on in NightWhere," Mrs. D said.

"From what you've described, that sounds pretty good for him. What's the downside?"

"He can't ever leave."

"Maybe he doesn't want to," I suggested.

"I've seen him in my dreams," Mrs. D said. "I know he wants to come home. They're milking him dry."

I chose to ignore the dream comment. I could have found a few choice barbs to puncture that. But somehow the picture of a guy watching scads of people doing all manner of sexual things, and the phrase "milking him dry" struck me as too funny to pass up.

"A guy's gotta rest between milkings," I said, trying to keep my lips serious. My face betrayed me.

"It's not funny," she said. "If you can't get him out of there, I'll never see my husband alive again."

I slapped myself mentally, scribbled a note, and then told her my price. She didn't blink, and handed me my upfront money—$500—in five crisp Benjamin Franklins. She provided photos of her husband, the address of her kinky friends, and the knowledge that invitations seemed to come mid-month and usually midweek. Since it was a Monday and the thirteenth of the month, I figured I should start a stakeout at the friends' house in about thirty minutes. They may already have gotten an invite… but chances were, it would be turning up over the next couple nights. I was already mentally making a list of things I'd need to keep me occupied in the car for the next few evenings, as I watched their mailbox. I had a *Victoria's Secret* catalogue already stashed in my glove box, but I had a feeling that this case was going to need something stronger. A bag of Doritos and a stack of *Busty Babes In Naked Peril* magazine (I was a lifetime subscriber) was going to be more like it.

∞

The invitation came on Thursday. I almost missed it—though I'm not sure how that happened (although I have to admit, the *Busty Babe* on page 134 did hold my undivided attention for several ecstatic minutes)—I never saw who delivered it. It was around 5:30 p.m. and I knew that within the next thirty minutes, one of the two would get home from work, so just to be safe, I got out of the car (parked halfway down the block) and took a walk to wake myself up for the next couple hours of stakeout. If they didn't receive an invite by 8 p.m., Mrs. D had said, there wouldn't be one.

As I was passing their house, on a whim, I reached out to unobtrusively open the mailbox. I'd checked earlier, after the post office truck had swung by, and all they'd had was an advertising circular for a chimney sweep and what looked to be a credit card bill. I hadn't seen anybody walking on the block for the last couple hours since.

Still…

My impatience was rewarded, because on top of the junk mail, was a bright red envelope. I slipped a finger between the loose end of the back flap and slit it open. An invitation was inside, as I suspected. It said very little, though every letter appeared to have been fingerpainted in bloody red on white paper. The text was obscure, but I knew what it meant.

You asked for it.
You have this chance to get it.
Come to 69 Angle Ave. in Riverside tonight at 9 p.m.
Be there.
—NightWhere

I folded and pocketed it after making sure nobody was out and about and watching. Then I got the hell out of Dodge.

More clichés. Sorry. I watch a lot of old movies when I'm not watching philanderers, perves and perps.

What does a guy wear to a sex club? Especially when he doesn't intend to have sex? I pondered that quandary for several minutes, and finally decided on a pair of faded blue jeans that looked weathered but not ragged, and a black button-down shirt. Part of me considered opening the shirt buttons extra low and donning a gold necklace, but honestly, I don't have the thick black chest hair to pull off the disco-stud gimmick and I hadn't been able to stomach *Saturday Night Fever* even when it was hip. I couldn't mimic it even with irony implied now.

I pulled on my favorite pair of leather boots, and slipped my secret weapon into the custom scabbard on the top of the left one. I didn't know what I was walking into, and I sure wasn't going to go there unarmed. Since I wore my black shirt untucked, I was easily able to hide my little Kimber Solo in the back pocket of my jeans. If they patted me down at the door, they *might* find the little handgun, but I was betting on not.

Booted and armed, I stood and looked in the bathroom mirror for a moment. I didn't hate what I saw. A little weathered maybe, but I hadn't let too much beer go to the gut. And there was still a feathering of dark hair across the dome. The furrows that hundreds of nights on stakeout had helped carve gave me a man-of-the-world look, I thought.

I'd probably get hit on tonight, I mused. Although, from what Mrs. D had told me, I wasn't sure I wanted the attention. Whips and chains looked great in glossy, tawdry magazine photoshoots, but I had no desire to feel the reality of their painful welts on my couch-conditioned skin.

Still, before I left the bedroom, I stopped at my nightstand and pulled out a square foil pouch with a rubber raincoat inside. I slipped it into my right front pocket.

Be prepared, the Boy Scouts had taught me.

I had a gun, a knife and a condom. What else could I possibly need?

⌘

I had a pretty good idea of where my destination was based on the address. Angle Ave. ran along the railroad tracks on the outside of town. There was a long stretch of small businesses, from auto mechanics to glass shops to lumberyards there. I had a pretty good guess that 69 Angle (I had to give them credit for their sense of numerical irony) was on the far side of the lake on the seediest outskirts of Riverside. That would certainly make the most sense. And Google Maps agreed with me. I backed out of my drive at 8 p.m. It was going to take me close to forty-five minutes to get over there, and I didn't want to be a latecomer.

Not that I expected (despite my right pocket preparation) to be a *comer* at all, in club parlance.

But I didn't want to be noticed as the guy who walked in last. I planned to get there on time, stake out my place on the wall, and then watch the flowers shuffle in. I'd do a little reconnoitering, get some hints as to the location of the Field of Flesh, and then slip out of the main club in the direction of that hidden room when the festivities were getting, shall we say, boisterous.

I noticed I was being followed about a half hour into the trip. The headlights had been following me for some time... maybe all the way back to my apartment.

I realized after three or four turns that the same lights had consistently sat there in my rearview mirror.

I was being followed? Wasn't that supposed to be my job?

Just to prove that I wasn't being paranoid thanks to my profession, I pulled off on an abrupt right turn into a small subdivision of beat-up old ranch homes. At the first stop sign, I turned left, circled the block and then exited back to the highway at the same spot I'd entered.

The lights stayed with me through every turn...though I noticed they faded back quite a bit.

When I pulled back onto the main road, it was only a few seconds later when the beams of my pursuer's headlights flipped out of the subdivision and resumed their path behind me.

Hmmm.

Who would follow me? Well...I supposed there were any number of potential "who's" out there. Open any file in my wide three-drawer file tower and you could find a couple people in every manila folder who had a reason to stalk me back.

Strange thing was...none of them ever had before now.

Hmmm, indeed. I decided the only course of action was to maintain my course of action.

The highway turned left and began to follow the edge of the bay. The businesses and buildings along the route dropped away until there was only a business sign every thirty seconds or so.

I watched the address signs though, as they slowly slipped down from 1500 Angle to 900, to 330, to 102 and then, just ahead, on the Bay side of the road, I saw a lone outpost.

The mailbox at the edge of its driveway read 69. Luckily, I'd already slowed down, anticipating that.

The lights behind me did as well.

Interesting. I shifted on the seat to feel the hard shape of the concealed handgun in my back pocket. Had the owners of the invitation witnessed my theft? Had the inviters?

I pulled into a long gravel drive that led back to a Quonset hut. It looked as if a giant coffee can had fallen on its side in the middle of an overgrown prairie. But despite the remote location, I was definitely not alone. There were at least three dozen cars scattered around the building.

My intent was to be unobtrusive, so I turned left before reaching the front of the metallic structure, and drove past several parked cars before pulling mine into an impromptu parking space. The tall grass scratched against my already tortured muffler as I slowed to a halt. I felt a twinge of concern over the beating my car was taking on gravel roads and weedy parking lots, but it was the lights in my rearview mirror that held my attention. My follower hadn't slowed when I pulled into the drive on 69 Angle. If anything, my pursuer pulled closer, and followed me right down the weedy path to pull in alongside. A silver Lexus. Nice—quietly confident money on wheels.

I popped my door open and stepped out; I wasn't going to be caught sitting down.

The door to the other car sprung almost before I was on my feet, and I saw the black lace of fancy, impractical headgear rise above the silver roof. And a cascade of equally impractical black locks flowed around it.

The head turned and I knew those dark eyes, even at three yards away in the dark.

"Patricia Delacroix," I said. "You are following *me*?"

"Shhhh!" she implored, a finger to her lips. She darted around the car, and I saw that she was very definitely dressed for the occasion. Black silk dress slit up past her hip, it seemed, thin shoulder straps that only got thinner on their way down, leaving plenty of room for her more than adequate, um, assets, to be displayed.

Her legs were spidered in fishnet, and as she moved closer, I realized that her heels had to have been six inches long. She was looking down on me, the moon shining cold over her right ear.

She slipped an arm around my shoulder and leaned in to whisper. "If anyone sees us, we're together," she said.

"I thought you can't go in?"

"I can't," she said. "Not through the front door."

She reached into her tiny leopard-skin handbag and pulled out a small business card. "But when you find him...I want you to call me. You might be able to let me in through a back entrance or something. And if not, I'll be out here, waiting for him."

"You followed me," I noted again. This time, she acknowledged it with a curt nod. "You might need me," she said. "I had to be here."

"I keep thinking that you don't really need me. You could handle this all on your own," I said. But Patricia Delacroix only pulled me close, pressing my face into the soft crook of her neck and forcing my eyes into the open invite of her cleavage.

"No," she whispered, pressing my face lower into that softness. As if smothering me with the thing she knew I wanted. "I absolutely *do* need you for this."

With that, she pushed me away, and put a finger under my chin, forcing me to look up into her eyes, not down the line of her neck and into her...

"Call me when you find Lucas. If you can find a way to let me in, I'll be out here waiting. Now...just...get *in* there," she said, pointing at the steel door of the Quonset hut. "Go find my husband." She sniffed, and closed her eyes for a moment, taking a deep breath. As if steeling herself, forcing the emotion at bay. "I want my Lucas back."

"I'll see what I can do," I told her. "But from what you've described, it's going to be tough picking him out in a 'field' of people."

"Field of Flesh," she corrected. "And you have his picture. Plus, they will likely have stripped him, so you'll be able to see his tattoo. I'm pretty sure that nobody else is going to have a tattoo of a man in chains stretched across his chest. It might take you a while, but you'll find him."

She had given me a photo of Lucas's tattoo in my office. I had to agree with her. The tattoo of the chained man on his chest was striking. Especially since the detail work put the droop of the tattoo man's penis right onto the O of Lucas's bellybutton. I'm sure it looked better when he was younger, but now? That bellybutton was sagging. I guess that worked in the favor of the man in chains, but...

"Stay out of sight," I warned and stepped back from her. And then I walked towards the front of the giant steel coffee can. My fingers stroked the invitation in my pocket and I felt increasingly nervous that they would identify me as an imposter as soon as I presented it.

When I reached the door, it was closed. A steel rectangle set in a steel half-oval...it was easy to think at first that it was not even an entrance. But I knocked; I could see the outline of the opening, even if there was no handle.

And a moment later my confidence was rewarded. The door cracked open. "Invitation?" a low male voice said from the slit of darkness beyond.

I held my red slip of paper out, and it disappeared inside the chasm.

The door opened, and a pale face peered out. "Come in, and sin," the man said.

I had no intention of the latter, but I was happy to hear the invitation of the former. I'm sure I grinned a sappy grin and nodded, as I wholeheartedly, and yet falsely agreed, "Yes, I will!"

But I had no intention of indulging. I was here for one reason. And one reason only. To discover the room where Mrs. D's husband was being held naked, captive and presumably against his wishes (though I, frankly, had begun to doubt the latter point). All I wanted was for this job to be over and my payment to be propping up the balance in my checkbook.

At least, that's what I wanted until I stepped into what was known as The Blue Room of a club called NightWhere. Then I have to admit, I began to want the job to last a while.

The first thing that struck me once I was inside was the music.

It was pulsing throughout the black-walled rooms. I mean *pulsing*. I could feel the low end of the bass shivering the cuffs of my pants. I think my thighs shook. Not an altogether bad sensation...but weird. A band played some kind of dirgey, throbbing anthem up on the dark stage, and all around the room along the ceiling, tiny lights blasted blue glare onto the floor and walls of the place. But it wasn't the light or the sound that held my attention, I'll be honest.

It was the breasts.

Lots of them.

Without any attempt at concealment.

Beautiful, bouncing breasts. There were women all around the main lounge area of the club dancing and disrobing...or disrobing and dancing... And I couldn't look away. I was here to find a man, but all I could do was look at...

Mentally, I slapped myself.

Boobs wouldn't pay the bills. Even really bouncy ones with

tattoos of flowers or skulls or Betty Boop. Though I saw those. And I certainly enjoyed watching them.

I walked past the bar and the dance floor and found myself in the super kinky zone, where a dozen men and women brandished whips upon people bound in chains, laid back on racks. I watched one woman, clad only in a black leather corset, twirl a wand with a half dozen leather straps on its end. She brought the tips of those straps in contact with an overweight balding guy's painfully white ass again and again, just barely lingering before pulling the straps away. With each stroke of the leather, he moaned as if in ecstasy instead of pain, though I saw the rising red trails on his pale flesh from her attentions. Her hand moved in an easy figure eight in the air, bringing the pain, then quickly teasing away before returning to slap again with six separate tongues a second later.

I leaned back against a black pillar and smiled. The air around me reverberated with the techno sounds of the darkwave band (they were playing on a small stage near the bar) but was also colored by the moans of dozens of people in the throes of various carnal pursuits. I felt as if I were standing on the set of a really dark, kinky porn film. In fact, I would never have guessed that a place like this existed outside of a prefabricated, calculated movie set. But this was inarguably real. A full frontal assault on sight, sound, smell and libido.

As titillating as the show was, I couldn't spend too much time enjoying it. The night was short, and somehow, I needed to strike up a conversation with someone who would know what and where this "Field of Flesh" was. But Mrs. D. had warned me to be careful. The Field was not something that the general populace of the club had any knowledge of, and those that did might be suspicious of some newbie asking about it.

It was like a poker game where I had some cards but they had not been dealt in an easy straight. More like an almost full house that needed the Jack of Hearts in the next deal or I'd have to fold and go home penniless.

There I go with the bad analogies again.

Anyway, I forced myself to look away from the woman wearing a Saran Wrap bikini (the plastic made her nipples stretch unnaturally wide, like a pair of lips pressed hard to a window).

She was kneeling and bobbing her head at the waist of a man in pinstriped suit (who wears Armani to a sex club?). I walked back towards the bar. A good investigator listens, before talking. Observes before diving into action.

I needed to hear some of the patrons—and I don't mean their moans of passion. The bar seemed the most likely place to pick up some easy information without having to probe too obviously. People talk at bars. Though I had to wonder why anyone in a place like this would be sitting at the bar for very long. There were definitely more interesting places to be in at this club.

"Well, hello stranger!" The bartender was on me before I'd fully gotten my ass on the stool. I looked up and saw two astonishingly round but proud breasts jutting over the bar in my direction. Twin Xs of masking tape covered her nipples, but aside from that, all the woman was wearing was a cascade of startlingly blonde hair and a skirt made solely of threaded beads. She tantalized the male eye with what showed briefly behind those beads with every step or bend she made.

"My name's Sin-D," she continued. "I'll be your server for the evening. What can I get for you? Cock-tail, or cock-tease?"

"Are they mutually exclusive?" I asked.

That brought a smile from between two cherry-red lips. Sin-D nodded. "We're going to get along just fine."

I ordered a whiskey on the rocks and when she returned with the glass, her lips were swollen in an exaggerated pout. She set the glass down, ice clinking and threatening to slosh over at the top. Then she pointed at a trail of liquid that was dripping down the side of one creamy, perfectly complected breast. Her skin looked smooth and unblemished as freshly fallen snow. "I spilled some of your booze on my boob," she complained. "Could you lick it off? I hate to waste good liquor. Or the chance for a good licker."

She leaned over the bar, and suddenly I had that beautiful boob right in my face. What could I do but kiss it? So I did. Her skin tasted like booze and vanilla, and I felt my concentration swoon. I could get lost here, I thought, still tracing the curve of her femininity with my tongue. Sin-D pulled away and winked. "You wanted both, so you got it," she said. "'Tail and Tease."

"I think I ordered the wrong kind of 'tail," I mumbled.

She leaned forward and licked the tip of my nose with her tongue. "Bad boy," she said. "If you want that kind of cock-tail, you'd better finish that drink and get out on the dance floor. This is the waiting zone, stud."

I nodded, but she was already moving away to help another customer. I could see the bare cleft of her ass revealed, twin globes shaking between the beads of her skirt as she walked down the bar.

Something stirred at my left, and I turned to see a cloud of black hair bending down over the stool next to me. A woman. She was setting a handbag on the ground, and when she straightened up, and slid onto the seat, I realized that she was a striking, if painfully thin woman. She might have been ten years older than me, or not. It was hard to tell. While her facial complexion was pure above the faded leather dog collar she wore around her neck, the skin of her arms and shoulders, and of the part of her back that I could see where her thin black dress dipped low, were crisscrossed with chicken-scratch scars. She looked weathered, but still desirable.

"Hey," I said as she settled in.

She raised an eyebrow and brushed back a strand of kinked raven hair from her forehead. "Hey," she answered. Her tone didn't invite further discussion. Her breath sounded rushed, as if she'd been running.

"Who won?" I asked.

She gave me a blank stare, and I thought the brown of her eyes held deeper mysteries than I ever wanted to plumb.

"The race," I added to clarify. "You sound like you've been running."

"Just wanted to get in here before they locked the doors," she said.

"They lock people out?"

Her eyes brightened, and she looked me over more carefully. "You're a virgin, aren't you!?"

I shook my head adamantly. "Not since I was twenty-seven."

"Didn't you read your invitation?" she asked. "If you don't make it here by ten, you're SOL. Everyone gets in, they throw away the key, and…"

"...then somebody yells 'Let's party like it's 1999'," I finished for her.

She gave me a piqued look. "Something like that."

A chipmunk-cheery voice and two bouncing breasts suddenly were back on our side of the bar. Sin-D leaned down, elbows on the bar with her hand on her chin. "What are ya havin'?" she asked my new friend. "Bloody Mary...or just blood?"

The thin woman gave her a "you can't be serious" look and then finally answered. "Alcohol first, blood later. Tequila Sunrise?"

When Sin-D turned away to mix the drink, the woman turned to me. "How are you with a flogger?"

"Inexperienced," I said. "I'm more of an observer."

"Figured," she said. There was an element of disgust to her tone that I couldn't miss. She downed half of the Sunrise as soon as Sin-D set it in front of her.

"Just remember," she warned. "If you spend your life watching, your life will pass you by, unlived."

"Is that from *Famous Quotes, Volume Two*?" I asked. My sarcasm was not appreciated. She cracked the glass down on the bar and stood up. "People who refuse to learn are doomed to remain dumb."

Part of me wanted to laugh at the ridiculousness of that declaration, but instead, I saw an entry here.

"I am not refusing to learn, but I don't have a teacher," I said. "This is my first time here...would you show me the ropes? Can you teach me *something*? I know there is more to this place than just this bar and the band and the whips-and-chains club over there." I pointed to the far corner of the room where the floggers were busily eliciting twisted moans of pain and pleasure. Their hands, and the leather straps they held, never seemed to slow. "Can you show me the secret side of NightWhere?"

I knew I was probably pushing it there, but what the hell. She looked like a woman who knew the score here, and she was challenging me...so I used it. If she believed what she said, then she should live by her words and show me the ropes. Although, preferably, without putting any of them around my wrists.

I saw the change in her eye. The spark of a challenge. She saw in me someone she could break in. She couldn't know that

I intended simply to hitchhike on her good (bad) nature to get where I needed to go.

"Come with me," she said, and held out a long, thin hand. I pressed her fingers in mine, and slid off my stool. Her fingers were warm. And firm.

She led me past the goth band, who, I noted with amused disinterest, seemed dressed exclusively in fishnets, even though they were all men.

The blue and red lights reflected strangely off the scars on her back, illuminating and accentuating them as if she were white cotton in a field of black light. When we reached the wall of racks, she was greeted warmly. Obviously she was no stranger to this section of the club. Two of the male floggers offered her their whips, but she put up her free hand and turned them down. "I have a date," she said.

I wasn't sure I liked the way they grinned when she said that. It made me fear for the wholeness of my skin.

We stopped in front of a large wooden door. It looked like the entryway to some medieval castle, all rough-hewn wood with iron straps inlaid, fastened by fat bolts. There was a guard there, or maybe a ghoul. Certainly he looked more like the latter. His skin was a sickly gray and he was bald and emaciated; his face lined with a dozen rivers of age. But when my guide nodded at him, he didn't balk. He stepped to the side, and opened the cavernous door for us.

When we stepped through, it felt as if we'd walked into another world.

While outside in the club, it felt modern, if dungeon-influenced, here, the medieval wasn't an influence, it was a fact. We *were* in a dungeon. A long stone hallway led away from the antechamber, its walls occasionally lit by the flickering orange light of a low-burning torch attached to the walls.

And the walls...they looked freshly painted...if the painter had been dipping his brush into a recently gored carcass. The hallway smelled dank, and metallic. But it wasn't empty, not completely. While there was nobody in sight, the echoes of screams and moans...and even faint cheers...reverberated out of the dark at us. I was suddenly both anxious, and afraid, to see what lay ahead.

"Let's start here," she said. Her voice was cool, soft and distant, though she held my hand.

She stepped into the doorway of a side room, and I followed. Inside, torches lit the dark gray rock-hewn walls with shifting shadows, but it was the floor that held my attention almost instantly.

A man lay naked there, in the center of the room. A ring of people surrounded him, though they were not lying down, but on their feet. They too were nude, and ranged from fat dumpy old women to hot, skinny chicks who looked like someone had just panty raided them and dragged them here from their sororities. Most of the younger women had the kind of full-body tans that said they were not strangers to tanning beds or beaches.

Oh, there were a few cocks dangling around that circle too, but I wasn't looking in their direction.

My eyes were on the taut belly that writhed and jolted on the floor.

And the weird colors that covered it.

Because the circle of bodies surrounding her were not just *holding* candles.

They were diligently pouring the byproduct of those candles in a molten stream onto the girl's nipples and belly and lower…

Hot wax dripped in a kaleidoscope of colors onto the nude girl's most sensitive parts, dying her in red and orange and yellow. With each drip of hot liquid, she twisted and groaned on the floor…whether in ecstasy or pain, it was hard to tell…but she didn't get up.

When one guy tipped his blood-red candle to rain over her pubes, and a trail of scarlet drops drew a line from her bellybutton to the swollen lips that opened below, I shook my head.

No way anyone was going to dribble hot wax on my Johnson. Not on your life. That said, I had to admit that I enjoyed the colorful view. And my guide knew it. She stood very close behind me, and after we'd watched the waxing for a couple minutes, her hand brushed across the front of my Dockers, lingering on the thickness that had grown there.

"You like the wax room?" she whispered into my ear. "I could arrange for you to stay here a while if you like."

I wanted to say yes, but I shook my head. "No, I would rather see more."

"As you wish," she said, and drew away from my shoulder, pulling my hand until I turned and followed.

We stepped back into the shadows of the long stone hallway, and moved silently towards the next doorway, on the right side of the hall. I could see the glint of flames escaping the room like skittering shadows on the wall opposite. We stopped just before entering, and my guide looked up at my eyes with a smile that was as cruel as it was amused. "It's warm in here," she said. "You're probably overdressed, so if you want to get more comfortable once we're inside…?"

"I'll be fine," I promised, but a moment later, I began to wonder as the sweat began to slip down the back of my neck. It beaded under my arms and instantly showed through in darker patches on my already black shirt.

"You saw 'wax' in the other room, but this is the Night-Where version of waxing," my guide told me. It only took me a moment to understand her meaning.

In the center of the room was a stone-bordered pit, with a heaping mass of glowing orange coals. Tongues of flame jumped in the air periodically from the incendiary heat, but it was the view beyond the heat that drew and held my eyes. Along the wall, a dozen men and women, stripped nude, were arranged side-by-side in a row against a stone wall, hands locked in cuffs and held up by chains bolted into the stone above their heads.

A ghoulish man wearing what looked like a black, tattered loincloth paced between the imprisoned, waving a long iron pole to and fro, seemingly idly. But then he turned suddenly and pointed the iron at one of the men in the midst of the chain-line. He thrust the iron rod at the man's chest and rolled it up across his nipples.

The sulfurous smell of singing hair filled the room almost instantly. The man shook and trembled beneath the rod, but didn't cry out. In fact, his penis grew visibly hard as the burning-hot rod rolled back and forth across his chest, smoke rising in its wake.

Now *that's* a pervert, I thought. Getting hard from being burnt!

"There are many things that can excite the human animal," the woman at my side whispered, as if reading my thoughts. "Watch."

I did.

I watched as the ghoulishly pale and bony man dipped his iron rod into the glowing pit, until the edge came out glowing electric orange. He waved that fiery rod around in the air a moment, and then brought it down to touch the pubic hair of the woman next to the man who no longer sported any chest hair.

In moments (and after a brief tortured scream), that black thatch of hair above her sex was nothing but char.

If I hadn't known better, I would have thought her screams of complaint were actually moans of arousal—her nipples hardened, and her hips bucked rhythmically as the molten metal burned the hair from her pudendum. I imagined that she came in part just to get wet—so that her orgasm could put out the fire above the lips of her sex. Part of me anticipated her torturer pressing the tip of that poker lower, and opening her up to the "heat" even more...but then I mentally slapped myself. What kind of sick ass would think of sticking a red-hot poker up a woman's...

The question was answered before I even finished mentally asking it.

Apparently a sick ass like the ghoulish gray-skinned guy in front of me.

Because that's exactly what he did to the next girl.

Damn.

Ouch.

But I had to admit, he was an equal opportunity impaler. He sterilized his tool in the red-hot coals, burnt off the pubic hair of a fat, pasty man on the end of the line, and then slapped the man repeatedly until he turned, showing us the prodigious white ass that he'd probably spent the past twenty years sitting on behind a dark wood desk. And then the ghoulish guy stabbed that cooling, but still orange-glowing poker right up the man's rectum with a none-too-gentle, well-aimed thrust.

I'll be honest? I didn't look away. I should have. But I didn't.

A hand cupped my testicles, and I looked guiltily to my left, only to meet the dark, amused eyes of my guide.

"What's your name?" I asked. Generally I knew the names of women before they cupped my balls.

"Why do you care?"

"Because I hate to call girls, 'Hey, bitch'?"

"Good point," she admitted, "sometimes we get irritable if you say that."

She stopped kneading my crotch to consider.

"My name is Andreisa," she said, tilting her head towards my obviously aroused cock with a raised eyebrow. "And I can tell that you are enjoying what I'm showing you."

I shrugged. "I've always enjoyed watching," I admitted. "But you all take it to a bit of an extreme here."

She grinned. "That's really kind of the point, isn't it?"

Andreisa took my hand in hers once more. Her skin was cool and smooth, and I have to admit, I enjoyed its touch. She pulled me from the room and back out into the hall. We walked farther away from the main room of the club, and passed several rooms without stopping. The sounds of whips and the clank of chains echoed from within the shadows of a couple of them, but Andreisa only shook her head. "Passé," she said. "I want to show you truly interesting places. With people who will haunt your dreams, doing things that will taunt your passions."

In my head, I rather thought that a simple bit of nudity with the occasional slap of a leather strap would do me just fine. But I went along with her. What else could I do...she was my guide in the strangest, seediest place I'd ever been in my life. I was not fearful of what she would show me next. I was anxious. Filled with undeniable desire.

"This will be good," she said presently, stopping outside of another room. "I want to show you what they do in here. I think you'll like it."

I followed her in, and instantly, the air grew thicker, humid with the scents of sex, and something else.

Maybe blood. Maybe something more grotesque.

The room was dark, and until my eyes adjusted, I couldn't tell what was going on in the murk. From the sounds, it was both brutal and ecstatic.

And when I saw what they were doing, my initial reaction was utter shock and denial. Nobody would agree to do that. Nobody would bend over, and bend backwards, to accept such a thing. And yet...

In the shadow room, people did. They writhed and moaned and screamed and allowed the worst defiling I have ever imagined to happen.

Through it all, I watched.

I almost didn't even notice Andreisa's fingers on my crotch, stroking me to a pathetic climax as I viewed and grew painfully aroused by the defilements celebrated in the room.

"I knew you were right for The Red," Andreisa whispered in my ear, as I gave in almost unconsciously to grind myself against her skilled and agile fingers.

"I don't know what you mean," I breathed, not even really caring what words I said.

"You are a man who understands the pure joy of watching pleasure, in all its forms," Andreisa said. "You were meant to be the audience to the perverse."

I nodded in uncontested agreement. I did know how to watch.

Later, when the sex in the room had subsided, and my pants were uncomfortably stained, Andreisa gently led me out of the room and down the hall again to the next point on her agenda.

"You like to watch," Andreisa whispered at me in the darkness.

"It's my job," I answered.

"But you *like* it," she pressed.

I nodded. "Yes,"

I can't deny that I do.

She led me down an incline of black floors and glistening red walls until I found myself in the midst of a disturbingly visceral scene. All around the room, a ring of people stood, watching. Looking down at the black center of the floor. Where seven men thrust into the torsos of seven men and women. They were not fucking the sex of their mates, but rather various holes carved into the bellies and sides of their partners...and in one case, a head.

Blood streamed and flowed in vicious visibility across the midnight floor, blooming in rhythmic beats around the fatal fucking...

"They're screwing them to death!" I said.

Andreisa nodded. "The ultimate rape fantasy," she agreed. Then she reached a hand around my middle and dropped her fingers below my belt buckle.

"Don't pretend to be offended," she said, kneading the thickness she found there.

I didn't say another word, but watched as the victims screamed, orgasmed (yes, I saw some visible evidence!) and bled out on the floor, fingernails clutching and marking the backs of their lovers/killers.

It was obscene and horrible and hideously erotic.

My pants were more damp than before when we left the room.

"There are so many rooms I think you will enjoy here," Andreisa said. Her voice was smooth but I heard the edge in it. Like a blade poised eagerly over a vein.

I took my chance.

"Is one of those rooms called the Field of Flesh?" I asked.

Andreisa was silent. I could almost feel her draw away from me. I knew instantly that she knew what I was searching for. And she didn't want to talk about it.

"What do you know about the Field?" she whispered. "Virgins aren't supposed to see the rooms I'm showing you, let alone…"

"I heard someone talking about it," I dodged. "Voyeurs, the Field…it all seemed to go together."

Andreisa nodded. Her hair bobbed with the shakes of her head, but her eyes never really left mine. They were beacons, no, searchlights, honing in on me. Measuring. Considering.

"I can show you where it is," she said. "But I wouldn't go there if I were you. It's forbidden. And they say that people who enter the Field never come out."

"Well," I said, "Maybe that's just because they don't want to leave!"

The expression on her face said otherwise.

"I can show you some other things that you might be more interested in," she suggested. I could tell that she was still hoping that I'd change my mind. Maybe I'd finally get horny enough to strip her down and give her a good flogging in one of the other rooms with hooks and chains and the heavy smells of leather and wax and oils and sex. But I shook my head. "I really want to see the Field," I said.

"They say it is the ultimate place for voyeurs," she said. "But we'll have to be quick. If any of the Watchers saw me take you to the Field..."

"I understand," I said. "I won't be a problem. But I can't stop thinking about it."

"You're never going to hold a whip for me, are you?" she asked.

I sensed the question was rhetorical, from the sadness in her voice.

"I had hoped that maybe, once you saw a bit of The Red..."

"That I'd want to bend you over?" I finished. I shook my head. "No, you have the wrong guy for that. I might watch some other guy bend you over...but it ain't gonna be me!"

Andreisa nodded. "I'm beginning to understand that." She looked around, and then took my arm and pulled me back to the bloody hallway. "All right, c'mon, let me give you a glimpse of a place that almost nobody ever sees. At least, nobody who comes back to chat about it. Most people in NightWhere never come here...but I'm told a lot of people do end up there. The Watchers take them."

When she said that, a chill shot through my gut. It didn't sound like the place I wanted to go, given every other enticing perversion I'd seen so far. But it was why I was here.

"Who are the Watchers?" I asked.

Andreisa laughed. "You *are* a virgin, aren't you? Haven't you seen those men here who are pale and bony...almost ghoulish? They walk the club and make sure that everyone is having a good time. They call the shots here. They're known as the Watchers, because they never take part in any of the fun...they just encourage it."

I followed her quick and quiet steps down the corridor, which grew ever more shadowed. The sounds of moans and twisted cries of pleasure disappeared behind us until all I heard was the shuffle of our feet across the stone. The place was like a crypt to begin with, but as the path wound along, the torches lighting the way grew farther and farther between. The air was cooler, damp, as if we were descending into the bowels of the earth. The titillation of watching the obscene began to wear off, and I began to grow nervous about Andreisa's intent. She seemed very accommodating…almost too much so. Was she really taking me where I needed to go, or…

The next words she said didn't make me feel any better.

"Here it is," she said, gesturing at two large, wooden doors. The path dead-ended into them. You either went forward, or turned around. The tops were both curved in an arch that met in the middle, and the wood appeared to be carved with a number of strange symbols. It reminded me of the entryway to a very old church, only…there were no symbols of doves or crosses here. There were eyes, and chains and strangely intersecting circles and jagged lines.

"This is the entryway to the Field of Flesh," Andreisa said. "And this is as far as I'll take you. I really would suggest that you just sneak a peek through the doors, satisfy your curiosity and then come back with me without going inside. I can show you so many other…exciting things."

As she said it, she slipped a hand across my belt buckle and down, trying to raise my lusts again. I took her hand in mine and squeezed it.

"Thanks for your help," I said. "But I feel like I really need to do this. Maybe I'll see you again in the club, later tonight."

She gave me a humorless grin and nodded. "Maybe," she said, as I released her hand.

I could almost hear what she was thinking. "Maybe…but I don't think so."

She turned away and disappeared around the bends in the corridor in a heartbeat. I took a deep breath and turned back to the doors. They were easily ten-feet tall, but when I reached out to pull the handle, the door swung towards me without a sound.

I stepped into the room beyond.

"Holy Mother of God!" I whispered. I stood in an alcove, but just a few steps ahead of me, the floor was much brighter. The room ahead seemed to stretch out forever, but it wasn't the enormity of the place that shocked me.

It was the bodies.

The field.

There were thousands of men and women ahead of me, all
of them tied to row after row of heavy wooden stakes. They all
appeared to be nude, but that wasn't the shocking part. It was
what their nudity revealed that was frightening. Just a few yards
ahead of me, a woman shivered and moaned faintly on her pillar.
She was missing her left arm. But it looked as if the arm had just
recently been severed. Blood flowed in a thick, rhythmic pulse
down her side from the ragged hole in her shoulder. It was collected in a trough near her feet, and sluiced away in the gutter.

Her other arm remained whole, and she was using it to
masturbate. Her moans seemed to be related to that activity,
rather than the fact that she appeared to be bleeding to death.
When her head raised momentarily from staring at the ground,
I thought for a second that her eyes were closed. But then I
realized that her eyelids were open. There were just no eyeballs
beneath them.

I looked away, only to have my gaze fall upon a man without
legs at all. He was strapped to the wooden pole with a harness.

His body wept blood from a dozen gashes that all ran paral-
lel his ribs. But like the woman next to him, his hand was busy,
masturbating himself with the lubrication of his own blood. As
he arched his chest in apparent orgasm, the slits in his chest also
opened, spilling more blood down his sides to splash in the gutter alongside his stake. This man had eyes, but he was looking
somewhere that I couldn't follow. His eyes were wide, but when
I stepped a few steps closer, he seemed stare right through me.

"Jesus Christ," I murmured. As my eyes slipped over the
bodies behind and around these two horrid figures, I quickly
realized that they were not nearly the worst abominations in
the room. Every body appeared to be missing some "pound of
flesh", and many were clearly getting off to some invisible porno
show that must have been playing in their heads. Others hung
limp, and apparently lifeless.

The most horrible part was that there were so many of them.
I couldn't see where the rows began or ended. There was no way
in hell I was ever going to find Lucas in this.

I looked from right to left, taking in the sea of humanity
ahead, and then looked back the way I'd come.

The door had closed as quietly as it had opened. I stepped

back to push it open, to escape back into the corridor to consider. I didn't think that I could do this job for Mrs. D anymore. And I had a really creepy feeling about being in this place. A sense of dread that I couldn't contain. Maybe it was time to give back the retainer, and cut bait.

The door wouldn't budge.

Great.

My heart froze. If I couldn't go back...then how was I going to get Lucas out of here if I actually managed to find him in this sea of bodies?

I thought about what Mrs. D had said. She'd talked about me finding a back door to the place and sneaking her in.

One bridge at a time, I thought, and turned back to the bodies. The first thing to do was actually *find* Lucas. Then we'd figure out how to get back out of the room. I suspected the former was going to take a lot longer than the latter.

I looked out at the field before me and considered my strategy. I wondered if the people were arranged here in some order. If they were staked in order of entry, presumably Lucas shouldn't be buried too far into the middle.

Only one way to find out.

Ask.

It's what a good detective does.

I walked up to a guy who seemed to have all of his limbs, though his body was a mess of scars and oddly formed bumps where the flesh hadn't knitted back together evenly. He looked like he'd survived a walk through the threshing machine.

"Hey," I said. "Can I ask you a question?"

One of his eyelids slowly raised, revealing a cotton-white orb behind it.

I swallowed hard, but asked my question. "How long have you been here?"

"Not long," he said. "And not long enough."

Great. That was really helpful.

"I mean...have you been here a week? A month? I need to find someone, so I need to see where they've put the most recent arrivals."

His head tilted slowly to the left, and he opened the blind eye again. "We reap. We rotate."

"How can I find the man I'm looking for?" I asked once more.

"Close your eyes," the man advised. "In the Field, you see what you wish."

I gave up and began walking down the row, looking right and left for a chest tattooed with a man in chains. This was going to be a long night.

I walked past men holding their entrails in slick fingers, and women massaging the raw meat holes where they had once had breasts. I saw an old, gray-haired guy with no lower jaw, and a beautiful blonde girl who looked right out of the sorority. Her body was flawless, but when her blue eyes turned to follow me as I stepped closer, she opened her mouth to smile...and a stream of blood slipped over her lips. She had no teeth.

Damn.

I passed what seemed like one hundred people bound to stakes when I finally came within sight of the shadowed wall on the other side of the room. The sight gave me comfort; I had started to believe that there really was no end to this chamber of horrors.

I reached the end of the row, finally, and then began to walk back. This time I counted the rows. When I reached the other side, I was pretty sure that I had just walked past 216 rows of people bleeding from any number of gashes and amputations. My guess was that there were at least that many going longitudinally as well.

My feet were going to hurt.

I started down the next row and caught my breath as I slowed down to stare at a tall redhead. Her hair was striking, hung in long curls down her shoulders and trailing strands almost all the way to her elbows. Her breasts were small, but her entire body looked to have been poured from cream—she was flawless and shockingly white. Without a freckle or mole.

And she was masturbating herself with a frenzy I had rarely seen.

I felt myself growing hard, something I would not have thought possible in this room of abominations.

She moaned and cried out, louder and louder, eyes closed the whole time. I didn't think she knew I was there, until she suddenly opened two amazing large green eyes. Cat's eyes.

"Is this what you're looking for?" she asked. I was taken aback, since nobody else seemed to acknowledge me. But she was looking straight at me. No mistake.

"Well," I began, and stopped.

She stopped rubbing herself and instead offered me her palm.

It was thick with blood, and pink, fleshy petals that I could only believe were the shredded lips of her labia.

"Take it and eat," she said. "A feast for the beast. My body is yours to enjoy..."

Her thighs were running with scarlet, and now I could see the ragged shreds that she had made of her sex. Pieces of her hung between her thighs like unstrung tampons.

I backed away from her bloody fingers and hurried down the row, eyes looking right and left.

Sexual cannibalism had never been a part of my fantasy landscape.

I was midway through the fourth aisle, and my feet were already killing me. I stopped to take a breath. This could take forever. I wasn't sure how many more glimpses of the grotesque I could take. And there was no place to avert the gaze; the abominations were everywhere. Blood and scars for what seemed like miles.

I closed my eyes and breathed deep. And then remembered what the first man I'd talked to had said. "Close your eyes. In the Field, you see what you wish."

If for no other reason than to try to wipe clear the images I would now see in my dreams forevermore, I held my eyes closed, and pictured the photo that Mrs. D had given me. Of Lucas's broad chest, overprinted with another man's chest in chains.

It was weird, but instead of just seeing that tattoo, I suddenly saw a hazy maze of bodies all around it. In my head, I was looking to the left, and about fifty yards down, the chained man tattoo almost seemed to glow in the distance.

I stepped towards it, and realized that while the bodies looked faint as ghosts around me, I was seeing them in their actual positions, relative to where I stood. Without opening my eyes, I reached out to a woman with long dark hair, and touched her shoulder. My hand felt her flesh; I wasn't dreaming that she was really there, just in front of me.

Nor was I dreaming that my hand now felt sticky.

I had an idle thought that no amount of soap was going to wash this place from my body.

I held my eyes closed and slowly threaded my way through the bodies, occasionally reaching out to touch one, to validate that the ghosts that I saw in my head were really there.

They were.

And in moments, I stood at the place where that glowing tattoo had lured me. I was afraid to open my eyes.

But I did. I was standing before a man.

It was Lucas.

And now I saw why the tattoo was glowing. Someone had carefully used a knife or a razor to trace the lines of his body art. They had painstakingly carved the tattoo into his skin. The flesh behind each link of the tattoo chains had been removed, turning the chains around his heart into three-dimensional weeping wound. A chain of broken flesh and blood.

Lucas's eyes were already wide when I opened mine, and the ghostly vision of all the abominations around us turned undeniably real. How I had been seeing him with my eyes closed...I didn't want to know. I'd never really believed in dark magic until the past hour. But in a room filled with bleeding people who clearly should be dead but seemed very much alive—and even happy with—their fate...I knew that something was at work here that I did not really want to understand.

"Were you looking for me?" Lucas asked. His eyes were piercingly blue, and his voice low. Soft with a hint of gravel. He would have made a good country music singer, I thought.

"Word on the street is you want to break those chains," I said.

He smiled. Slightly. "I think my chains have already been broken," he said. "But I would like to see my wife again. Is Patricia here?"

I shook my head. "She's outside. I'm supposed to call her now that I've found you—she sent me in to rescue you...she said they'd never let her past the door."

"Hmmm," the other man said. "They might have let her in, but probably not out again."

"I didn't know if I was really going to find you," I said. "The rows seem to go on forever."

Lucas shook his head. "Not forever. There are 216 rows."

My eyes popped wide. "How did you know that?"

He smiled. "It's a special number. Six times six times six. There are never more and never fewer voyeurs watching here. The Field must always have exactly that number of people in it."

"What happens if too many die?"

"Nobody dies here."

"But I've seen them—there are people bleeding to death all around us."

"We bleed so that NightWhere lives," Lucas said. "So long as we are connected, we will not die."

"That's insane."

Lucas smiled, grimly. His face grew distant. "It is beautiful. The things I see every time I close my eyes…"

I heard murmuring coming from behind me. As if the field was growing agitated suddenly. "Let's just get you out of here," I said, bending to look behind him, to see what chain or rope tethered him to the wooden pole.

There was nothing there. His naked back pressed against the wood, but there appeared to be nothing keeping him in place.

"You can walk away from this at any time!" I yelled. "Why are you just standing there?"

"No," he said. "There are things you do not see. Run your hand down the outside of the pole."

"And doing that will release you?" I now imagined that he was held by a line of hooks on the inside back of the pole, fastened deep inside his skin. Maybe by tripping a switch that he couldn't reach, those invisible bindings would be released?

I didn't see any such button or switch, but I grasped the pole and slid my hand down it. As I did, I heard laughter from one of the bodies beside me. I ignored it, as Lucas fell away from the pole, his body collapsing with a grunt on the stone next to me.

"Damn," he breathed. "My legs don't want to work. It's been a long time."

I pulled my hand from the pole to help him up, but found

my hand wouldn't budge. I yanked it again, and then pulled my arm so hard I could feel my wrist bones threatening to crack.

"Help," I called to Lucas. "Now I can't get my hand free."

"No," Lucas agreed. "You can't."

He was slowly bending his legs at the knees, stretching and unstretching them as he kneaded the muscles with his hands. "There are many ways into the field, but only one way out. There must always be 216 times 216 bodies to bleed. Forty-six thousand, six hundred and fifty-six pairs of eyes to watch."

"Please help me," I said. "You can't get out of here anyway. The door I came through is locked."

Lucas shook his head. "It's a one-way door," he said. "If you come in through it, you cannot go back out through it. You have to find a different way."

I suddenly realized why Mrs. D had hired me. It wasn't to find Lucas, it was to trade places with him. Now that I'd walked in…Lucas could presumably walk out.

"I can't stay here like this," I complained. "My hand is glued to the bottom of the pole!"

Lucas laughed. "Don't worry," he said. "The Harvester will be along soon. He'll get you up. With his blade he'll strip those clothes away, and set your blood free. You are lucky—you will be able to see things here you've never even dreamed of. You will watch the most beautiful, horrible things…"

The air seemed slowly to be filled with whispers. At the same time, Lucas's face grew fuzzy and my vision instead filled with the images of men and women bound to iron racks with chains. They writhed and bled and groaned in obscene orgasm as a handful of young nude women with some of the most perfect breasts and bellies I had ever seen proceeded to flog them steadily. Bloodily. Mercilessly.

I blinked to try to clear my vision, and vaguely I could see Lucas leaning over me, rifling my pockets for my phone. I saw his grin when he found it and held it up in front of his face.

"Thanks, man," he said. "I enjoyed it here for a while, but I really wanted to still do more than watch. This is something of an unorthodox way of leaving the Field, but it plays by the rules. An eye for an eye, your blood for mine. One voyeur in, one voyeur out."

The whispers in my head grew louder, a growing wind of moaning voices, all saying what sounded like the same thing. Lucas limped down the path, and just as he faded from view, I saw a dark shadow turn the corner, moving towards me. A tall man in a black cape and hood. Carrying a scythe.

I put my feet against the pole and pushed, trying to rip my hand from its grasp, but it was as if my flesh had grown into the wood. I felt my shoulder pop, but the hand would not rip free.

The visions Lucas had promised filled my head then, marvelous visions of blood and breasts and sex and pain that turned orgasmic.

I almost didn't feel it when the grim Harvester's blade descended.

At the same time, I finally realized what I had been hearing at the edges of my perception. It had been a fuzzy but persistent chant. And now its words were clear.

That drone in the back of my head had been the sound of forty-six thousand people whispering and moaning one word:

"Welcome."

I knew without a doubt that I wasn't going to be leaving, and so I closed my eyes, and thought about what I wanted to see.

What I *really* wanted to see.

FAUX

AARON STEC VISITS the zoo every Friday at lunch. I've watched his routine for weeks. He stops at the eco-friendly fast food stand around the bend ("Soyburgers save lives!") and chews his meal thoughtfully while peering over the lion pen. It's a fine simulation of Africa. If you can ignore that the verdant fields are painted on rough concrete, and the endless vistas of hunting ground are cut short by false ravines, electric fencing and a concrete path of gawkers. In my mind, I see his blood spurt with his every careless bite.

Barriers won't stop me. I thirst for Aaron's blood. I've yearned to slash razor claws across that soft pale neck for too long.

He stands here again today, gazing at the lazing pride in the pen, and doesn't notice my advance, four-footed and quiet between the faux rocks of the enclosure. Why would he, a deceitful king of human industry who credits no foe with intelligence, ever consider that a lion, a cunning king of beasts, could have the brains to slip across that deep ravine of its prison, scale the concave concrete wall and leap the electrified wire? He is a man who fears no man, and certainly no beast. Yet something draws him here, every week, to stare.

His Achilles' heel.

I can almost hear his blood sluicing in arrogant pumps through each vein as I pad quietly on the hidden path meant for zoo attendants until I can smell his unsuspecting, cologne-primped, pinstriped body.

The lion pen is not the main attraction at lunchtime. The pride is lazy, hiding in cool shadows. I wait until the other visitors, a mother and toddler, retreat from the rails. Then he's alone, chewing his faux beef, lost in treacherous thoughts, staring at this faux Africa.

I steel myself and spring. The distant cheers from the dolphin show drown out his cry of surprise. I claw buttery jowls and neck; Aaron's life blooms, free at last on the pale concrete walk.

I waste no time soaking in its warmth. Clutching the collar of his pretentious suit, I drag him out of sight before finishing the job, slashing ebon razor claws again and again across his pompous throat and face, until those pale, sightless eyes are glazed in crimson.

Overkill.

When I'm through, there's little to identify Aaron Stec. My paws ooze blood, the fur of my throat glistens. I rise from his savaged body and roar.

With a flick, I hook claws in the hidden zipper and exit my disguise, kicking bloodied fake fur to the ravine.

Aaron Stec was more than a mark. He was my ticket out of America, the land of the faux free. A hit these days is hard, with cameras recording every corner, security systems tracking every mosquito. But Aaron's ambitious protégé wanted him dead at any cost and paid up front. I'll fly to the unfettered skies of Africa in the morning.

A shame I can't free the slumbering lions below with me.

THE PUMPKIN MAN

WHEN THE LIVELY summer breeze turns deathly chill and the lush emerald leaves of August crumble with autumn age, the Pumpkin Man comes to town. It happens every year. One day, the gravel lot on the corner of 5th and Maple is bare, littered only with broken glass and tufts of dandelions and thistle. The next, and the lot is full, covered in gourds of all shapes and sizes. Piles of warty yellow squash tumble next to row after row of well-creased pumpkins, most of them fiery orange, but some still betraying the green veins of a fruit that had been picked just before prime.

When word filtered through the school that the Pumpkin Man had arrived, we got on our bikes and rode straight from school to see. We went there every day for a month, until one day, right after Halloween, we'd turn our bikes around that corner and find the lot was vacant again, littered only with the husks and leavings of gourds gone by.

The year I turned thirteen, we had been anticipating his return for weeks when it finally happened. On the very first day of school, Steve Traskle had said, "The Pumpkin Man will be here soon."

One day, early in October, the day finally came.

The word whispered its way across the school like fire in a field of browning wheat. I heard it first from Dave in English class, and then from Belle in History. By lunch I'd heard it a dozen times, "He's here. The Pumpkin Man is back!"

The school day took a month to pass. I watched the minute hand on the homeroom clock move from notch to notch, each minute taking an hour to tick by. When the 3 o'clock bell rang to announce the day's dismissal, I was already half out of my seat, anticipating its clamor. Billy and Carl were right behind me, and the three of us pushed our way down the crowded hall and out to the bike rack in record time.

"Goin' to Maple?" Steve asked, racing up behind our little gang.

"Yeah," I said, not looking up from the combination of my bike lock.

"Can I go with you guys?"

"If you can keep up," Carl said. He yanked his ten-speed around and stomped the pedal as if he were jumpstarting the engine on a motorcycle.

"Let's go, girls!"

We were off.

∞

The thing about the Pumpkin Man wasn't that he appeared and disappeared each year with equal mystery and stealth. Nor was it that he brought a thousand globes of orange and yellow for us to take home and carve. You could get a pumpkin at the Save-All if you just wanted something to draw a face on.

"Oh man," Billy whispered, as we skidded our back tires around as one, and stopped to stare, a gang of four, at this year's display.

The thing about the Pumpkin Man wasn't the pumpkins he brought to town, but the faces he carved on his pumpkins. In the midst of the sea of fire-bright globes that covered the white gravel of the lot at 5th and Maple was a long wooden stand. It stood as tall as a man, and as long as a house. And lining the half dozen shelves within its overhang were special pumpkins.

Carved pumpkins.

Pumpkins with the most evil grins and scowls you've ever seen scored into a gourd. At night, he put candles in all of them, and the darkness at the edge of our little town was broken with a hoard of devilish teeth and slanted, glimmering eyes. It was as if the very door to hell had been opened, and the armies of Lucifer were poised to feast upon our innocent souls.

"Damn," Carl said as we stared at the offering for this year. Even in the daylight, the jagged orange-rind teeth gave me a shiver. Somewhere, someone was whistling a strangely discordant tune.

"Twisted as hell," Steve agreed.

We stashed our bikes on the side of the lot and stalked for-

ward, eager to get closer to the frightful carvings that seemed to
have blown in overnight with the brittle oak leaves. If the days of
a stifling sun and cool blue pools were past, than this was a fine
substitute, we thought.

I moved past a row of grinning, leering faces, stopping finally at a particularly evil-looking gourd. Its eyes were almond-
shaped, narrow but long, and its teeth leered like daggers waiting to strike. It was a pumpkin with the soul of a rabid rat.

"Help you, boys?"

Steve pulled his fingers back from touching one of the
scowling gourds as if he'd been bit.

"Just looking," Carl said, answering for all of us. His voice
shook a little, and I could understand why. The Pumpkin Man's
creations weren't the only creepy thing in this newly filled lot.
The Pumpkin Man himself was a frightening sight to behold.
Wisps of ice-white hair curled out from his ears like mist, and
his eyes, piercing blue, looked too tight together, as if someone
had rolled two blue marbles as close as they could. His lips were
pale and long, and his neck was thin as a turkey's. But it was
his hands that made you look twice. The Pumpkin Man strode
slowly between us and the pumpkins, and as he did, he trailed
one long finger across the green stubs at the top of each gourd.
That finger seemed white as a bone, its nail dark as snails.

"See something you like? Ten dollars for any of my babies."

He grinned at us then, showing teeth brown as candied molasses.

I shook my head and moved away from the display. In years
past, I'd never come face-to-face with the Pumpkin Man when
I'd perused his lot, and now, I found, he gave me the creeps
more than his carvings.

Steve, Carl and Billy caught up with me a few minutes later,
as I wandered around a four-foot pyramid of orange globes.

"'S matter, man?" Carl asked. "We were talking to the
Pumpkin Man back there after you split. He told us some cool
shit. Like how he models his carvings on animal teeth, and people too. Why'd you leave?"

"Just felt like it," I dodged, and soon we were talking again
about how cool the carvings were, and about which of the hundreds of pumpkins we'd get our moms to come buy in the next

week. Carl had already picked out one on the edge of the lot, based on its "totally cool warts". The thing was basically flat on one side, and half yellow, but it didn't have a smooth patch of skin on it anywhere. "It's a mutant," he boasted.

Behind us, the Pumpkin Man stood, arms folded across his chest, smiling.

A mutant, I thought.

⚬⚬⚬

I didn't go back to the no-longer-vacant lot at 5th and Maple for a few days after that. I'm not sure why; everyone at school was a-buzz with the cool faces the Pumpkin Man had brought for us to see this year. And there were always new ones. Each day, he chose a gourd to create another feral face to replace whatever pumpkins had been purchased from his display. And each new fearsome face was different, unique. He didn't carve from a mold, that was for sure. His imagination was apparently full of haunting, harrowing teeth and eyes.

It was probably the second week in October; the nights had come early, full of thick gray clouds, and the trees already seemed skeletal, their leaves fled with fright at the onset of an early winter. I was bicycling home from Carl's after dinner. It was only seven o'clock or so, but the sky was already devil blue, and I pulled my jacket close as I pedaled around the bend at 4th and Maple. Ahead, I could see the glow of candles, and the leer of a hundred hungry faces.

The twisted patch of the Pumpkin Man was waiting.

I pedaled faster, past houses wreathed in corn stalks and fake spider webs, windows aglow in orange lights.

As I reached the lot, I slowed. The row upon row of glowing, fiery gourds lit the darkening fall of night, but did so in stillness. There were no shoppers perusing the Pumpkin Man's lot, nor a Pumpkin Man to be seen.

I'm not sure what possessed me, but I braked my bike and laid it quietly on the rocks at the front of the lot. Then I walked in between the rows of uncarved, unborn pumpkin faces until I stood again at display of carved pumpkins, staring at the gourd

I'd honed in on the week before. The rat-faced pumpkin. Its teeth still made my skin crawl as I stared into its flickering eyes.

Something about it drew me, and despite the goose bumps on my skin, I stood there, alone in the dark, and returned its hellfire gaze. That's when it happened.

"Eeeeerrreeeeech!"

I jumped five feet in the air. The screech had come from just behind the pumpkin trailer, and it raised every hair on my head. It sounded like something had died.

In front of me, a hundred flickering faces leered. But they stared quietly, unmoving. I looked behind and to the side, and saw only the shadows of pumpkin piles. A haze of cloud slid past the moon and even the shadows grew darker.

My heart pounded so loud I thought the neighbors must surely hear me from down the street, but I forced myself to creep down the aisle of candle grins to the edge of the makeshift shed. There was a dim light coming from behind the display stand, and I quickly saw why.

The Pumpkin Man was carving.

On a makeshift table, his hands moved from side to side. A flash of silver cut the air and then the sound came again.

"Eeeeerrreeech!"

The pumpkin was screaming!

His blade cut the skin and with deft motions he carved a sliver from the gourd, tossing it to the ground.

Again and again he plunged the blade into the pumpkin and each time I heard the noise, though the cries grew weaker. I was rooted to the ground, watching him from behind, his shoulders pumping and swiveling, his body alive with the fury of his work. He dug a long thin furrow in his creation's mouth, and gave a soft cry himself when the knife caught.

"Rrreeeaaahhh" cried the pumpkin as he brought the knife out, and flicked another shard of shiny pulp over his shoulder. A piece bounced across the gravel near my feet. I don't know why, but I couldn't resist; I bent to pick it up.

The Pumpkin Man whistled something then, some off-key tune, as I turned the slick skin of the filleted gourd between my fingers. It was gross, sticky, and I dropped it back to the ground and carefully retraced my steps around the corner of the pumpkin display stand. In the light of the flickering, evil pumpkin faces I held up my sticky fingers and gasped.

They were coated in red.

Blood.

I turned and ran as hard as I could from the place. I didn't even stop for my bike.

Nobody could understand why I wouldn't go on the daily forays to the Pumpkin Man's displays. The next day, I stopped by the lot just fast enough to retrieve my abandoned bike, and then went out with Steve to look for Rusty, his German Shepherd. The dog had gotten out the day before, and while that wasn't unusual, this time it hadn't come back. Steve tried not to show it, but he was near tears. We combed the woods on the west side of our subdivision for hours, going up one dirt trail and coming down the next, yelling "Rusty? Here, boy!"

Looking for the dog kept my mind off the pumpkin display, but only for a while. The talk of the Pumpkin Man was ever-present at school.

"He's got a real cool one today," Carl told me just a couple days after I'd heard the pumpkin cry. "It's creepy—like a werewolf or something. It really looks like it has a snout full of nasty teeth."

"Try sticking your hand in 'em," I suggested, brushing past.

"I'm serious, man. You should see this one…it's one of his best."

A week passed, and the October rains hit hard. The trees lost their leaves all at once, and the ground was a mess of brown, soggy piles. Nobody visited the Pumpkin Man for a couple days as the rains kept us dodging from car to school and back again. When it all passed, and the days grew dry, the winds picked up and the days grew ever darker. Winter was just around the corner, and we pulled out our heaviest, ugliest coats to hide from the chill. My bike hadn't been out of the garage in almost two weeks.

"Let's go see what the Pumpkin Man's been up to," Billy said one day after class. It was just before Halloween, and everyone eagerly assented. Except for Steve, and me. Steve's dog had never turned up, and he hadn't talked much once it became clear that Rusty wasn't coming back. And I hadn't been to the corner of 5th and Maple since the day after I'd held the shard of a bleeding pumpkin in my hand.

But it was a rare sunny day, and Billy and Carl and Dan were almost running for the bike rack. Steve and I followed, but didn't say much.

We pedaled past the towering piles of soggy leaves, and the wind shifted, blowing a crisp reminder of early winter across our necks. I shivered and pumped my feet harder to keep up.

"Good to see you, boys," the Pumpkin Man said in a voice sharp as cat claws as we walked up to the display of carved gourds. "Which of my little beauties would you like to take home today?"

Despite the light of the waning afternoon sun, I thought the pumpkins seemed unusually grim. There was a darkness behind all of those razor-shorn eyes, and a hunger in their ragged, sharp-edged teeth. Their hollowness called out to be filled. Called out for blood. A chill shivered my spine at the thought.

"Got any vampire pumpkins?" Carl said, and the man laughed.

"Can't say that I've killed me any of those."

"Have you ever tried to carve a Freddy Krueger pumpkin?" Billy ventured.

The Pumpkin Man shook his head, and clouds of wispy hair flickered at his temples.

"I only carve from real life," he said. "See this one?" He pointed at a rat-faced pumpkin much like the one I'd noticed almost three weeks before. This one was a recent creation, but still aging fast. Its teeth curved inward, and a faint scum of mold covered the dark spots on the surface of its skin. Soon it would cave in on itself in decay.

"I used a squirrel for this one," he said. "Note the teeth."

We nodded at his ingenuity, and stepped away. Maybe we all felt a little creeped out by a man who dedicated his life to carving pumpkins. And then Steve stopped at one of the newer creations. The one that, despite its round, veined surface, seemed to have long canine teeth, and a snout.

"It's just like Rusty," he breathed. I saw the wetness in his gaze, and punched him in the shoulder.

"It's a pumpkin."

"I used a dog for that one," the Pumpkin Man called.

Steve choked and balled his fists. "C'mon," I said, and pushed him to leave. The others followed. Behind us, I heard the Pumpkin Man start to whistle.

∽∾∽

"I don't know what he does," I told Steve later, as we sat by the tree in his front yard. My butt was cold and damp from the leaves, but we didn't retreat to the warmth of his house. We had secrets to share.

"I was there looking at the pumpkins," I said. "It was the day Rusty disappeared. I heard a screech, like something was dying. When I went to look, I saw him carving a pumpkin, and when I picked up what he threw away from it, my hand was covered in blood. Something's not right about the Pumpkin Man."

"Let's check it out," Steve said.

"What do you mean?"

"Tonight. Let's see how he does it." His eyes glimmered with unshed tears and he turned away. I knew he was thinking about Rusty. All I could think about was the spine-curling scream of a mutilated pumpkin.

∽∾∽

We left our bikes at the Thompsons, two houses away from the vacant lot which was now filled with pumpkins. It was dark, after 8 p.m., and the moon was nowhere to be found. I shivered beneath the heavy down of my olive-green coat. I'm not even sure if it was because of the cold.

We threaded our way between the piles of warted squash and miniature gourds and beach-ball-sized carving pumpkins. We stepped carefully, not wanting the crunch of gravel to give us away. In moments, we were face-to-face with the blazing wall of flaming, smoking faces.

The rat-faced pumpkin seemed even more shriveled than this afternoon, the curl of its teeth leaving it look gummy, geriatric. The snarling dog-faced gourd caught Steve's eye again, and I had to pull him away.

"C'mon," I said. "He'll be back here."

We stepped around the back of the pumpkin shed the same way I had two weeks before, but this time, the Pumpkin Man was nowhere to be seen. The carving table was there, unused in the midst of the empty clearing.

"Maybe he's back here," Steve whispered, pointing to a small pickup truck trailer. You couldn't see the pickup from the street with all the pumpkins and the display shed, but now it was obvious how the Pumpkin Man got around. He could pack everything into the truck and then sleep in it as well.

Steve stole around the side of the truck and disappeared into the shadows. I waited for him to round the other side of the rusting hulk of a vehicle, but he didn't reappear. The night only grew more still. Then something snapped. I froze.

From nearby, I heard a now-familiar whistle. This time I recognized the tune. It was "Nowhere Man" by The Beatles. I retreated from the pickup until the rear wall of the display stand was at my back.

That's when I saw him. The Pumpkin Man sauntered around the side of the truck where I had been expecting to see Steve. Something was clutched in his arms. It was covered in a brown blanket or tarp. He kept whistling, seemingly calm, but whatever he had trapped was wrestling and kicking like hell.

He dragged the covered form over to the table, sat down, and with one hand scooped up a pumpkin and set it on the table. With the other, he forced the form in the blanket down on the table next to the gourd.

I'm not clear exactly what happened then. It was dark, and the Pumpkin Man's back was to me. And I was scared. But I know this. From the depths of the night I heard Steve cry my name. And then, the Pumpkin Man's arm raised up high in the air. When it came down, a flash of silver against the sky, I heard the most piercing scream I've ever heard in my life, before or since.

The blanket thrashed and kicked against the Pumpkin Man's body as he wedged it tight to the pumpkin on the table, and dug his blade into the gourd again, and again. Dark shapes flew in the air as he gouged chunks from the pumpkin and tossed them aside. On the table, a new face took shape, and I struggled to keep my teeth from chattering, as I watched him draw eyes and a smile that were hauntingly familiar. The light was poor, and the Pumpkin Man's back hid his work, for the most part, from my spying eyes.

But when the screaming faded to gasps, and the Pumpkin Man dropped his now-still blanket of inspiration, I saw a shrieking face more horrible than any of the laughing, scowling faces on the stand directly behind me.

On this pumpkin, captured in abject terror, the Pumpkin Man had carved Steve's crying face.

⚮

I never saw Steve again. The kids at school talked the next day about the amazing new pumpkin that the Pumpkin Man had on display, but I didn't go see. I already knew what it would look like.

The police came to our house on Halloween night, and asked if we had any knowledge of Steve's disappearance. They asked when I'd last seen him, and wrote carefully in their notebooks when I told them that we'd been at the Pumpkin Man's just two nights before, and that the Pumpkin Man had carved Steve's face into one of his creations. Had carved *Steve*.

They didn't believe me. I knew that they wouldn't. Even my parents shook their heads. That's why I didn't even bother to go to my dresser, where the shriveling shard of a pumpkin triangle rested, hidden away in my top drawer. I had picked it up from the ground, the night the Pumpkin Man carved Steve into a pumpkin.

I think he knew I was there that night. At one point, he looked over his shoulder, and smiled a horrible toothy grin in my direction. He started whistling again then, as if he knew I could never do anything to stop him.

And he was right. Who would believe a kid that says a pumpkin carver was killing stray dogs and children to make his grotesque creations all the more real?

But I still have the last piece of Steve they'll never find. Shriveled like leather in my drawer.

Its sunset skin is still faintly smeared by a dull, violent red.

THE TAPPING

THE TAPPING AGAIN. Every night, the tapping.

And every night tapping louder than the one before.

The wind howls around my window frame like the fabled hounds of hell, but louder still, the tapping shatters the breath-held stillness of my room. I'm afraid. Afraid that I won't make it through this night.

And afraid that I will.

∞

I made a grave mistake, pun woefully intended. And learned a thing or two in the aftermath, not that it will do me any good now. But maybe this tale will help someone else. You, perhaps. Maybe this will save you from the ghoulish trap that I have sprung. God, I can only hope that someone will find this and steer left of the devil. Here's what I have learned:

Never take your friends for granted, one day they will be gone.

Never take an oath beneath the orange stare of a full moon.

Never take a dare to disturb the sleeping bones of a tomb.

The last might seem obvious, but marinaded in three martinis well into Halloween night, I was open to anything. So was Al. The sweat of intoxication glowed on his forehead like the sheen of death, and Ramondo played on both of our sorry states. Which is no excuse, because he'd downed at least three beers before we met up with him at the Excelsior. We made a motley crew—I was recently divorced, Ramondo couldn't seem to settle on a single pair of legs, and Al couldn't seem to *land* a single pair of legs. And so while all of our other friends carted kids around to costume parties and trick-or-treating, the three of us had met up for a cocktail—or five—at Excelsior. Not surprisingly, given the occasion, our conversation turned to the macabre.

Ramondo was poking fun at one of our workmates, who generally seemed about as aware of what was going on around her as a blind narcoleptic.

"You think Maria would notice if one of her trick-or-treaters today was an actual skeleton, instead of a kid wearing a painted shirt?" Ramondo asked.

"Naw." Al grinned. "She'd drop a couple Milky Ways into its hand and not even notice when they fell through the bones to the sidewalk."

"You're assuming she'd hear the doorbell in the first place," I said.

Ramondo laughed and tilted another Genuine Draft. "Yeah, she'd be too busy feeding her cats to pay any attention."

Al shook his head and raised his glass. "We're making fun of the old girl, and really we should envy her. I wish I could be so happy in my own little world. Here's to oblivion."

"To oblivion," Ramondo and I replied, and downed another swig.

The conversation continued in this vein, until the dim strands of orange-bulbed Halloween lights strung across the bar seemed very bright and everything shone with a golden aura. I was very drunk. And Al was nearly comatose. He seemed to end every word with an "s".

"I'll tell you what we ought to do," Ramondo finally vouched, one great, black caterpillar eyebrow trembling as if it were considering wriggling right off his forehead. "We ought to go down to Resurrection Cemetery and check out one of those crypts."

"You mean those little stone houses they put the bodies in aboveground?" Al slurred, and Ramondo nodded, his mouth widening into a dangerous grin.

"We could get ourselves a real skeleton hand. I bet tomorrow at work, we could stick it out, shake hands with Maria, and she'd never know the difference."

What can I say? It sounded good at the time.

Resurrection was just down the street from Excelsior, and we decided to take a little walk. To anyone on the street, it probably looked more like a big stagger.

Excelsior was on the end of a low traffic street, partially due to it sharing the neighborhood with a cemetery, and by this time of night, all the trick-or-treaters had long since counted their candy and gone to bed with the start of new cavities. The street was silent, but for the gusts of October chill, and the rattle of chocolate wrappers across the sidewalk. We didn't care.

"Does it have to be a whole hand, or just a finger bone," Al slurred, at one point, and Ramondo was adamant.

"No half-assed bones," he declared. "You ever try to shake hands with a finger bone? We need the whole hand. In one piece!"

The cemetery gates were locked. They stood ten feet tall, sharp-edged green metal bars locking into a beveled, curved iron door that was as much decorative as imposing.

"Looks like they want to keep us out," I said.

"Or keep the dead folks in," Al mumbled.

"I can pick it," Ramondo said and went to work on the lock with a paperclip he pulled from his pocket. I didn't ask. He has some skills I don't want to know about.

The wind whipped up and I hunched over, pulling my coat tighter.

"Shoulda brought one for the road," Al said, and then burped. I didn't think he needed anything else for the road but a driver. But I said nothing.

"Got it," Ramondo announced, and with a shove, the heavy metal gates swung inward with a slow-building screech. I looked around, fearful of discovery, but the street remained dark and silent.

The three of us ducked through the entry and presently stood at a crossroads just inside. Three dark asphalt roads led away from the gates, one directly to the heart of the cemetery, the other two encircling its borders like grasping arms.

The shadows of row upon row upon endless row of praying, prostrating memorial statuary reached out towards us; the moon was late in rising, and its full orange eye lit the entire landscape with a bloody light. A night bird fluttered somewhere in the distance, and I trembled.

"We're heeeere," Al announced, and I elbowed him.

"What?" he asked, cocking an angry brow my way. "You

think I'm gonna wake the dead?"

At that exact moment, an owl shrieked, and he jumped as much as I.

"Maybe."

Ramondo turned to look at the two of us and laughed. I hated that laugh. The slight upturned snarl of that long lip, the bright white of perfect teeth that he flashed briefly, quickly, like a striptease. The jaded, cynical smile that attracted women to lick at his face like lemmings following a mad rat over the edge of a cliff. There was nothing wholesome in Ramondo's smile, and maybe that's why chicks dug it—at least at first. Whatever its attraction, I hated it when that sardonic grin turned on me.

"Livers showing their true colors?" he crowed. "Lily white?"

"Bone white," I said. "Like the skeleton hand I'm gonna bitch slap you with. But what's the bet? What's the prize? If we all come back with a bunch of bones, who wins?"

Ramondo nodded and put a finger to one pouty lip. Another trait women seemed to go for. Maybe it reminded them of a Chicano Elvis or something.

He dropped to a crouch after a second, and with a loose stone drew a white X on the asphalt.

"Okay," he said. "Here's the mark. First one back to the mark with a complete," he looked at Al, "*complete*, skeleton hand wins."

"And the winner gets?" I prodded.

"The mutual respect and admiration of the other two," Al offered.

Ramondo snickered. "I think graveyard violation is worth more than a little respect. Actually, perhaps it doesn't deserve any respect at all," he said, laughing again. "How about fifty bucks from each of the losers?"

"Steep," Al said.

"So hurry," Ramondo responded.

I just nodded. I wasn't sure how I was gonna get in and out of a tomb the fastest, but I knew I sure as hell wanted to get this over with as fast as humanly possible.

There was a moment of silence, and then the wind gusted and chilled my ears in shivery squeal.

"So are you both in?" he asked.

I nodded. Al shrugged. His eyes seemed glazed and I wondered if he was going to puke.

Ramondo extended his arm and nodded at the top of his hand.

I laid my palm on his knuckles and after a moment, Al's covered mine.

"Swear," Ramondo said.

"Damn," Al replied.

"That's not what I meant," Ramondo said. "Swear that we will all break into a tomb tonight, on Halloween, the night that all souls twist restless in their sleep. Swear that you will sever the hand of someone long since gone to their heavenly, or hellish, reward. Swear that you will return to this X with that hand, ready to shake with the rest of us...and eventually, Maria."

I may not have mentioned it before, but Ramondo also had an annoying sense of the dramatic. Another reason the girls liked him. Some girls, anyway.

"Swear," we all murmured.

The moon seemed to paint our joined hands a sallow orange and we pulled away from our clasp as something fluttered again in the distance. To my ears, the cemetery seemed strangely restless this night. But I shrugged the thought off as the product of a guilty mind.

"Who wants a paperclip?" Ramondo asked then, and pulled a half dozen shining slips of metal from his pocket.

"You working as office help on the side these days?" I asked.

"Cheap help?" Al echoed.

"Take it or leave it, fellas," he said, and we both grabbed for a clip. The last time I tried to use a paperclip to get through a lock was in high school when I'd been grounded and gone out anyway, without my keys. As I'd been picking the lock of my own house, my dad had turned on the outside light, thrown open the front door and nearly clocked me to the carpet with his fist. I wasn't looking forward to this attempt, but it couldn't be much worse, I thought. After all, if a corpse answered the door to my lock picking this time, it couldn't possibly pack as much of a wallop as my dad.

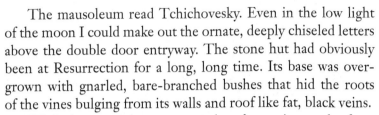

The mausoleum read Tchichovesky. Even in the low light of the moon I could make out the ornate, deeply chiseled letters above the double door entryway. The stone hut had obviously been at Resurrection for a long, long time. Its base was overgrown with gnarled, bare-branched bushes that hid the roots of the vines bulging from its walls and roof like fat, black veins.

We had separated, one to a road, and gone in search of our hand bones like ghouls, heads dipped low and legs creeping. Ramondo took the center path and Al the right. I took the left. I'd always been a liberal at heart.

Soon I spied the squat stone hut perched behind a row of six-foot marble statues in the shape of a weeping Christ, a cheerful mother Mary and a score of harping and praying angels. I ducked beneath a low-hanging tree branch, sending a litter of dead brown leaves to the ground and stood still, holding my breath before the double doors. Its shadow stretched long and dark across the graves to the right of its doors, and I felt naked on its stoop, standing stock still at the lock, ready and armed with a paper clip to brave the inner crypt and disturbed the dead.

If the world hadn't been spinning, just the tiniest bit, I'm sure I would never have continued.

But the world *was* tilting, just a little bit, and my arms seemed both light as air and heavy as lead, and my lips burned with the bitter, secret, pine power of gin, and I pulled out the paper clip and stuck it inside the small padlock holding shut the entrance to the Tchichovesky family's crypt.

I had little hope of tripping this lock fantastic; its hook was rusted and dark, and even if I could fool the mechanism inside, I doubted whether I could convince the metal to part from where it falsely joined.

The moon fell across my shoulder, and a tree branch somewhere nearby moved back and forth, making it feel as though the dead themselves were sighing and leaning and breathing across my shoulder as I picked and twisted at the innards of the padlock with my small metal barb.

My flesh shivered and I shoved the paper clip deep into the

lock like a spear, jamming and twisting it with neither finesse nor delicacy.

And it sprang.

I couldn't believe my eyes. Not only did the lock trip, but the U lifted away from the shank and I had easy, free clearance to the tomb.

Shit.

I was far more prepared to try, fail, and pay the $50 than I was to venture inside the black house of death. But I was also enough of a competitor that I couldn't intentionally throw the game.

I slipped the lock from the clasp and let it drop to the ground. And then I pulled the aging steel door open. It creaked far louder than the cemetery gate, and for a moment I didn't breathe.

The stones around me stayed still, angels and saints frozen in timeless gazes, staring, witnessing my unholy violation. The wind slipped like scarves around the trees and whistled. There was no more safety outside than in, I concluded and threw the door open wide to the wind.

Stepped inside.

Gasped.

The air was heavy and cold. Stale. Foul.

The breath of the crypt.

I waited 'til my eyes adjusted, wondering if rats awaited my prying fingers. Slowly, the moon shadow proved bright enough to light the crypt, and I stood before the bronze marker holding the name of a long-dead corpse.

Benito. 1902-1946.

I grasped at the handle of his deathly bed and pulled. Pulled. Felt a muscle gasp in my back and pulled again. Icy sweat slid down my back, whether from fear or exertion, I don't know.

In moments, Benito's casket lay exposed before me, slipped from the hollow confines of his stone bunk bed, and I stared at the dirty cover. Was I really about to rob a grave for $100?

Yeah, an inner voice whispered. *Get on with it.*

There were clasps on the edge of the wooden frame and one by one, my hands slipped along the edge of the lid and threw them.

Did I really want to do this?

Get it over with, the voice in me screamed, and I propped both palms against the coffin lid and pushed upward.

Another creak, a wooden scream, and the lid was up, and my nose assaulted with a rush of stale fetid air like a hammer blow across the skull.

I gagged, sneezed, and cursed, but refused to let go of the lid.

I stared down, in the pale, diffuse moonlight, at the mummified vellum skin of a man once called Benito. He still wore the dusty dark shards of a suit, its buttons caught and reflected the faint light of the devil moon behind me. His palms were crossed over his chest, and I shuddered.

They were at peace.

Clutched together.

Skeletal white.

"I'm sorry," I remember saying, and reached in to grab his right hand.

I pulled, and the arm lifted, the dust of his decayed, forgotten flesh rising in the air like a cloud. The suit sleeve pulled back, revealing a worm-eaten white—now grayish—shirt, and I pulled hard on the hand, crumpling in my hand like popcorn.

But the hand wouldn't separate from the arm bone.

It lifted and shook and dust clouded the narrow space...but the hand remained connected to the dead man beneath me.

"Damnit, let go," I cried, and I do mean cried. Tears were streaming down my face but I would not, could not stop. I propped the coffin lid up and held the dead man's dead arm over the edge of the coffin. With my left hand I brought my palm down in a karate chop to sever the hand from the wrist.

There was a snap and a pain in my hand from a sharp stab of bone and it was done. I stood there, in the center of a mausoleum, holding my prize.

The bony hand of a man some sixty years gone. The hand that had once, perhaps, driven spikes to build a railroad, or whipped up a horse to pull a plow, or caressed the breast of a lover and stroked the brows of his children. Now reduced to a $100 prize.

"I'm sorry," I said again.

The wind howled on cue, and the door behind me slammed shut with a crash.

At the same time, the coffin lid fell.

I was holding the hand of a dead man. In the dark.

Both feet in his grave.

Something outside sounded like laughter. Something in my head screamed and screamed and wouldn't stop.

I fell to the floor and cried out, begging, "Please, please, let me go."

It was quiet then, in the tomb, and I waited, breath drawn.

There was no sound at all. With the door closed, the wind was silenced; all sound from outside was cut off. It was me, and the hand, and the coffin.

That was all.

I wanted to scream out. But my throat was closed.

And then.

A knock.

Behind me.

On the coffin lid.

And another.

"No," I whispered. "There's no one here."

Silence. For a moment. And then a tap on the lid. Inside the lid. I turned to stare at the dead man's box in the faint light that slipped through the small barred window in the door. I watched the dust lift and twine with each tap like swirling spirits in the near-black shadows of the tomb.

Benito wanted his hand back.

"No," I gasped again, and lunged toward the door.

I flung it open and lunged out into the icy chill of the October wind. The cemetery seemed suddenly angry, watchful, and I dashed through the long grass, stomping hard on the soil of sunken graves until I reached the paved roadway. I looked back at the mausoleum, for a second, and saw that the door swung open in the breeze; it opened wide and then slammed shut in the wind.

I waited at the X Ramondo had marked on the roadway for an hour.

Once, I thought I heard someone cry out. But it was faint, perhaps only the shriek of another night bird. Another moment and I thought I heard the teeth-grinding drag of metal on bone.

And another time, I thought I heard something slam. Probably the door of the crypt I'd plundered, opening and slamming shut in the wind, I told myself.

But when I heard the laughter behind me, the horrible, heavy throat-gasping laughter coming from the road on the left, I ran through those forced cemetery gates, back to the land of the living.

I ran through the open cemetery gates and past the low orange glow of the Excelsior.

I ran past the healthy homes of seductive sleeping suburbia and past the sinking row houses of the wrong side of the tracks slums.

I was crying and wheezing and very, very sober when I reached my home, and once inside threw both locks on the front door immediately behind me. Lightning flashed outside as I mounted the stairs, and shed my clothes. I lay in bed, cowering beneath the covers, every shadow a ghost of coming death.

And soon, very soon, the tapping began.

They were light, at first, the sounds. Branches on the window, I told myself, though that didn't help me sleep.

Tap. Tap. Tap.

Hour after hour, all night long. Eventually, when my heart couldn't pump in double time any longer, the steady rhythm of the tapping lulled me to sleep sometime before dawn.

The next day, when I woke and the cleansing rays of the sun washed through my windows, I laughed and told myself we had all been drunken fools. Still, I shivered when I stared at the bony hand lying on my dresser that said I'd won the bet. I showered and dressed quickly, eager to compare stories with my friends on how they had fared the night before. Who had run home first, I wondered.

I left home in such a rush, I forgot to take my trophy with me. But neither Al nor Ramondo showed up that day to work.

∽

The tapping that night on my bedroom window grew louder, though there was no wind or storm in evidence. I pulled the sheets up to my nose and prayed to all the saints for forgiveness. The bony rhythm was not slowed by prayer. I could almost see the whitened digit drumming slowly, persistently against the glass.

Tap. Tap. Tap.

But I dared not throw the curtains to look.

∽

The next day passed and at lunch I called Al. I called Ramondo. Their answering machines gave the ghosts of their voices and a machine gun's report of beeps.

I lay in bed staring at the white knuckles of Benito on my dresser, and shuddered. My eyelids had barely shut when the tapping began again at my bedroom window.

This time, from my dresser, I could have sworn I heard an answering staccato response:

Tap-tap. Tap-tap. Tap-tap.

I pulled the covers over my head and hid.

But I couldn't hide from the sound.

In the morning, the skeletal fingers were spread, like a wave, on the floor of my room. I used a towel from the bathroom, and carefully picked it up, depositing it back on top of my dresser with a series of bony clicks.

∽

He's here again tonight.

Rap, tap-tapping on my window panes.

I can feel the stab of each tap throughout the room, each crack like the sound of his hand snapping against the hard edge of his coffin and I know, I know, the glass will break soon and let him in.

Should I be brave and open the window? Open the front door and let him in? Will he kill me quickly, if I do? Will he thank me if I give him back his hand, and let the door slap shut, safely, behind him?

Tomorrow, if I live through this night, I think I'll finally take Benito's hand and offer it to Maria to shake. It's the only thing left to do. It's why we did this. It's why we all will die. Someone should finish the job.

The irony is, whether she shakes my hand or Benito's, whether Maria realizes it or not, she will be clutching the bones of a dead man. Once disturbed, I don't think he will rest again. Not without my punishment.

Even now, behind me, I can hear him again.

A question. An accusation. A demand.

Tap.

Tap.

Tap.

THE WHITE HOUSE

"THERE IS NO poetry in death," Mrs. Tanser said. "Only loss and rot, stink and waste. I never could understand those gothic romantics who celebrate the dark and lust after the cycle of decay."

The little girl in front of her didn't say a thing, but nodded creamy, unblemished cheeks as if she understood.

"I suppose that doesn't make much sense to you," Mrs. Tanser continued, running a powder-coated finger up the girl's cheek. "You came here hoping to sell cookies and to visit my nieces, and here I am talking to you about death! But I can't deny death, mind you. Everything has its place. And every place, its thing."

The older woman laughed, and stood up from the table. Her plate of thinly sliced apples remained untouched, uneaten, the brown creep of time already shadowing the fruit. The girl's plate, however glistened with the juice of apple long gone.

Mrs. Tanser ground a pestle into a tall bucket that squeaked and shifted on the counter as she worked.

"Well, I'm sorry my nieces Genna and Jillie aren't here any longer. They only came for a visit, so I'm glad you got to meet them. Perhaps you'll have the chance to be with them again soon. But I talk too much and time passes. Too fast, too fast. Eat my apples, dear. Waste not, want not."

The plate slid across the table. Mrs. Tanser raised a silver eyebrow as it did.

"You are afraid of this house, aren't you?"

The child nodded, slowly. Her eyes were blue and wide, and the reflection of the older woman's methodic grinding and pummeling of the substance in the bucket glimmered like a ghost in their mirror.

"I can't say that I'm surprised. Quite the reputation it has. I didn't realize that when I moved in, but now it makes sense what a steal it was. I knew there was something wrong when the Realtor quoted me the price—you could see it in her face. She was afraid, that silly woman was, not that she knew why. A beautiful old mansion like this, perched on the top of the most scenic hill in town? I have to admit, I didn't care what was wrong with it—for that price, I thought, I could fix it. And then I moved in, and started teaching down at Barnard Elementary, and I found out why that girl was scared. You know, she wouldn't even walk into the house past the front foyer?"

Mrs. Tanser laughed. The pestle clinked against the top of the bucket, and a hazy cloud puffed from the opening like blown flour.

"The one warning that woman said to me was, 'You know, it's a bad place for children.' I didn't even ask why. 'I don't have any,' I told her. That shut her up. Or maybe it didn't, I didn't care. I walked up those gorgeous oak stairs that wind out of the living room and up to the boudoir. I wanted to see it all, with or without her help. She didn't come with me."

Mrs. Tanser stopped her grinding then and considered. "Would you like to see the upstairs?" she asked.

The little girl shrugged, and the older woman dropped the pestle.

"That settles it. Genna and Jillie aren't here, but I can still show you the house. Come on upstairs. I'm going to show you the most beautiful four-poster bed your little eyes have ever seen. The girls loved it! It may be the *only* four-poster bed your little eyes have ever seen."

The girl rose from the table, hands held straight at the sides of her red-and-green-striped skirt. She wanted to leave, felt embarrassed that she'd been coaxed into staying somehow. Her freckles threatened to burst into flame as she waited for Mrs. Tanser to wash her hands in the sink.

"C'mon then," Mrs. Tanser said at last, and led the girl back towards the front door she'd come in. Her backpack from school still lay abandoned on the floor nearby. Mrs. Tanser put a foot on the first varnished step, and then paused.

"What's your name again then, young lady?"

"Tricia," the girl answered, in a voice high as a flute song.

"Tricia," Mrs. Tanser announced, waving at the crystal jewels of the chandelier above, and the burnished curves of the banister on the second-floor landing above.

"Welcome to White House," she said. "Welcome to the House of Bones."

At the top of the landing, Mrs. Tanser stopped again. "This house was built in 1878 by Garfield White," she announced. "I looked it up. He was a railroad man, made his living helping folks move their steel and wood and food and such from one place to the next. Why he settled here, in the middle of nowhere, I'll never know, but there you go. Everything has a place, and every place a thing. He built this place, and put his wife here in it to raise their son. Maybe he thought she'd give the boy a good upbringing here, away from the corruption and sin of the cities."

Mrs. Tanser motioned the girl to follow her down the hall to the dark-rimmed doorway of a room.

"That woman spent her time in here, so the stories go, day after day after day while her Garfield rode the rails making his fortune. He stayed out on those rails more and more, hoping maybe to gain his son an inheritance."

The older woman stepped with a click and an echoey clack into the room. The walls were papered in a pattern of whirling pinks and blossomed yellows. But the garish sidelights did little to detract from the majesty of the enormous mahogany bed that dominated the center. Its rich posts rose from lion claw paws on the floor to taper in spears to within inches of the faded ceiling. A translucent gauze of yellowed lace hung between the posts and darkened the space with ghostly light.

"The more her husband stayed lost on the trains, the more his wife stayed lost here, in this very bed," Mrs. Tanser said.

"Go ahead, sit on it yourself and see why!"

Tricia stepped into the room but stopped at the edge of the mattress, which was nearly as tall as her.

"Use the step," Mrs. Tanser said, pointing to the dark wooden box near the girl's feet. "In those days, you wanted to sleep as high above the ground as you could. Rats, you know."

Tricia hopped up on the step with the mention of rodents, and rolled her body onto the heavy down mattress, smiling at the caress of the silken blue comforter that covered it.

"They called it the White House, and not because it was in Washington, D.C.," Mrs. Tanser said. "But it was anything but white inside. Mrs. White kept all of the drapes pulled shut, and spent more and more time here, in this bed. They say she was trying to make it feel like nighttime inside, so her son would sleep. Had the colic, and cried all day long. But pulling the drapes did nothing to calm the boy, and after a while, Mrs. White went a little bit mad, I think. Day after day, night after night, her baby cried, cried, cried and she paced this floor with him, pounding his tiny back and begging him to burp and then *screaming* at him to burp."

Mrs. Tanser shook her head.

"That boy never saw that nest egg his father was out putting away. When Mr. White came back from one of his long trips down the rails, he found the house dark, and all the shutters pulled. I probably shouldn't be telling you this, you being a young girl and all—but you've probably seen worse on TV. Oh the things they show on that tube." Mrs. Tanser shook her head brows creased in dreadful sadness.

"When Mr. White came home that day, he walked up those same stairs you and I just did, and knew right away something was wrong. I won't say more than this, but the smell was in the air, and he was no fool. He rushed to the bedroom and threw open this door and…"

Tricia's eyes widened as the story unfolded.

"…when the light streamed into the pitch-black room, he found his wife and his son, here in the shadows. Only they were in no condition to leave. The poor boy was hung from his tiny neck right off of that pole there," Mrs. Tanser pointed at the right pole at the foot of the bed. "Mrs. White had tried to quiet him by wrapping a sheet around his head—but when he didn't quiet, she'd finally snapped. She hung him by his tiny neck like a Christmas ornament at the foot of the bed, and when he finally quieted, she lay down on the pillow and went to sleep. When she woke, and realized what she'd done, she took her own life, using her husband's straight razor.

"If I took the sheets off this bed you could still see the marks of her blood. Nobody's ever changed that mattress. She lay down right there, where you are, and cut herself again and again and again until she couldn't cut or scream anymore."

Tricia leapt from the bed as if it had turned to a stove burner.

Mrs. Tanser grinned, wrinkles catching at the corner of her eyes like broken glass.

"She used that blade so much, they say she had to have a closed casket. Can't imagine cutting your own face with a razorblade myself, but, I can't imagine hanging your own baby, neither!

"There's a reason they started calling this place the House of Bones. But that came later. Mr. White kept this place for almost thirty years after his wife killed their son and herself here. And he never remarried. In fact, he may have been dead for a year or more before the town grew the wiser. He was gone for long periods at a time on the railroad, and it was only when the spring winds brought a tree down on the west wing of the house that someone from the town realized it had been months and months since Mr. White had been seen. When they looked into it, they found out that he hadn't been out on a rail for more than a year, and that's when someone thought to look in the basement."

Mrs. Tanser looked at the trembling girl and shook her head.

"I'm sorry, I'm scaring you. My home does not have a cheery history, I must admit. But it's fascinating too, don't you think?"

The old woman shook her head. "C'mon downstairs, and I'll buy some of those Girl Scout cookies. A lady needs her vices, huh?"

The doorbell rang. But there was no silhouette showing through the stained purple glass in the front door of White House.

Mrs. Tanser answered the ring, nevertheless, and smiled as she saw the pale features of the girl on the landing, shivering and yet waiting outside. So small, she couldn't even send her shadow through the glass.

"Come in, child," she insisted. "You'll catch your death of cold. I don't believe your mother lets you go out like that in the fall chill."

Tricia entered the house again, driven by a feeling she could not have explained. The house scared her to death. Mrs. Tanser was strange. But interesting. A welcome diversion after a boring day at school.

"I didn't think you'd come back after the story of Mr. and Mrs. White," the teacher exclaimed. "Sometimes I feel like I am just the steward for this house. I have to give its history, no matter how twisted it may be."

She motioned the girl into the kitchen, a room colored in orange walls and burnished counters.

"You're probably hoping for my nieces, but I'm afraid they're not around to play with you right now. Can I cut you an apple?" Mrs. Tanser asked again, and Tricia nodded.

"Good."

After a while, the older woman went back to her grinding, pounding work at the counter, and talked to Tricia from across the room.

"Hmmm...where did we leave off last time? How it all began, I think. Yes. I suppose you're wondering, what happened after the Whites lived in White House?"

The girl nodded, and Mrs. Tanser barely waited for that response.

"Mr. White was found in the basement. I won't go into how his disposition was, other than to say that his funeral did not boast an open casket. The house was eventually sold to another family, and life went on—for a time."

Mrs. Tanser brushed the dust from the lapels of her maroon collar. It smeared like dried milk across her chest.

"You can't hide the past," she said. "Nor can you hide from the past. What is, *is*, and what was, *was*. The next people who bought this house pretended that the Whites hadn't killed themselves here, and as a result..."

Tricia looked up from her slice of apple with a keen gaze of expectation.

"Well, they didn't consider the fact that they might also spend their lives—and deaths—here.

"Sometimes," Mrs. Tanser said, eyes looking far, far away. "A mother's love is not endless. In fact, it doesn't even really begin."

The older woman rubbed a tear from the wrinkles at the side of her eye, and forced a grin. "Silly old woman I am," she said. "You're just a girl and you can't even begin to understand the twists and cul de sacs of a mother's love. I had a tough one, is all, and even now I can hear her scolding me. I've met your mama at the PTA, and she's not like that. Not like that at all. You're a very lucky girl.

"So where was I? Oh yes, the next family. A pastor, the father was, come here all the way from Omaha. Why *here*, again I'll never know. This must be the end of the line for some folks, and they just don't know it. Hell, why would they come here if they did? Something draws them though, because no matter how many young folks try to escape this town after they graduate, the place keeps growing. Back in those days, before the Great War, there were just a couple hundred here, and the Martins moved into this house with a huge welcome from the townsfolk. For a time, Pastor Martin even held services right here in this house—in the sitting room I believe—until a proper parish chapel could be built down in the center of town.

"All that holiness didn't settle things apparently, though, in White House. Because the pastor and his family came to a similar end as the Whites did. Things were happy here for a few years, and the Martins had two children, Becky and Joseph. But, just like Mr. White, Pastor Martin's vocation began to consume him, leaving Mrs. Martin here in the house all alone with the children day after day. The story goes, that Mrs. Martin got bit by the green bug, and started thinking that Pastor Martin was spending far too much time down at the new chapel in town. There's no telling if it's true or not, but she thought the pastor was making time with a pretty little hussy in the back pew, while she was trapped here, in this old, cold house with two screaming kids.

"I'm talking too big for you, aren't I?" Mrs. Tanser said noting the confused expression on the girl's face. "The pastor's wife thought he had gotten a girlfriend, is the thing. And he was married to her and she didn't want him to have a girlfriend. So she locked little Becky and Joseph into a small room at the back of the house. Someone, probably Mr. White, had added on, and built the room by hand. It wasn't completely true. Sometimes,

Pastor Martin would come home at night and hear those kids screaming in the back of the house, and when he'd let them out, they'd tumble into the house proper shaking and blue with cold, because none of the seams of that room were level. The outside could leech in easily, hell, you could see the grass waving in the wind through the gaps and the draughts on this hill in the winter are something horrible, I have to tell you. Even asleep in that big four-post bed upstairs, I put an afghan on top of the covers in December. Can you imagine how cold it must have been for those children when they could actually see the outside through the cracks in the walls?

"Anyway, Pastor Martin yelled at his wife many a time for how she treated those children, yelled so loud the people a mile down the hill in town could hear him and mark his words. And she'd yell right back, and accuse him of taking the Lord's work to the devil, not to mention that tart Beatrice Long. She thought he was making time with a church whore."

Tricia put a hand over her mouth to stifle a yawn, and Mrs. Tanser pushed the plate of apples closer to the girl.

"I'm going on too long, aren't I? Let me speed it up for you some. An old woman can go on. One day Pastor Martin came home and for once, the house was quiet. His wife told him the kids had gone to stay with friends in town for the weekend, and he heaved a sigh of relief. The noise had really begun to get to him, and that, as much as anything, was why he'd been spending more and more time at the chapel. The Martins reportedly had a lovely dinner, and even broke out a bottle of wine to celebrate their brief 'vacation' from the children. Pastor Martin tried to get romantic with his wife, but she waved him off of that. 'You wouldn't want to make more of the little screamers, would you?' she said."

Mrs. Tanser paused, looking quizzically at Tricia's moon-round cheeks. "That probably doesn't mean much to you yet, does it? Hmmm."

"Well, it came to Sunday, and Pastor Martin spoke after the church service with the folks his children were supposedly stay-ing with, thanking them for their hospitality. But they looked confused at his thanks, and told him that they would be happy to have Becky and Joseph over any time, but they hadn't seen the kids these past few days.

"Pastor Martin was upset by that, and after the last service, headed home in a rush. He wondered if he'd gotten the family wrong that the kids were staying with. When he entered the house, for the third day in a row it was completely silent, but Mrs. Martin waited for him at the table.

"'Sit,' she insisted. 'Eat.'

"He sat, but asked her where the children were. Mrs. Martin smiled sweetly, and ignored him, fixing herself a sandwich and then pushing the plate towards him. 'Light or dark?' she asked.

"'Both,' he said absently, and as she put the meat on his plate, along with a long crust of bread, he asked her again. 'Where are the kids?'

"Mrs. Martin smiled that strange little grin again and nodded, as he lifted the bread to his mouth and chewed.

"'You're eating them, dear. Becky's light, and Joseph's dark.'"

Tricia's eyes went wide and she set the piece of apple she held back on the plate, uneaten.

"Horrible, hmmm? Apparently Mrs. Martin had used that back room to turn her children into cold cuts. When he screamed and beat on her for her horrible crime, she only smiled and smiled, and told him to make more with Beatrice Long. Back then, in a town this size, they didn't have asylums, and so Mrs. Martin never actually left this house. Pastor Martin locked her in the room she'd killed her children in, and fed her meals at morning and night. She never came out of there again, and whenever he'd break down and cry and ask her 'why' all she would say was 'the house needs strong bones'."

Mrs. Tanser grinned. "Creepy, hmm? Want to see the room?"

Tricia's eyes widened.

"Oh don't worry, the Martins are long gone from there. Come along, I'll show you."

Mrs. Tanser led Tricia through a hallway and a long, dark sitting room to a white door. She turned a latch and a metal bolt clacked audibly before she turned the old round knob.

They stepped through into a small, dark room. It had no windows at all, but still was lit. The sun beamed in through hairline cracks in the grout between the stones that had been shaved and stacked to form the addition. Shadows played like anxious ghosts on the walls and dust motes rained in lazy dances as the wind shifted and groaned outside.

"This is it," Mrs. Tanser said. "The infamous White room. They think that Mr. White built it with his own hands, and used the bones of his wife and son as the grout between the rocks. Mrs. Martin followed his lead. The paint you see in here? The reason the room is so white? She ground up the bones of those two kids after carving them up for lunchmeat here in this room. She used the dust of their bones to paint this room an everlasting off-white."

Tricia stared in horror at the walls. "The paint is...their bones?"

Mrs. Tanser nodded. "It seemed a sacrilege to paint over the remains of those poor souls, so the room has been left exactly as it was when Pastor Martin sat down here in the middle of the room and...well...there's no delicate way to put this. He blew his brains out with a hunting rifle. Lord knows where he got it, a man of the clergy and all. Someone wiped down the ceiling and wall over there..." She pointed to a shadowy stain to their right.

"But all in all, the bones of those children are still right here, chalky and white, for anyone to see.

"Oh my dear, you're trembling; you're white as the walls. Come here, I'm so sorry. I'm an old woman and talk too much. I forget myself. And you, just a 5th grader and all. Let's have us a soda pop, hmmm?"

Mrs. Tanser pulled the wide-eyed girl from the room and bolted the lock once again.

"Don't need any of those summer breezes or restless ghosts getting in," she mumbled, and then shook her head. "Darn it all, there I go again."

The massive door opened with a long squeak. Mrs. Tanser peered through the foot-wide opening with a suspicious look on her face. Then her eyes lighted on the tousled hair of Tricia.

"You're probably here to see my nieces, aren't you?" she asked.

The girl shook her head. "No, ma'am. I don't know them."

"Don't know them?" Mrs. Tanser looked confused. Then she slapped a palm to her forehead. "My oh, my, that's right. They came a-visiting a while before you came a-visiting. And you've been too polite to correct an old woman before."

She opened the door wider and motioned Tricia inside. "Sometimes it's all a blur," she confided, and pushed the door shut.

"I remember now. I've been giving you the history of the house, and fattening you up on apples. Not the best choice for fattening, I'll give you, but it's what I have. No chocolate cakes up here on the hill!"

Mrs. Tanser motioned her into the kitchen.

"Where were we last time? I told you about the Whites and the Martins... There were others too. But then in the '50s, they turned the place into an orphanage."

Mrs. Tanser laughed. "I know, it sounds ridiculous. A house where children kept dying in horrible ways. A house where children's bones actually painted the walls white—and they turned it into an orphanage. But there you go. I wonder if they ever even saw the irony."

The rhythmic sound of a knife on stone filled the kitchen as Mrs. Tanser cut the girl an apple.

"Here we go," the older woman said, pushing a plate in front of the girl. She stared at the ceiling a moment and then grinned and nodded. "Forty-seven."

Mrs. Tanser scooped the core of the apple and a couple seeds from the counter and threw them in a waste can. "Forty-seven children in all disappeared while this house was an orphanage. That's what I found out down there at the village hall. God knows why the town didn't have this place bulldozed, but, then again, who cares so much about orphans?"

The old woman shook her head in obvious disgust and then motioned for Tricia to follow her.

"Grab an apple," she said. "I want to show you something."

Mrs. Tanser led the way past the dining room and a dark hallway and the horrible room of bone paint, with its locked door. She stopped at another door, this one painted dark as a 2 a.m. shadow.

She pulled a ring of keys from the depths of her apron and explained, "Sometimes at night, I hear voices from in here. Terrible voices. Men howling. Children screaming. When I open the door, they're never there…but I keep it locked anyway."

She pushed the door open and stepped inside. Tricia followed, though hesitantly.

The room expanded to fill the eye with a vista of beautiful stonework and a floor of intricate mosaic. Like most of the house, the predominant color was no color. The room hurt the eye in its melding of cream and vanilla and starving, emaciated white. It also ascended three stories in the air and ran as deep as a football field.

"Over here," Mrs. Tanser called, and led Tricia to a corner. She reached down to the floor and pulled on a small cord that poked out from beneath the shards of tile. A hidden trap door opened upwards at her pull.

"Look," Mrs. Tanser pointed, and Tricia leaned in to stare down into the gap.

The trap secreted a small cubbyhole, maybe eighteen inches deep and a foot wide. Its bottom was hidden by dozens of small white pebble-like shards. They covered the bottom and stacked on top of each other like a pound of gravel.

"Hold out your hand," Mrs. Tanser said. As Tricia did, her arm visibly shook.

The older woman squeezed her outstretched palm and grinned. "It's okay. They can't get you here. Their time was a long time ago. Now. You see these?" She turned the girl's hand palm side up and ran a finger across the top joint, on the other side of the fingernail.

"I'm not sure what they intended, but I believe that little stack of bones down there are the top joints of all those missing orphans' fingers."

Tricia ripped her hand away and gasped.

Mrs. Tanser shook her head. "They say down in town that those orphans disappeared, but it's no mystery where they went."

She let the trap fall down with a smack that echoed through the too-still room.

"Just look around you," she said and gestured at the intricately laid floor. "Those kids never left this room. Their bones are here, laid into the walls and the floor and the ceiling. Those kids built this room."

Tricia's eyes had now widened so large that the whites of her eyes were circled in red.

"Yep," the old woman sighed. "You're standing on them."

The girl screamed.

"Just bones," Mrs. Tanser said. "I wanted you to see, to understand. This house has a bad reputation, and rightly so. I'm sure those voices I hear coming from this room are from all those innocent orphans who had their fingers cropped off, and their bones ground down to shards of decorative tile."

"It's this house," she said and shook her head, pulling Tricia closer. The girl didn't fight her embrace. All she could think of was that she was standing on the chopped-up bones of dead people.

"Everyone who's ever lived here has felt the need to add to the house," Mrs. Tanser said, and pulled the girl towards the back of the long room.

"The White House was large by the standards of the 1800s when Mr. White built it, but there have been many rooms added since. I showed you the draughty room last time you were here. And this room—which I think was probably a gymnasium for the orphans—was built over a long period. There are others. In the basement is a small closet that I believe was painted in the paste of a child…its colors are faded and dulled now, but it looks to be a mad swirl of mud and blood and bone if you stare closely. There's a shed on the back of the property that has window frames that are rounded and made of what looks to be rib bones. And the lock on that shed is a primitive thing, but it seems to be made of an arm or a leg bone that drops into place and holds the door fast."

"There's no way the Realtor could have warned me," Mrs. Tanser said. "There's no way she could ever really have known—she wouldn't walk inside much past the front door. I wish she could have told me what I was in for. But the house… once you're here…"

They walked across the long bone mosaic room, and the chatter of Tricia's teeth began to reverberate through the silence.

"It's okay, child," Mrs. Tanser said. "I just want to show you one more room."

At the back of the long white room she stopped, and reached out to turn the latch on a door that only announced itself as thin seams set in the wall. It opened outward at her touch, and a cool breeze hit them as it did.

"I think that some of the rooms people added to the house were afraid to show their real colors," Mrs. Tanser said. "The people knew what they were doing, on some level, and they bleached the bones and carved the bones and crushed the bones into paste and mortar and paint."

"But when the house told me...when I realized what I would have to do, I made a pledge to myself to be true to the children who came here. The people who grew this house. They shouldn't be hidden in pieces, I said to myself, but celebrated. After all, everything has its place. And every place, its thing. The things that build this house, have their place. They had life, and in death...they grow the White House in rooms of bone.

"And this house...must have its thing. These days...that's me."

Mrs. Tanser picked up a hammer and raised it above Tricia's head. She breathed deep as the girl squealed and tried desperately to run. Her screams rang out like bullets scraping metal. But Mrs. Tanser's other hand held the small girl fast. A trapped animal.

"You'll live here forever," she promised. "And I promise you'll hardly feel a thing. I can't believe the torture some of these kids must have gone through. I could never be so cruel."

Tricia screamed again. A horrible, larnyx-shredding sound. But she couldn't break free of the old woman's grip. Mrs. Tanser lived only for the house now, and Tricia had never felt such desperate strength before. The veins of the woman's hands stood out blue and serious above the small girl's reddening fingers.

"I came to this town because I loved children. Genna and Jillie didn't want to stay here either," she whispered. "Look at them up there."

She nodded at two tiny skulls shrieking in silence on the wall. "But what could I do? I adore children. The house… This house…it never relents…

"Hold still," Mrs. Tanser said. "I want your face to stay this beautiful, always."

Tricia twisted and turned, staring at the bone-white eye sockets and jaws of the handful of splintered skulls that lined the half-constructed wall of the small room like fractured masks. Those perfect, unblemished bone faces screamed silently in chorus with her, as Mrs. Tanser turned to make her kill.

"It's going to take a long time to finish this room," the old woman lamented. "But I will finish my room. Everything has its place. And every place, its thing. This room is mine."

She brought the hammer down.

Star on the Beach

"No, I don't!"

He caught my hand in mid-throw before I could let go and cast the shell back to the ocean. It had an odd shape, apricot and cream in spirals, I'd noticed, but it was not so strange as to make me want to keep it. Still, when the wiry little Cuban boy gripped my arm and yelled no, I listened.

"What?" I barked, and released my grip on the shell. He scooped it from the sand excitedly and said, "Star, star!"

I shrugged and went back to shoveling sand with my whole arm into the shape of a wall.

∽

We'd met on South Beach.

Miami.

Home of skates and tons of sand…and…T&A. I could literally taste the sex in the air. Or was that just the ocean?

After a long walk down the beach from my hotel, where I'd left my wedding ring in a drawer under a stack of underwear, I'd finally convinced myself to turn my attention to the earth, instead of the well-displayed (and endowed) but unachievable women. Like countless men before me, I'd taken to architecture to release my creative urges, building phallic representations of my unsated lusts from the earth.

Sand castles.

I was building sand castles instead of scoring some choice 36-24-36 when the teenage brown-skinned boy joined me.

"You build?" he asked.

He took my nod as an invitation and soon both of us were shoring up sand walls to protect an unimpressive, tentative squat tower from the crush of the ocean.

Story of my life.

'Til I dug out the shell.

Then he freaked.

"It's just a shell," I said, but he kept on.

"Star, star."

He forced it out of my hand, chocolate eyes serious with concentration.

"Keep." He nodded.

I stuffed it in my pocket and went back to shoring up a beleaguered moat wall. We worked in silence until sunset, he pointing to areas gone weak and smiling with teeth as white as the moon when I filled the gaps with sand.

When the sun set and the conga music began filtering over the berm from Mango's on Ocean View, I announced that I had to leave.

He looked alarmed.

"Some time?" he asked.

English came hard to him and he struggled with each word.

"Some," I admitted. "But I need to meet some friends from work for dinner."

I don't know how much he understood, but he motioned for me to follow.

He took me farther down the beach than I had gone before—past the rows of hotels to the very end of the island.

"How far?" I asked and he only nodded his head quickly and said, "Yes."

Finally, he turned and grinned at me and nodded again.

"Now, now," he said and ran up, away from the water and in between an old boarded up shell of a building. Maybe it had been a small motel, I thought, though they didn't seem to have anything else around here. He pointed to a mound of sand and then to my pocket.

"Star," he said and without question, I gave it to him. But he refused, instead motioning for me to place the shell at the top of the pile. Or the bottom. Who could tell? Once placed, he clapped his hands and began shoveling sand off the center of the mound with cupped hands. After a moment, I took the hint and joined him. The sand slipped through my hands like water, but still I scooped, armful after armful, some sliding back as soon as I'd removed it. But little by little, we made progress towards his undescribed goal.

Her belly was bronze.

Beautiful.

And more than a bit frightening when I realized what it was we were digging up.

Again, the kid egged me on.

"Okay, Okay." He nodded and proceeded to uncover more of her perfect, nude body.

She was like every celluloid queen I'd seen strutting up and down the beach, playing volleyball in bikini suits too small to cover all of their privates at any one moment.

Her nipples jutted round and proud from out of the sand-like copper ice cream cones, her thighs looked taut and strong and her oil-gloss pubes shed sand like liquid gold.

I was in awe. And scared to death.

The kid was uncovering a dead body. A beautiful dead body, but dead, nonetheless. We hadn't yet seen a face and there was no way she'd been breathing under all that sand.

And then he did the worst thing.

Pointing at me, he began to rock his hips back and forth. Then he'd stop, motion at my crotch and grind in her direction again. It looked silly, coming from a boy. What could he know?

"No way!" I said and he smiled again, pointing to himself.

"Me?" he asked.

I shrugged and he dropped his shorts to reveal his finger-sized erection. It may have been small, but he knew what to do. In an instant, his twelve-year-old hips were slapping with dog-like speed against the half-buried body.

I couldn't look at him, not really, and walked away in the middle, but he caught up to me a few minutes later, slapping the shell back to my hand.

"Star," he said.

I looked closer at the shell this time. It wasn't a starfish… wasn't like any shell I'd ever seen before, really. I shoved it in my pocket, wondering what I should do. I didn't want to report a body. That was local stuff…and I didn't want to be involved. I was just passing through. Have a few drinks, build a couple sandcastles, slip my ring back on, and head home. No entanglements.

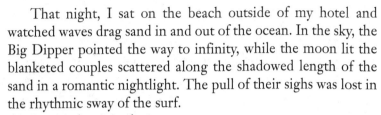

That night, I sat on the beach outside of my hotel and watched waves drag sand in and out of the ocean. In the sky, the Big Dipper pointed the way to infinity, while the moon lit the blanketed couples scattered along the shadowed length of the sand in a romantic nightlight. The pull of their sighs was lost in the rhythmic sway of the surf.

I wanted to join them.

I wanted to plunge into the ocean.

I wanted to plunge into her.

Night birds scattered like ghost crabs across the sand as I restlessly walked the midnight coastline, the occasional rotted coconut washing in from the deep like a dark skull, tangled vines like veins trailing from its shattered brainpan. Sea foam sucked the sand from beneath my toes and shoveled shells and secrets home and gone again. The full moon reflected off the receding waters in a shining beacon.

There were eyes on me.

Silent eyes. Nervous and lustful.

The eyes of nocturnal birds and stone-white crabs and furtive humans coupling nervously in the shadows, their lovemaking open to any, yet seen only by the stars. I could feel them all, watching me, secret yet bright in the night.

In my mind, I wondered about her. Had she been one of these hidden women? Brashly naked and stealing sex on the beach in the midnight hour. Had her lover taken her hard, with liquid cries and writhing need and then, at the end, throttled and buried her, far from the surf and the crabs and the pounding feet of screaming kids and jogging businessmen?

How had the kid known about her? Had *he* buried her? Had it really happened at all?

The ocean breeze was warm and humid but goose bumps covered my neck and spine and I shivered. Without looking back, I strode through the mostly empty beach chairs and made my way back to my room. On the way in, I stopped at the bar and ordered a drink. Bombay gin martini. Evaporate-on-your-tongue dry. Extra olives.

A fuzz of alcoholic evergreen filled my eyes and nostrils and eventually, moon shadows kissing at my bed, I slept.

The next day was a maze of hotel room meetings and end-less, pointless committee discussion. I cinched at my tie often, and desperately wished that I could be one of those carefree pa-trons who I saw during breaks in the hallway, sandals slapping the tile as they headed, shorts-decked and chest bare, towards the sun-haloed doors leading to the pool and the beach. The day seemed endless. And then, it was 6 p.m., and a reception was playing itself out near the pool, and I…slipped away after five handshakes and a Chardonnay.

Free.

Back in my room, I thought of heading down the crowded pavement of Ocean View towards the clubs and restaurants, and then decided not to. I could eat anytime. The ocean, however, was not an option near my home. Without a second thought, I pulled on my still slightly damp swimsuit, slipped on an unbut-toned paisley shirt, and slipped my key into a pocket. I was leav-ing suit-ville for swimsuit-ville.

I made a wide circuit around Chardonnay and Cheap Beer city (the stuffy reception by the pool) and quickly found my feet in the sand and my face kissing the salt breeze. The sun was slipping low on the horizon, but not setting, and I started south once more, the same direction I'd gone the night before. In mo-ments, I'd settled into a sand-kicking rhythm, sometimes bend-ing to examine an interesting shell, but mostly heading straight south along the surf, reveling in the feeling of escape and adven-ture. I didn't stop until I'd reached the curve of the bottom of the island.

Now the sun was setting, and the beach was draining of pa-trons. I could see the line for the crab shack not far off, and hear the slight jingle of steel drums somewhere along the line of eateries and greeteries.

The ocean would soon be empty as sun worshippers turned their bodies to bait. Why else had they bronzed their skin, if not to attract prey?

I was alone on the end of the island.

I was yards from the buried woman in the sand.

It struck me that this was the moment I'd been waiting for all day.

I started up the beach, away from the ocean and towards the space between the buildings where the boy had taken me the day before.

I started towards her.

Sometimes it's funny how we fool ourselves. How we focus on other distractions while moving towards a goal.

I'd been moving towards her since my first sip of gin the previous night. I'd been putting it off, and steeling myself for it at the same time. And now, hands in the sand near a slight hill in the otherwise level beach, I began to dig.

Slowly at first, then faster, suddenly tasting the desire I'd denied the day before. Would she smell when I uncovered those tawny thighs today? Of fish or carrion? Would I take her anyway?

I wasn't sure what I intended—or at least, wouldn't admit it to myself—as I continued to scoop armful after armful of sand away.

And then…

"No, *no!*" came the voice.

"Star, s*tar!*"

A hand pulled me back from the mound, shoved me over and I saw the Cuban boy, eyes bulging and flashing with excitement.

He pushed me again, hard, and I fell back from the dig, not expecting such passion.

"Star," he said and pointed at my hip.

Now I wished I had stayed at the reception. I could have drowned my lusts in liquor, like usual, and avoided such a scene.

Hands felt me up as the boy ignored my resistance and felt along my thighs, ferreting out my pockets to see if I still had the shell from the day before.

Since I'd been thoroughly drunk and exhausted when I'd returned to my room the night before and hadn't emptied my pockets before stripping and falling into bed, the boy found a reason to smile. Reaching past my slapping hand, he extracted the orange—and-cream shell he'd given me with such ceremony during yesterday's sandcastle excavation.

"Star!" he proclaimed, and placed it on the portion of the beach where I imagined her head would be rotting.

I could almost see the crabs feasting on her eyes beneath the sand.

I no longer felt like continuing the excavation…in fact, I wondered why I'd come here at all. She may have looked pretty yesterday, the bits that I saw, but after all, she'd been dead.

The boy didn't waste time, however. After dragging the shell from my pocket, he proceeded to drag me to the mound, pushing aside more and more sand and grinning flashes of white teeth in the slowly creeping twilight.

"Much fun," he proclaimed at one point, and pointing at my swimsuit, made his own crotch push forward and back.

Then he dove back into digging in the sand, and, I regret to say, I followed suit. I'm not sure if I wanted "much fun", but I did thirst to see her golden thighs and belly one more time before I flew home.

I was not disappointed.

My hand suddenly scooped against a layer that did not give, and I found myself moving sand away from succulently bronzed flesh.

A buried woman's thigh.

The boy laughed and dug into the work with renewed vigor.

At one point he chuckled at me and pushed his swimsuit forward and back three times.

"Much fun," he said again.

This time, I insisted on unburying her face. Call it morals or curiosity. I knew by now that I was going to do what the boy had wanted me to yesterday.

She was too beautiful to waste.

And, damn me to hell, but she certainly was in no position to complain.

We left the shell above where I imagined her hair trailed beneath the sand, but uncovered the slight jut of her jaw and the thin line of her nose. Her eyes were closed, but seemed wide with promise, and her lips, despite the scrub of sand, still looked ruby red as if slathered with raspberry lipstick.

There was no smell, as I'd feared, and I longed to put my tongue to those lips and my body to the rest. She was a perfect specimen of beach fuckability. She was what the bleach blonde, electric bikinied girls skating down Ocean View wished they were. And she was buried and silent in the place where she should have been queen.

She was mine.

Mine and the boy's.

This time, though, the boy could wait.

I looked around the beach to see that no one was around. Like the night before, this stretch was a wasteland. The waves crashed against empty sand yards away, and nothing but salt air disturbed the sand grass that led away from us towards the empty road. Ignoring my provocateur, I pulled my shorts down.

With one hand slipping through a mountain of loose sand, and the other massaging her gorgeous, perfect breasts, I slipped myself between her sandy thighs. I needed no more foreplay than to look at her body.

I could almost feel the slippery lubrication of excitement from her, as I entered her, missionary style. And how appropriate that was. Wasn't I bringing satisfaction to the dead? A true vocation of the saintly.

Yeah right.

This wasn't religion, except in the sense that I worshipped her perfect body.

Perfect *dead* body.

At some point in my plumbing of her soft, clinging depths, it did occur to me that I was knee-deep in necrophilia, with a minor as an accomplice/victim.

Try getting out of the charges *that* could bring.

No matter how the courts looked at him, he was an anchor on my neck. As I came, violently, in an intense and satisfying series of shudders and groans (the boy giggled), I determined that no matter how he'd found me today, he would not see me tomorrow.

When I came here. Double entendre intended.

"Much fun," he enthused, as I slipped my sloppy, half-flagged dick out from the beach babe. Beached babe. Babe of the beach.

No matter how you cut it…

I edged back as the boy edged down his trunks. He was going to have a go, too?

Given the stretching I'd given her, I severely doubted whether the kid was going to feel much grip on his drill. Though, of course, he was willing to try.

It didn't take him long. Fast hips, boys have.

Then junior was asking me to help him rebury her.

We scooped in silence, and when the mound was complete, he grinned at me once more.

"Star. Much fun!"

He nodded politely at me then, and I think I bowed. Then we separated, him slipping through the dunes to climb his way back to the road, me heading back towards the line of the tide. I had a half mile or more to go, and the sun was already just a red glow on the horizon. I would follow the waves back to my hotel.

The next afternoon, I considered my attack. I didn't want the boy to beat me to the mound. Nor did I want him to join me. There are some things a man likes to do without an audience. At least, I do. I figured, the night before, I'd probably walked past the boy playing on the beach and he'd seen and followed me. This time around, I wanted no spectators.

Instead of following the surf, I walked down Ocean View until I reached the crab shack. Only then did I venture out onto the sand. I knew the buildings where she lay were right there, at the end of the island. I didn't expect to have any problem locating them, even though I came at them from another angle.

And, as it turned out, I was right. As soon as I got near the surf at the south end of the island and began following its line north, I spotted the buildings. Hell, I spotted our footsteps from the night before. Apparently, the boy and I were the only ones who knew of the girl beneath the sand.

Well, tonight, she was mine.

I hurried up the beach (as fast as one can hurry when scuffing through powder-thin sand) and found the mound we'd built the night before. I thought briefly of my wife and kids back home.

Briefly.

Then I began to uncover her.

There are some things in life you simply have to go for. And this was one of them. An average guy like me will never have a South Beach girl. Shit, we're barely able to even look at one, let alone ever score. And right now, I had my own babe of the beach lying right here, willing and open for my lovin'.

Okay, so she was dead.

She was still perfect.

Dead.

The thought *did* register. Don't think it didn't. I'm not that kind of freak or perve. But...she'd felt like a live woman. And she hadn't smelled. And...damn, but her boobs were everything I'd ever wanted. I knew if she'd opened her eyes, she would have laughed out loud at what was "taking" her. But, as long as her eyes were closed...my dreams were made flesh. Her flesh.

I dug fast.

I wanted her again.

Once more.

I had to leave in the morning. I'd jet back to my sweet, if sometimes naggy, wife, and my lovable yet loathable kids. I'd find my shag carpet still musty, and my aging German Shepherd still uncontrollable.

They loved me, the lot of them. And I loved them. But there are some dreams a man should get to live, once or twice in his life.

This was one of them.

Dead.

Minor detail.

That made her willing, right?

I laughed, a little nervously, and scooped sand faster. My suit already displayed a painful tent of anticipation, and I wanted to set the main pole free.

The waves crashed nearby, a lulling, relaxing sound. From far away, I could hear voices, cajoling and laughing shouts. The revelry of early drunken fun.

My fun was here.

And my time was now.

I pushed away a length of sand with my entire arm, and found the lower length of her leg.

The bone lifted with the force of my scoop.

The bone and a putrid soup of blackened, reeking flesh.

I gasped and fell back, staring at the white long bone, replete with gooey strings of tendons still clinging to it like wisps of gum. There it lay unearthed atop the white sand, and from the hollow I'd lifted it flowed a dark, stinking mess of liquid flesh.

The stench was ungodly. Puke mixed with rotten hamburger. Fresh sewage blended with old fish. I rolled away from the smell and felt my lunch struggling to escape. When I dared to peek back at the pit I'd dug, I saw dozens of black leeches climbing the lip of the pit to escape towards the surf.

Yesterday, I'd fucked her like a virgin, today she was a flowing mass of rot.

Was I at the wrong tomb?

I looked around, and saw the mounds of what could have been a dozen other burials. Scattered around between the abandoned buildings were other mounds, but there was only one trail of human evidence. The footprints of one pair of small feet and one large led from the beach and ended here, at this coffin of sand. The trail of the boy and me.

Was this some sick joke? Had he buried a woman here before bringing me to the spot and later replaced the body with… no. That was even more ridiculous than fucking a perfect (*dead*) woman lying beneath the beach.

I thought of his insistence over the placement of the shell and realized that today, I hadn't set it at the head of the mound.

Reaching into my pocket, I found it still there in my suit.

Was it really the "key" that allowed one to unlock the hidden beauty within the sand? If so, had I "killed" her?

Was I losing my mind?

I moved to the head of the mound and held the shell in my hand. If it had worked before, would it again? The sea breeze was spreading the stench of the rot I'd uncovered and I coughed, hard. I forced a swallow to keep from adding my own spew to the smell in the sand, and without another thought pressed the shell to the ground.

The sand shook beneath my hand.

Something pushed upwards under me and I fell backwards. From far away I heard a keening, a hellish wail like sharp nails dragged across a slate and the throat of a pig at the same time. From the pit I'd dug, a spray of black ichor erupted, and the sand we'd so carefully piled yesterday began to shift and sift away from the center of the mound.

The sound grew louder and then with a puff of expelled sand, exploded from a muffled wail to a clear siren at my face. She was alive again, but she wasn't remotely human. Her tentacles drew her from beneath the sand like wriggling, slapping snakes.

I rolled away from the mound as the first gray octopus-like tentacle lifted from where I'd expected her gorgeously tan arm to be, and slapped against the sliding sand. Then another snaked to the surface, then three more, and five.

She screamed and screamed from five purpled beaks set below dozens of spider-black eyes as she came to ground, and I could see the reason. Below her enraged mouths was a blackened, shriveled stump, and from it, in sync with her screams, pumped the stinking black blood, staining the sand.

Tears came to my eyes, as I watched her writhe in pain, jabbering and screeching from all of her mouths and using several of her arms to try to stem the flow of her blood. As she fully emerged from the pit, I saw that her skin was a delicate gray sheath that looked as if it would barely be able to hold in the long coils of intestinal tubes and shuddering organs within. But as she tumbled across the sand in horrible, audible agony, the vellum-thin skin cracked and blistered quickly in the Miami sun, and her elastic arms brushed and beat at her segmented body. One of her sucker-pod fingers split off as she slapped the top of her bulbous head and in seconds another stream of runny tar stained the sand from the broken appendage.

I had injured her before, by not using the shell. Now I had sealed her death by forcing her to ground half-formed. She was burning away.

"I'm sorry," I whispered. "God, I'm so sorry."

She screamed again, an elephantine bellow, stepped up in pitch, and swiveled towards me as I spoke. She bled from all her arms now, and the skin on her head seemed to be sinking inward. But still she moved towards my voice, dragging her disintegrating body at me with definite unfriendly intent.

I rolled as a tentacle slapped the sand where I'd been seconds before. It broke off and lay there on the ground, a bubbling, fishy mass of gray and black. I didn't stick around to watch, but rolled out of the way of another grasping sucker pod and then half-ran, half-crawled out of her reach.

Her cries had been deafening, but as I turned back from what seemed a safe distance, I realized they were lessening. She no longer moved forward, and not all of her beaks were opening to cry. Only three of her arms were raising and falling, trying to drag her bulk forward. Then only two. As I began to move back towards her, the last arm fell to the sand, and one mouth feebly keened, a thin, heart-wrenching wail.

I knelt nearby, and staring into several of her lidless, black marble eyes, I apologized again.

"I never meant to hurt you," I said.

She cried.

As did I. She was burning away in the sun, and sorry or not, it was my fault. I had betrayed her, betrayed my wife with her...

"I'm sorry."

It wasn't enough.

"Starrrr!"

I heard the cry behind me and knew its owner.

The boy grabbed my shoulder and shook me.

"Star? *Must* use star! No, no no!"

He was crying now, and threw himself down in front of the creature.

She seemed to respond to him, her tea-kettle cry settling to a quieter hiss.

The boy reached out and touched one of her beaks, and then turned to shoot me a black stare.

"All gone," he said, and pointed at the other mounds. "No more much fun."

The creature went quiet as he stroked its mouth, and settled farther into the earth.

He stood up and walked over to the demolished mound that she'd exploded out of. In a second, he'd found the shell and shook it at me.

"No more star. No more change. No more."

He shoved it in my face and then stuffed it back into his own pocket.

The creature was now little more than a black bubbling stain on the sand. I tried to put my hand on the boy's shoulder, but he shook me off.

"Go," he said, choking on his grief. "Find your own."

I backed away, thinking of the beauty beneath the sand, of the boy I'd shared her with. Of the boy I'd stolen her from.

Forever.

Thinking of how I'd found perfection, and then ruined it. Thinking of how I would feel if someone had done that to me. I stared at the pale band of skin on my left hand. The cruelest part was, I already had my own. I didn't need to find it.

I didn't know what she was, or how he'd found her or what the shell was. But as the boy dwindled to a brown speck in the distance, my feet began moving faster and faster. I had to get home. Before someone or something else got there and ruined it for me. I already had found my own.

I began to run. I hoped I wasn't too late.

MY AIM IS TRUE

ALONE, HE WATCHES. Every morning, his eyes stare out through that wide pane of glass, waiting for me.

Fearing me.

Wanting me.

His vigilance seems never-ending. Every day, every night, he stares out from the soft cushions and artificial warmth of his living room, trying unsuccessfully to fathom the hidden places from his protected vantage. Once he did catch a glimpse of me, and as his heart triple-knocked in unwound tremors, his coffee slopped in rich oily stains on the back of his couch. He shivered, and swore, and settled back to staring through the window. Since then, I've been more careful.

We have spent a lifetime watching for the other.

Every day, the hours slip by and his eyes search the trees across the road, peer suspiciously at the cars coasting past. Has that Chevrolet been down this road before? Has it been down once too often? Is the dark shadow of that driver me?

He stretches across the back of the couch at noon like a cat in the sun, letting the heat seep into his skin day after day. He sleeps there in the shadows of midnight, letting the chilly light of the moon steal that heat back, degree by blue degree. He rarely leaves the safety of his haven. He rarely tastes the winter in the breeze, or the summer in the rain.

Today is different.

Today he lets his guard down, and steps away from the glass. He takes a walk through the hidden path just outside his tiny house. It's overgrown from disuse with aging thistles and white-dotted stalks of Queen Anne's Lace, but I slip from my place in the forest across the rutted road from his couch, and push through the brush to follow.

Something snaps and rattles loudly and I stop, furious that my cover may have slipped, that the noise may have alerted him and he may have seen me. But through the brown leaves of last year's uncut grass, I see he is walking still, down the long, thin stretch of unkempt lawn.

I stoop to find the cause of the alert, and find it crushed beneath my foot. Orange and faded, handle snapped and missing. A child's rattle. The inner beads have rolled and scattered in the dirt.

I move on, past the rusted tricycle and the muddy, single shoe of a roller skate missing its back wheel. The tattered pages of yellowed magazines cling to the bushes on the side of the yard, but despite the holes and rips and weathered fading, I can still make out the alluring contour of a bare breast on one page, a seductively curved thigh on another. A pile of broken beer bottles glitters in the dirt nearby.

I've lost him now, and step up my pace, leaving the weeded path near the house and stepping into the open expanse of his backyard. The ground is littered with broken glass, dented hubcaps, rusty nails and faded wrappers between the hoary tufts of sickly broadleaf. Dandelions sprout in proud distain between stretched and twisted condoms; ants scuttle over cigarette butts, leaving sticky wads of long—lost gum to feast on mounds of gray, matted fur. I stop at one shapeless mound momentarily to consider, but can't tell from the remains whether it was dog or cat. In the end, I suppose, it doesn't matter.

I press on, and pass the graying wood shed where he spent many hours at tool craft in his middle years. A two-legged table leans against its wall, and I wonder which holds which up—the shed, or the table. A paint can is tipped over on the ground just beyond, spatters of grayed tint leaking in a hardened mold on the ground.

Just beyond the shed, I see that he has strayed from the narrow confines of the yard. A ripped shred of his T-shirt hangs from the bramble bush that borders his lot. A hank of graying hair shivers faintly, like a spider's web from the twist of another barbed branch. I follow his leavings into the scrub, and something glitters on the ground in a shaft of late-afternoon sun. A gold band. His wedding ring. I slip it into my pocket; he'll want it back.

Through the thorns and treacherous bog land I follow, weaving in and out of sun and dark like a prayer. And then I see him at last, far ahead and getting farther. He's running now. He must know I'm here.

Somehow he's slipped back onto that thankless plot of earth he's called home for most of his life, and I follow, never losing sight of the glint of dying sun on his balding pate. I can hear him breathing hard now, and just steps away, he sinks to the earth at the bank of the river. He falls on all fours and stares at his reflection in the water. His eyes are dark pits in the folds of age that have turned his once hard, tanned brow to hoary ravines. His tears slip into the river's current like a rain of broken promises and lost dreams. He doesn't even stir when my reflection joins his in the chocolate murk of the river.

"Already?" he asks quietly, and I nod.

"I should have done more," he whispers, rolling an old, well-chewed bone between his fingers. "Explored. Tried. Gone outside."

Again, I nod, and bend to kiss him.

He shivers in surprise, but accepts my solace. I slip the ring back on his finger, and he begins to cry.

"It's time," I say.

It's all I ever say.

This time he nods, and hangs his head in offering.

Pushing back my cowl to ensure my aim is true, I raise the ancient scythe high enough to touch the moon and then bring it crashing back to earth, sending his wrinkled head rolling to the edge of the river. The boatman will be by soon, but I don't wait.

Our paths always lead to this, but rarely cross. I have many more barren yards to walk.

FISH BAIT

"NOT THE BEST stuffed fish I've ever seen," Wayne ventured, staring up at the five-foot-long trophy on the bar's wall.

"You got that right," whispered Terry, who raised an eyebrow in lieu of pointing upward. "It's some kind of small shark, right? They fuckin' nailed it to the damn wall!"

While normally a mounted fish had an almost plastic, fake sheen to it thanks to the preservatives the taxidermists used, this one's skin was marred by an array of ragged, uneven scars. The silver of its belly, interrupted by the rusty head of a nail, shaded into a deeper hue at its top fin, where another nail head intruded. Its whole form was wrinkled, shriveled. Worst was the head. An empty, desiccated eye socket topped a gasping mouth that looked poised to snap with a row of twisted, yellowing teeth.

"Hope the beer's a bit more appetizing," Wayne agreed. "Though I suppose anything'd taste good at this point." He shrugged off a backpack and nodded toward the bar.

"What do you want?"

Wayne and Terry had been hiking and camping in the back end of the Rockies for the past five days. They'd left their car with an old friend of Wayne's in Estes Park and trudged immediately off-road through the deep woods of the national park system with the intent of getting as far from civilization as possible. They took a bag of beef jerky, some canned beans, and an illegal handgun to hopefully add some game to their diet. They had no jobs and figured to return to civilization only when hunger drove them to a road to hitchhike back to their ride. Terry had hoped they might disappear for most of the summer.

"Whatever's on tap," Terry said. He scratched idly at the growing black stubble curling across his cheek.

Wayne nodded and walked across the stained wood floor to the bar. A dirty-blonde bartendress in red plastic glasses, who apparently had an issue with underwear (as in, it was obvious that she wasn't wearing any), nodded at him and bent over to grab two glasses.

Terry could see the blur of tattoos beneath the edge of her stained, white, ribbed tank top as she turned. He wondered how her faded khaki shorts stayed up. He had seen the triangular edge of her hips when she faced them, and the pants barely hung off her ass when she bent. He wasn't surprised to see Wayne try to score small talk with her while she filled the glasses at the tap.

As he turned to carry the two glasses back to the stools of their table, the bass pound of Heart's "Barracuda" segued to Seger, and Terry found himself humming along to a life-on-the-road song. He was liking this bar already.

They'd been camping just a few yards away from a small gravel road the past two nights, not realizing how close they were to a town, in the dark mesh of branches and brush. The trudge of their boots across the rocky ground, the whisper of the wind through the cathedral of pines, and the steady hiss of a nearby mountain-runoff stream were all they heard. But this morning they'd stumbled across the gravel road, and Wayne had suggested following it downhill a while to see where it led. After only three long curves, they'd found themselves entering the town of Winston, population fifty-seven, according to the faded wooden sign.

The town seemingly consisted of a bar, a three-aisle grocery, a handful of scattered shacks, and a tin silo that was apparently a nondenominational church (it bore no name, but a silver cross dominated the air above its silver doorway).

"I'm not impressed," Wayne had said as they stood at the mouth of the town, sizing it up.

"Well, we can at least restock and grab a beer," Terry answered, nodding at the neon Coors sign just a few meters and three decaying buildings away.

"I suppose."

They'd passed the tin church and what appeared to be a private house before stepping up the wood-plank steps to enter the bar. A sign above the door labeled it as *Carioca Morte*.

"I hope that means death to karaoke." Wayne had grinned.

"Whatever," Terry said. "As long as they have beer. I can't believe we forgot to pack alcohol."

"Where there is Coors, there is a hangover," promised Wayne, and they pulled open the rough-hewn wooden handle of the bar door.

They were well on their way to hangovers two hours and four beers later. While they'd been sitting, the bar had begun to fill with a strange mix of overalled rancher types and tattooed, punkish youth. As a band began to set up a xylophone and assorted guitars and amps in the corner, the loosely clad bartendress slipped out from behind the bar to sidle over to their table, tanned belly swaying ever so slightly as she walked. Terry smiled as he noted the blue-etched shark that threatened to swallow her bellybutton with its teeth.

"Hi there," she said, flashing a line of teeth beneath a face of pale freckles. "I'm Jasmine. Glad to see you boys in here tonight. I'm guessing you ain't from any place near."

When neither answered quickly, she offered, "Get you boys something from the kitchen?" She held up a small order notepad. Terry thought the edge of her chin looked as thin as a nail. He shrugged away the image of his tongue licking it.

"Can you get me a burger?" he hazarded, and Wayne took a sip of his beer before answering.

"Got a menu?"

"We can do burgers and dogs," she said. "And catch of the day is salmon. Cook fries it if you care. We don't print a menu. We just make what we got."

"Got any tilapia?" Wayne asked and grinned when she looked at him sidelong, confused.

"It's a fish," he offered. "How about some catfish?"

"Out," she answered. "Wanna try a bit of shark?"

"Ya got shark but not tilapia?" he teased. "You're not exactly sitting on the ocean. I think I'll stick with the land bound. Gimme a burger, grill the onions?"

She nodded and headed to the bar, where she spoke to another bartender, a man in a black-and-red-checked shirt. The man's face was long and marred with pockmarks and a patchy growth of beard. The arm of his shirt hung loosely on the left side. No hand protruded from its dangling sleeve. He disappeared through a door beneath the shelf of whiskey and vodka bottles.

The music had begun alternating between Woody Guthrie and Nine Inch Nails. Then some cow-punk band started in, an earthy female singer vouching psychotically, "I only love pieces of things that I hate."

"This place is weird," Wayne hazarded.

"Fuckin' A," Terry agreed. "We camp as far away as we can walk tonight, I'd say."

"We don't eat something soon, and I ain't gonna be walking past the church," Wayne said.

"Was thingin' the same thing," Terry slurred.

Both men leaned away from the table and their bottles of half-drank Coors and stared about the bar, noting the women with multiple piercings and deep-cut cleavage, and the men in worn jeans and T-shirts that boasted logos by Chevy, Harley, and lesser-known businesses. Terry focused in on a woman who kept her arm slung over the neck of a thin man in a faded blue button-down shirt. Her eyes seemed on fire, glinting with humor and energy, as she jabbered away at the table next to them, occasionally pressing an open palm to her electric bright T-shirt. *Eat me*, it said in bold black letters. *I'm part of an unbalanced nutritional diet.*

The B-52s warbling about a "Rock Lobster" abruptly stopped mid-song, and a swarthy man with a peg leg stepped to the mic and said something in Spanish. Several in the crowd laughed at whatever joke he'd told.

"Hello," he said, switching to English. "Welcome, friends."

Terry thought his black eyes were staring straight at them. "My name is Petey, and we'll be playing for you tonight. Just like we do every night." He chuckled to himself then, white teeth flashing in the dimming light.

The bandleader nodded and the drummer took brush to snare as a white-haired man began to plink out a Cajun-sounding melody on the xylophone. Terry noticed a jagged scar down the center of his forehead that led to a misshapen blob. Half his nose was missing. *This is a band that's seen the low side of down*, he thought.

Not too much later, Jasmine reappeared at their table, tummy provocatively displayed as she balanced two plates. Steam rose from piles of fries and two bun-clad burgers.

"Eat up," she announced and slid the plates to the table. "Get you boys anything else?"

"Naw," Wayne drawled, imitating her accent. "Not unless you're on the menu."

"Special of the night," she returned. "Only it's not night yet. You'll have to stick around and see." She winked and pulled an unlit cigarette from behind her ear. Wayne laughed.

"We got a good show tonight," she offered. "You oughta stick around." She pointed the unlit smoke at the sign over the door at the back of the room. It was a simple poster, black on white. Its text offered little, simply boasting *Carioca Fish Bait Fridays. No deposits, no returns. 7 p.m.*

"What, you have some kind of bottle contest here tonight?" Wayne asked.

"No, it's more of a game," she said, winking a wide, blue eye. "And we take bets on the winner."

"What kind of game?" Terry asked. "Chance? Betting? Cards?"

"Yes," Jasmine said, twisting a kinked strand of wild honey hair between her fingers. She gave them a friendly, freckled grin. "All of the above. I'll let you know when they start."

Then she turned and wove through the growing crowd back to the bar.

"What the fuck?" Terry grumbled.

"Yes," Wayne said. "The operative word is fuck."

"Get over it." Terry shook his head. "The looks of that... you'd be going where every man has gone before."

"I may not have packed heavy," Wayne said, "but I did pack protection."

Terry rolled his eyes. "What, you were hoping I'd bend over one night?"

"Naw, I figured you'd bend over in the morning!"

Terry threw a french fry at him. "Get over it. We need to head outta here and set up camp for the night."

"Just eat your burger. We'll be fine."

"I'd suggest you eat your burger," Terry said. "Cuz you ain't gonna be eatin' her."

Wayne just grinned and took a large bite out of his bun. A splat of grease swam across his plate.

"We'll see."

The two ate in silence for a while as the band moved from New Orleans jazz to a strange Mexican-sounding rhythm with a psychedelic twang.

Behind the bar, Jasmine was talking animatedly with the other bartender, waving around her still-unlit cigarette and then tapping it against the bar in a strangely nervous habit. Every now and then she'd lift it to her lips and reach for a lighter, but she always dropped the lighter back to the bar and then continued to tap the unlit tobacco in an unheard drumbeat.

Someone nearby tossed her a pack of matches and yelled, "Consummate the damn relationship with that thing, already!"

Grinning, she struck a match and lit up. But after just a couple puffs, she put the smoke back out and slipped from behind the bar.

"Getcha another?" Jasmine said, suddenly at their table again. Terry raised an eyebrow in surprise as she put a warm hand on his shoulder.

"Next round's on the house," she said, amber eyes twinkling. "You boys put plenty in the kitty for tonight, if you know what I mean."

Wayne grinned, made an inappropriate comment about kitties, and agreed to another round as Terry pinched his midsection, trying to unobtrusively clear his head. The pinch cleared the fuzziness for a moment, but he wondered if he could really soak down one more and still manage to walk back into the wilderness and stake up a tent.

"Getting late," he ventured as Jasmine's tattoos swayed their way back to the bar.

"Hmm." Wayne nodded, taking another bit of his thick burger. "We may not need to camp tonight."

"Keep dreamin'."

"From dreams are memories made."

"You're crazy, you know that?"

"No more than you. Fuck, the whole reason we're out here is that you couldn't keep your little piece of ass happy."

With that comment, Terry knew Wayne was officially drunk, but it hurt nevertheless. After his breakup with Rochelle, he'd pretty much gone the nose-dive route, at least by the judgment of society. After sulking for weeks and getting written up at work, to the point of being put on a thirty-day probation after nine years of service, he'd cashed it all in and walked away. As it turned out, Wayne had just gotten fired from the lumberyard for insubordination ("All I did was pee on his shoes," he'd complained) and had no prospects himself. So the two had emptied their apartments, thrown their belongings into a cheap storage cubicle, and hit the road.

"Who needs a roof when you have the national forest?" Wayne had said as they drove up the long, winding road into the mountains, weaving in and out of the snail-paced tourists.

"Not me," Terry had agreed less than a week ago.

"You boys gonna play?" Jasmine asked, returning with two mugs of amber.

"What's the game?" Wayne asked.

"Fish bait," she said.

"That's you, right?" Wayne grinned. Terry groaned, waiting for the sound of a slap. But the waitress didn't miss a beat.

"Nope," she said, adding with exaggerated sultriness, "I hate getting wet. But I like to watch."

"You're killing me," Wayne laughed. "So what's the game?"

"It's a floor game," she said, pointing through the doorway at the back of the bar. "We've got a floor laid out with a grid. Two players try to stake out their territory by placing little black rocks on the corners with each turn."

"Can you put the rocks anywhere?" Terry asked.

"Exactly. But once they're down, you can't move them. The goal is for one player to completely capture the board by surrounding and locking up territory."

"Kind of like a human version of Go." Terry smiled. Jasmine looked blank.

"It's an ancient Oriental board game," he explained.

She shrugged. "The loser gets a dunk in the tank out back."

"What does the winner get," Wayne asked.

"A date with me, if he's good." She winked. "You boys in?"

Terry started to decline, but Wayne cut him off.

"Wouldn't miss it. When does it start?"

From the bar came an awful clanging. Terry looked up and saw the bartender bashing a spoon against a cowbell with his one good arm.

"Right now," she said. "C'mon."

Wayne was out of his seat before Terry could say another word. Reluctantly, he slid off his stool and followed the two of them—and most of the other patrons—into the back room.

The Fish Bait room looked much like the outer area of the bar, only there was no bar. The rough-hewn plank floor was painted in an interconnecting lattice of black lines laid out in a square grid nine rows deep and nine rows across. The walls were paneled in rough, unfinished pine and bare, except for a handful of stuffed fish, which were nailed to the far wall in descending size. Terry thought of a cartoon he'd once seen where a minnow was being eaten by a fish that was about to be snapped up by a shark, which didn't notice the whale looming behind it. The room stank of brine and rotting fish.

The crowd lined up along the walls, and the one-handed bartender stepped into the center of the room.

"All right then," he yelled. "My name's Bruce, as ya'll know, but we got us a couple a' newcomers, so let's make 'em feel welcome and let 'em in on a little game of Fish Bait, eh? Do we have any volunteers for t'night?"

The bartender pushed a low-seated pair of glasses back up his nose, scanned the room for the briefest time, and then shook his head.

"Tell you what, let's keep the odds fair here and let these two gentlemen try a game betwixt the two of them. C'mon out here, boys, and let me teach ya how it's done."

Terry held up his hand to decline, but Wayne stepped instantly onto the game field.

"We got us a shy one." Bruce grinned, looking directly at Terry. "Watch us a bit," he said. "Then you can play the winner.

Jasmine, bring us the pieces."

Jasmine pushed through the crowd to a wooden box in the back of the room and returned lugging two nets. One held what appeared to be a couple dozen starfish, while the other was filled with dark green turtle shells.

"Goal is simple," he explained, handing the turtle bag to Wayne and keeping the starfish for himself. Jasmine uncinched the netting for him, and Terry couldn't help but admire the curve of her barely hidden ass as she crouched. He still couldn't make out what it was, but the dark sketch of something intricate seemed to rise from below her waistband. Its outline just missed touching the edge of her well-worn shirt. He could almost see her skin through patches of the tight shirt.

"Place a piece on any line intersection," Bruce explained. "I'll do the same. It won't seem like much at first, but after a while you'll see that we're fighting to control the board. Whoever does that and blocks out the other player until there are no more moves wins."

"You're on," Wayne said. He dropped his first turtle to the grid with a confident grin.

"We'll make this a practice round," Bruce said and placed his starfish close to a corner.

Terry watched and nodded at the deceptive simplicity of the game. He saw how Wayne plotted to cut off the bartender's pieces and soon decided that unless the one-armed man was really stupid, he was angling to lose. After only fifteen minutes the game was decided.

"Hey, hey!" Wayne yelled and came over to high-five Terry. Then he stepped up to Jasmine.

"So…do I get that date now?" he prodded.

Her eyes narrowed, but the corners of her lips lifted. She pulled a cigarette from her mouth and blew a cloud of smoke into his face. This time the smoke was lit.

"That was a practice round. See if you can beat your friend for the real thing."

She reached down and picked up a turtle shell, shoving it into his hands.

Wayne quickly dragged Terry onto the playing field, and Bruce handed over his bag of starfish.

"Loser of this round goes in the tank," the bartender warned.

"Fish bait," the crowd yelled.

Something in Terry's stomach clenched. A grizzled old man with a cane and a black eye-patch leaned forward and whispered something in Wayne's ear.

Wayne smiled and nodded, looking up at Terry. "Gonna feed you to the fish," he threatened.

"Keep thinking with your worm, and it's going to get bit off," Terry retorted and placed his first piece.

This time the game seemed to go longer. Terry struggled to stop the alcohol from clouding his mind. He pinched his side again and again, willing the pain to clear his head. He was determined not to let Wayne win, if for no other reason than because he'd forced him into this. Wayne always got the girl, and this time Terry aimed if not to get her, to at least stop Wayne from going there.

He drew a diagonal line across the board, and Wayne placed a series of disconnected turtle shells. But when they started filling in the holes, for a while it looked like Wayne had the game. At one point he cut off four of Terry's starfish, and the crowd drew a collective breath. "Fish bait," someone squealed. There was laughter.

But Terry had grown up playing chess, and this little diversion was something he'd counted on. This was a more fluid game than chess, but he was working toward a strategy; he had tried to focus Wayne on the small part of the map while he angled his attack. He ignored the loss of pieces and closed a line across the upper center of the grid.

"Give up," Wayne enthused, closing another gap and missing the larger strategy that was about to encircle his pieces.

"Go fish," Terry answered and dropped the last piece of his trap in place.

"No fuckin' way!"

"Gotcha." Terry grinned. Behind them the crowd began to chant.

"Fish bait. Fish bait. Fish bait!"

A heavyset man with a white goatee and piercing blue eyes stepped out of the crowd and put a hand on Wayne's shoulder. He pushed him a step forward and pointed.

"Time to take a dip," he said. His voice was low, but Terry could still hear it above the crowd's chanting. "Take a walk through that door."

The crowd surged forward onto the playing field. Bruce and the white-goateed man began to push Wayne forward.

"All right, all right!" he yelled, shrugging off their hands. "I'll take my punishment." Then he turned to Terry, a flare of anger lighting his eyes.

"Don't think I won't get you back for this," he hissed. He'd always been a sore loser when it came to women.

Jasmine slipped past Terry then and put her arm around Wayne's shoulders.

"I'll dry you off," she promised.

As she went by, Terry froze when he finally got a good look at the tattoo on her back. It was an octopus. But that wasn't what made him freeze. The reason he hadn't been able to make it out from a distance was because it was so twisted. It writhed in coils and strange twists across her lower back, one tentacle reaching its sucker cups toward the crack of her ass, another testing its way around her side, as if in search of her belly. And the reason it was so twisted was that it had been drawn to hide the scars.

The teeth marks.

Wayne's frown slipped away with Jasmine's promise, and he started through the doorway to the dunking tank.

Terry looked from the ragged pink lines of scar tissue across Jasmine's back to Bruce, the one-armed bartender and the one-eyed old man next to him. He finally noticed that most of the people in the bar seemed to bear the track marks of life-threatening accidents. An Indian man shook his head as if in ecstasy, bobbing to a beat that no one else could hear. Not surprising, since he was missing an ear—and a quarter of his skull.

Petey, the bandleader, hobbled into the midst of the crowd on his one leg, the wooden stump of his fake foot clomping louder than the growing chants of "Fish bait."

A woman in a blue tank top with frizzy brown hair pushed past Terry to be in the front of the spectators. When her left boob crushed warmly against his arm, he turned to look at her and saw the right half of her shirt hung loosely, with no flesh to hold it up.

There was almost nobody here, he realized, who wasn't visibly, horribly disfigured. Something was very wrong in Winston.

"Wayne, don't," he suddenly screamed and pushed past the tank-top woman and the peg-legged bandleader.

But Wayne had stepped through the dark doorway.

"Keep going," Bruce advised and put his hand on a switch at the side of the door.

"Is there a light in here?" Wayne called, and the bartender threw the switch.

The room came to life, and Terry could now see that Wayne stood at the end of a diving board. A plank of wood extended out over a vast pool of water. Lights blazed down from the unfinished beams of the ceiling spotlighting blue water. Terry pushed Jasmine out of the way and tried to see better. He couldn't tell how deep it was, but the room looked like a poor man's gymnasium. A narrow wooden walkway led around the long stretch of water. Somewhere a pump hummed.

Here was where the smell he'd noticed in the game room came from. That room had smelled, but this room stank. Of fish.

Rotting fish.

"Wayne, don't," he said again, pushing past the bartender to stand alone in the doorway.

"I'm going in," Wayne said, holding his nose and dramatically waving with his one free hand as he fell backwards into the pool.

Two shadows darted out of the corners of the tank before Wayne even hit the water.

"Oh my God," Terry whispered.

"Fish bait!" roared the crowd, who had filed around Terry to stand on opposite sides of the plank along the narrow walkway surrounding the tank.

He stood at the safe edge of the plank, just inside the room, and watched as the two dark shapes shot forward, the edge of one telltale fin breaking the top of the water just as Wayne's face disappeared beneath the blue. His eyes were closed as he sank toward the bottom of the pool, holding his nose. But even from where he stood, Terry could see them pop open wide as the shapes converged on the bait. Wayne thrashed then, and his hand left his nose as he screamed beneath the water and tried to pull himself with one wild arm to the surface. Something dark colored the water where his other arm had been seconds before.

Terry could see the pale fingers of a hand disappear down the maw of one monstrous gray mouth. "Oh God, no," he cried, falling to his knees at the edge of the plank in time to see the other shark bite down on Wayne's midsection. The water bloomed bright in blood, and for a moment Terry couldn't see a thing. Then the sharks wrestled the body to a clearer section of water, and he saw the winding coil of his friend's guts unfurl as one hungry fish snapped at the delicate flesh and pulled.

"Fish bait!" roared the mangled crowd in appreciation.

Wayne's head was shaking from side to side, his mouth wide and shrieking bubbles. But all Terry could hear was the crowd and the splash of shark tails as the hungry creatures breached the water and angled down for another bite.

In moments the water was still. Terry was weeping, utterly in shock, unable to move.

Someone touched his shoulder. He looked up into the unnaturally bright eyes of the goateed man.

"Sorry about that, son. They've really grown up, it seems. Used to be they just got a piece of you, not the whole package."

Jasmine bent down to wipe the hair and tears from his eyes.

"I'm glad it was him and not you," she said. "You're a pretty good player. Wanna go another round? I'm sure someone will want to take you on, and since they've had dinner, the loser oughta be able to get dunked without losing a limb."

"Get the fuck away from me, you freak!" Terry screamed and pushed her back.

"What is with you people?" he yelled, looking at the parade of limbless, scarred locals lined up around the pool. Until his outburst, some had been clapping and cheering. "How can you do this to someone?"

"Not much else to do out here." Bruce shrugged. "Passes the time."

"Pass this, you fuck," Terry screamed and barreled into the man, forcing him three steps down the plank. The bartender flailed for balance, reaching for the edge of the plank with the ghost of his hand and only catching the edge of it with the smooth scar of his stump as he tumbled headfirst into the bloody soup.

Goatee man leapt forward and punched Terry square in the face. The pain arced behind his eyes like a white-hot poker.

"You push someone in, you go in yourself," his deathly voice boomed across the pool.

Terry fell backwards, slamming his head against the wood. He started to slip off the side but caught the edge of the plank with a foot as he struggled to clear the red stars from his eyes. His nose felt on fire, and his head pounded with heat. A heavy foot stomped on his calf and Terry screamed, kicking back blindly at his opponent, who only took the opportunity to kick him again.

"Give it to 'im, Gordon," someone yelled. "Fish bait!"

He began to slide off the plank and grappled frantically with both hands and a foot to hold on. Below him he saw the sharks circling the bartender, who flailed about with purpose. Bruce rounded on the sharks and kept them at bay with a series of well-aimed underwater kicks and punches. Some of the crowd had gathered at the point closest to him and urged him on, calling to him and holding out their hands. Terry also caught a glimpse of Wayne beneath the water, eyes and mouth wide open, his face miraculously unharmed. The rest of him looked as raw and torn as if he'd been chain-sawed.

Then another kick sent his feet off the plank, and Terry dangled dangerously from his fingertips, his feet beneath the water.

Gordon's voice boomed again. "Shoulda taken your winnings and gone."

A heel ground into his left hand, and Terry screamed, yanking it away. But before the big man could crush his remaining grip, Terry pulled himself up as hard as he could with his remaining arm and managed to swing a leg back up to the board.

"No you don't," Gordon laughed, but Terry was fast.

He reached with both hands around the wood and pulled, levering himself back up to the topside of the board. As the burly man reached down to grab him and throw him off, Terry struck. He kicked as hard as he could, catching the man right in the kneecaps and then shimmying backwards toward the game room as Gordon yelled in agony and fell to a crouch.

Petey came from somewhere and tried to stop him, but Terry kneed him in the balls, collapsing the wiry bandleader awkwardly over his fake leg. He dove around the other doorway back into the bar, grabbed his backpack, and was almost out the door when Jasmine stepped in his way.

"Wait," she implored. "We could have fun. This'll blow over. Don't leave."

He shoved her back, but she grabbed a beer bottle from the bar and raised it over her head.

"Don't make me use this," she threatened. By now some of the rest of the crowd had piled back into the bar and were right behind her.

"I won't," he agreed, raising a hand in surrender before slumping his shoulders to let his pack rest on the floor. The Indian with the chunk missing from his head stepped toward them. Terry could see that whoever'd sewn him up had done a pretty poor job. His cheek and forehead were crisscrossed with leathery scars. He looked like Frankenstein's monster.

Terry lunged out with one foot, kicking the sultry waitress right in the shark tattoo above her belly button. She gasped and fell backwards, disrupting the gathering crowd and bowling over Frankenstein. Terry yanked the door open and dashed out into the night. He dug around in his pack as he ran down the gravel of the main street and found the cool butt of the pistol they'd packed to hunt with. He pulled it out, shoved it into his waistband, and dropped the pack so he could move faster. They were right behind him.

"Fish bait!" they screamed. "Come back, worm!"

He ducked off the road into the forest and lay down behind a bush, hardly daring to breathe as he heard the tromp of several feet crash by. Then he stood up and slipped back toward the road. He knew he'd never survive out here if he got lost in the woods. And before he left this town, he had a debt to settle.

Terry slipped up around the side of the bar and listened at the voices arguing within. From the woods he heard the call and response of his hunters.

He stepped up to the wood porch of the bar and went back inside. Jasmine, Petey, and Gordon looked up as he came in.

"Take a walk," Terry said and motioned toward the game room.

Gordon pointed at the swell of his knees. They'd had to cut off his pant legs and had been applying a towel filled with ice when he came in. "I ain't walking nowhere thanks to you."

"Help him," Terry said to the other two. "I mean it."

Petey got up and started toward Terry, who leveled the gun straight at his face. The bandleader thought better of the attempt and stopped. He helped Jasmine lever Gordon up.

"The others will be back here in a couple minutes to deal with you," the injured man warned, white goatee wagging like a tail.

"Won't matter," Terry said. He herded them back to the game room. "Walk the plank," he insisted.

"We won't all fit," Jasmine protested.

"Walk," he said and fired a shot at their feet. The sound was like an explosion, and the trio jumped forward as one. Two others were across the room, bandaging a wound on the bartender's half arm. They stood up.

"What're you thinkin'?" an older woman said, hands on her hips. "That man has got no chance against the sharks with those knees. That's not fair."

"It wasn't fair what you did to us," Terry said, turning back to Gordon. "Get in."

"No. You can shoot me if you want."

Jasmine tried to grab at Terry, but he swatted her away with the barrel of the gun, catching her on the side of the face. She went down hard and rolled off the plank to splash into the water.

"Now," he insisted. "Go now and I'll give you a chance."

Petey was crying. Terry aimed at his head, and the man lifted his fake leg over the edge and toppled in.

"Go."

Gordon was the last man left, but he wasn't standing. The big man began crawling toward Terry, pulling himself sideways to keep the weight on his hip instead of his knees. Terry aimed the gun and shot him in the thigh. Gordon screamed and grabbed at the wound. He rolled in agony, hit a swollen knee, and screamed again, and this time fell off the plank, making a satisfying splash.

The old woman was coming around the pool, and Terry aimed at her. "You too."

Bruce lay in the arms of another woman across the pool and didn't say a word as the old woman slid quietly into the water. Terry could hear someone crying.

The dark shapes came again from the corners, converging on the fresh bait. There was a scream, and a cherry bomb exploded in the water. And then another.

Terry stood and watched for a moment and then aimed his pistol at the thrashing, watery fight. He pulled the trigger once, and then again. And then twice more, for good measure.

Terry thought of the Fourth of July. The smell of gunpowder overpowered the stink of fish temporarily. As the echo of the shots faded, four bodies moved as one toward the edge of the pool. Two gray shapes drifted motionless.

"You killed them." The bartender's whisper could be heard from across the pool.

Terry left the room and grabbed Wayne's backpack from the bar. He risked a last glance back at the bloody pool, where Jasmine clutched a wounded leg and the other two were trying to pull Gordon's bulk from the water.

"Fish bait," he yelled. He didn't realize that he was crying.

Then he slipped out of the bar and ran down the gravel road until the first rays of dawn shone on the horizon and he couldn't run anymore. He yearned to see the headlights of a car, to hear the welcoming sounds of an FM radio. But the road was empty, and the woods remained still around him. In his head he only saw the face of his friend, wide-eyed and dying beneath the water. He only heard two words, repeating over and over and over.

"Fish bait."

CAMILLE SMILED

CAMILLE SMILED. I thought so, anyway.

And then she sighed.

It was faint, light as baby's breath. But I swear I heard it.

I stroked a wisp of black hair from the marble-smooth slope of her forehead.

"Wake up, honey," I whispered. "Talk to me, baby."

It had been days since I'd last heard her voice, and the house felt deadly still without the sparkling tinkle of her laughter. As if the whole world was holding its breath, waiting. I didn't know if I could stand another day of it.

Hour after hour I'd waited by her bedside, pacing, praying, bending to listen for her heart at her breast, holding a mirror to her lips to see if she breathed. I straightened the handwoven necklace that voodoo queen Madame Trevail had sold me, down in her tiny shop hidden near the French Quarter. I centered its small pouch of leaves and clippings and extracts of God only knew what until it rested like a teabag in the small of her neck. Then I reconsidered and moved it out of that pale hollow, thinking that its miniscule weight might choke her tiny throat as it rested in that most delicate of settings.

"Wake up," I begged again, and stared at her tiny frame, so still and frail there on the bed. She wore her finest dress, a yellow chiffon summery thing that my wife Annabel had picked. "It brings out her eyes," she'd said.

If only I could see those eyes now. It seemed like forever since they'd gazed up at me, so wide and blue, and turned my scolds to dust. She had one of those faces, one of those looks, that melted any offense. She was going to bring a lot of men to their knees someday, I knew.

"Jack, come to bed," a voice spoke behind me.

I turned and Anna was there in the doorframe, her eyes red and swollen, her fist stifling a yawn.

"She sighed," I explained.

"She didn't." Anna's voice sounded brittle as spun glass.

"She did, I heard her. She'll wake soon, I know it."

Anna cried, a low stifled moan, and I went to her. This was a pain we shared, a fear we couldn't live with. I couldn't bear to see her suffer, though I felt the same empty pit in my soul. I pulled her close, cushioning her head to my shoulder.

"Believe, Anna," I whispered through the tangled web of her raven hair, so like her daughter's.

She pushed away.

"Believe?" she hissed, shoving again at my shoulders. I retreated toward the bed but she kept coming.

"Believe in what?" she yelled. "Our daughter is not going to wake up again, why can't you understand that?"

She stomped to the bed and grabbed Camille's dress with both hands. The sound of ripping fabric filled the room and Anna turned to me with the shredded lemon chiffon still gripped in her hands.

"Look at her," she cried, pointing at my eight-year-old daughter's undeveloped chest. The porcelain-white skin was hideously broken by accusing blushes of purple and midnight blue. Black, oozing stitches held my daughter's chest together from the ruin that the fender of an '87 Ford had made of it. My daughter would never grow up to wow the boys with her bosom. She would never have one.

"Cammy is dead, Jack," Anna wailed. "When are you going to accept it? When are you going to take her back to the cemetery, where she belongs?"

Her voice had risen to a dangerous boiling-tea pitch.

"I can't stand to see her anymore," she cried, laying her face on the ugly dark crosshatching of Camille's chest. "I can't stand to see you like this anymore."

"Anna," I began. She shrugged off my hand and rushed from the room.

I turned back to Camille, and tried to draw the shreds of her dress back to a seemly covering.

"Wake up, baby," I said for the thousandth time. I thought I saw her eyelids crease, just slightly and I leaned forward, anxious.

Her eyes opened.

Maybe it was the press of Anna's touch, or her tears or the

violence of her actions. Maybe the voodoo sachet I'd hocked my second car to obtain had just taken its time. But for the first time in days, my baby's beautiful crystal-blue eyes stared up out of that tiny angel face and into mine. Only they seemed dulled, lacking that ocean-deep warmth I remembered.

"Cammy?" I said, bending to hug her.

She clubbed me in the side of the head with her fist.

"Huh?" I gulped and fell to the floor, more out of surprise than hurt.

Camille sat up in her bed, and looked down at me on the floor. Her expression remained blank.

"Honey?" I said, rubbing my ear. I could feel the heat of swelling as a flood of blood rushed through my earlobe. It felt like a bee sting.

Camille lifted a foot over the edge of the mattress, and then stood, walking slowly, stiffly past me to her dresser. She stood there staring at the mirror and didn't move. I thought she was looking at her face, but then as I eased off the floor, I saw that her finger was tracing the long jagged paths stitched into her chest. Her skin shone with the glossy smear of something liquid, something leaking, where her finger had passed.

"It will all be okay now," I said. She leaned in toward the mirror, and then turned. A split second later I realized that it might not all be okay.

I barely saw her arm in the air before her pet rock caught me right between the eyes with the force of a major league fastball.

When my vision cleared, she was gone. My head was aching, but my heart felt worse. Something had gone horribly wrong. My beautiful daughter, the little flower who meant more to me than life, would never have hurt a fly, let alone her daddy. But her first two actions upon waking from a sleep deeper than death were to try to hurt me.

Bad.

I gingerly probed the thick bump on my forehead.

Was my daughter dangerous?

Was my daughter alive?

A ragged blade of ice serrated my brain when I turned my head, but gritting my teeth, I grabbed hold of the mattress and pushed myself to my feet. Gingerly, ignoring the pain, I padded out of the room. I had to find Camille. Before she hurt herself.

Or someone else.

I pushed open the door to our bedroom, and saw the pale moon of Anna's cheek setting into the pillow. One hand grasped at my untenanted pillow, and her chest moved slowly, rhythmically. She was already asleep.

I pulled the door shut and took the stairs down to the front room, praying Cammy was still in the house.

And afraid to find her if she was.

The great room was all shadows and floating fear, and I forced myself to put one foot in front of the other to cross it. I had to get to the light switch, but what if my newly resurrected daughter came at me when I couldn't see her?

With each step, I paused to listen, but my heart's insistent pounding drowned out any ambient noise. The house seemed silent. I found the wall near the front door and slid my hand along the frame, looking for the switch plate. I could feel the draught of cold seeping in from outside through the seam in the doorframe, but it wasn't as cold as the ice in my belly. The hair on the back of my neck stood up, and I pushed my hand fast up the wall, at last connecting with the switch.

The light on the end table near our couch blazed on, blinding me for a moment. I turned and pressed my back to the door, ready for whatever might come at me.

But nothing did.

The room was empty, still. The morning newspaper still lay open on the center cushion of the couch, and the TV remote hung halfway off the coffee table, where I'd left it hours before.

Then I saw her.

Camille stood, unmoving, in the arch leading to the kitchen. Her eyes stared straight at me, yet she seemed unaware of anything. There was no recognition in her gaze. No life in her smile. She seemed like a living doll.

There was, however, a long silver carving knife in her hand. It was the knife I used to carve Thanksgiving turkeys, and it looked ludicrously large in her grip, its point just barely above the carpet as she held the shaft in her tiny hand. I knew exactly who and what it was meant for.

"Cammy," I said, trying without success to level the tremor in my voice. I had to be calm. She was just a child. My child. "Baby, what's the matter? Everything's okay now, you're with Mommy and Daddy again. I brought you back because I loved you."

She began to walk toward me then, placing one delicately sculpted foot in front of the other, her ghastly white toes glowing in contrast to the taupe of the carpet. She said nothing.

"Cammy," I tried again, trying to think of what would entice her. "Let Daddy…get you a nice bowl of ice cream. Does your tummy hurt?"

Her feet sped up and she was across the room, raising her arm with the clear intent to pin me with her blade to the door.

"Baby, stop," I begged, but she didn't.

As the knife flashed into motion, I acted, sliding down the door and throwing my body to the right. The knife clacked against the wood behind me. When I hit the floor in front of the end table, I rolled away, coming up in a crouch, ready to move again. She was already upon me, raising the knife for the kill.

"Cammy, no," I cried, and instead of rolling away from her, I launched myself *into* her, tackling her at the knees at the same time as I brought my palm up to grasp her thin forearm. She fell backwards with the unexpected slam of my weight, and the floor reverberated with the smack of her skull on the carpet. She didn't move.

I almost let go of her arm to cradle her head, parental concern overriding self-preservation, but Cammy didn't miss a trick. Her stillness had been a feint. The knife began to slice towards my throat as I hesitated, and I pushed away from her just in time. Something warm was suddenly dripping down my chest, but I didn't pause to look. She was already on her feet again, free, and coming towards me.

"Stop," I cried, putting the coffee table between us, and desperately looking for something I could use to hold her back, without hurting her.

She held no similar concern. Face blank of any emotion,

my little baby walked around the coffee table, knife raised high, ready to slice without remorse into her daddy.

I grabbed one of the couch cushions and thrust it out at her just as she struck.

"No," I yelled, and pushed the cushion—and Cammy—backwards until her feet tangled and she fell again. This time, her back slapped on the decorative oaken strip of the couch front and I heard something crack.

Then she was lying still again on the floor, eyes open, and still empty. This time, she stayed down.

The hall light flicked on and Anna appeared on the steps, one fist shoved into her teeth, stifling a yawn.

"What's going on down here?" she demanded, hand and yawn serving muffle her words.

I looked down at our baby lying on the floor, the knife lying just inches from her hand.

"It's Cammy," I said, still fighting for breath. "She's alive again."

Anna said nothing, but continued down the stairs until she was standing just a couple feet away. Her cheeks glistened in the dull orange light.

"She's dead, Jack."

"No, honey," I argued. "After you left, she woke up, and she punched me and then she ran away, so I came down here to find her and..."

"*Stop!*" Anna screamed. "Our daughter is fucking *dead*, Jack. She's dead, dead, *dead*. I don't know what you're doing down here with her body; I don't want to know. I can't stand this anymore. I can't stand you. Put her back upstairs. And tomorrow, you're taking her back to the cemetery. And I don't want to hear any more about your voodoo black magic bullshit. This is too much."

My wife ran up the stairs then, leaving me standing there, staring at the unmoving form that once was my baby, on the carpet.

"Cammy," I whispered, kneeling down next to her. But she didn't answer. The hair stood up on the back of my neck as cautiously, I touched her cheek, and felt the side of her neck. She was cold to my fingers. There was no pulse. After a moment, I traced the soft skin of her eyelids, and then pushed them closed. Slipping my hands beneath her neck and knees, I lifted my baby from the floor, and carried her back to her room.

She didn't move as we walked up the stairs, and didn't blink as I laid her once again upon her bed. There was nothing to show that, just minutes before, she'd been trying to stab my life from me.

I closed the bedroom door behind me, but didn't turn out the light. As I crawled into a bed gently shaking with the slowing sobs of my wife, I was trembling. I lay there for hours, listening to the subtle shifts and creaks as the house settled. I was waiting. I was anticipating the tiny footsteps in the hallway, ready for the slow creak of our bedroom door as it opened, revealing the form of my killer baby with the empty eyes and silver sharp blade.

It was a very long time before I fell asleep.

The sunlight hurt my eyes when I opened them. I blinked out a tear and reached out for Anna, but she wasn't there. The sheets were rumpled with the absence of her weight. The clock gleamed 8:14 in electric blue LED.

I pulled on my sweatpants and shambled into the hallway, hearing the sounds of breakfast echoing from the kitchen.

"Anna," I called, and my wife answered with more cheer than I'd heard from her in a week.

"Down here, hon," she said.

The air was alert with the smell of burning butter, and pancakes. I winced. Cammy's favorite food.

And when I stepped into the kitchen, I saw why.

Cammy was seated at the table, in her usual place. Anna looked up from the griddle and smiled. She finished flipping a cake and then met me at the doorway, kissing my cheek with a flutter.

"I'm sorry I doubted you, honey," she said. "I don't know how, I don't wanna know how, but she's back. Oh Jack, it's a miracle!"

I looked over to the table, and saw the same blank stare from my daughter that had haunted me the night before.

Or was it blank?

Was there just a hint of knowing there? A thinly veiled glint of malevolence?

"Anna, we have to talk," I said, reaching for her arm to pull her out of the kitchen.

But she slipped away with a giggle.

"Sit," she said. "Breakfast is served."

Reluctantly, I took my place at the table, and Anna came right behind me, a plate of steaming pancakes in her hand. She stabbed three with a fork and slid them to Camille's plate, and then did the same for her own before handing the rest of the platter to me.

"How are you feeling this morning, sweetheart?" I ventured.

Cammy didn't answer. Instead, she picked up the butter knife and held it poised, just over the top of her golden-brown cakes.

"No, baby, let me," Anna said, and pried the knife from her hand to cut the cakes up with deft precision.

As she did so, Camille slowly raised her head and met my eye. Her lips parted, just slightly, and it seemed that she gave the faintest hint of a grin. Then it was gone.

A shiver ran down my spine.

When Anna went to work on her own plate, our daughter sat still, unmoving.

"Aren't you hungry?" I ventured.

Anna reached out to stroke Camille's hair.

"She's still in shock, I think," she said. "She probably just isn't hungry."

"Not very talkative, either," I said.

Anna set her fork down with slow deliberation. When she looked at me, I could see the tears threatening in her eyes.

"Leave her alone," she hissed. "What did you expect from her? This is going to take time."

Then Anna forced a smile and ruffled Camille's hair again. "Try to eat something, sweetheart."

Camille didn't look at her plate. Her eyes remained pinned on mine. But slowly, her right hand lifted a fork, and stabbed a square of pancake sopping with maple syrup. She raised it to her mouth, pushed it between her lips, and swallowed. She repeated the act a second, and a third time, pushing the pancakes past her lips and gulping them down.

I never saw her chew.

After breakfast, I pulled Anna aside at the sink. Camille remained at the table, staring unmoving at the wall behind where I'd been sitting.

"Something didn't go right," I whispered in her ear. "Maybe it took too long to raise her, I don't know."

Anna grabbed the front of my jacket. "She was dead, Jack, what did you expect?"

"Just be careful today," I said. "When she woke up last night, she gave me this." I pointed to the bruise already well-formed on my forehead. "And then, before you came downstairs, she came after me with a knife."

Anna shot me a disgusted glance and shook her head sadly.

"I don't blame her. Go to work, Jack."

Not knowing quite what else to do, I did.

Over the next few days, Anna continued to work with Camille, coaxing her to eat, to dress, to talk. But while the child remained pliable, she also remained wooden. She only seemed to move when pushed to do so, and the light I remembered so well in her beautiful blue eyes remained dull.

She stared straight ahead at all times, unblinking.

I found myself avoiding her, sitting in the kitchen when she was on the couch, and vice versa.

"Go play with her," Anna insisted one night as I read the paper at the kitchen table. "You did this. You're the one who wanted her back. And you've done nothing but avoid her ever since she woke up."

There was nothing I could say to that. So I nodded, and went to sit in the front room. I put my arm around the bony shoulders of my dead daughter, and stared for a while at the TV with her. It might have helped if the set had been turned on.

We sat silent that way, her and I, for a long time, as Anna clattered about in the kitchen, cleaning up the remnants of dinner. She sounded abnormally loud, every drawer slamming hard, and every dish clattering on the counter. Then came a crash, glass breaking in the sink, and I heard Anna swear. The catch in her voice sounded dangerously close to hysteria.

"Are you okay?" I called out. "What broke?"

"Just a glass," she answered.

That's when I realized that Camille had turned her head. She was staring at me.

Just staring at the hairs on my neck, with the dogged, unwavering attention of a mounted deer head.

It was creepy. Goose bumps broke out on my arm, and I realized again how cool and clammy her neck felt against my skin. Cold as riverbed stone.

I pulled back my arm and stood up.

"I'm going to see how your mom's doing," I announced, and left her frozen grin behind.

∞

"How are you?" I asked Anna later on, as she settled into bed beside me.

She shook her head. "I can't say it," she said. "It's too horrible."

"I know," I said. "I wish I'd never...I'm sorry."

Still later, I came awake suddenly in the pitch-black of night as Anna snored heavily beside me. Something felt wrong. I knew it before I opened my eyes. The air tasted feral. And icy.

I slit my lids open just a hair, and took in as much of the dark room as I could. I caught the faintest whiff of something both sweet and sour.

Something sparked near my face and I sat up like a shot.

Camille stood by the bed.

A knife protruded from the pillow where my head had rested just a second before.

A breath hitched in my chest. She had almost put the blade

right through my eye as I slept. She hated me. Camille seemed capable in her new pseudo-life of almost nothing. But one thing she had proven.

She wanted me to be as dead as she.

I slid my legs to the floor and took her by the shoulders, leading her away from the bed and back to her room. She did not resist. Except for the dull movement of her feet, she didn't show any sign of life, whatsoever.

When I tucked her back into her own bed, and pulled the covers back up to rest on her frail shoulders, a tear bled from my face to fall glistening on her chin. She made no move to wipe it off, only stared straight ahead, at the ceiling. I rubbed it away with my forefinger, and felt my skin crawl. I now had a horrible revulsion at the touch of my daughter's skin.

When I left the room, her eyes remained open. Unblinking. Unfeeling. Dead.

I locked the bedroom door behind me, pulled the knife from its sheath in my pillow and slid it beneath the bed. Sleep didn't come for a long time. In my head, I replayed scenes from the past year, when Cammy had been full of beaming sunshine and infectious laughter. When she had laughed at my funny faces and begged me to bounce her on my knee like a bronco pony. When she had kissed me and said, "I love you, Daddy."

When she had been *alive*.

Then I remembered her calm in death, as all around her quiet body people moaned and cried. She'd lain there in a coffin built just for children. Anna's mother had moaned tediously about the horror of the thing, proclaiming to any that would hear that they should never need to build wooden boxes for kids. But, as I finally pointed out to her, they do, and Cammy had hers, and her face had looked small yet peaceful on the cloud-white silken pillow.

Now she had neither the joys of life nor the peace of death.

I was the reason. As the gray light of dawn slipped in through the bedroom window, my mind finally slipped into a troubled hour of sleep, soothed only by images of black blood and newly filled graves.

I knew what I had to do.

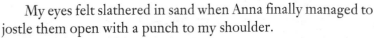

My eyes felt slathered in sand when Anna finally managed to jostle them open with a punch to my shoulder.

"Get up," she insisted, "you're going to be late for work. And why did you lock the door last night?"

I didn't answer her question, but stumbled as fast as possible from shower to closet to car. When I passed Camille, already sitting motionless at the kitchen table, I couldn't meet her eyes. I didn't want to see what was, or wasn't, in them.

The day passed in slow motion. Every time I looked at the clock it seemed that only another five minutes had passed. I could barely hold my head up, but still, I welcomed the crawl of time. Anything to avoid what I had to do when I got home. All through the day I replayed the images of Cammy's gravesite on the night I brought her home. Of how I propped the industrial flash on the side of the loose dirt, and of how each shovelful rose with the ache in my back to join the growing pile beside the flash. Of how, after what seemed like hours, I finally reached the wooden gleam of the top of her deathbed, and of how my fingers fumbled at the clasps to free my baby.

It all had to end.

It *had* ended, and I'd refused to believe it, thinking that somehow Madame Trevail and her voodoo could cheat the reaper. In some way, I supposed, it had. But the reward was worse than the loss it answered.

When I finally pulled into the garage that night, I hit the button to close the door behind my car, but didn't immediately enter the house. Instead, as the chain ground through its heavy cycle to bring the garage door to the ground, I opened the trunk, lifted the false bottom that hid the spare tire, and pulled out the heavy tire iron that fit the expandable jack. Then I replaced the bottom, and lined the surface of the black carpet floor with black trash bags from my workbench.

I pulled a long spade from its rest on a round hook in the garage wall, laid it on the plastic, and shut the trunk.

Then I hefted the tire iron in my hand and slapped it lightly against my free palm. The sting from just that slight touch said it would easily do the job.

But could *I*?

Taking a deep breath, I assured myself that I could, and turned the doorknob to enter the house.

The foyer was dark as I stepped inside. I slipped off my shoes in the small mud room between the garage and the living area and opened the door into the great room. The room where I had almost been skewered not so long ago by my dead daughter. The TV and lights were off here too, which was unlike Anna, who normally lit the house up before dusk, but I could see light beaming from the kitchen.

"Anna?" I called.

The only answer was a faint thump.

Something was wrong here. The air screamed with the electricity of evil, and my stomach clenched. Why hadn't she answered? Where was Camille? Part of me had hoped to find her planted here, unmoving, in front of the television while her mother fixed dinner.

But there was no warm smell of spice or stew in the air. The house felt empty.

I crept across the front room carpet until I reached the entryway to the kitchen. The hanging fixture on the far end of the room over the kitchen table was on, and I could see something resting on the tiles of the floor, something that peeked into my view from just beyond the edge of the cabinets. Something pale and fleshy.

Something that looked like a bare toe.

I stepped into the kitchen and flipped the florescent light on. As it flickered to life over the counter and I moved closer and closer to the table, the shadows lifted and the light...*oh God*, the light. It burned the image into my brain forever. I wish to God I could forget it.

Camille sat beside my wife on the floor. My daughter's face was blank, but her hand still held the weapon. Cold steel tempered in the heat of life. Silver wetted and warmed with her mother's blood.

Anna wasn't dead yet. She reached out to me from the floor as I gasped in shock at the tableau. Blood streaked the pale skin of my wife's fingers; her entreating arm was streaked and spotted with gore. I could see Anna's lips moving, trying desperately to say something to me as her eyelids fluttered, struggling to stay conscious.

She never got out a word.

Her hand dropped back to the awful, bloody wound on her stomach. The beautiful skin of her belly, that soft flesh I'd kissed and caressed for so many years, looked as if it had been punctured and ground through by a dull can opener. Bloody shreds of skin peeled back and wept life as her fingers grasped and struggled to hold the slippery wound closed. I could see something undulating beneath the skin, beneath the blood.

Something creamy. Something soft and pink.

I gagged as the realization hit. Anna was holding her very guts in.

She wheezed and coughed, then, her whole body shuddering, and a stream of crimson spat from between her lips. A heavier flow sluiced from the ragged slice in her neck, running like thick juice to ripple on the tile. Her eyes held open firmly and locked on mine for just a second, and my heart froze. Then she seemed to shiver, and her pupils rolled back in her head until I could see only white.

A keening, pitiful cry came from her throat before gagging off to a painful, gargling choke. Her beautiful raven hair stirred a broth of blood as her whole body shook. Before I could break my paralysis and kneel to hold her, she was still.

"Anna," I cried, and fell at her feet and crawled through the warm stickiness of her blood. Ignoring the silent presence of our daughter, I pressed my ear to her chest. There was no sound, no breath.

Her face was still, her features quiet. I looked into her eyes, hoping for some spark of life, but already, their luster was gone. With a fingertip stained red in her blood, I closed her eyelids. At last, I realized my own danger, and looked up.

"Why?" I whispered, sitting back on my haunches to stare at Camille. My daughter sat at her mother's head. Her empty eyes didn't stray from my own.

I hadn't expected an answer and I didn't get one. I sat there for some time, waiting for the tears to come. But they didn't. I couldn't quite fathom that Anna was really dead. This shredded, bloody mess on my kitchen floor couldn't be her. And the deadly child couldn't be ours.

I stood up, and started towards the phone to call 9-1-1 for the police, or an ambulance, whoever you have to call when these things happen.

My hand was on the receiver when I stopped.

What could I tell them?

That my dead, eight-year-old daughter had brutally murdered my wife with a knife while I was at work? I pulled my hand back and looked at Camille, who scratched at the back of her neck.

How could I explain her? Who would believe me?

"Get away from her," I yelled at Camille, who had bent over to touch her mother. "Isn't it enough you killed her? Are you going to drink her blood now, too?"

I walked back around the counter from the phone to shoo her away and stopped.

Camille's hands were around Anna's neck.

And in those hands, was the charm I'd bought from Madame Trevail. Camille had not been itching her neck, but removing the magical talisman. She fastened it deftly around my Anna's throat, and the small sachet of voodoo herbs and magic lay in the wound there, soaking up the blood from her ruined neck like a sponge.

"What are you doing?" I cried and started towards her.

Camille picked up the knife and pointed it at my heart. I backed away to safety behind the counter.

What was she trying to do? First she slaughtered her mother, and then she dressed her with the charm that would bring her back to life? Would it work? Would Camille guard the body until it did? And if it did, then what? Would Anna reborn be as deadly as her daughter?

There were no answers from Camille, whose dead eyes followed me without a blink. We were at a standoff.

It occurred to me, finally, that when I had entered the house, I had done so armed. The tire iron lay on the floor now, abandoned, soaking in the blood next to my wife's thigh. Slowly, I stepped back around the counter and knelt down at her feet, edging forward, hoping to get close enough to snatch the weapon before Camille realized my intent. She remained at my wife's head, knife in hand, and watched my progress, but didn't stir.

My heart leapt with victory; my hand was nearly on the weapon, but I moved too slowly.

Anna's body shuddered. Her eyes flickered open.

Then my dead wife sat up, blood still oozing sluggishly from the gash in her neck. The salmon loop of her inner organs threatened to spill from the grinning lips of her open belly, but she didn't seem to notice.

"Anna?" I whispered, backing away from her and Camille until my back hit the wall of our kitchen.

My wife's eyes met mine, and I knew that I was lost. There was a darkness resident there, the same vacant emptiness I'd seen in our daughter's. Anna's hand reached out to grasp the tire iron, and I shuddered.

"Honey?" I begged, as Anna stood up from her deathbed of blood.

She raised the iron rod over her head.

Behind her, my daughter followed, bloody knife in hand.

Anna brought the tire iron down as I dove away, embedding its curved end in a chalky puff of drywall.

She pulled it from the hole and kept coming, her purpose clear.

I fled the room, stopping at the garage door for a split second to look back, to see the ruin of everything in my life that had mattered. To see the tortured, gory body of my wife still staggering toward me, intent on braining me with a tire iron I'd meant for my dead daughter. To see the horrible picture now forever etched in my brain—the image of my daughter, holding a knife still dripping with the blood of my wife.

There was no question of her expression.

Camille smiled.

LIGEIA'S REVENGE ON THE QUEEN ANNE'S RESURRECTION

THE SOUND SENT a shiver to the very marrow of his bones. It was high-pitched as birdsong, yet something deeper lurked inside. A melody that yearned for response. Demanded a duet. It soared high and free and then trilled and swooped, lower and deeper until the earthy lust of its contralto made his knees grow weak, and that which hung between grow strong.

Donato walked to the edge of the ship's rail and stared out at the black ripples of the ocean. The sky was cloaked in dirty clouds, but now and then the faint beam of the moon shone through, and he could just make out the rocks of an island in the distance.

He knew the sound came from there. And he knew why.

Benito.

The First Mate slept belowdecks with the rest of the crew, but that afternoon, he had taken a small boat to the island. And when he came back, he'd bragged again and again of his (mis) handling of a mysterious lone woman they'd found there.

"Her name was Ligeia," Benito had crowed at dinner. "She was asleep in a cave near the ocean when we found her. Beautiful thing she was, too. Breasts like soft melons and hair so long and dark, you could wrap it around you for a blanket. I had Antonio get some rope and he tied her arms behind her head while I took care of her feet."

The burly man had laughed then, absently scratching the long twine of his rusty beard. His eyes glinted with humor and violence. "Antonio had no head for the business though, did ya, boy?"

The younger crewman turned red. "I just didn't want it that way," he said softly.

"You a pansy, boy?" one of the others laughed. Someone punched Antonio in the shoulder. "You take 'em where ya find 'em, ya fool."

Benito laughed. "And that's exactly what I did. Damned woman started singing in the middle of it all, so I put a sock in it; ripped off me own sock I did and stuffed it right into that big mouth of hers. Put me off the kissing, cuz my socks don't smell too good. But I don't need the kissing, not when I've got me the rest of a woman to work on. And I tell you, she was a good one to work on..."

∞

Donato stared at the lonely rocks and heard the song begin again. The melody tugged at his heart, and he put a foot up on the deck rail. *He could climb over and swim to the island and...*

The slap of his own hand across his face stopped him. Donato slapped his face three more times, trying to shake loose from the spell of the song.

His stomach quaked. What had Benito awakened? He knew the stories of the wicked creatures that sang a man to death— luring him to his watery grave.

Donato wouldn't have it.

He walked to the mast and pulled a cord of rope from the deck. He wrapped it around his ankle, tightening it before fashioning a noose to slip his hands through. He held the rope with his knees as he positioned his hands, and then let go; the slack pulled back up into the sail and pulled his arms up with it.

He didn't want to think about what the men would say when they found the night watchman tied up by his own hand, but he refused to follow the song into the water.

The song stopped.

And then it began again, but now it sounded...closer.

Donato closed his eyes and wished it away. But it was too close to ignore.

When he opened his eyes, she was there. Naked and dripping with seawater. Her eyes were black and deep as night. Her breasts were full and lush, just as Benito had described. Donato longed for just one taste...

She stared at him for a moment, sizing him up. And then, she sprinted away, down the stairs to the bunks.

"Wake up!" Donato called, but instead, the Siren's song drowned him out. She sang from the depths of the ship, low and sensual, and then high and sharp. One of the men screamed, but was almost instantly silent.

Donato shook his head and cried. He was supposed to protect them. He was the Watchman. But he didn't know. He hadn't thought she'd come aboard…

She returned to the deck a few minutes later, walking backwards slowly, and motioning with her arms. Languid, easy motions, as if she swam through the air.

Benito followed. Caught in a dream. Sleepwalking. He followed her song, and the sweet promise of her smile. She pulled him right into her arms at the edge of the deck, and her song stopped briefly, as they kissed. His arms wrapped around her, stroking her flanks and back as he kissed greedily. She returned the embrace, but her intent was less erotic.

She kissed him *hungrily*.

And presently, as Donato watched, she kissed his neck until it bled.

She painted the deck red with his life, and when he was dry, she picked up his body and tossed Benito over the side.

Ligeia paused just before following him into the sea.

Then she pulled her leg back over the side and walked slowly across the deck to Donato. She ran long, sensual fingers over the rope that bound his wrists, following it up to where it held him to the mast. She looked confused at first, and then smiled, faintly.

She touched his cheek with those fingers, and pressed her lips to his in a gentle kiss.

"Not for you," Donato heard her say, though her lips never moved.

She leaned in and bit the rope that held his hands with her teeth. A moment later, his bonds snapped, and Donato fell forward. He couldn't feel his arms at all, and he sank as low as he could against the mast, his feet still bound in place, pins and needles beginning in his arms as the blood flow returned.

Ligeia ran a hand through his hair before walking to the edge of the ship. Donato watched the flesh of her ass shift as she walked, and even without the drug of her song, he was entranced.

As she lifted one leg over the side of the ship, Donato heard someone yell from below.

"Antonio?" the voice called. "What's happened? Oh God, Antonio no. Oh no!!"

Ligeia caught Donato's eye in the murky light of the moon. The black vengeance of her soul sparkled in her eyes for that moment, and she grinned, showing a mouth full of sharp, dangerous teeth.

She sang one low, sonorous note that filled Donato's heart with sadness.

And then with a faint splash, she was gone.

Green Apples, Red Nails

I KNEW SHE was a witch the moment she offered me the apple. How else could she have known what the perfect lure would be for a man like me? She must have cast a spell and looked inside my head at all of those moments I've kept hidden in the darkness of shame and pain.

And then she'd shown up at my porch to gloat.

I had no idea who she was, or why she had chosen me, but I opened the door to let her inside, anyway. She shook her head. "You need to clean house first, before you are ready for me," she said. Her voice was cool, but smoky with promise. Red lacquer gleamed in the fading afternoon light as her long fingernails dug faint trails across the skin of the apple. It slipped in slow motion anticipation from her grasp to fall into my waiting hand.

"Look inside. The answers are there," she said with an ever-so-slight raise of her brow, and then she turned and walked away, down the uneven sidewalk path and up the hill that led from our slum of a subdivision and into the bramble woods that bordered the entry to town. I watched the pendulous sway of her rear as she slowly stepped from concrete square to square, never looking back. I wondered again, why she'd chosen me. And wondered if she came from that house that nobody in town would ever visit without the aid of a big money bet and a bottle of liquor for courage. The house in the woods. The House of the Lost, they called it during late-night whispering conversation.

I closed the heavy door to my rundown ranch and tossed the apple a foot in the air, catching it easily before throwing it higher. And then higher again. When it nearly touched the ceiling, I almost fumbled it on the way down, so I stopped and set it down on the kitchen counter next to a handful of other green apples that I'd just bought from the store that afternoon. Then I looked around my little hovel and wondered what was so desperately in need of cleaning before she would deign to step into my home. The stained brown couch was empty but for an afghan on its back cushions that my late grandma had knitted me. The old thrift shop coffee table in front of it had a stack of magazines and an empty Coke can on it, and the TV remote. The carpet was worn but uncluttered, and the kitchen counters were empty but for a stack of junk mail, my coffeemaker and the coffee and sugar canisters. I didn't keep much of a house, but I did keep it neat.

I stared at the green apple there in the middle of the counter. How had she known? What did she want? A tear wriggled loose from the corner of my eye, and slid down my face as I remembered so many things best left forgotten. "The answer is inside," she'd said. I thought about that for a moment, and shivered at the thought of biting into the apple. I thought of the fairy tales and a poison apple. Instead of eating it, I took a heavy cleaver from the utensil drawer, and held it for a moment above the stem of the unripe fruit. Then I brought the knife down cleanly, easily dividing the apple in half. It fell in two pieces and I stared at the center, where the seeds should have been.

The apple was hollow at its core. A small worm lifted its head from the rotten brown pit in one half of the apple, and then put its head back down, content to continue eating the apple's heart out.

The unripened fruit was already rotten.

What was she trying to say?

∽

The hurting began early. It wasn't dramatic or extreme. You hear stories about these schizophrenics and street bums and mass murderers and how their childhoods were so cliché over-the-top bad. You know what I mean—"Oh, well, his mama slept with every man in town while her son played Tonka trucks next to the couch as she gave head to the guy who would later sodomize the poor kid repeatedly once his mom had passed out from a steady daylong series of complex cocktails of sperm chased with vodka. Yeah, it's no wonder he turned to collecting severed heads when he grew up."

Well, my mother wasn't a junkie whore and I didn't live in a rat-infested tenement. I have no horrible story to tell about why I ended up living a lonely life in a forgotten town. I can't even talk about a Bonnie & Clyde robbery spree or a bat-shit-crazy murder trail. I was nobody, am nobody. But I still felt the hurting, regardless. Maybe it wasn't dramatic enough to make me famous, but it hurt still. And most people would probably hear the story and laugh and say, "Well, get over it." If it were only that easy! You just never know what thing is going to stay with you for life.

My parents and I lived in a typical suburban house with a mutt of a dog and a chain-link fence and meatloaf on Wednesday nights. Memorably unmemorable. But I can remember the first time I really hurt inside. The kind of hurting that stays with you for life and creeps out in the night during those moments when you're truly alone. The hurting didn't come from a beating from Dad or a lecture from Mom. My parents never hurt me. Hell, sometimes I wonder if they even noticed I was there. And maybe that was hurt enough, I don't know. They had their own lives to sort through, and I probably didn't ever even tell them about the girl with the green apples.

I was twelve or thirteen and really getting interested in girls when Allysa Romano, an 8th grader who looked more like a high school senior to me, promised me a peek beneath her blouse. She told me to meet her in the picnic clearing at Busse Woods, which I did. Busse Woods was one of those dark quiet places…where furtive people met in shadows to do shadowy things before parting, without a word. So I was excited and scared to go there. But how could I resist Allysa, with those long wavy locks and eyes that always seemed to be laughing at secret jokes? When I arrived, she was holding two green apples. She grinned when she saw me, and slipped them inside the bra beneath her yellow T-shirt. "Wanna bite?" she asked, and when I nodded, albeit hesitantly, she smiled. "I need to see what I'm getting into," she said. "Take off your shirt first."

I argued a bit, but finally peeled it off and asked her to do the same. She shrugged, and dropped the yellow tee to the ground. I could see the green of the apples pushing out of her white bra, the soft flesh of her smooshed breast trying to escape from the opposite edge.

"Now your pants," she said. I hadn't expected things to go this far, but now I was excited, and horny and it didn't take much before I was standing naked in front of her.

"Hmmm," she said, sizing me up and down with an eye that had more of woman than girl in it. She walked around behind me as she talked. "You might be a little green yet, I think."

"Your pants?" I asked, a little breathless and cold but still warm with the queasiness of excitement in my groin.

"You still want a bite?" she asked, leaning against my naked back from behind. I nodded, and I felt her hands brush against my skin. "Hold out your hands," she said, and when I did, they were suddenly filled with something cool and hard and round. The apples.

"Eat up!" she laughed, and grabbed her shirt from the ground. At that moment, the woods suddenly released a mob of taunting, hooting, laughing girls from my school. As Alyssa put distance between us, a hail of apples suddenly rained down on me from the hands of almost a dozen creatures whose wickedness was masked in braids and barrettes. One of them rushed up close enough to slap me in the ass as I wheeled about, scrambling to find my clothes and still, unconsciously, clenching the hard bitter skins of the green apples that Alyssa had left me. When I got home later that afternoon, eyes still red with the residue of tears, I found that I still clenched one green apple. When I bit into its skin, the tart juice only served to make my eyes tear up again, and I threw it on the ground of my backyard. It was much like me—unripe and unready. And bitter.

∽

Shaking away the memory thirty-five years gone, I threw the rotten apple in the garbage and put on my shoes to take a walk. Not too surprisingly, my feet led me down the same path I'd watched the woman leave my house. When I came to the path leading into the woods, I hesitated, but not for long. I wanted to know. Did someone live still in The House of the Lost?

When I was a kid, we used to dare each other to run into the woods on Halloween and egg the old gray frame shack that hid in the middle of the trees like a canker on otherwise healthy flesh. Only the bravest of the brave trick-or-treated here, and there was a time in grade school when I had been dared to visit the House of the Lost on Halloween.

I had reluctantly agreed, and dressed as a hobo, had walked into the forest after dark with a flashlight, to ascend the creaking steps of the old house's porch. I had knocked on the door and a woman had answered the door. She wore a black pointed hat and for a second I almost ran when I saw the yellowed fangs and the horrible warted nose of a witch beneath the hat.

And then she had lifted the mask to reveal a softer chin and warmer lips. And green eyes. With a long-fingered hand, she answered my "trick or treat" by offering me a taffy apple. "Made it myself," she said, before letting the mask slip back over her face and giving out a hideous cackle. Not knowing what to say, I backed off the porch and then ran back to the sidewalk.

"She gave me this," I said to my cronies who'd dared me to brave the dark. I raised the caramel apple in the air with a flourish and then put it to my mouth for a bite.

"No, don't!" Tom had yelled as I bit into the fruit and the sour juice of a green apple coated my tongue. "It might have razor blades in it! Or pins!"

I spit the piece on the ground and threw the rest of the apple into the forest. "You're right," I said, hoping that there hadn't been poison in the sour juice. I spit and we'd left the witch behind.

It had looked like a death house three decades ago. And as I approached it now, at dusk, I saw that it hadn't gotten any better with age. The green of moss obscured the black of its peeling shingles, and paint hung in strips from the eaves beneath. In the side yard to the left of the porch, a broad but short tree hung heavy with green apples. So. Now I knew where the "witch" got her stock. I wondered where Allysa had gotten hers. And all these years later, I still wondered why.

Some hurts never heal.

The two windows on either side of the front doorway were dark, betraying nothing of what was inside, and I smiled at myself. Fool, I thought. Why would a beautiful woman live here? Whoever she was, her "magic" was a knowledge that she shouldn't have of me. Not true magic at all. What her purpose was, I didn't know, but as I stood there in front of the old house as shadows fell deeper by the second, I was suddenly certain that there was no witch, and the rotten green apple had no more meaning than the green apple I had carried home from my public shame in the forest clearing so many years before. There was no magic here, only the sadness of decay.

I was turning away from the porch when a light flickered on inside.

"I've been waiting for you for a long time," a voice said from the doorway.

I turned back and faced my witch. She had the green eyes just like the witch I'd seen on my Halloween trip here in high school, and from just an hour or so earlier, on my porch. She couldn't have been the same woman, and yet...

"What do you want from me?" I asked.

"What do you want from me?" she said, countering my question as she used one hand to pull aside her long emerald robe. It shimmered faintly in the moonlight as it moved, and revealed the naked shadow of her breast and belly behind it. I could see the wide cone of her nipple still soft and unaroused. But the promise of her body stirred an instant reaction in me. And that reaction made me angry. I could imagine the feel of her velvet skin slipping against mine, her lips brushing my ear and promising so much. And I hated her for teasing me that way.

"Just leave me alone," I said, and suddenly ran from the forest. Behind me, I heard the gentle titter of a woman's scornful laughter following me.

That night, I dreamed of Alyssa. She led me into the forest again, and this time she didn't offer me apples at all, but instead unbuttoned her white blouse and dropped her private school plaid skirt, before kicking aside her panties and bra to stand nude and white before me. Her breasts looked smaller untethered than they seemed in her sweaters, but my eyes were drawn to that soft black down at the crux of her thighs. She slid a hand behind my belt and made a fist around what she found there.

"Use it or lose it, my friend," she said. And the next thing I knew the dark locks of her hair were tickling my naked legs and Alyssa was using it and abusing it with wanton heedless abandon.

Something in me snapped and I was no longer the frightened, humiliated boy that Alyssa taunted, but instead, I was filled with power and raw lust. I grabbed her by the hair and hauled her from my lap to push her back up against a tree. I bit her nipples like the skin of an apple and thrust myself inside her as the bark of the old tree scraped against her skin. She shifted and I twisted her around to make her hug the tree then as I used her from behind and laughed as she cried and slid down the tree trying to escape the force of my thrusts…But then she suddenly changed and stood up, taller than me, and older. Her hair was still dark but her eyes were the green of emerald and her breasts heavier and thick. With a hand she reached down and grabbed my penis and twisted until I screamed.

"Look inside," she said. "The answers are there."

And then I was standing naked in a forest, holding two green apples.

I woke up cold and shaking. What the hell was going on? The images of the dream just kept cycling through my mind, the tease of a past that never happened juxtaposed with the modern face of the witch. Why was this stranger in my dreams suddenly? Why was she at my door? My heart pounded as I thought about the red daggers of her fingernails releasing her robe to let me see her nakedness. I remembered a time that I had gone outside to the park nearby, wearing only a robe. Perhaps she was simply letting me know that she knew what I'd done… But I didn't think anyone had seen…

It took me a long time to go back to sleep.

∽∾

I had a girlfriend once who called testicles crotch apples. She didn't last with me long; she was uncouth and wanted to do disgusting things. But that term stuck with me a long time. How could you sully the sweet purity of an apple by comparing it to sweaty hairy balls? I didn't like the way she tried to put mine in her mouth…it felt strange and made me nervous every second that she was going to bite down.

I almost had a wife once. We got very close in college and I wanted her to move in with me. But in the night, when she stayed in my bed, she insisted on sleeping naked, rubbing herself on me and the sheets like some rutting feline. I had to wash my linens after she stayed over every time. She wanted me to put my tongue in places that were obscene. And I don't mean in her mouth—though she eventually said some things that could only have come from the gutter. I realized too late that as sweet as she looked on the outside—the apple of my eye—she was rotten at the core. Just like the apple the witch brought me.

I'm rambling. I'm unnerved. My life was fine until she showed up yesterday. And now everything seems…unsettled. Old memories coming back. Old hurt. I need to get past this and just go to work. When I come home, I'm sure it will all be fine. No apples, no witches, no temptations for things of the flesh that are filled with well…foul mortality. Juices and stench and bitter and sweet and…

I'm rambling again. Just…never mind.

∽∾

When I got home, she was waiting for me.

"Did you taste my apple?" she asked. It almost sounded like a double entendre.

I shook my head. "No, I chopped it up and found a worm inside. Was that supposed to be a message of some kind?"

"Only if you know how to read it," she answered. She held out her hand and offered me another apple. This one was green on one side, and brown and soft on the other. There were holes in the skin, and I could feel liquid seeping out of the rotten side to trickle across my fingers. I threw the thing to the ground and wiped my fingers off on my pants.

She smiled. "Do you prefer your rot to be exposed on the outside?"

"Why are you here?"

"Because it's nearly Halloween," she said. "And this year, since you haven't been able to do it yourself, I thought it was probably time to stop you."

"Stop me from what?"

She pulled another green apple out of the pocket of her robe. She held it in front of her, staring at the green mirror of its smooth skin as if into a mirror. "There's always one, isn't there?"

I cocked my head, wondering what she was getting at.

"Always one perfect young apple, waiting to be plucked."

"You're not making any sense."

"You're not asking the right questions," she said. Her lips split into a smirk, and the light flickered with humor in her eyes. She didn't blink. "Why don't you come back to my place, and I can explain?"

"I don't even know your name," I laughed. A little nervously, I might add.

"Beth," she said. "It's my middle name, but it's what my mom and dad always called me. I don't know why they didn't use the name they gave me. In any case...does that help?"

"A little," I said. "But I still don't know you."

"Ahhh...but you have known me," she laughed, a quiet but tantalizing sound. "You have known me deeply."

"I don't think so," I said. "Please leave."

"Suit yourself," Beth said. "But you are not going to give out a green apple this year. I'm going to make sure of that."

She turned and stepped away from my tiny porch. "Come back to the house," she said. "I think you'll be glad you did."

I shut the door on her words and her face. And her apple.

Then I sank down in my kitchen chair and tried to figure out just what she meant. It was almost Halloween, and every year, I did give out an apple. To most of the kids, it was your standard candy bars and nickel prizes fare that I tossed into their bags when they came to my door dressed as lions and tigers and zombies, oh my. But there was always one. A beautiful, perhaps haughty little girl with some makeup on her face to augment the princess costume, or the fairy dress. There was only one, but when I saw her, I knew. And I gave her a green apple.

I don't know how it started. I don't know why. But I'd been doing it for as long as I could remember.

And now a witch was going to take issue with it? I shook my head. My private Halloween award was none of her business. But like any female, she somehow supposed she could make it so.

I stood up and decided that this would stop, right here and tonight. A woman would not meddle in my life again. Women were only good for one thing, I'd found.

The hurting.

I slipped on my shoes and walked to the edge of the forest, where there was a path through the brush that led to a witch's home. It was time to peel this particular apple.

∞

The old house looked darker tonight than it had before. More abandoned. More desperate. Perhaps it only reflected the emotion of my own soul. I stepped onto the gray wood of the porch and it creaked loud in the silent night. I stepped forward and the steps echoed in the night. A ghoul creeping towards the door.

When I opened the screen to pound on the heavy wood of the door within, it fell back at my touch. Open. I didn't think, I just moved with it. I stepped inside. The wood creaked shut behind me, but I didn't move.

She was there on the floor just inches from my toes. Naked. Bloody.

I stared at her corpse and willed myself to breathe. Her chest had been stabbed repeatedly; seven deep red rents opened the skin beneath her shoulders and into the swell of her breasts. I couldn't help but look at them; her nipples floated there atop blood-spattered breasts as if they were only waiting for me to suckle and I almost bent to do so before something in the back of my head reminded, *She's dead!*

I don't know what I was thinking. But I know that after staring at her for a minute or two, I finally stepped past her and moved farther into the house, stepping slowly down a dark corridor, worried that I would trip and fall headlong through the rotting boards of the floor. The house stank of dead things and mold. Rotting wood and sour animal droppings. This was a crypt and an outhouse, not a home. How could I have even imagined that Beth lived here? Witch or no, she'd been putting me on for reasons she'd apparently taken to the grave. In coming here to wait for me, she'd run afoul of someone more evil than this house.

"I should have guessed that a dead body wouldn't phase you," a soft voice whispered from behind. I whirled to find Beth standing just inches away, the blood glistening wetly on her skin like the polish on her nails.

"But you're…" I began, and she pressed a finger to my lips. I could feel the dent of her nail on my lips for minutes after she took her finger back.

"I know what will phase you though," she said, and with that she stepped closer, slipping a long silky arm around my waist, the daggers of her nails trailing up my spine to my neck. Her hand held the back of my head and she pulled my face in close to her own. I could taste her breath, sweet and tart, the cider of apples ripened and soft. She pressed her lips to mine and I gasped. She was so soft. I wanted to lose myself in her mouth, and for a moment I gave in to her and pulled her body close. I could feel the heat of her blood soaking through my shirt as her breasts molded against my chest, and the delta of her thighs rubbed up against the bone of my hip. Another "bone" between us began to grow as I realized that no matter what the cost, I wanted this woman. This seeming witch, whoever, whatever, she was. I wanted her red nails to dig into the flesh of my back as I pounded against her, and in her until…

A spike of ice shot through my heart and my eyes opened to see the glimmer of green in hers. She was smiling even with my tongue in her mouth, and suddenly the taste of her was of vinegar and rot, sour and rancid. You could never trust a woman. I shoved her away, and she laughed, stepping back easily to watch me.

With one hand she rubbed the stab wounds in her chest, and drew the new blood down to smear across her belly and nipples. She painted her flesh in her own blood, and then reached a bloody hand down to cup the thin pink lips of her sex. She held my eye, and made sure that I was watching as she slipped first one bloody finger and then two inside herself, using her own blood as lubricant. And as she performed a dirty sex show for me, her tongue slipped out of her mouth to rest against her teeth, and her eyes rolled back to show their whites as a stream of black began to leak out from between her fingers. The rot of years slipping out from her uterus. The room filled with the stench of decay, as if someone had just upended a wheelbarrow full of week-old roadkill on the floor.

I backed away from her as she climaxed, spilling the liquefied core of her womb to the floor with each groan.

Things on the floor ground and crunched beneath my feet but with my back against the hallway wall I edged away until she was out of sight, and found myself in the kitchen. The light of the moon streamed in just enough to paint the forgotten space a ghostly blue-white, and I looked for something to use against her if she came near me again. I felt around carefully for a drawer. When it opened, I found a coil of thin twine, instead of a drawer full of knives and utensils. And next to it, a short, serrated knife with a wooden handle. I pulled both from the drawer and was about to turn when two hands slipped around my waist.

I jerked around, knife at the ready, but it passed through thin air. Twin green eyes stared up at me from chest level.

"Is this better?" a child's voice asked, whispery and suggestive. "You could never handle a real woman, could you? You always were too stuck on me."

I stared at the heavy red pout of her lips, too old for her age, and the kinked raven hair that trailed across her shoulders in feathery wisps. Just like Beth, she was naked, with seven stab wounds crossing her chest.

"You're not her, you can't be…" I began. She laughed, and lifted one black-smeared finger and drew it across my cheek. I flinched, but not before her dead blood had marked me.

She changed, and then her face was older, and her nose an inch from mine as she pressed her body against me, pinning me to the counter. "I am her," she said. "And I am me. And I am the witch who lived here before us all. And I am here for all of the girls you've given green apples to over the years. You could never grow up inside...and you stopped them from having the chance."

She stepped back a pace and her face looked momentarily sad. "They never did anything to you," she whispered. A tear slipped down her face, and as it fell, I saw it change from clear to red to black. "I was sorry once," she said. "But I'm not anymore."

"Who are you?" I asked, gripping the knife tighter, getting ready to add to her wounds if that was what it took to escape this madhouse.

"I am Allysa Beth Romano," she said. "And you killed me when I was only seventeen. I never got to grow up and have children. I would look like this now, if I was still alive. But you didn't let me."

"I don't know what you're talking about," I said. "Allysa humiliated me so bad I didn't talk to anyone for months in 8th grade. But we went to different high schools. I never saw her again."

"Not true. You knew where I lived and you followed me all through high school, looking for a way to get your revenge. And one night, as you were spying on me and my friends, you heard them dare me to go into the witch house after dark on Halloween. And you went there yourself and waited for me. You forced me to take my clothes off in the dark, and when I fought back you stabbed me. And when I screamed, you stabbed me again and again until I was quiet. Then when you heard my friends coming you pulled me down into the cellar and hid with me there until they left. I was the first body you buried here. But not the last. Not nearly the last."

"You're crazy," I said. My voice choked as somehow visions of everything she said streamed past my eyes like some crazy film reel shot by a drunk.

"Am I?" She smiled but there was no humor in it. With one hand she reached out and grabbed my wrist. With her nails she gouged into the flesh of my wrist until I couldn't resist anymore. "Drop it," she said, and the knife fell to the floor.

"Come with me."

The pale moon of her ass shifted in front of me as she held my hand but walked ahead into the dark. She led me to a closet in a back bedroom. "You brought me here, the night you killed me. And when you hid with me in the closet, you found this." She pulled up a trap door in the floor, and then forced me to walk down a creaking wooden ladder ahead of her.

The basement smelled rank with rot and mold and Beth pushed me forward until we reached a wall. Then she guided my hand to a shovel leaning against the cinderblock wall. She pointed at the dirt floor all around us, and from the faint luminescence that seemed to glow from her bloodied flesh, I could tell that the ground was uneven.

"They are all here," she said. "Every girl you ever gave a green apple to."

"No," I said. "I gave those apples to the girl with the best costume each year. I never…"

"You gave the apple to a girl who was alone, and looked, in your twisted mind, somehow like me," Beth corrected. "You told them how much you liked their costumes and told them you'd picked the apple fresh from the tree just that day, and encouraged them to taste it. And once they did, the drug you injected worked fast. Oftentimes, they never even left your porch before they went to sleep. And then you brought them here, to strip them naked and do the thing to them that you always wanted to do with me. The thing you could never do with any girl who grew into a woman."

I protested but the world seemed to spin around me as I saw the faintest memory of a dark-haired girl with the red lips and red nails of a street hooker standing on my porch. She was wearing a nurse outfit, and chewing gum when she said, "Trick or treat."

I saw the girl dressed as Princess Leia, dark hair pulled in ram's horn buns up on the side of her head, and I wondered what she would feel like when I…

I saw the girl wearing a brown paper bag; she called herself the bag lady…I saw the girl wearing so much Saran Wrap that you couldn't really tell there was nothing but skin beneath it… and then I remembered how that plastic wrap had looked when it had been pulled tight across her face, smearing her wet features into a garish mask of silent screams as I laid myself on top of her and pretended that we were married…

"You can dig them up now," Beth said. "If you don't believe me."

"What do you want from me?" I said. I kept looking at the ladder, trying to gauge how many steps of a head start I'd need to vault up in without her having the chance to pull me back down.

"It's not what I want," she said. "It's what *they* want."

She pointed at the floor of the cellar and I saw the dirt shifting in a dozen different spots around the room. Dirt was lifting and rolling and dust rose on its own into the shadowed air and then a skeletal hand appeared from beneath the earth just past my feet. I gasped and stepped back, but there were now several hands protruding from the floor, and then they were scooping at the earth, white bones on black earth, shoving aside their graves until all around me the cellar filled with the forms of dusty skeletal girls. Before my eyes their bones filled with blue-white flesh, and all as one they looked at me with unblinking serious eyes. Eyes that didn't bleed with anger so much as finality.

"You know they call this the House of the Lost," Beth said, still the only ghoul who spoke, though from the faces of the girls who were stepping towards me, there was no need for any other words. "You picked a strange place to bury your dead," she said. "A witch did live here once back when we were kids…and the ground still bears the power of her curses."

A hand reached inside my shirt and another slipped between my jeans and my belly. Their fingers were cold and hard. My belt began to loosen and I pushed them away, but only for a moment. Four icy hands gripped each of my arms and pinned me to the wall.

I tried to struggle and kick, and for a moment, I actually pulled one fist off the wall and connected with the face of a girl with buckteeth. She bit me and I screamed just as someone else kneed me in the groin. It didn't take long before I was stripped naked and the ghostly flesh of all of my girls pressed me to the wall.

Beth laughed, and reached out to finger the thing that had betrayed me all of my life. "It never did grow up, did it?"

And then she was the Allysa I remembered again, the sparkle in her green eyes still full of both humor and the cruelty that only children can display, before the pain of life has taught them the real weight of the hurting.

She guided my hands down from the wall and back to the shovel and flanked by naked ghosts, she pointed at a spot in the earth that seemed relatively level. "Dig," she said. "And make it deep and wide. You're going to have a lot of company."

I dug. The cellar earth moved easily, but my hands were quickly raw. The sweat poured off my head but I didn't feel hot. Every time I looked up from the earth I saw the empty eyes of all the girls I'd buried here on Halloween nights past. All the girls I'd loved. In my own way.

Under their silent eyes I stepped the shovel down again and again and dug the grave deep. I didn't protest when Allysa put her hand on my head and told me lie down in it. I knew there was no point; they were not going to let me leave, and honestly, I'm not sure I wanted to. After a time, maybe that hollow place inside you just grows so much that the shell left around it simply doesn't care to move anymore.

"Do you know what day it is?" Allysa asked, as I crouched down in the damp earth. I shook my head, momentarily confused.

"It's Halloween," Allysa said. "Your day of green apples."

I lay down and waited for the girls to join me. I figured when Allysa had promised company that they planned to torment me even beneath the earth for my crimes.

But then something hard hit me in the head. And something else bounced off my chest. I reached out and found the smooth skin of an apple. I held it up and saw the glowing eyes of the girls peering back down at me from the edge of my grave.

"Take a bite," one of the girls said. And then another said the same. And another.

"Take a bite," the whispered in unison, over and over again, as more and more apples rained down on me, painfully bouncing off my knees and hip and ribs and face. I held the apple to my mouth as the grave began to fill with the fruit. It was cool and hard against my skin, and soon I could feel nothing but the weight of green apples against my chest.

I bit into the apple in my hand, and the taste was sour and sweet, both at the same time.

Just like a woman.

I looked up and saw the girls above me growing into women, their pert breasts and boyish waists filling out and curving and their eyes lengthening into organs both sultry and feral. The apples continued to rain down on me until I could no longer see the beautiful dead nudes above me who were stoning me in fruit that should have still been maturing on the branch.

"All wasted," Beth's adult voice came from somewhere far away. "All of it wasted like apples gone wrinkled and brown, left to rot on the ground untasted."

All around me the immature fruit began to change, growing older, ripening. The smell of vinegar filled my nose and then I was drowning in the scent and drip of bitter age, covering and crushing me until I cried out again and again that I was sorry.

But there was nobody left to hear or care. They were all dead.

TO EARN HIS LOVE

WHAT BETTER WAY to spend Halloween night than to watch a witch in action?

I shivered as the cinnamon-sharp autumn wind cut through my denim jacket, but the thought of the coming night made me warm...and a little scared. Marshall had asked me to sneak in and watch before and I had, thinking the whole while that it was all just a put-on, that my older buddy was ditching me in a draughty shack for kicks. But I'd gone along with it, hiding behind the wooden crates for an hour, and sure enough, she had shown up. *She* turned out to be Miss Carny from 4th period English! What the heck was going on here, I'd wondered, but Marshall showed up right after and the two had begun their strange erotic magic without a word.

Marshall never called her Miss Carny. He just said "the witch". She'd called him to her a couple other times since that night, but Marshall hadn't invited me to watch again. Understandable, really. I don't think I could do what Marshall did with the witch while anyone else was watching. The time I had watched, my heart had nearly stopped as I saw my teacher savagely strip her clothes and then buck and shriek beneath Marshall on the floor. As soon as he had been spent, she had pushed Marshall off of her. Then she'd reached between her legs with a flat hand, and scooped a sticky mixture of their lovemaking out. She'd walked, boldly naked, across the shack and used a wooden spoon to scrape the goo from her hand and mixed the junk into a mason jar with other, dark and fuzzy things. After a few minutes of concentration, she'd turned back to Marshall, still lying on the floor, and smiled.

"Se-magic," she whispered. "Your semen seed will draw his interest. You will bring him to me." She'd groaned as if in orgasm at her own words then, a deep, throaty sound that made me cringe.

Marshall thought the "he" was a wizard, but I was sure it was the devil. Marshall thought their trysts were, in his words, "awesome", but when I watched them together, my heart shriveled up in my chest. It was evil.

But exciting.

So I was going back tonight. Marshall said she had promised him something special tonight, the culmination of all their heaving magic. As his silent partner, he wanted me to see what the witch would create. It would be easier for me to get out of the house this time—I'd just say I was going trick or treating. Ma would say I'm too old for that, but she'd let me out anyway.

∽

It was dusk when I set out across the graveyard and ducked into the foliage beyond. I hoped I could find the trail again. The wind had calmed, but the night felt colder than ever. Leaves rustled slightly overhead, and their fallen brethren crunched loudly beneath my feet. I'd started out early, not wanting to risk the witch getting there before me.

At last I found the trail. It was recognizable only because it stood as a narrow lane in the woods without trees. Something had cut out the forest, but hadn't stripped away the grass and weeds. I waded through the chest-high stand of brush, all the while moving farther away from the edge of town. And then, as the last deep red of the sunset slipped away from the sky, I was there. At the shack.

The witch's shack.

It was made all of wood; old wood bleached gray by the years and leaning slightly to one side. A chimney slanted from one side, and branches and rotting leaves all but covered the roof. The glass of the windows was spider-webbed and splintered from the sport of young explorers. I wondered if any of them had blundered into this decrepit cabin after dark. When the witch was here.

I pushed the squeaking door open and stepped inside, waiting precious minutes before moving. When my eyes had adjusted enough to tell my thudding heart that no one was there yet, I walked across the spongy, sagging floor and secreted myself behind the topsy-turvy stack of wooden crate boxes, as I had last time. It wasn't long before I was shivering, both from cold and, I think, fear. Why had I come here? I knew this was wrong. Miss Carny was evil. The evidence was all around me. Bottles of magic-stuff lined a shelf on the far side of the one-room shack near the fireplace. The floor was scuffed, not only with wear, but with circles and triangles and strange symbols. Miss Carny was more than some child molester (though the molesting was mutually enjoyed). She was a witch. I'd seen it in her eyes over the past couple months in school. They seemed slanted, slightly. And a weird gleam seemed to focus from them on certain students, when they were causing trouble. That look always silenced the room. I suspected it wasn't a natural thing.

The door slammed open, and I jumped, almost giving myself away at the start. But the protest of the hinges safely masked any noise I made, and it swung closed again. She was here.

Her arms were piled high with tree branches, which she dumped into the fireplace across the room. Thank God! I praised silently at the thought of heat, and then bit my tongue as I thought of the inappropriateness of that calling. The witch, I thought, would be calling on a different deity tonight.

As she bent over the fire, nursing the kindling to hellish life, I squinted at my watch. It looked like another half hour or so until Marshall was supposed to get here. I was starting to wonder if I could hold out that long. My butt was going to sleep on the cold floor, and the spider webs stretching from the boxes to the half-boarded up window over my head were giving me the creeps.

Soon the fire was crackling, throwing red-and-orange shadows at the walls behind me, if not any heat yet. The witch was busy. I watched as she got down on the floor, on her hands and knees and darkened the symbols already carved there with a marker. It occurred to me that she didn't look like any witch I'd ever read about. Her face was young (for a teacher), and her eyes were…stunning. They flashed a piercing aqua blue that was, literally, spellbinding. I had had a crush on her last year, when I started at Pierson High. After I'd seen her naked with Marshall, and watched her strange mixing and magicking after, I'd become afraid, but yet, still drawn by her. She wasn't much taller than me (maybe five six or seven, I'd guess) and she still had a thin, high school girl figure. And her hair… God, it trailed in kinky black ringlets down her shoulders and down her back. In school she wore it tied up and pony-tailed, but now, it hung from her shoulders to the floor, masking the characters she drew from my sight.

I couldn't believe that she didn't somehow sense my presence, so close to her, but she worked diligently just a few feet away from me. I could see most of her through a crack of space between two of the crates, and had to keep reminding myself to breathe as I stared at her. The heat was starting to seep into my corner of the room, and I was starting to relax a little, when she stood up and surveyed the floor.

Don't come here, I begged, but she walked over near the fireplace and opened a cabinet set on the floor. She gathered some things and then walked back to the largest circle in the floor. There was a pentagram inside it, and outside of it, squaring it off, were four smaller circles with strange geometrics inside each. Then I saw what it was she had gathered.

Knives!

With practiced ease, she threw one at the floor, and it stuck, at just a slight angle, right inside one of the smaller circles. She missed the second circle, but levered it out of the floor and threw again, this time hitting her mark. When she was finished, four gleaming silver daggers ringed the large circle. She grabbed a bag from near the door, and then knelt in the circle again. She took a tape measure from the bag, and adjusted it to what looked like about two feet. Then she set a candle at the tip of the internal pentagram on the perimeter line of the center circle. Measuring an exact length each time, she proceeded to space out twenty or thirty other candles, all the color of burnt cherries. When she was finished, she clicked a lighter, lit a spare candle, and used it to light the others in the circle. Now the center of the cabin was bright, and the place was beginning to reek of the tangy wood smoke mixed with the flowery, sweetly musky fragrance of the candles.

What was she doing? I wondered, starting to become afraid for my blithely horny friend. The last time I'd been here, they had done it about where the circle was, but there no candles or knives were involved.

She walked over to the row of jars then, and pulled one down. I thought, from its place on the shelf, that it was the one I had seen her mix before. It looked the same, anyway, when she walked back to the circle and began spreading its dark, muddy contents with her finger on the floor. She traced the triangular patterns within the candle-lit circle, mumbling something to herself the whole time. Then she stood up and stared at the door.

Just stared.

Unmoving.

What the hell, I thought. My legs were cramping up, but I didn't dare move. And she was really creeping me out now, staring blankly at the door like the walking dead or something. And then she spoke in a language I could understand.

"Hurry, my darling," she murmured.

Marshall knocked on the door; unnecessary civility, I thought, but the witch strode from her circle to answer it.

"Trick or treat," I heard him say, and the witch laughed.

"Both," she said, and a spike went through my stomach. I was becoming very afraid of her promised surprise.

Not Marshall. He stepped inside, and the breeze from the door told me how warm the cabin had quietly gotten. I shivered, and hugged the corner close as he walked into the room just a few yards away.

"You won't need the mask tonight, Marshall," the witch laughed. I peered through the crack at that, and saw her pull a rubber Frankenstein face from his head. He really didn't get it. He called her a witch, but I realized then that he was only humoring her. He took the sex, but didn't believe she was anything more than a kinky teacher.

I did. More than ever, at that moment.

"Tonight we shall call up a real monster," she said, wrapping one long, slender arm around his shoulder.

"Good spread for Halloween," Marshall observed, walking to the candle circle.

"Yes. My book says it must be on Halloween. The other times were to get his attention, but the night of calling must be Halloween. If we are lucky, we have gotten his eye, and he will hear *our* call tonight."

"What book?" Marshall asked, playing along. I could hear in his voice that he didn't care. He just wanted to get her undressed.

"This one," she answered, picking up a small, dark-bound book from inside the canvas bag that had held the candles. "This is where I learned how to call him. I found it last year when I cleaned out my grandmother's attic, after she'd died."

"So that's like your spell book?"

"And more," she said. "Grandma had it hidden in a locked safe. I wouldn't have even found the safe if I hadn't needed to have the roof redone before I could sell the house. When the builders removed some rotted wood, they found the safe sealed up in a wall. And I found this," she held up the book, "in the safe."

"Cool," Marshall said. "So are we gonna do it in the circle tonight?"

"Yes. Take off your clothes and lie down."

As Marshall tossed jacket and flannel shirt to the side, Miss Carny also began to remove her clothes. Her own long coat hit the floor by Marshall's. She wore nothing, I soon saw, beneath a sheer black blouse. Her breasts were breathtaking; deliciously pendulous and darkly nippled. I could see the gooseflesh on her white skin in the dancing arcs of firelight. She kicked off her shoes and shimmied out of her jeans. Her naked thighs and buttocks created an uncomfortable stirring in my pants. They both stood naked in the circle now, and she ran a fingernail from his chin to his already pointed penis.

"Hmmmm," she smiled. "Lie down now. I'm going to paint you before we begin."

Marshall didn't even flinch. If he got sex out of it, she could probably tattoo him and it would be the same.

He stretched out on the floor, and she straddled him, using her finger to trace circles and squiggles on his chest and belly, periodically dipping her finger in the same black mixture she'd used on the pentagram. When his body was a mess of black hieroglyphics, she placed the black book above his head.

"Don't move," she cautioned. "Don't say a word."

Marshall grinned, obviously thinking this another part of her kinkiness that he could take advantage of. So, spread-eagled and naked, in the center of a pentagram, Marshall was mounted by a witch. Her foreplay amounted to a brush of lips against his, and then she was slowly rocking atop his crotch. My pants suddenly seemed incredibly restrictive as I watched her breasts jiggling faster and faster above Marshall's muddied chest.

Suddenly, she dropped her hands to pin his wrists at the edge of the circle. Her hips never stopped bucking, but her face lost some of its look of pleasure. She began to read from the book above Marshall's head. Strange, tough-tongued stuff. It was no language I'd ever heard.

"Gutta, hruth sreighvit ciccilis tor," she growled.

Marshall eyed the breasts bouncing just out of reach of his mouth, and chased them unsuccessfully with his tongue.

Her guttural reading continued, her voice gaining in volume as her hips' motion grew wilder. As she read, I began to feel strange, almost dizzy. I thought it was the scent from the candles, or maybe just the combination of autumn cold and fire. But as her voice rose to a scream, her figure swam out of focus. I steadied myself on the floor with my hands, praying that I wouldn't fall into the boxes in a faint.

Which is exactly when it happened.

As I swayed, and she screamed, the witch suddenly reached above and ripped a blade from the floor.

"I love you," she cried out, and then brought the blade down straight into Marshall's amazed and open mouth.

His screams were horrible. He started thrashing, but the knife had gone all the way through the back of his throat. He was now pinned grotesquely to the floor, with blood spurting and bubbling down his cheeks. I was frozen by the horror of the scene. It was really too late to help, I realized. Marshall would be dead in minutes. There was no way out.

She took another blade then, and again held it high above her head as she said, "I love you."

She brought that one down on his chest, and then she was awash in his blood. His screams were already subsiding as she drove the third knife into his belly. As she raised the fourth knife over his groin, and again pledged her love, I realized that she wasn't proclaiming her love for Marshall. She was calling "him".

As Marshall's movements died down to a few feeble twitches, the witch knelt at his side, and dipped her hands into his opened belly. They came away dripping crimson, but instead of holding them away from her in disgust, she began methodically to paint herself. Her cheeks acquired geometric rouge, her neck crude stars. Around her left breast, she drew a circle, and then bisected it, sketching a bloody nail across that creamy flesh, across the wide nipple and back down. She repeated the process with her right breast, and then began to smear the blood without regard for form, until her belly and thighs were a bright, slow oozing paint of blood. Then she raised her arms above her head at the center of the circle and chanted some of the same things she had screamed moments before. Again I began to feel dizzy. But this time, as her chanting rose in volume to a scream, I didn't fall back. I found myself standing up.

No! I railed against myself, but my limbs suddenly were not my own. She heard me rise, and stepped backwards. I saw the recognition in her eyes, the sudden fear that another of her students was about to ruin all her plans.

"You! What are you doing here?"

"You called me," I said, but the voice was not my own. It was heavier, throatier. My hands began unbuttoning my jacket. Hands ignored my commands and flung it from me and then ripped off my shirt. They quickly dropped my pants and I stood cold and whitely nude before my bloody teacher. The witch.

I could feel my erection stirring, though my stomach was aching in horrific complaint.

"You have possessed the boy?" she asked, and squinted at me, looking deeply into my eyes. I felt a heat in them, and she seemed to see something about them that convinced her. For without another word spilling past my unwilling lips, she dropped to her knees. Her naked skin glistened with blood, and the body of my best friend lay gutted behind her, but the demon within me discounted that. I strode forward, pushed her shoulders with unhuman strength and was on top of her in an instant.

"You have earned my love, woman. And now I will give it," my throat growled.

Her mouth opened in rapture as I began to work my groin against her own.

"Yes, master," she cried. "Take me, I am yours."

I laughed. An evil thing. A sound I hope never to hear again. In it I heard barbed wire sawing through bone. The snap of a neck as the noose constricts. The scream of a man dropped into boiling acid. Its tone opened her eyes, and she, perhaps, had a few seconds of time more to realize her mistake than poor Marshall had. But the knife was already in my hand, dripping Marshall's lifeblood on her already crimsoned chest.

"I love you," I laughed and brought the blade down.

She didn't struggle nearly as much as Marshall had.

As her last moans gurgled to a hush, I stepped outside the cabin. The cold air whipped my body with lashes of ice, and I cried out inside for clothes, for warmth. The demon the witch had called didn't seem to notice. My mouth opened again without my permission.

"I love this night," my voice yelled to the stars as my legs began walking away from the shack and into the forest.

I couldn't have disagreed more.

I couldn't wait for this night to end. My best friend was dead. I had killed my teacher (at least, my arm had). What if they locked me away for the murders?

And then a thought colder than the Halloween wind struck me. What if the possession didn't end with this night?

Inside my stolen body, I began to cry.

STILL, THEY GO

I LOVED HER, but I wanted to kill her. Maybe that's what saved her life. Maybe that's what doomed mine.

I always was indecisive. Maybe just once, in those interminable, circular arguments when she'd called me an ass and I'd called her another word for a dog, if I'd just had enough backbone to answer her slaps to my face with an all-out punch to the jaw, things would have worked out differently. Maybe then, she would have respected me. I know, it's heinous to hit a woman. But I've got the flip side for you: spare the rod and spoil the child. And too often, Janice acted like nothing so much as a brat.

But I never put her in her place. Not really.

Janice is moving out today and there's nothing I can do to stop her. She doesn't even look back as she pulls the last suitcase through the door. I remember that one…it was mine. She always made fun of me for the color, as if having a purple case was somehow unmanly. I always said the color made for an easy spot on the baggage claim.

She would snort. Now she had no qualms with walking away with it, as I watched. Billy followed her, a beat-up brown box in hand. I wondered if I'd ever see him again. He was so tall now. All grown up.

All grown up but not quite a man, I'd like to tell him. But he wouldn't listen if I tried.

I remembered when he was just a boy, sitting here on this couch next to me. Janice hadn't wanted the couch, so she was leaving it behind, though she'd emptied the rest of the place. I'm glad because this couch holds a lot of memories for me. I think a piece of my soul is lost in the lint between its cushions.

When Billy was just six, he'd sat here playing a video game on the big screen TV. Racing cars. He was so cute at that age…particular in a precocious way. Determined. Caught up in his realistic-looking NASCAR race, he passed two cars and moved quickly closer to usurping another. As he neared the turn at the end of the track he suddenly shouted out, "I'm coming for you, bitch!"

Bitch? I thought to myself...*at six years old? Really?*

I put a hand over my mouth to cover the laughter, and silently thanked God his mother wasn't home to hear him. And then I donned my fatherly mantle and asked, "Billy, where did you hear that?"

"I dunno," he'd said, never taking his eyes from the race. Not realizing he'd done something wrong.

"Billy, you shouldn't say that," I said, still stifling a grin. He'd been so earnest! "That's a bad word."

Now he looked at me. His expression changed radically. Chagrined.

"I didn't know it was a bad word," he pleaded. He looked terrified. Horrified that he had unknowingly crossed the line.

"Just don't say it anymore," I said. "It means a mean, horrible, selfish woman." In my head, I added, "like your mother".

A few minutes later, he was passing another couple of cars and he yelled again, "I'm coming for you!" Only this time he didn't add the "bitch". That made me smile again. He was a good kid. Earnest. Wanting to please. He'd make a good shoe someday for some woman. She'd step and step and step on him and he'd smile and kiss her for it. The thought curdled my stomach.

Now he was a teenager. A few weeks ago he'd sat next to me on this old couch, playing another game, this one with swords and monsters and life points. His black hair curled and kinked in waves across his collar and masked half of his cheek so I couldn't see his eyes. But I knew how intent they looked. Sometimes he didn't know that there was anyone else in the house, let alone the room. He certainly hadn't noticed I was there.

It had been a long time since anyone noticed or cared that I was there.

The house was silent for a long time after Janice and Billy moved out. As the days and weeks went by, every now and then people came over, but they never stayed. When the front door closed and the evening light turned to night, it was just me.

Alone.

Here on the couch.

Sometimes I paced, trodding up and down the stairs to the bedroom. Sometimes I stood in the kitchen and remembered the meals we'd had there together. Isn't that what family is about? Communal meals, stories shared, the day remembered, together.

There was no togetherness here anymore.

There was just me.

I remembered the time when Janice had loved me. Sometimes it seemed like just yesterday. Other times, it seemed like a lifetime ago.

But she *had* loved me. She had held me to her bosom and comforted me when I cried, and held me to her bosom and fucked me when I'd been excited.

Every good thing in my life had rested there, in those two snow-white globes of soft flesh, each crowned in a pink kiss.

It was thoughts like that that made me suicidal.

I never really had the balls to kill myself though. I mean, if you snuff out your thoughts…how can you look at your situation and nod that you did the right thing, or crow, because you did the wrong? Self-assessment is part of who I am. I couldn't stop that process, even if it meant living here in this godforsaken empty house until the end of time.

But then, one day, I was no longer alone.

They came into the house like an army. Trevor and Amy and Sam. A handful of others marched behind them, all carrying boxes and dressers and lamps and more. My couch was dumped on the front lawn, as a bigger, softer settee took its place. The last piece of my former life was gone, but still, I remain here.

I listen to their banal conversations and typically pointless arguments and I remember when *my* family lived here.

I remember when I *lived* here. Before that night when Janice lost the last vestige of civility and began throwing things at my head, a lamp, a paperweight, a shoe. I ducked and rolled on the landing, laughing at the ridiculousness of it all, and my amusement drove the anger in her to a blinding heat that she couldn't control. She kicked at me and then ran at me with both palms outstretched, screaming, "Get the fuck out of my life, you asshole!"

Her hands had connected with my still laughing chest, and I imagine my eyes popped open in that last second when I realized that she had toppled me, and that there was nothing behind me to stop me from back-flipping over the low railing at the stairs. The last thing I heard was a scream, whether it was hers, or my own, I couldn't tell you.

And then I was here again.

Only, I wasn't really *here*.

I watched Janice wrestle with her guilt until she couldn't stand it anymore. Her obvious remorse gave me no feeling of vindication. I couldn't comfort her, and I couldn't take any comfort in her. Yet she was right there all the time. Crying on the couch next to me. The couch that was now out on the curb.

I wonder how she is. Has she found another man to replace me? Someone who didn't laugh at her when she screamed like an idiot? Someone who loved and accepted her fully, unconditionally, despite her faults? That's what she always said she wanted.

I wonder how Billy is. Has he found a girl yet? Would I like her?

I'll never know. When I was a kid, we always said that "Grandma went up to heaven, and she's looking down over your shoulder, protecting you in whatever you do."

I don't think that's true. Because all I'm looking at is a bickering bunch of strangers in my house, painting all of my walls obnoxious colors and filling my rooms with furniture that has that faux Scandinavian design that defines so much of the crap you can buy at the Ikea store.

All my life I hated Ikea.

Now that's what I'm going to look at all my Death?

Life sucks and then you die...

...and then it just gets worse.

VOYEUR

IN THE BEGINNING, he'd only wanted to watch.

They didn't know he was there and he got an amazing rush just from being there, hidden, silent in the dark.

He knew it was wrong…but where was the harm?

He looked down at the bruised and lolling face beneath his knees and answered his own question.

There. The harm was right there.

"I never meant…" a voice in his head complained.

"There's meant and there's did," another voice answered.

Ron didn't have an answer for either voice. What was done was done.

Now he had to deal with the evidence effectively, or perish. He didn't intend to perish. He enjoyed his life too much for that.

There was irony there, but he refused to look it in the eye. Any more than he would look at hers. Sometimes if you ignored something long enough, it went away. He told himself that, but still, the vacant eyes dragging along on the ground between his knees didn't stop sightlessly staring.

The solution to his dilemma had come to him with deceptive ease. Just a few weeks before, he'd been down on the beach, playing Hacky Sack with an old college pal in between long pulls on some long necks. They'd wandered down the beach a bit, talking and walking, until the open area between the hill and the ocean narrowed and narrowed and then finally disappeared.

There was nobody down there, and rightly so. The beach transformed into a hill of black, gull-shit boulders that climbed twenty feet in the air before slipping back down and into the bay on the other side.

"What's your porn star name?" Gary had asked him, as they perched against the rocks and watched the surf crash and spray.

"I've never done porn," Ron had answered.

"Obviously," Gary had laughed. That laugh had stabbed Ron in the heart, but he'd only smiled.

"You take your favorite sweet thing, and pair it up with your favorite spice," Gary explained. "So that makes me Peppermint Pepper."

Ron had thought a minute, and then grinned. "I guess that makes me Honey Ginger."

"You sound sexy," Gary laughed.

He was rewarded with a punch.

Ron had changed the subject then. "Ever go inside a cave?"

Gary had shrugged. "I don't think so, why?"

Ron had pointed at a think black crevice in the wall of rock that rose from the beach to the road a hundred yards above.

"Because I think there's one right there."

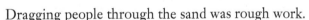

Dragging people through the sand was rough work.

"Maybe next time, if you decide to filet your date, you'll wait until you're closer to your destination?" the voice in his head taunted. Part of him considered that and nodded at the logic. The other part wanted to slap himself across the face…only, that would mean letting go of her arms.

A voyeur saw things in flashes. Pictures. Frozen moments that he held on to in his mind, and enjoyed over and over again. Sometimes sexually. Sometimes not.

Snap.

"Smells like dead fish in here," Gary said as they stepped inside the water-weathered edges of the rock and entered the chasm. The sound had deadened almost instantly, along with the light. But Ron could still see his sandals leaving imprints on the damp, dirty sand as they wound inside the rock and plumbed the hollow path within.

Ron dragged Aurelia Anne inside that very opening now. Part of what had attracted him to her was her name. How could you resist a girl named A.A.? She had been gorgeous and autonomously sexual. He had not been able to look away. Now he didn't want to look at her at all.

He hadn't dragged her all the way down the beach.

He'd parked along the roadside above, and let her body roll down the hill. Expediency was called for. Still, the nervousness of that moment as he pushed her body over the edge...would she make it down the hill? Would someone pull over near his car above and see what he was up to? Would somebody that he couldn't see on the beach below intervene when he reached the bottom to drag the body inside the rocks?

His armpits were sodden when he'd reached the bottom of the hill and reclaimed the limp grip of her slender fingers. Those fingers he'd watched so many times through her window, glistening with the moisture of her own desire...

Ron shook away that image before it froze in his mind, and concentrated on dragging her inside.

The thing about chasms near the ocean is that they are carved and worn by time. Well, really, the ocean over time. And water can be relentless...and unexpected. When Ron had explored the crack in the black rock face with Gary, they had only walked inside a few yards, until the darkness hid their steps... but before they had left, Ron had seen the place where the water had worked its way deeper into the heart of the hill. He'd see the place where the walls disappeared, and the sand fled down...

The best place to hide a body is a place where it will never be found.

That's the mantra of murder, but really, so few murderers ever find that special place. And that's how they are unmasked as murderers. People always seem to stumble over the bodies. Without the evidence, all you can ever be is the accused.

Ron didn't intend to be seen as either. There was nothing to connect him to A.A. and he was going to dispose of the evidence in a place that it could never be found.

He stopped for a moment to click on the flashlight he'd brought, and tucked it into his armpit, before picking A.A.'s cold hand back up again. He dragged her into the darkness, which slowly unveiled its secrets to him, as the soft light sought carefully ahead.

Snap.

"Did you bring a rope?" Gary said.
Ron shook his head. "Why?"
Gary pointed. "Because if you take a step thataway, you're going to be mountain climbing."
Ron had looked over the edge. "That's the toboggan slide to hell, right there."

He stood at the toboggan slide now. And A.A. was going down. He expected that she wouldn't be coming back up. Ever.

"You were good to watch," he whispered, and sent her on her way.

As she went, he felt something shift in his pants pocket, and heard a metallic clatter.

Ron swore and slapped at his jeans where his cellphone had been. The pocket was loose. Empty.

"Are you fucking kidding me?"

He stood there on the edge, for many minutes, trying to decide what to do. The evidence would never be found, he was sure. Not down there. But still...he couldn't leave his phone there with the body, could he? In case, somehow, it was found? Ron shook his head.

This endless night would never end.

He drove back to his house, and retrieved the rope coiled in the garage. Rope he'd fantasized about on occasion for other purposes that had nothing to do with climbing down steep rock falls inside an ocean cavern. He slipped a beer from the fridge into the pocket of his jacket and returned to the car.

Snap

"What are you doing here?" she yelped. With sex-damp hands she sought to cover her breasts, but that only left other parts unveiled. Her hands floundered, not knowing what to hide.
"I just wanted to see you," he'd answered.
"Pervert," she screamed, inching away from him. He saw the steak knife still lying on her dinner plate, on the table next to the bed.

He knew that was where she was inching towards.

He beat her there.

"I just wanted to watch you do it," he cried.

A.A. screamed and reached out to grab his hands before he could act.

But she was too late. He knew that her voice had to be silenced.

It was the warmth of her life, coating and caressing him, that opened his eyes...

He found a heavy boulder to tie one end of the rope to, and then Ron was ready, hand over hand, to follow it down. He'd taken a class last year in rappelling, because he'd always fantasized about going on a solo mountain climb. A man against the world, surviving and climbing and moving to a new high...none of the latter had ever happened, but he still knew the drill. Push with that foot, let go with your hand, grab and weave...

Ron worked his way down the hidden cliff in the dark, until his feet finally touched the bottom.

His arms goose bumped. Shivered.

It was another climate here. Cool and still. Humid. He shook, and ignored the message. He didn't care if it was cold— he had to do something here.

Ron shone the flash around the place where he had landed. The naked body of A.A. lay just to his right, blood still oozing from the wounds of the blade. And probably some nicks she'd received from the rocks on her way down.

Great, he thought. An evidence trail.

"Only if anyone else ever climbs down this slope on a rope," his inner voice reminded.

"Won't matter if they do," he said aloud. "By then, A.A. will be long gone."

It only took a few sweeps of the light for the glint to reflect back at him the image of his phone. He bent and swept it back into his pocket.

He wanted to leave right there and then, but the pale skin of A.A. lay just to his left, reminding him of why he was in this position.

Ron looked up the tall slope that he'd climbed down and shook his head. "Not far enough, darlin'," he whispered.

JOHN EVERSON

He looked around for another crack to drag the body too. Another place where it could disappear farther into the earth. He'd come this far...someone else might as well—and he didn't want them finding his object of affection if they did. So he'd best make her even harder to find as she rested. He imagined that somewhere near here, the ground shifted again, and A.A. would be beyond the touch of anyone.

He pulled her toward a dark crack in the rock nearby, assuming that would be another fall, deeper into the earth, but as he walked, his eye caught on something else. Something that glinted in the orange light of the flash.

"What are you then?" Ron murmured.

The wall of rock was not *all* rock. There was something buried in it. Something glassy. It glinted in the light of his flash, but disappeared when his light slipped to the side. He moved the flash back.

"Weird," he whispered. He was deep beneath a tall rocky hill...he couldn't think of how anything could have gotten accidently buried this far down.

The glass orb in the rock did not answer. But it did seem to respond to his flash. The crack in the wall suddenly glowed red.

Ron raised an eyebrow and stepped back. When nothing happened—no sound or sudden laser beams extruded—he stepped closer again. But this time he used his hammer and a piton and knocked some of the rock loose around the crack. The fissure quickly grew until he could fully see the source of the red light. It was a round bit of glass, no bigger than a quarter. But something moved inside it. As he hammered at the wall, the focus of the light shifted. Almost as if it were an eye.

Looking at him.

"What the hell are you?" he whispered. If this was some kind of detection system (who would install a detection system in the well of a cliff?) then it had seen him climb down and retrieve his phone. Right after a dead body came rolling along.

Ron put the piton on the center of the red light and hit it as hard as he could with the hammer.

His wrist vibrated, but the light did not wink out.

He tried again. And again...but the glass eye did not fracture or dim.

Ron decided to find out what the hell the thing was attached to. If he couldn't put it out head-on, maybe it was connected to a recording device of some kind.

He started chiseling away at the edges, but quickly realized that his climbing hammer and a piton were not the right tools for the job. He was going to need to come back. Again.

∞

He had never wanted to become the man he was. And when the sun shone bright and he had to face himself, as he did now in the rearview mirror, he wasn't sure he recognized the stubbled, drawn features that looked back.

He'd started peeping when he was a teen; the woman next door left her windows open all the time. And he had reason to believe that she wanted him to see. She'd undressed right in front of her window too many times for him to believe otherwise. And there were several times that he was sure she had seen him watching. Her eyes had seemed to catch his, and her lips had moved into the faintest of smiles…but she had not stopped the erotic things she was doing. Teasing. Touching.

After she'd moved away to another state, he realized that he couldn't go back to just looking at magazines. Or even videos. He needed to see a real woman…but it was best when the women didn't know he saw. It excited him the most if his objects of excitement didn't know that he was there, spying on their most private moments.

Not having too intense of a social life, or really, any social life at all…he became an accomplished window watcher. It became a game to plot out the private lives of the women who lived around him. And eventually, thanks to the easy access provided by one of his "performers"…he found that the erotic rush was even more intense if he was actually in the house with the woman.

He found that it was not too difficult to get into a girl's closet when she wasn't home. If she had a regular routine, the escape unseen was equally easy.

Over the years, he found his eyes closer and closer to their naked bodies…never quite touching.

Until he had bathed in A.A.'s blood.

The five minutes after that bath had given him the most intense orgasm of his life. And now, instead of feeling sick and scared at having taken a woman's life…he found himself imagining what Erin would feel like, naked and bleeding out against him.

And Carolina.

And even Fran, who might be a challenge. Unlike most of the women he watched, she was twice his girth. She'd crush him if she fell the wrong way. Still, she knew how to pleasure herself…and by doing it in his invisible presence, she knew how to pleasure him.

What if she bled on him as he…

Ron shook Fran's folds (and the image of her crimson folds) from his mind and concentrated on descending the rope again into the black space below. This time he had brought not only sledge and chisel, but a full-sized pickaxe. He would see what had been buried/installed here.

He started slowly, worried about missing with the sledge and destroying whatever the device was that lay hidden behind the rock. An hour later, he wasn't being so careful any longer. None of his misses had appeared to damage the dark metal structure ensconced behind the rock. And so his excavation work had grown increasingly bold. The rock floor around him was now covered in shards of broken stone, and he no longer worried that he'd break the machine.

Now he just hoped he could dig it out.

His arms felt swollen and his back twinged threateningly when he bent, but still he kept slamming the sledge into the rock.

Volcanic. It was darker than limestone, and almost glasslike in the way it smashed.

This thing in the wall, had been covered by a volcanic eruption, he decided. When was the last time a volcano had erupted in Northern California?

Ron shook his head. The idea was impossible. The last one was almost one hundred years ago, and that was nowhere near here. That would mean that this machine had been in the ground long before there even was a machine age…

No. He couldn't consider that. Ron shook his head.

As he did, the red eye moved.

Well, the light from it did, anyway.

"The fuck?" he whispered, and stepped away from the device, sweat streaming down his cheeks and neck and back. Ron wasn't used to physical labor…he was going to pay dearly for the past few hours.

He gasped and bent to rest with his hands on his knees, drawing in air as if he'd been holding his breath. Fast and hard. But even as he struggled to calm his breathing, he didn't take his eyes off the machine. A weird, black steel cylinder that seemed impermeable to his axe. Or, apparently, molten rock. Ron eased himself down to sit and kicked his legs out on the ground.

The light of the red eye seemed to shift, and follow him. The beam of its gaze was like a sniper's laser sight on his chest. It made him nervous. More than just nervous. And that laser slowly moved upwards, slipped across his neck and chin until he blinked as it hit him in the eye.

"Knock it off," he yelped, as if the thing could understand him.

But…weirdly, as he said it, the red light winked out, leaving his eye streaming.

"Um…okay…" he said, once he'd blinked away the tears and focused on the thing again. He'd chopped out a hole in the stone wall about two feet wide and four feet high, and he hadn't found its edges yet. But he had held its constant attention.

This was the first time its "light" had turned off.

Ron moved closer to the machine, and brushed away some of the debris that shielded its rounded face. He couldn't tell how much more of it was buried in there, held fast by the freeze of molten rock, but he guessed it was a lot.

When he leaned in to stare at the strange dormant glass eye—the only thing that marred its face—he was rewarded with a sudden light. A red beam that caught him once again straight in the eye. He felt himself falling.

But…

He did not move.

His body was locked in place, though he felt as if he were in freefall.

As the red light slipped around and through his vision, permeating and coloring his sight, he began to relive every moment of his evening with A.A. It felt like watching a film unwinding in slow motion, yet, it was over in a heartbeat. His memories were a film fed through the wheel in fast forward. A contradiction; slow motion in light speed.

The vertigo was intense.

And bizarre…

And then *gone*.

That's when he did fall. Flat on his ass.

He swore. And stared at the silent, lightless, metal canister half-unburied in the wall.

"You did that on purpose, didn't you?" he whispered. "You intentionally made me fall."

Ron had nothing to help him deal with this. His liberal arts degree hadn't addressed the issue of finding intelligent artifacts in cave walls while disposing of murder victims.

The machine was definitely there. But what did he need to do with it, that was the question.

In his head, he had a new vision.

He saw himself touching A.A. He stroked her chest and bent in to kiss her full, rich lips. He'd watched her for so long, given up so many nights to be with her, yet always distant.

And then she was close. A cold, bloody doll in his arms.

Ron shook that image away. He'd enjoyed the blood, he had to admit that. But he never wanted her to die. If they were dead, they were hard to watch…

He stood up, and shook away the vision.

The device stood silent, inside the wall. The light remained on, still looking at him. Ron didn't attempt to change that.

He had realized that this was not some security device that someone had secreted underground. This wasn't connected to some government secret probe. The rock he had excavated said this thing had been here for a thousand years… Maybe more. The rock had not been rubble, but had been molded around the device like concrete. It had to have been trapped by some volcanic eruption…long before anything on Earth had had eyes or metal skins.

Ron looked at the device again, and shook his head.

"You're an alien, aren't you?"

The red light winked on again, and swiveled about the room, until it connected with his face. And then, oddly, it settled, and slipped up across his cheekbones until it beamed directly into his eyes.

Ron realized that its strange gaze didn't hurt. Instead, it seemed to bring on memories in his head. Images of girls he'd long ago seen buried crossed his eyes. He smiled at the images, remembering times that he'd spent outside their windows, watching. Touching himself. Lost in his solitary ways. Lost in their beauty… He forced the pictures back, and picked up his tools.

"I'll see you later," he promised.

And with that, Ron grabbed the rope and climbed out of the pit—both metaphorical and real. But as most people know, in the end, all that matters is what's real.

What was real to Ron was Erin.

She lived a few blocks away from him, and after the last twenty-four hours, he needed the comfort that only a familiar girl could provide tonight. A girl he knew, and trusted. He'd watched her try on five pairs of earrings some nights. He'd watched her paint her toenails other nights. But the best nights were when she'd pull on a light silk robe and then reach into the bureau next to her bed…

It felt right to him when he thought about watching her.

Ron stepped across her lawn in the darkness and felt for the familiar handle of her garage door. She had never seemed to realize that the back side door was unlocked. And for the past year he had used that door to slip, unseen, into her house. Once he was in the garage, it was a game of silence to slip his way into the kitchen. And from there, through the rest of the house… including her bedroom. Especially her bedroom.

While it was always nice to get into position in a closet or bathroom before the woman he was peeping on might enjoy slipping out of her clothes, thinking she was alone…he'd always ended up following Erin into her bedroom, which made his visits to her more challenging. She got home early…he had to keep an eye through the window to see when she might be headed into the back room.

Tonight was different. Instead of watching, he strived to be waiting. He realized on his way to her house that for him… overnight, the game had changed.

When she dropped all of her clothes to the floor and walked down the hall to the bath and reached an arm past the curtains to turn on the shower…he was waiting. She shrieked when he grabbed her arm, and pulled her in with him.

She only cried for a minute.

And then his blade found her skin, and crying wasn't in the cards.

She opened her mouth to scream, but all that came out was a whisper. And a gurgling hiss.

"I've been watching you so long," he whispered. She tried to claw out his eyes, as if that might obscure all of those past peeps.

He slapped her away, and then showed her his knife.

Well, really, the blade of a pruning shears. Better than a knife really. Certainly longer. He smiled to himself as he considered that they could prune both bushes *and* bones.

"What do you want?" she whispered through dying lips. Every time she spoke bubbles escaped from the wound he'd made in her throat.

He ignored her wild eyes and rapidly unintelligible pleas. Suddenly he didn't want to watch anymore. He wanted to punish. He wanted to hurt her, make her pay for all those nights that he'd gone home alone. As if his social ineptitude was somehow Erin's fault. Suddenly that beauty he'd enjoyed spying on for so long brought up a torrent of fury. On the spur of the moment, he decided to remove her ears with a couple swift, bloody swipes of the shears.

When the pink curls of her earlobes lay bleeding on the floor, Ron began poking the blade between her lips to address the tongue. He maybe should have taken care of that first, in hindsight. She kept trying to make noise… He couldn't get both ends of the shears in her mouth at the same time, though he'd definitely stabbed something while he was trying…blood was pouring past her lips now in a river. He abandoned trying to snip her tongue and instead decided to trim her fingers. And then her toes. No more earrings or rings or painted nails for her. Erin's struggles quieted after they had both slipped a couple times and fallen hard against the tiles. She'd struck her head, and his blade had pierced her breast, and then her belly as they went down. The blood was dark and steady as it passed the steel ring of the drain.

When the tub was littered with pieces of the girl he'd once lusted for, he pulled Erin's body to him, and turned off the water. She was still warm, even though an hour had passed. When he pressed his nakedness against her, and she bled out the memory of who she had been all over him; as he bathed in the lifeblood of a woman he had watched for years, Ron experienced a moment that could be explained as nothing less than euphoria.

"Only God could give me this," he breathed, pressing himself into the secret places of a woman who once had been beautiful. He thought this end was oddly appropriate; she had always enjoyed getting off in the shower. He of all people knew that.

He pressed the blade of the shears into her neck and then drew it lower, pulling hard until she was opened in a way he had never imagined a knife could do.

Her blood quickly coated the bathtub floor. Ron closed the drain and lay down in it, and held her body to him, enjoying its weight and subservience. And its warmth. She was finally his, after what felt like a lifetime of watching.

He knew that she would never leave him. Couldn't leave him…

Later, when he woke with the stickiness of her blood congealed and cold on him, he rolled her off and looked around at the evidence that could expose him. He realized that the room was full of his conviction. Fingerprints. Bits of her skin. Smears of her blood. He stopped feeling sexually excited and instead worried about collecting all of the pieces of toes and fingers and skin. He showered and rinsed the bath as good as he could, and then gathered her body, and its loose bits in a sheet he found in the towel closet.

It was probably long past time to leave.

When Ron dropped her body into the pit ahead of him, he saw the red light of the eye below follow the corpse. After he climbed down and rolled the body down into a deeper crevasse, the same pit he'd sent A.A.'s body into, he stepped over to the thing in the wall and let it stare him deep in the eye.

"You're just a watcher, like me, aren't you?" he whispered.

The thing didn't answer. But suddenly Ron felt as if he was falling again. And the images of his moments with Erin passed before his mind's eye in that same weird duality of speed and crazy slow, slow, slow motion.

Snap.

Every pore on her neck was clear. Blood bubbled out from the slit he'd made there. The fear streamed from her blue eyes, the realization that this was absolutely going to be the last time she got in...or out of the shower. She had never been more beautiful to him...

He saw it all clearer now than he had a few hours before, when it happened.

He'd never wanted Erin to fear him. He'd only wanted to enjoy watching her. But watching suddenly wasn't enough for him anymore.

"You've been watching a lot longer than I have," he said, retrieving the pickaxe that he'd left leaning against the wall. "And you haven't had much to see. I bet you're ready to do something more."

He swung the pick and brought down several chunks of rock. It felt good to slam the thing into the wall, and Ron soon moved in a steady rhythm, as sweat streamed down his back and legs. After a while, there was a good pile lying in front of the machine, and Ron lay the pick down on the ground, breathing hard.

"Huh," he murmured, when he finally looked up. For the first time, he could see the entire side of the "watcher" in the wall. He'd cleared the right side of the cylinder, and could actually see the top of the thing as well.

There were markings on its side, and he squinted hard to make out what they said. They weren't regular characters...more like telegraph signs. Blips and jags. It looked like CZAVNˉM.

"Is that supposed to be your name? I'll just call you Zav, if that's all right," Ron said. The light of the red eye shifted until it was locked with his own.

For a moment, Ron felt himself suspended in a darkness that was blacker than black. A darkness that was palpable, heavy, and eternal.

And then he saw something else. Something very familiar.

He saw himself stabbing at the rocks with the pickaxe.

Only, he saw the image from Zav's point of view.

Ron shivered. The thing had just been in his head; it had just showed him what it wanted, he was sure. And he could understand it. How long had it been locked inside this wall?

He lifted the pickaxe and set back to work, this time without pausing for breaks. After an hour or so, he had it fully exposed.

Zav stood about six feet tall and two feet wide. A man-sized bullet of midnight metal. The only thing that marred its dark surface was the red eye, and the lettering: CZAVNˉM.

"Well, there you go," Ron said, dropping the pickaxe as he looked the thing up and down. "Free at last."

The red light held his eye again, and Ron suddenly felt the earth move beneath his feet. A rumble. Almost like an engine starting.

And then Zav was somehow out of its hole in the wall.

"You can move," Ron whispered.

The black sides of the cylinder flickered, and two long metallic rods extended from its sides. A second set followed, extending from Zav's middle. And then a third, from its base. The creature had six "arms" suddenly bending in front of it. And each arm ended in a clawlike "hand". They snipped independently at the air of the cave, and Ron found himself shrinking away from his mechanical "pet".

"It must feel good to be free again," he whispered. "But what are you? Why are you here?"

The arms reached out and gripped his wrists in a handcuff vise.

"What are you doing?" Ron gasped, pulling in vain against the thing's grip.

The red light caught his eyes, and he saw things that he recognized. Things from his dreams. He saw beautiful women naked. Pleasuring themselves and then...bleeding.

Cut.

Crying.

He saw Erin's eyes, wide and panicked.

He saw A.A.'s mouth open to a scream that he silenced.

He saw a knife cut. Stab. Trim.

Something cold slipped down his left leg. And then his right.

"What are you doing?" Ron whispered again, more afraid than he'd ever been in his entire life. "I helped you!" He suddenly understood the look in Erin's eyes when she'd found a hand grabbing her by the arm in her shower. Her supposed-to-be-unoccupied shower.

His jeans slipped to the floor; Zav had cut through them with its claws. The cold of the cave made his bare thighs goose bump. He felt the cold of metallic fingers tracing the inside of his legs, and then sliding coolly across the low sling of his testicles.

At first Ron was afraid. Yet trapped.

And then he gave in. There was suction. And movement. And clear intent.

Zav wanted to bring him to orgasm.

He was being jacked off by an alien voyeur that had lain dormant inside the wall of a subterranean cave for centuries... maybe eons.

Ron didn't protest. He couldn't move anyway, so instead of fighting, he closed his eyes and enjoyed the strange, but amazing sensation.

When Zav's grip suddenly turned from stroke to snip...Ron screamed.

Before he could begin to try to escape, six black-steel arms set to work on his fingers and toes.

Something drew a line of cold pain across his neck, and then his belly.

"Zav, no," he pleaded, but the rush of warmth that preceded the wave of pain told him it was already too late.

The alien had carved him up the same way he'd done Erin. It had followed his blueprint for human interaction.

It only took seconds before he lacked the strength to scream.

"No," he gasped, air hissing through the slash in his neck. "It's not like this. We're not like this."

Ron's mind suddenly filled with a barrage of images. The collection of an alien voyeur.

Snap.

A blur of space; darkness passing. A fiery flight. Jungle. A million plants and trees straining to reach the blue sky he'd just fallen from. Animals. Some screeching, hunting. Others quietly eating, hiding. The eye focused on each animal in turn. A freeze frame. Then a flurry of white text in some unknown language materialized next to the frame. And then a predator emerged, and clawed at the animal, pinning it. The image faded, and the eye focused on something new. Something reptilian, with teeth. They killed and were killed. Again and again, a rapid succession. Cataloguing creatures, and hunting…

Zav carried Ron's body across the cave and tossed it down the crevasse to join Erin and A.A. CZAVN'M was trained to observe, learn, and fit in. It had seen what was required. It fulfilled.

For the first time in a millennium, CZAVN'M left the cave.

It was ready to finally carry out its mission and join the local culture. It knew what it needed to do to fit in; it had seen enough.

THE HOLE TO CHINA

THE HOLE WAS deep enough to step into now. It was slow going, with his shovel, which was meant more for moving sand than packed gray dirt. He'd broken the edge of it already on a rock that had been hidden in the ground.

Jeremy had started digging the hole on something of a lark two days ago. He'd been sitting there behind the shed, searching for water bugs under the green-stained flagstone piled up near the weedy back fence, when he found the faded blue shovel lying in a patch of weeds. He'd picked it up and used it to dig into the trails of an ant colony at the edge of one of the bits of flagstone, and after he'd unearthed the nursery (and a thousand tiny white eggs) he had just kept on digging.

Tonight after dinner, he'd come back to work on it again. When the yelling began, he simply slipped out the back door of his house and took refuge behind the old rotting wood shed at the back of their lot. Just as he had on many nights after his father came home. His parents never noticed. They were too busy threatening to strangle each other.

The spot behind the shed was as far away from the house as he could get and still be in the backyard, which he was forbidden to leave without explicit permission.

He could still hear them inside the house.

Once one of them started, it would go on and on. It made his stomach twist in a particularly unpleasant way. It felt both empty and like he had to throw up all at the same time, and he hated it. But nothing he did could get them to stop. He used to try to intervene, begging his parents to stop fighting because they were scaring him, but he either got yelled at, slapped or sent to his room. Usually all three, actually.

So lately, he'd come out here until the voices in the house quieted or it got too dark to see. Usually the latter happened before the former.

"Whatcha digging there?" a soft voice asked.

Jeremy jumped. He turned to see a woman standing on

the other side of the fence. She had long black hair that spilled over her old T-shirt. Freckles spotted her nose and cheeks. She looked older than his mom, but not by a lot. He thought she looked happier than his mom. But that wasn't hard. Nothing ever made his mom happy.

"I didn't mean to startle you," the woman said. "I was just doing a little yard work and saw you over here."

Jeremy nodded, but didn't say anything. He had never seen the woman before, though she looked friendly enough.

"My name's Roxanne," she said. "But you can call me Roxy for short."

"I'm Jeremy," he said.

"So what are you digging for, Jeremy?" she asked again. "Looking for worms?"

He shook his head. "I'm digging a hole to China," he blurted out.

The woman had a nice smile. When she did, there were all these little crinkles that stretched and made her eyes look happy.

"That's going to take a lot of digging," she said.

He nodded.

"It might be easier to buy a plane ticket," she said.

He shrugged. He didn't have enough money to buy a plane ticket. But he'd heard if you dug far enough, you'd go right through the center of the earth and end up in China. And that would be about as far away from here as he could get...which sounded good to him. It might take a long time, but he had nothing else to do.

"Tell you what," the woman said, leaning closer to him over the fence. "If you want, I can give you a better shovel to use."

Jeremy's face perked up. The blue plastic shovel was kind of a pain. But then he frowned. He wasn't supposed to talk to—or take things—from strangers.

It was almost like the woman read his mind.

"Don't worry," she said. "It's just an old shovel. It used to be my husband's—I got it for him to dig his own hole to China. He left it behind when he went."

She grinned at some private joke and held up a finger. "Wait there, I'll be right back."

She disappeared from view, and Jeremy felt a little uncomfortable. He thought about slipping back around the shed and going back to the house, but at that moment, he heard his mother's voice escalate again. "...care what that *bitch* says, you can just..."

His father's voice crescendoed in answer to Mom's shrill taunts. "...shut the hell up! I've got half a mind to..."

Jeremy decided that it was better if he stayed where he was. He wondered how fast he could get to China with the strange woman's shovel. Probably faster than with the old broken blue plastic one. He heard her moving things about in the shed next door. He'd never seen her there before; he'd never really seen anyone in that backyard before. But he knew the shed. It was older than the one in his yard. You could see the places where the wood was rotting away. The birds had built nests inside it, and sometimes he sat here behind his own shed and watched the birds fly to the roof of the decaying structure next door and disappear inside. There were a couple of missing shingles and you could see the dark spots where the wood had gone soft, letting the sparrows peck their way in.

"Here you go," the woman said, interrupting his contemplation of the neighboring shed's rotten roof. He hadn't seen her pop back up at the fence line, but she was holding a small spade with a wooden handle. The part used for digging into the earth was polished and shiny.

"That looks like gold," Jeremy said, taking the proffered shovel from her hands, and lifting it to look closer at the exceptionally clean metal that was supposed to get dirty with earth.

"It's copper," she corrected. "It's very strong, and it's perfect for working in the earth. It can be your bridge from here to China!"

"Wow, thanks," Jeremy said, unable to take his eyes off the garden implement. "But I don't know..."

"It's not doing anyone any good in my shed," the woman said. "Use it whenever you want to dig, and when you're done, just set it back on this side of the fence, right here," she said, pointing at a spot to the right of an overgrown mulberry bush that dropped so many berries in the summer that the grass near the fence turned purple.

"Okay," he said slowly, but his face still betrayed his unsurety.

"Don't even worry about cleaning it off," she said. "I'll do that before I put it away in the shed. I'm just happy someone else will get some use out of it."

The woman's face beamed at him; her lips were wide and the freckles made her look as if she were a girl just about to laugh. "Dig your way to where you want to go," she said softly, and then slipped away from the fence.

Jeremy took the shovel to his hole, and pushed the spade into the earth. It seemed almost a crime to get that perfectly burnished tip muddy, but after the first couple shovelfuls came out of the ground, he didn't worry about that too much. He couldn't believe how much better this was than using his plastic hand shovel. The spade seemed to cut right into the earth like a spoon into mashed potatoes. In five minutes he had moved as much earth as it had taken him to move in an hour with the hand shovel. The hole was growing wider and deeper, and now when he stood in it, his belt was below the edge of the ground.

"Jeremy!" his mother called. He heard the back door slam, which meant she had stepped out on the patio. He climbed out of the hole and hurriedly set the shovel back over the fence where the woman had instructed. He hoped it would still be there to use tomorrow. He hated to give it back so quickly, but he knew the meaning of that voice. Time to go in, clean up and get ready for bed.

"Jeremy, get in here!"

It had gotten dark out over the past few minutes—he hadn't even realized. But now he could see the moon peering through the violet sky just over the top of the roof next door. Jeremy took one last look at the hole, and then turned to walk toward the house, where his mom was waiting.

He wished he could just stay out here, and sleep in the hole.

The shovel was still there on Tuesday night, which was good because the arguments started before dinner was even on the table. Mom spit nasty words under her breath that he knew he wasn't supposed to say and Dad pantomimed strangling her when she turned her back. Jeremy wolfed down his spaghetti and asked to be excused from the table.

Mom's cheeks were flushed and she nodded quickly; he didn't waste a second slipping off his seat and setting the plate on the counter.

Thanks to the shovel, by the time it got dark, he had dug down three more feet. It was getting difficult to get the dirt out of the hole now, because the edge of the ground was now above his head.

"I'm going to have to dig some stairs," he said to himself. If he went any lower, he wouldn't be able to pull himself out of the hole!

He started slicing furrows into the existing walls, and slowly carved out four stairs into the existing sides of the hole, so that he could step up them and dump the dirt out onto the growing mound along the back of the shed. After stepping up and down them a few times, he realized that he needed something else.

A bucket.

Half the dirt was falling off his shovel by the time he got it above ground. He needed something to put it in. And then he could get more dirt out than just a shovel full at a time.

Jeremy climbed out of the hole and went to his dad's shed. There were lots of buckets in there; he picked out the biggest one he could find—an old white one that used to hold tar or something for the driveway. It had a long silver handle and should be able to hold several shovels-full at a time. He heard his parents' voices echoing in the shed. They weren't whispering anymore.

"...*frigid bitch...*" "...*perverted asshole...*"

There was a lump in his throat as he heard things he knew he wasn't supposed to. It scared him when they got this way, which happened more and more these days. Once upon a time, the fights had been infrequent, a hot blowup now and then, and the rest of the time, Dad had rolled around on the floor with him and Mom had made dinner, kissed both of them and called them her boys.

It seemed like a long time since she'd done that.

Jeremy closed the shed door and walked back around it to the hole carrying the bucket. He tossed it down into the dirt and picked up the shovel, intending to follow.

"How's it going?"

It was Roxanne. She was leaning on the fence; a long lock of kinked black hair trailed over to rest against the gray wooden slats on his side.

"Hello, Miss Roxanne," he said. Mom had always taught him to address adults as miss and mister.

"Just Roxy, please," she said. Today she was wearing glasses—they were sort of squarish, and had emerald arms that disappeared into her hair. Roxy stared at him over the top of the glasses. Her eyes were brown, and he thought she looked amused, somehow.

"How deep did you get?"

Jeremy smiled. "I'll show you!" he said, and stepped into the hole. He was proud of how far he'd dug in the past two evenings. He stepped down his newly carved stairs and disappeared temporarily from sight. Then he popped back up, just bringing his head above ground.

"You look like a gopher," Roxy said with a laugh.

Jeremy laughed. "Can gophers dig all the way to China?"

"Maybe," she said. "It depends how much they want to get there."

"I want to get there."

The smile seemed to slip from her face just a little bit, and she nodded. "I know," she said quietly. "You just keep using my shovel whenever you need it. You'll get where you want to go."

The dirt slipped under his feet just then, and Jeremy stepped down a stair to regain his balance. When he stepped back up, Roxy was gone.

On Friday night, Jeremy's dad didn't come home. Mom ordered pizza for dinner, and they sat at the table in silence. Jeremy kept looking at the empty chair to his right.

"Where's Dad?" he asked finally.

"Hopefully six feet under," his mom said, and shoved another bite into her mouth. It looked to Jeremy like she was attacking her food, not simply eating it. He didn't ask any more questions.

Without Dad, the house was quiet. Jeremy felt his stomach work itself into knots; somehow the silence was even worse than the yelling. He stole back out to the yard, and found the copper shovel waiting for him again on the other side of the fence. It looked as if Miss Roxy had cleaned it for him; the blade was gleaming in the fire of the sunset.

There were now thirteen steps leading down into the hole. Instead of going straight down, it had to kind of angle its way deeper and deeper, to allow for the steps. But he was making progress. It was like he entered another world when he stepped all the way down the bottom of the hole. The sky grew farther away and the air was cooler. Damp. Sometimes dirt fell from the walls and landed on his neck, making him shiver and jump. He wasn't the only one working down here. Bugs were busy digging holes too. They scurried about on the walls, ducking in and out of tiny tunnels in the earth. He didn't mind working alongside them, so long as they kept to themselves.

Jeremy thrust the spade down hard into the dirt. He came back with a big hunk of dirt and dropped it into the white bucket. Without pause, he shoved the spade down again. He wanted to get to China more than ever now. A tear ran down his cheek and he rubbed it angrily away on his sleeve.

The bucket filled up fast.

He picked it up, and hefted it step by step to dump out above on the growing mound. It was almost a relief to get back down to the bottom of the hole. He felt safer here. It was his own space. Nobody yelled or did bad things to each other here… because…it was just him.

Jeremy hefted the bucket up the steps a half a dozen times. It was starting to get dark outside; the sun had disappeared behind the houses, and there was a faint breeze ruffling the leaves of the trees around him. He looked towards his house. The lights were on in the kitchen, but there were no voices coming from inside. The quiet was refreshing…but eerie. Jeremy wondered where his dad had gone. Maybe he'd decided to go to China too. But he'd probably get there a lot faster since he'd driven away in their Ford Escort. Driving had to be faster than digging.

"How's it going?"

Roxy was there at the fence again. Jeremy shrugged. "Okay, I guess. I think it's going to take a really long time to do this though," he said.

"I think you're closer than you think," she said.

"But China is all the way on the other side of the world, and I'm still just a few steps down."

Roxy smiled. "I'll tell you a secret. There is a whole network of tunnels beneath our feet that lead to wherever it is you want to go. I think your hole has almost reached them. And once it does…you can go to China…or anyplace else you want. As long as you really want it."

"I do," he said. "I want to be anyplace but here."

Roxy nodded. "Then I'll let you get back to it. Right now—when the day is gone but the night is not quite here? That in-between time? That's the best time for digging to where you're going."

She grinned, and Jeremy could see her freckles bunch up around her nose. "Good luck," she said. And then she walked away, through the tall grass in the yard behind his.

Jeremy stepped down into the hole again, carrying the white bucket. He thought about what Miss Roxy had said, and pushed the shovel into the dark earth near his feet. He might be close! The thought made him dig faster. And he filled the white bucket in no time. The dirt trickled over the edge of the rim, and he decided to try to put one more shovelful on top. He pushed the spade in once more, and this time, when he put his foot on the copper edge of the spade, it sank down easily into the ground. When he brought it back up, there was dirt on the shovel…and a hole where the spade had been. A hole that went much deeper than the little bit of dirt he'd lifted out.

He pushed the shovel in near the edge, to widen the hole, and as he did, chunks of earth broke away and fell into the black-ness below.

"I bet this is one of the tunnels Miss Roxy was talking about," he whispered. He moved around the hole in an ever-widening spiral, shoving the spade down and letting the earth fall away. In just a few minutes, he was looking at a four-foot wide hole that went…nowhere.

Well, it went somewhere, he supposed. But he wasn't sure just where. Everything below his feet was black...but when he laid down on the ground and looked down, he could see stars. Faint pinpricks of light in the darkness below. If he dove through the hole...he'd be in space!?

"You made it," a voice said behind him. Jeremy jumped. She'd surprised him again. Miss Roxy was standing there behind him. Her feet were on the last step.

"It's outer space down there," he said.

Miss Roxy shook her head. "It's whatever you want it to be. If you want to go to China, just picture it in your head, and jump into the hole. That's where you'll go."

"Did your husband go to China?" Jeremy asked.

She shook her head. "I dug the hole for him, and then when he could see the stars, I asked him what he thought hell looked like. He thought about it for a minute, and then described a really horrible place full of fire and impaling spikes and..." Miss Roxy stopped speaking for a moment and shook her head. "Things you don't need to know. When I was sure he had a good picture in his head, I gave him a little push, and away he went. I hope he did end up in the place he imagined...he was a bad, bad man."

"I don't want to go to hell," Jeremy whispered, scooting back from the edge.

"No, no, sweetie, I would never have given you the shovel for that. I want you to go where you want to go."

"I want to go to China," Jeremy said. He stood up, his eyes welling with tears. "I don't want to be here anymore."

Miss Roxy nodded. Her face was serious. "Think of China, then," she said. "Close your eyes and picture it really good in your mind."

Jeremy screwed his eyes shut and held them that way. In his head, he imagined the place that he'd been thinking about for months every night when he laid down to sleep. In his mind, there were beautiful tall buildings with flags and banners waving in the wind. Horses marched along stone paths and dogs frolicked in the grassy square. All around him, short people walked hand in hand. Hardly anyone was taller than Jeremy, but everyone was friendly and kind.

"Do you see it?" Miss Roxy asked softly.

Jeremy nodded, but didn't open his eyes.

"Good," she said. "Just take a step forward, and you'll be there."

"I'm afraid," he whispered.

Miss Roxy put her hand on his shoulder. "Is the place you're thinking of nice?"

He nodded.

"Is it where you want to go?"

He nodded again, faster.

"Then I'll help you," she said, and gave him a gentle push.

~~*~~

When Jeremy's mother stopped yelling out the back door for him, and instead stepped out of the house and into the backyard, she immediately walked to the shed. She knew Jeremy had been digging back there lately. She'd let him do it since it kept him out of her hair.

"Jeremy!" she yelled, stepping around the back. "You are so going to be grounded."

But when she turned the corner to the back of the shed, Jeremy wasn't there. The evidence of what he'd been doing remained, however—a mound of dirt was piled up near the fence, and the hole in the ground where it had come from was nearby. It looked as if Jeremy had dug down two or three feet in the dirt. The broken blue plastic shovel he'd apparently been using lay abandoned next to the hole.

She called her son's name once more, and looked around at the rest of the yard, and then at the neighbor's house next door. The place was overgrown with weeds; nobody had actually lived there since the murder, years ago. After the wife had gone missing, the police had questioned the husband, but never came up with enough evidence to arrest him. When they had finally come around with dogs, they'd unearthed the body of his wife, found buried beneath the floor of the broken-down shed. Ironically, by the time they discovered the whereabouts of the missing wife, the husband had gone missing. And he had never been found. Most people assumed he'd fled the country to avoid being arrested.

Jeremy's mother shivered in the breeze and looked up at the old, empty house next door. It may have been a trick of the rising moon...but there appeared to be a face in the upstairs window. A woman's face.

The woman seemed to be smiling.

Jeremy's mother looked away and around the darkening yard once more, calling angrily for her son. When she glanced back at the window of the house next door, the woman had vanished.

Just like her husband.

Just like her son.

She stared at the hole Jeremy had begun to dig. She remembered when she was a kid, how the other kids used to say that if you dug down in your backyard really deep, you could dig your way all the way to China. Once in her life, she'd really believed that was true. Once, she'd believed a lot of things were true.

A tear crept down her face, followed quickly by another.

God, did she wish she still believed that now.

She wished she could dig a hole to take her far away from here.

All the way to China.

ABOUT THE AUTHOR

JOHN EVERSON is a staunch advocate for the culinary joys of the jalapeno and an unabashed fan of 1970s European horror cinema. He is also the Bram Stoker Award-winning author of *Covenant* and its two sequels, *Sacrifice* and *Redemption*, as well as six other novels, including the erotic horror tour de force and Bram Stoker Award finalist *NightWhere* and the seductive backwoods tale of *The Family Tree*. Other novels include *The Pumpkin Man, Siren, The 13th* and the spider-driven *Violet Eyes.*

Over the past 25 years, his short fiction has appeared in more than 75 magazines and anthologies and received a number of critical accolades, including frequent Honorable Mentions in the *Year's Best Fantasy & Horror* anthology series. His story "Letting Go" was a Bram Stoker Award finalist in 2007 and "The Pumpkin Man" was included in the anthology *All American Horror: The Best of the First Decade of the 21st Century.* In addition to his own twisted worlds, he has also written stories in shared universes, including *The Vampire Diaries* and Jonathan Maberry's *V-Wars* series, as well as for *Kolchak: The Night Stalker* and *The Green Hornet.*

His short story collections include *Cage of Bones & Other Deadly Obsessions, Needles & Sins, Vigilantes of Love* and *Sacrificing Virgins.*

Learn more about John and sign up for his e-newsletter mailing list at www.johneverson.com or connect on Facebook at www.facebook.com/johneverson.

Its roots are old... and twisted!

THE FAMILY TREE

© 2014 John Everson

The blood of the tree is its sap.
It has sustained Scott Belvedere's
family for generations. It's the secret ingredient behind the family's intoxicating ale and bourbon,
among other elixirs.

But only when Scott inher-
its The Family Tree Inn, deep
in the hills of Virginia, does he
learn anything about his family,
its symbiotic history, or the mam-
moth, ancient tree around which
the inn is literally built.

And after he stumbles upon
the bony secrets hidden in its

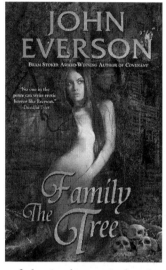

roots, while in the welcoming arms of the innkeeper's daughter, he realizes that not only is blood thicker than water—it's
the only thing that might save him from the hideous fate of his
ancestors...

Enjoy the following excerpt from
The Family Tree:

PROLOGUE

IT WAS ALWAYS dark here. The heavy, inky dark of a windowless
cellar. A root cellar, where the pale insects scurried in the center of the floor, unconcerned about being discovered. The light
rarely caught them.

They hunted and nested and lived and died unseen.

Just as he lived here…unseeing.

Sometimes he didn't even bother to open his eyes for days on end. He didn't miss it too much; the sky came to him every day in dreams anyway.

When he looked inside his mind and allowed himself to simply drift…which was more and more these days…he could feel another skin.

He could feel the air slipping and kissing with the hint of coming spring through his arms and hair like a gentle caress. He couldn't move, not really, not like he once remembered. His limbs were leaden. Locked in a rictus that belied the life within. And yet, he enjoyed the most freeing sensations every day. Swaying in the wind, with his eyes locked on the sky. Heaven was in his sight…though he was not the one doing the seeing.

Not really.

His body changed in the dark.

Sometimes he felt the shiver of veins distended, contracting. Sometimes he imagined his hair had twined around his legs; he felt the tickle of movement.

Growing pains?

Insects?

He couldn't tell. It was dark, and he didn't move.

Couldn't.

Though he was naked and below ground, it never felt cold to him. The air here was damp with the breath of the earth, and he could feel the pulse of life, ever-present. It moved through veins he could feel, but not see. It was the gift of the earth…the blood of the tree.

Time passed slowly here. But that urgency of getting to the next thing? The desperate striving? The planning for tomorrow? He'd given all that up, and he felt he was a better man for it. If he could still call himself a man. Here, he was a quiet provider. The heart of the house. In his soul, he was at peace.

And now and then, he woke and she came.

A dream of lilac perfume and fiery hair.

He couldn't move…but she did.

She moved a lot—in beautiful, sensuous ways.

She moved like heaven in the dark.

Sometimes, he even opened his eyes to gaze at her in rapture.

He needed nothing more.

The Family Tree **is now available.**
Read it today!

More Great Titles from Dark Arts Books!

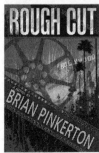

Rough Cut, a novel by Brian Pinkerton (2017 reissue)

Synchronized Sleepwalking, a fiction collection by Martin Mundt (2016)

The Dark Underbelly of Hymns, a fiction collection by Martin Mundt (2013 reissue)

Cage of Bones, a fiction collection by John Everson (2013 reissue)

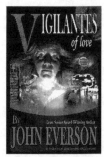

Vigilantes of Love, a fiction collection by John Everson (2013 reissue)

The Crawling Abattoir, a fiction collection by Martin Mundt (2013 reissue)

Four-Author Anthologies only from Dark Arts Books

Discover amazing new fiction from our critically acclaimed original anthology series!

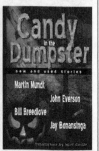

Visit www.DarkArtsBooks.com

Made in the USA
Lexington, KY
19 July 2017